PRAISE FC

"An emotional story packed with deceptions, secrets, and intrigue. Diana Awad's dark and twisty thriller will keep you guessing until the very end!"

—Laura Griffin, New York Times bestselling author

"A masterful exploration of marriage, secrets, and identity that will leave you questioning how well you really know those closest to you. Diana Awad crafts a thriller that is both heart-stopping and heartbreaking."

—Mindy Kaling

AS FAR AS SHE KNEW

AS FAR AS SHE KNEW

A Novel

DIANA AWAD

MINDY'S BOOK STUDIO

This is a work of fiction. Names, characters, organizations, places, events, and incidents are either products of the author's imagination or are used fictitiously. Otherwise, any resemblance to actual persons, living or dead, is purely coincidental.

Text copyright © 2026 by Dora Mekouar
All rights reserved.

No part of this book may be reproduced, or stored in a retrieval system, or transmitted in any form or by any means, electronic, mechanical, photocopying, recording, or otherwise, without express written permission of the publisher.

Published by Mindy's Book Studio, Seattle
www.apub.com

Amazon, the Amazon logo, and Mindy's Book Studio are trademarks of Amazon.com, Inc., or its affiliates.

EU product safety contact:
Amazon Media EU S. à r.l.
38, avenue John F. Kennedy, L-1855 Luxembourg
amazonpublishing-gpsr@amazon.com

ISBN-13: 9781662536595 (hardcover):
ISBN-13: 9781662532627 (paperback)
ISBN-13: 9781662532634 (digital)

Cover design by Joanne O'Neill
Cover image: © KOEN VAN DAMME / Adobe Stock; © Arfa Affan / Shutterstock

Printed in the United States of America

First edition

For Taoufiq

A NOTE FROM MINDY KALING

I'm thrilled to tell you about a book that kept me up way too late for several nights straight. If you love suspenseful domestic thrillers that also pack an emotional punch, *As Far as She Knew* is the perfect read for you.

Let me set the scene: Imagine discovering that your marriage of twenty-three years—a marriage you believed was rock solid—was built on lies. That's exactly what happens to Amira Abadi when her husband suddenly dies, and she finds out about a house she never knew existed. But that's just the beginning.

What I love most about this book is how it goes beyond the typical thriller formula. Yes, there are jaw-dropping revelations and mounting tension that will keep you turning pages, but there's also a deeply moving story about family, identity, and the courage it takes to face hard truths. Amira's journey felt incredibly real and relatable, even as the danger around her intensifies.

The author, Diana Awad, brings her experience as a former television journalist covering mysterious disappearances to craft a story that feels authentic and compelling. Every time I thought I had figured out where the story was going, another layer would peel away to reveal something even more intriguing.

Trust me on this one—this is the book you'll want to discuss with your friends over coffee, dissecting every discovery and debating what you would do in Amira's shoes.

Don't be surprised if you find yourself staying up late to read "just one more chapter." I know I did!

Chapter One

My husband died on a cold summer night.

Later, when I discovered the truth, and the haze of shock and disbelief melted away, I wished he were alive so I could kill him.

I found out my husband was dead via one of those middle-of-the-night phone calls that is always bad news. It came through on the landline, a number that no one, except for telemarketers and the pharmacy, ever used. They initially tried to reach me on my mobile, but only Ali and the kids got through when I silenced my phone.

I was in too much of a sleep stupor to process what was happening. The stranger's voice vibrated into my head, somehow both intimately close and yet coming from a distance, hurtling into my ear.

"Is this Mrs. Abadi?"

"Yes?" My voice was muffled, creaky with sleep. I didn't bother to correct the routine mispronunciation of my last name. He pronounced it "a body" rather than the correct "a baddie."

"Do you live at 1620 Merry Pines Circle? Are you married to Mr. Ali Abadi?"

I shifted in bed, growing more alert. Why were they asking about Ali? Why did they have our address? "Who is this?" I asked sharply.

I tried to remember where my husband was. My mind went blank at first. Then it came to me. He had a business thing with the local TV station where he worked as an occasional contributor. Dinner with sponsors. It was supposed to run late.

"Ma'am," the voice in my ear said, "I'm Officer John Wheaton with the county police department. We are outside your front door. We tried knocking and ringing the doorbell, but no one answered."

I awkwardly pushed myself into a sitting position. "You're where?"

"At your house. We didn't want to alarm you by banging on the door."

I hadn't heard anything. The fan that I ran in my bedroom every night took care of that. Which was usually the point. I couldn't sleep with my college kids, home for summer break, tramping up and down the stairs at all hours, closing doors, and talking too loudly. Long gone were the days when I could force them to go to sleep at a reasonable hour.

I stumbled out of bed, almost tripping on the corner of the sheet that caught my foot. I threw on the first thing I saw. The baggy T-shirt and elastic-waistband shorts I'd worn the day before. My usual uninspired work-from-home uniform. A whiff of body odor hit me when I tugged the cotton top over my head.

I stopped myself from turning on the upstairs hall light. I didn't want to wake the kids. By then, it registered that something was wrong. I gripped the banister when I reached the stairs, and somehow managed to get to the front door without pitching, face-first, down to the landing.

I fumbled around for the key and finally turned it into the lock. I was surprised by the shock of cool air that blasted over me when I managed to fling the door open. It was late July, when the days were hot and muggy in Virginia, even in the middle of the night. But it was like nature had adjusted the temperature to meet the moment.

The uniformed officer stood on the doorstep, his face contorted into a mask of practiced sympathy, as if he'd done this too many times before.

"I am sorry," he said, "but there's been an accident."

Chapter Two

Before

"*Yalla*, come on, Amira!" Mama poked her head into my bedroom, trying to hurry me. "They're going to be here soon."

"I'm almost ready." I made a show of taking my time, slowly pulling the brush through my long dark hair, which was blow-dried flawlessly straight. At twenty-one, I wouldn't be caught dead acting excited about meeting a guy with husband potential. I was a soon-to-be professional woman with a college degree.

But the knot in my stomach told a different story. I was nervous. A marital prospect had apparently seen me at my second cousin's wedding a couple of weeks earlier. His mother had called my mother, and now he and his family were coming to meet us. It wasn't my first meet and greet, but the encounters had accelerated lately. This was my third time meeting a potential husband since graduating from college a couple of months before.

"I don't know how you stand it." My younger sister, Lulu, lounged on my bed, examining her split ends. "It's like you're a horse up for market. Next thing you know, he'll be checking your teeth."

"The way I choose to view it is that *he* is on display for *me* to accept or reject," I told her, very pleased with my liberated-woman outlook. "It's all in how you see things."

But I was feeling the pressure. Most girls my age in our local Palestinian community were already married or at least engaged. I'd finished college. Marriage was the next step. At least according to my parents. Being a spinster made you an object of pity, and I didn't want anyone feeling sorry for me. Besides, I wasn't the type of girl who rocked the boat.

The doorbell rang. Lulu and I looked at each other. She popped up from the bed.

"Your stallion awaits!" she said, pushing me toward the bedroom door.

The first thing I noticed about Ali Abadi was his height. He was tall. And he had nice eyes. Kind eyes. Framed by dark lashes so lush that they almost looked fake.

His handshake was big, warm . . . and a little limp. When I teased him about it later, Ali protested that he was trying to be polite. It was a classic clash of East and West embodied in a handshake. An Arab man was impolite, forward even, if he shook a woman's hand too firmly. In America, a loose grip meant the man was a wimp.

I liked the way he dressed, in dark jeans and a button-down shirt. Respectful but not too much. At the previous meet and greets, the potential husbands wore suits. It smacked of trying too hard. There was no competition. Ali exuded cool. He was relaxed and confident, with a laid-back attitude and easy smile.

We went for a walk to escape both sets of parents, who were busy trying not to stare and pretending not to eavesdrop. There were no sidewalks in our suburban Virginia neighborhood, so we walked along the side of the quiet street. I wanted to know everything about him.

"There's not much to tell." His voice, deep and warm, slightly gravelly, sliced through me like a hot knife through butter. "I'm a CPA. I work at one of the big accounting firms in DC."

"Do you like being an accountant?" He didn't strike me as the accountant type. And I couldn't imagine working with numbers all day. Words were my thing.

"I do enjoy the work. I find it satisfying when everything adds up." So maybe he was a little bit of a nerd. A hot nerd.

He shared some of his experiences growing up in Northern Virginia. His parents, like mine, were immigrants, but he was born in the States. After playing sports in high school, he'd gone to James Madison University and lived the frat boy life. I liked that he was as Americanized as me.

"High school athlete. College frat bro," I said flippantly. "Sounds like you were a party boy."

"I won't lie to you." A shadow crossed over his face. "I used to drink."

I was taken aback by how seriously he took my teasing comment. "I was just kidding."

"I don't drink anymore." He frowned and momentarily seemed very far away. "I don't like the feeling of losing control."

"You don't drink at all now?" The young people in our Arab American community, the ones who were Muslim, were a mixed lot. Some were religious and never touched alcohol. Others went wild in college only to give up drinking once they had families. Some never stopped.

"No. I don't drink at all." He shook his head and then smiled, as if mentally shaking off whatever memory had gotten ahold of him. "Now tell me more about yourself. I know you just graduated. What's your next step?"

I was more than happy to leave his sudden dark mood behind. "I'm finishing up an internship at the Smithsonian. I'm hoping to get a full-time job there."

"I don't think I've ever met anyone who works at a museum. What kind of work do you do?"

"I help set up new exhibits. Mostly on the writing side with the informational panels that explain what the display is about."

"That sounds interesting," he said like he meant it.

"It is. I love it." I pulled my sweater tighter around me, against the early-fall chill.

He noticed. "Are you cold? Should we go back? Or I can run to the house and get you a jacket."

"No, I'm OK." I didn't want him going anywhere. Not even for a few minutes.

We started down a slope in the road. "I've been out of school for three years. I own a town house at Tysons Corner." He got straight to the point. "My parents are really pushing hard for me to get married."

He didn't have to tell me why his mother and father were so eager. Many Arab families tried to marry off their kids as soon as possible. Settling down young helped avoid the temptations of American life, which, God forbid, included marrying a non-Muslim.

"What about you?" I asked him. "Do *you* feel ready to get married?"

"Yes. I do. Absolutely." He answered in a firm, declarative way. As if he was speaking as much to himself as he was to me. Then his voice softened, and his slow smile made my insides warm and dreamy. "Especially now that I've met you."

Of course I melted. That night, as I replayed our conversation over and over again in my head, I remembered the strange feeling that fluttered through me when I first laid eyes on Ali. It was almost like a flicker of recognition, an instinctual knowing that this encounter was unlike any other.

"It's *kismet al-naseeb*." Mama sighed happily when I mentioned the sensation to her and Lulu. "Your soul immediately recognized your fated mate, even if your mind didn't."

Lulu rolled her eyes. "Oh, *please*."

I laughed it off, but meeting Ali made a believer out of me. The concept of a fated mate secretly struck me as deliciously romantic. And, despite Lulu's skepticism, I couldn't wait to live out my very own fairy tale.

Chapter Three

Now

Muslim burials are fast.

Ali died on a Thursday and we buried him on Friday, the Muslim Sabbath.

"Yes, it's good." Ali's brokenhearted mother mercilessly rubbed the tears from her ruddy cheeks. Her grief seemed to deepen her accent. "There will be a lot of people there for Friday prayers. The more people who do the prayers for the dead, it's better."

My heart broke for my mother-in-law. Ali was her only son. Losing my husband was inconceivable enough. Losing my son was beyond imagining.

After Friday prayers, worshippers were invited to stay and join Ali's family and friends to complete the prayer for the dead. We were not regular mosque goers, so they were all strangers to me.

"Excuse me," one of the worshippers said to the young man beside him after completing the prayer. "Who is the deceased?"

"His name was Ali Abadi," Adam, our nineteen-year-old son, told the man. "He was my father." My son had cried when he first learned his father was dead. Now he mostly seemed shell-shocked, like he was walking around in a haze. Who would guide him into manhood now?

I barely knew how to pray, but I went through the motions with the other women. A wife should be among those to send a man off after he dies. After all, who was closer to him in this life than me?

Maybe his parents and siblings loved him more. Or at least as much. Who knew? How can you quantify such a thing? But I was his day-to-day. His person. After twenty-three years of marriage, Ali and I were embedded in each other's DNA. If that part of me died with him, who was I now?

In the days after the funeral, the flowers came. From friends and faraway family, from my work and Ali's colleagues, a couple of arrangements from more distant acquaintances whose kindness was a surprise. The local TV station where Ali occasionally appeared as an on-air financial consultant sent a huge bouquet.

The honeyed fragrance of the flowers, scents of celebrations and epilogues, of comings and goings, quickly enveloped the house. The cloying odor made me nauseous. I didn't water any of them. I had no interest in keeping alive things that represented death.

About a week after the accident, I was home alone debating what to do with one of the more elaborate arrangements. Adam was at the gym, and Ayla's friends had come to take her out for lunch. Everything felt surreal, the three of us still in varying states of shock.

Since the funeral, Adam had stuck to the basement playing video games, while Ayla locked herself away in her room. Although my son was quiet, mostly retreating into himself, he was also eager to talk about his father, remembering anecdotes that made us smile despite our devastation. Like the times Ali got technical fouls for yelling at the ref while coaching the kids' youth basketball teams.

Ali, usually so even keeled, was never as excitable as when he was coaching. Seeing his unlikely transformation on the sidelines always made us laugh. Well, it amused me after the fact. While it was happening, I was embarrassed from where I sat among the other parents.

Ayla's reaction to losing her father was vastly different. She'd completely withdrawn, rarely coming out of her room. So far, she didn't want to talk about Ali. Friends and family had delivered several meals that she barely touched. My heart wrenched whenever I recalled how she'd reacted when I told her about the accident. She ran to the bathroom and threw up. Afterward, she slumped on her bed hugging herself, shaking uncontrollably. "It isn't true," she'd moaned. "It can't be."

Ayla had always been a daddy's girl, in many ways closer to her father than she was to me. She wouldn't let me hold or comfort her. I told myself grief takes different shapes. That I should let Ayla process her loss in her own way. After all, it had only been a few days since Ali's death.

Besides, I was barely coping myself. Mostly I was numb, like a stranger watching my life unfold from the outside looking in. I didn't feel much of anything from that safe distance. Nothing could hurt me so badly that I couldn't go on. Despite the fuzzy feeling in my mind, I knew instinctively that I had to keep it moving for the kids. Falling apart wasn't an option.

Now, as I studied the floral arrangements, the doorbell rang. Probably more bouquets being delivered. Or food or another thoughtful gift.

My next-door neighbor Claudia, who I walked with a few mornings a week, had already sent over a lasagna. And the Goldmans, who lived across the street, left a generous bag of groceries on the doorstep. I was lucky to have so many caring people in my life. Nicki, my closest friend, set up a meal calendar that would keep us fed for the next month. My high school bestie, Rula, sent an enormous bouquet and way more food than we could eat from my favorite restaurant.

I sighed. How was any of this real? The night the officers came to tell me that Ali was dead, I was positive they were wrong. It had to be a case of mistaken identity. Ali's Honda was in the shop the night he died. He was driving a loaner car from the dealership when he crashed. Surely that had confused authorities. I still waited to hear the jiggle of his key in the lock when he came home from work.

The doorbell rang again, rattling me out of my thoughts. I found two uniformed officers on my doorstep. Fear streaked through my limbs. My legs almost buckled. The last time police showed up at the house turned out to be the worst night of my life.

"Mrs. Abadi?"

"Yes." I could barely choke out the words. "Has something happened? Is it the kids?"

"No, no. Nothing like that. I apologize for alarming you." He was short and square shaped with a full head of dark hair. He looked like someone who laughed a lot, so his current somber expression seemed out of place on such a jovial face. The other officer was taller, thinner. I barely noticed him.

"I'm Officer Torres with county police," the shorter man continued. "And this is Officer Bailey. We're wrapping up our investigation into your husband's traffic accident. We have a few questions for you."

"What could I possibly know? I wasn't there when he . . . crashed."

The officer smiled reassuringly. "Would you mind if we come in? This won't take long."

I showed them into the living room, the formal space near the front door where we rarely sat except for when guests were over. Flower arrangements littered almost every available surface, giving the room a funereal feel.

"All traffic accidents in the county are investigated," the officer began once we were seated. "In your husband's case, there were no tire marks at the scene."

"I see." I blinked and tried to focus. My mind tended to wander these days. "What does that mean?"

"That Mr. Abadi didn't try to brake."

"The police . . . the other officers who came to my door on the night Ali died . . . said he crashed into a tree."

"That's correct." He regarded me expectantly. Like a teacher waiting for a prize student to come up with the right answer.

"And?" I prompted, wishing he'd just spit out whatever he was trying to say. I could barely put one foot in front of the other. This was no time to test my analytical skills.

"Was your husband depressed?" His measured gaze focused on me. "Was he having trouble at work? Were you two, maybe, having issues in your marriage?"

I gave him a blank stare. "Like what kind of issues?"

"Did you fight a lot? Did you have any money troubles? Anything that might have caused him to become mentally unstable?"

"Ali wasn't depressed. He was the most stable, even-tempered person on the planet." My husband's quiet, easy smile flashed in my mind. My heart felt like it was cracking. "Why would you think otherwise?"

"It appears he drove straight into the tree and didn't brake or swerve to avoid crashing."

The implication of his words finally hit me. "What are you saying?" My voice rose. "You think Ali drove straight into a tree on purpose?"

The compassion that filled his dark eyes made me irrationally angry. "We have considered that your husband's crash was the result of suicide."

"Well, you're wrong," I shot back. "Ali wouldn't kill himself. We're Muslim. We don't kill ourselves. It's a sin."

"And was your husband very religious?"

"No." Neither of us was. "But that's not the point. I'm telling you that my husband didn't kill himself. He had no reason to. We had a loving marriage, our kids are in college and thriving. We both had good jobs." My voice cracked. To think of Ali as in the past was more than I could process. "Is that all?" I asked, suddenly exhausted. I couldn't wait for them to leave so I could bury myself under the bedcovers.

"Yes." He rose. "For now."

"Can't an accident just be an accident?" I asked.

"Sure. It *was* late at night. Your husband had worked all day. It's possible he fell asleep on the road."

That didn't sound like Ali either. He was too conscientious a driver to doze off behind the wheel. "What if he had a medical incident?"

"We're waiting for the toxicology report," the officer said. "Maybe that'll shed some light on things."

I led them out to the foyer. "Ali wasn't a drinker. He hadn't touched alcohol since college."

"The tox screen is standard procedure," the officer reassured me. "It'll be several weeks before the results come back."

"Ali didn't use drugs either. The man hated to even take Tylenol."

I showed them to the door. Officer Torres smiled and said goodbye, but I registered the skeptical slant of his mouth. The idea that Ali killed himself was as ridiculous as discovering the earth was flat.

Call it instinct, intuition, or whatever it was, but I knew with everything in me that Ali hadn't taken his own life.

Chapter Four

The weeks following the funeral were a fog.

I fought the urge to retreat and sleep for a month because I didn't want the children to feel like they'd lost their mother too. I forced myself to get out of bed every morning and go through the motions. Mostly I was still numb. Like a boat that was adrift with the shore in the hazy distance.

"It's your brain protecting you from unbearable pain. I looked it up," Lulu said authoritatively. My sister always searched for answers online. She believed Professor Google solved pretty much everything. "The numbness can last a long time."

I worried about what that meant. How much more nightmarish could life get once the numbness wore off?

The last days of August approached, and the children departed for the fall semester of college, Ayla for her junior year and Adam as a sophomore. They seemed eager to go: Adam finally emerged from the basement, and Ayla hurriedly packed and left as early as she could, a full week before classes started. As if escaping the house would distance her from reality. Maybe it was for the best. I hoped returning to school would breathe some life back into her.

But once my children left for college, the full force of how alone I was hit me. The house felt too quiet. Empty and cavernous. For the first time in my life, I lived alone, which left me feeling vulnerable and exposed. How many people—from neighbors to the kids' friends and acquaintances—were aware that I was on my own in this spacious house?

My anxiety was most intense at night, in the dark. Before Ali died, I preferred sleeping in a pitch-black room. Ali had even hung blackout curtains for me. But now I kept the hallway lights on overnight. Awakening in the dark, blinking my eyes open and not seeing anything, felt like death.

I detested the idea of being a wimp, a grown woman behaving like a scared little girl. Sometimes, at night when I felt jumpy, I'd try to call my best friend Nicki but usually got her voicemail because she went to bed early. Nicki and I had met as college interns at the Smithsonian and talked almost every day. It occurred to me that we hadn't spoken much in the weeks since Ali died. Why was that?

I didn't dwell on it. I was too busy sleeping during the day. The morning I picked up copies of Ali's death certificate, I came home before noon, slid under the covers, and stayed there until the following morning. Death is a tiring business.

There was plenty to do when I wasn't sleeping. A swirl of documents arrived from Ali's accounting firm, involving pension payments, life insurance, and reimbursement for the earned vacation time he never got to take. Suddenly, it was only me responsible for everything. Ali was an accountant who took care of all the finances. I had only a vague idea of how much money we had saved or invested.

I deferred to Ali in almost all financial decisions, not because he insisted but because finances bored me. The only investment I ever suggested, on a whim, was holding on to our town house after we moved farther out into the suburbs, but the idea had made Ali nervous.

"Money is going to be tighter with all of the expenses that come with the new house," he said. "I don't want to carry two mortgages."

My instinct turned out to be right. Our new house would be paid off if we'd held on to the town house for just a few more years. It never occurred to me that I might have a knack for making sound investment choices. That was Ali's department.

My focus was on the kids and my contracted work with museums. I specialized in researching and writing explanatory introduction panels and title cards for exhibits. Ali cooked sometimes on weekends and always helped clean the kitchen, except during tax season, when he worked late every night.

For the most part, though, we naturally fell into traditional roles, a separation of duties that lasted our entire marriage.

"How is it possible for the mortgage to be overdue?" I stared at the letter from the bank postmarked two weeks earlier.

"Did you say your house payment is late?" Lulu asked as she walked into my kitchen and set her overstuffed purse on the table. My sister carried her life in that worn leather tote. She found me sitting at the kitchen island, staring at stacks of official-looking correspondence littering the counter. "That's not good."

"No kidding." I was surprised to see her. "You didn't say you were coming by."

"Just checking in on you." She eyed the piles of envelopes laid out before me. "That's a lot of mail."

"I've kind of been avoiding dealing." I set the bank notice down. "But I started to stress that I might be missing something important."

"You think?" Unlike me, Lulu was the chief money manager in her household.

"Just be happy that I finally have the energy to go through this junk." A lot of the correspondence was addressed to Ali, which made sorting through it even more depressing.

"You have at least been paying the bills, I hope?"

I nodded. "Most of them are still on whatever autopay system Ali set up. And I pay any bill that comes in the mail—water, gas, electric, property tax for the cars."

"Time to put on your big-girl panties!" After weeks of coddling me, my sister had switched to more of a tough love approach. She studied the notice I'd placed on the island. "Didn't you say the mortgage is paid automatically?"

"Yes. Ali set it up."

"What day of the month is your mortgage due?"

"I'm not sure." There was a lot I didn't know. Without Ali, all the grown-up, real-life stuff felt overwhelming. We'd been like two sides of a house, holding everything up. How was one lone wall supposed to bear all of that weight on its own?

Lulu shot me an incredulous look. "You *still* don't know what day your mortgage is due? It's been almost two months since Ali died."

"Forty-three days, to be exact," I retorted.

The doorbell rang.

I popped up. "Saved by the bell."

"Are you expecting someone?"

"Yeah, some guy from the accounting firm is coming by for Ali's work laptop."

"Why do you still have Ali's work laptop?" She followed me into the foyer. "You'd think the firm would want it back quickly. There's got to be sensitive financial information on it."

"Beats me." I wasn't about to admit that I'd ignored emails from Ali's accounting firm requesting that I mail his computer back. The laptop was such an integral part of Ali's life. Returning it felt like losing another piece of him.

"I can't believe the company sent someone to pick it up in person," she said.

"They emailed a label for me to send the laptop back, but this colleague of Ali's offered." I neglected to mention that the firm probably sent the man over to force the issue, since it took me weeks to respond to their emails.

Lulu retreated back to the kitchen just before I answered the door. It was my first time meeting Jake Barnes in person, but I felt like I knew him. He was a work friend Ali had often mentioned, and they occasionally golfed together. Jake's kids were younger than ours, and, over the years, Ali enjoyed passing several of Adam and Ayla's hand-me-down bikes, scooters, and skateboards to the Barnes children.

"You really didn't have to come all the way out here." I reluctantly handed him the laptop, swallowing against the ache in my throat, trying not to think of the transfer as another erasure.

"It's no problem." Jake was physically fit and balding on top, with a band of dark hair curving around the sides. His manner was pleasant, but his watery blue gaze was watchful in a way I found a little unnerving. "I live pretty close by."

We chatted for a few minutes. "We really miss Ali around the office," he told me. "He was always so kind, always asked after the kids."

"I hope they're enjoying the bikes."

"Very much so." He smiled, but I still felt scrutinized. Maybe he wanted to assess whether I seemed sad enough for a widow. Or Ali had talked about me over the years and now Jake was finally able to sync what he'd heard with the person standing before him.

"Well, I'd better get going," he said after a brief pause. "Do you happen to have the mail label for the computer? The firm likes to check all that stuff back in."

"Of course. I left it in Ali's office." I ran upstairs to retrieve the label. I could still feel Ali's presence in the guest bedroom where he'd set up his desk. Going in there made me feel closer to him.

"Thanks," Jake said when I handed over the label, his gaze briefly flitting to the staircase behind me in the foyer. He shifted Ali's computer to the other hand. "Listen, if there's anything else you need to facilitate through the firm, I'd be happy to be your liaison."

I couldn't imagine what business I had left with Ali's firm. Right after the funeral, there'd been that swirl of documents and payouts from the company.

"I can give you my number," Jake offered. "Only if you'd like."

My first instinct was to say no. The information was obviously in Ali's phone, which the police returned to me after the accident, along with his wallet, wristwatch, and wedding band. It felt strange and surreal for all his personal effects to be here after he . . . poof! . . . vanished off the face of the planet.

"It's a good reminder that you take nothing from this world but your good deeds," my sister-in-law Julia had reminded me. Ali's younger sister had surprised her family when she joined the Muslim Club in high school, becoming so devout that she took to wearing a headscarf, the only woman in her immediate family to do so. Both of our families were more culturally Muslim, following many of the conservative social customs while not being very religious. Julia was a year older than me and one of the best people I knew.

But now, rather than go through Ali's phone again—and experience the unwelcome wash of grief that would undoubtedly accompany that walk down memory lane—I exchanged mobile numbers with Jake and promised to call if I needed anything.

"And you can always reach me at the firm." He provided that information as well. I recognized the familiar number, except that Jake's extension was different. My chest felt sore as I punched the digits into my phone. I used to call Ali's line all the time. He often silenced his mobile at the office so his meetings wouldn't be interrupted. Even though I hadn't dialed the number in months, the thought that I'd never call Ali at work again made my throat swell.

"Ali had a whole other life," I remarked to my sister as I watched Jake walk back to his car.

Lulu, who'd stayed out of sight in the kitchen, came over to look out the window with me. "What do you mean?"

"All spouses do. Think about it. Ali spent a third of each day at work." We made our way back to the kitchen. "He was at the firm for ten years. He had full friendships with people I've never met. Look at Jake; he's a complete stranger to me."

"Is that guy a good friend of Ali's . . . um . . . was he a good friend?" It still didn't come naturally to any of us to refer to Ali in the past tense.

"Ali talked about him sometimes, stories about his kids' sports activities. One of them is supposedly a lacrosse prodigy."

"Was he at the funeral?"

"Jake? I'm pretty sure I saw him there." Even though the entire day was a blur, I vaguely remembered Jake extending his condolences to me and the children. We buried Ali so quickly—the day after he died, in accordance with Muslim tradition—that many of his colleagues didn't find out about the funeral until it was over. Some had been away on their summer vacations.

"I've got to go." Lulu grabbed her tote. "It's time to pick up the kids." My sister had three girls, all much younger than my Ayla and Adam.

I stared at the mortgage notice glaring up at me from the counter. "I guess I have to call the bank."

"They won't bite." She dug her keys out of her bag. "You'll feel much better once you've cleared up any confusion."

After she left, I forced myself to dial the bank's customer service number. It took effort. I resented having everything dumped in my lap. It wasn't logical, but handling tasks that Ali used to take care of was like repeatedly getting hit over the head. A reminder that he was really gone, his absence permanent.

"Your husband has been dead for *how* long?" the bank representative asked in a way that reminded me of a doctor with a terrible bedside manner. "And it took you this long to notify us?"

"Yes." I didn't bother explaining that I'd barely been able to get out of bed up until a week or two ago, much less deal with the bank.

"Hold on," he said before I could ask about the mortgage. "I'm transferring you."

The bank apparently had a whole section devoted to "survivors." The representative assigned to me was named Martha. She had a warm, comforting voice edged with a hint of a southern Virginia lilt. Her serious tone, her consideration, her "I'm so sorry for your loss" made my throat swell. I sipped from the straw of my water bottle to keep my emotions in check.

Ali and I kept separate primary bank accounts. Our work checks were deposited into our respective savings and checking accounts. That's how Ali set it up, and I never asked why, since both of our names were on everything. Martha, the rep, confirmed what I already knew.

"Your name is on all of the accounts, so you have complete access to your husband's funds," the rep told me. "We'll need to close his savings account and move the funds into yours. Would you like me to also close his checking and move the balance to you?"

I wanted to hit "End Call" and hurl my phone against the white speckled countertop that Ali and I picked out together two years before. Ali had balked at the price, but the old laminate that came with the house had cracked and peeled so badly that I insisted on replacing it.

I released a long sigh. If only I could go back to those days when I did normal things that didn't include taking Ali's name off accounts. Soon there'd be no trace that he ever existed.

"Can I keep his checking account open?" I couldn't bear to close it.

"Sure, honey. I'll just put it in your name."

Hearing Martha clicking away on her computer made me relax a little. She was nice and understanding, her voice soothing. She didn't seem like the type of person who'd judge me for being financially clueless. "Will any automatic payments that my husband set up continue to be paid through that account?"

"Yes, everything that's set up should continue."

"The thing is that I got a notice that my mortgage is overdue."

"You did?" I heard the frown in Martha's voice. "Let me check."

"Thank you." Lulu was right. This wasn't so bad. I really shouldn't have put off dealing with the finances. I could do this.

More clicking sounds through the phone. "Here it is," Martha said. "The mortgage has been paid automatically on the fifth of each month for the last six months."

"So it *is* up to date?" I was confused. "Then why did I get a late notice?"

"I'm not sure. I'll tell you what," Martha said. "I see here that the payment goes to our mortgage department. This bank holds your loan."

"Yes, that's right," I said, trying to prove to Martha that I wasn't completely oblivious. "I cosigned the mortgage papers when we purchased the house sixteen years ago."

"Then this should be very easy to clear up," Martha said. "I can transfer you to our mortgage department. They'll have all of the answers that you need."

Unfortunately, Jim, the mortgage guy, wasn't nearly as comforting as Martha.

"Could you tell me about this notice?" I asked after being transferred to him. "It says my mortgage is overdue, but the rep I just talked to said it should be up to date."

"What property is that?"

"My house is located on Merry Pines Circle."

"Hmm." His polite tone carried an undercurrent of impatience. "Yes, the mortgage on Merry Pines is up to date."

Relief whooshed through me. "So it *is* a mistake."

"But," he continued, "the mortgage for the house on Cozy Glenn Lane is in arrears."

"The what?" What the hell was he talking about? Impatience rippled through me. The last thing I needed was for some bank screwup to needlessly freak me out. "There's obviously been some sort of mistake. My house is on Merry Pines Circle."

"Just a moment," he said. "Let me look into this." More sounds of fingers tapping a computer keyboard.

"I was right." He sounded very pleased with himself. "There are two mortgages for the separate properties."

"Excuse me?" I spluttered. I obviously hadn't heard him right. "Are you saying we're paying a mortgage on a *second* house?"

"Well, Mr. Abadi was. Your name isn't attached to the loan."

"Wait a minute." His words didn't compute. "Just to be clear. You are saying that my husband has been paying a mortgage on a totally separate property and the loan is only in my husband's name?"

"That's right," he chirped. "His, and a holding company by the name of Five *A*'s LLC."

The Five *A*'s. That's what we called ourselves. Ali, Amira, Ayla, and Adam. The fifth *A* was for Abadi. A family business, obviously. Being an accountant, Ali must have set it up for tax reasons or some other business purpose. But that didn't explain why we were paying for a house that I knew nothing about.

"And you are sure the mortgage for that second house is coming out of a joint account?" I asked.

"It *was*. But that account, the one paying the second mortgage, has run out of money. That's what triggered the notice you received in the mail."

I blinked. "Could you give me the address of the second property?"

"It's located at 104 Cozy Glenn Lane."

"In what city?"

"Durham, North Carolina."

"*Where?*" Ali had never been to Durham. As far as I knew.

"North Carolina."

"When did he get the house?"

"The mortgage was taken out eight years ago. Your husband has made regular payments since then."

Chapter Five

Before

After that first meeting, Ali and I decided to have lunch the following weekend. That date went on for hours, melting into dinner. The weekend after that, we drove out to Skyline Drive to see the changing of the leaves.

We walked on a trail for a couple of miles before settling on a rock with a view of the mountain range and national forest. The weather was crisp, the fall foliage an explosion of bright reds, earthy browns, and vibrant oranges.

Our conversation flowed. We were discovering that we liked, in broad strokes, the same things—reading, traveling, and trying new restaurants. He was also a movie buff. It was one of those rare perfect days that sticks in your memory.

"One day," he said, looking out, "I want to bring my kids hiking here."

Ali loved the outdoors. That was one area where we diverged. I wasn't a fan of bugs or getting too dirty or sweaty outside of the gym. My hair frizzed and my cheeks got too red. But I was ready to change my ways for this enigmatic man with gentle eyes and a deep, quiet laugh. Fortunately, I quickly came to look forward to the hikes—they were like a meditation—and I didn't have to pretend anymore.

After we had children, weekend hikes became a family ritual. Ali would pull up a map and select a new place to explore. We'd walk along the water at Ball's Bluff and Ali would tell the kids about the Civil War battle that had raged there. Or we'd reach the top of Sugarloaf Mountain and Ali would say, "Look at that view! Was that worth the effort or what?"

But then the kids got older and sports and school obligations got in the way. Once Ayla and Adam learned to drive, it was all over, except for the reluctant special exception for Mother's or Father's Day, or a birthday—one of ours, never theirs.

The pieces of family life loosened and fell away until one day, years later, we wondered how treasured family rituals faded without a proper send-off.

"Why did we stop doing the family hikes?" Ali asked one Saturday morning when Ayla and Adam were in high school. He drank his coffee while scrolling through the news feed on his mobile. The kids were asleep upstairs and wouldn't emerge before noon.

I stood to get a second cup of coffee. "Your children got better offers."

The family hikes eventually reverted back to couple outings, just Ali and me again. Like in the beginning.

As we made our way back to the car on that first visit to Skyline Drive, Ali paused after opening my door for me. He did that throughout our entire marriage. Always a gentleman when most men in our generation had forgotten about such things. Or never learned them.

Ali leaned in and gave me the slightest kiss; it was like a feather, just the faint brush of his lips against mine. But it was enough for lightning to flash through me.

"I just wanted to check."

"Check what?" I asked, my body still pulsing from the thrill of his kiss.

"I enjoy spending time with you. You're easy to talk to." He smiled. "I wondered if the chemistry was there too."

"And?"

"Wow," he responded. "Just wow."

"And how," I added breathlessly.

He laughed a little, looking at me with eyes that glittered with appreciation. "You're a surprise."

Up until that point, I definitely had a crush on Ali. I think I fell in love with him that afternoon. The memories of those early days, of that first kiss on Skyline Drive, have a shimmer to them, as if my mind dusted them with golden glitter. The excitement of connection, of undeniable physical attraction, of the idea that this man might be my forever person, was powerful.

And I was happily intoxicated by it.

Chapter Six

Now

"How could Ali buy an entire house without you knowing?" Lulu asked when I called her after talking to the bank. "It's not like that's a small purchase."

I sighed. Since Ali's death, nothing made sense. "You know I never checked the finances. That was Ali's department."

"I understand that, but a *house*?"

"Maybe it's an investment property."

"Even so, how could you not know about it?"

"It beats me. I'm obviously an idiot."

"No, you're not." Her tone softened, the new tough love approach swiftly abandoned.

Instead of making me feel better, Lulu's tenderness put me on edge. "I need to find out who lives in that house and what the deal is. Maybe we get rent from it." I still spoke in *we*'s, as though I were still part of a couple.

Lulu paused. "Did you try researching the address online?"

"Yes, but nothing comes up. The address appears, but there's no picture of the actual house and I can't tell who owns it."

"That's weird. You'd think Google Maps or some real estate website would have a decent picture of it. Maybe it's a private gated community? What are you going to do next?"

"What choice do I have?" I'd racked my brain. "I have to drive down there and find out what I can. If there's a tenant, maybe they have some answers."

"Ali is literally the last guy in the world I'd expect to keep a big secret like this."

Lulu's tone, her willingness to voice her assumption that my husband deliberately hid a significant purchase, threw me off. I hadn't even gone down that path. I'd automatically assumed there was a reasonable is-that-all explanation for why Ali was paying for a house I knew nothing about.

I trusted my husband. He was a solid guy, a good husband and father who lived a routine life. Work during the week. Lawn care and coaching kids' games on weekends. A couple of vacations a year. And he seemed content.

But Lulu immediately assumed Ali had been up to no good, even though she liked him and they always got along. Our husbands had been close. Khalid, Lulu's husband, and Ali were opposites in a lot of ways. Khalid was outgoing and very social with a wide circle of friends, while Ali was more introspective and maintained a smaller, tighter friend group. Still, they bonded. Our families took vacations together.

"You're assuming the worst," I said accusingly. I wanted her to reassure me, to tell me that I was being silly.

But she didn't. "I don't know what to think, except that when a husband buys a house without telling his wife, that raises a lot of red flags."

I winced. "I'm going to take some days off work and drive down there." Ali wasn't capable of lying about something of this magnitude. I was married to the man for twenty-three years. I knew him better than anyone. Sure, we argued and got frustrated with each other from time to time, but what couple didn't? Ali never once gave me any reason to doubt him. He and I clicked from the beginning. We *got* each other.

"You're not going alone," Lulu said. "I'm coming with you."

"But you've got the kids."

"Khalid will drop them off in the morning," Lulu assured me. "I'll ask their friends' moms to take them after school until Khalid picks them up when he finishes work."

"What about your work?" Lulu was a freelance graphic designer who arranged her hours around the kids' schedules.

"Don't worry about it. Just give me a day or two to arrange everything, and then we can get on the road."

That night I got into bed early and was scrolling through my phone when I thought I heard footsteps.

I tried to ignore it. The house creaked a lot, even though it wasn't that old. I never noticed the noises when Ali and the kids were around. Now that I lived alone, every rustle or groan was amplified. Sometimes it felt like the house was in conversation with itself. I called Nicki. Hearing her voice would make me feel less alone. The call went to voicemail. I dropped the phone by my side, feeling a little stung, unable to remember the last time we'd talked. Why wasn't Nicki calling? She was at the funeral and had set up a Meal Train. But since then, I barely heard from her.

Something buzzed and vibrated next to my thigh. I startled, my muscles stiffening, until I realized it was my phone. Someone was calling. Maybe Nicki? But then the name of Ali's accounting firm popped up on the screen. My heart jumped. For a split second, my brain believed my husband was calling.

But it wasn't Ali's extension. It belonged to Jake Barnes, Ali's colleague. He must be working late. But why would he call? As far as I knew, I had no business left with Ali's firm. The insurance money had been paid out, the pension benefits sorted.

"Amira, how nice to hear your voice," Jake said when I picked up. "How are you and the kids managing?"

"As well as can be expected, I suppose."

"I'm calling because there's a box at the office of Ali's personal effects collected from his desk. I can drop them by on my way home from work whenever is convenient for you."

"Oh. I forgot all about his office things." Shortly after Ali died, I received an email from his firm telling me his things had been boxed up. Did I want them? Where should they be sent? I meant to answer but got distracted. Everything was such a blur right after Ali's death. When I circled back weeks later, I couldn't find the email.

"Is there a day next week that's most convenient for you?" Jake asked.

"I don't want to trouble you."

"It's no problem. I'll be out of town Monday and Tuesday, but I can bring it by when I get back, if that works for you."

I didn't want to wait that long to get Ali's things. What if there was information in them about the secret house? But getting the box sooner meant picking it up myself, and I couldn't face going to Ali's office without him there.

"Sure," I finally said. "Any time that is convenient for you is OK for me. I work from home, so I'm here all the time."

"Great. I'll get in touch once I'm back, and we'll set up a time."

"Thank you. It's very nice of you to go to the trouble."

"No problem. It's my pleasure," he reassured me. "Talk to you soon."

When I disconnected the call, the house was eerily silent. A chill ran through me when I pictured all the empty rooms—including the basement with its sliding glass doors. There were lots of points of entry if someone tried to break in. Would I hear them?

I slipped out of bed and made my way downstairs to make sure all the doors were secured, including the ones leading to the basement and garage. Hurrying back upstairs, I locked my bedroom door behind me. Checking and rechecking the doors and windows was a habit I'd developed after Ali died and the kids went back to school.

I was a little paranoid now that I lived alone in a big empty house that used to bustle with family activity. I hated feeling nervous and uneasy in this home I'd made with Ali and the children. I'd lovingly decorated each room, but now, at times, I was afraid to go into certain spaces at night. I definitely never went near the basement.

My sense of isolation was heightened by the absence of a couple of my closest friends. Aside from Nicki, I also never heard from Rula, my high school bestie, anymore. Before Ali died, we'd check in at least once a month.

I'd always viewed myself as a strong, independent woman. But was I? I married so young that I'd never been on my own. I felt like I was failing a critical litmus test regarding what it meant to be a self-reliant grown-up.

———

Two days later, Lulu and I were speeding down I-95 south on the way to Durham. Lulu drove my old van because I was too distracted, staring out the window while she listened to a crime podcast. As the trees zoomed by, my thoughts went to the last time I'd driven this route.

It was years ago, when Ali and I took the kids to Myrtle Beach for spring break. Longing panged through me. If only he were here. This mystery surrounding the house in North Carolina would be cleared up by now. *But would it?* a voice inside me asked. If Ali were alive, the house might very well still be a secret. He'd had eight years to tell me about it. I'd never felt more confused or unsure of what to believe.

I read once that pilots become disoriented, unable to distinguish up from down, when they lose sight of the horizon. Ali was my horizon. Without him, everything felt upside-down.

When we were about twenty minutes outside Durham, my mobile buzzed.

"Where are you?" Ayla demanded to know when I answered.

My sister and I exchanged a look. "I'm with Lulu. You're on speaker."

"Hi, sweetie," Lulu said.

"Hey, Auntie. Why are you guys in North Carolina?"

"How did you know—?" And then I remembered. In high school, the kids had secretly activated location services on my phone so they'd know when I was close to home if they were at the house doing something they shouldn't. When I found out, I didn't bother to turn off my location. Why shouldn't my children know where I was? I had nothing to hide. At least I never had before.

Obviously, I couldn't tell my daughter the truth. I scoured my mind for a plausible reason to be in North Carolina. "We're going to see the Biltmore House," I said. Lulu shot me a questioning look.

"What?" Ayla said.

"It's the biggest house in the United States."

"Why are you going to see it?"

"Biltmore is a museum." I warmed up to the lie. "I'm curious to see how they write their exhibits—the introductory panels and object labels."

"It's a good thing she's getting out," Lulu added. "Your mom could use the distraction."

Ayla's voice quieted. "Are you still depressed, Mom? I mean—" She paused when she realized how the question sounded. "You know what I mean, right?"

Lulu mouthed, *Sorry*. Irritation roiled through me. The last thing Ayla needed was to worry about me, especially since she seemed to be coping badly with Ali's death. They'd been so close. Ali coached Ayla's house basketball team for several years and ran countless developmental drills with her at the local gym. With Ali gone, both Ayla and Adam needed me to be strong and steady for them.

"Yes, honey. I'm fine," I reassured her. "Obviously, still getting used to . . . everything. But much better than I was. I'm OK."

"Maybe Adam was right. We shouldn't have left you all on your own, alone with nothing to do."

That was the thing with kids. They assumed you had no life without them—no unique identity, no interests or aspirations—as if your life started and ended with them.

"I do have a job," I reminded her. "I'm fine. Promise."

I was anything but fine, but I didn't want Ayla to worry. Even though the closer we got to Durham, the more anxious I became.

"How are you?" I asked.

"Fine." Her tone was clipped.

"Have you thought about seeing a counselor?" I said, desperate to make sure she was OK. "I called the university, and they have people you can schedule an appointment with. It would help you to talk to someone." She certainly wasn't talking to me.

"OK." Her tone cooled even more. "Bye, Mom."

"Love you, honey," I said.

"Bye." As soon as Ayla hung up, I hit the settings icon on my phone.

"Biltmore House?" Lulu said.

"What else is in North Carolina?" I replied. "It's all I could think of."

Lulu's eyes went to my mobile. "What are you doing?"

"Turning off my location settings. I don't want Ayla and Adam to be able to track my every move. Especially not now."

"How is Ayla doing?"

"I'm really worried about her. She won't talk about Ali at all. She's losing weight. I don't think she's eating well."

"I'm sorry you have so much on your plate." Lulu paused. "I asked Khalid about the second house. He swears he knows nothing about it."

"Did you think he would?"

Lulu shrugged. "I just thought I'd check."

About twenty minutes later, we pulled up in front of 104 Cozy Glenn Lane. The house was located in a leafy historic neighborhood near the city center. My heart thumping, I stared at the quaint white Victorian with cedar shake siding and a wide front porch. It wasn't big, but it had character, which is more than you could say about our tract home in Northern Virginia where all the houses looked alike.

"It's pretty," Lulu said.

"Ali didn't like Victorians. He said they looked too old-fashioned."

"Ali didn't live in it." It was what my sister didn't say that permeated the air.

"Why don't you just come out and say what you're thinking?" My words were knife sharp. For the first time, I gave voice to an unthinkable possibility. "You suspect that Ali has a secret girlfriend in there, don't you?"

I turned away to study the house's waist-high spiked black iron fence because I couldn't stand to see the expression on her face. The sympathy, the worry, the concern that she was dealing with a fool in denial.

Was I a fool in denial? I shook my head against the thought. There was no way that Ali was sneaking around behind my back, committing the ultimate betrayal. It just wasn't who he was.

But then again, what did I know? I was never suspicious when Ali worked late. Never checked up on him or went through his phone. Having never dated before, I had zero idea what signs of cheating to look for. My inexperience put me at a serious disadvantage. Ali had had relationships before marriage. Me? I was totally clueless.

"I don't know what's going on." Lulu chose her words carefully. "But whatever it is probably isn't good. Otherwise, Ali wouldn't have kept it a secret."

"You knew how he was." I swung my head back to look at her. "How can you think the worst?"

"Ali was a great guy. But he was also very reserved. He didn't talk much."

"And that makes him a lying cheater?" I snapped.

"All I'm saying is that your husband wasn't exactly an open book. And don't get mad at me." Her face reddened. "I'm not the one who bought a secret house."

Tears stung my eyes. What had Ali done? Why was I hundreds of miles from home parked in front of a cute house that he bought without telling me? I reached for my insulated water bottle and took a gulp to keep from crying.

"What do you want to do?" Lulu asked in a more conciliatory tone.

I wanted to drive away and keep going until I arrived back in a world where my husband was still alive. I took a deep breath. "Well, we didn't drive almost five hours to sit in the car and stare at the place. I guess I have to knock on the door."

"What will you say when they answer?"

I swung my car door open. "I have no idea."

Lulu shut off the engine. "I'm coming with you." I felt a stab of gratitude to have a fierce sister who never let me down. Friends like Rula and Nicki may have drifted away after Ali died, but Lulu was steadfast.

My legs were like sandbags as I approached the fence, walking through the open gate, down the smooth stone walkway lined by bushes of spiked purple flowers. On the porch, outdoor furniture, dark wood with plush white cushions and tasteful throw pillows, was arranged on a patterned rug.

I'd envisioned this house in my head, my mind keeping it at a safe distance. But seeing it in person, verifying its existence, put every cell in my body on alert. Someone had made this house a home. A living, breathing person with apparent good taste lived here. My mind desperately grasped on to the hope that there was a good explanation for the existence of this house with an obvious feminine touch.

I wanted nothing more than for Ali to put his arms around me and reassure me that everything was OK. He'd been my safety net for more than half my life. My reason for feeling secure in the world. Who would catch me now?

"Ready?" Lulu prompted softly as I stood, unmoving, in front of the door.

No. But I forced myself to knock anyway. My heart beating hard, I rang the doorbell too. We waited without speaking. All I could hear was the sound of my shallow, rapid breathing. No answer. I rang the doorbell several more times and was disappointed, and relieved, when no one answered.

"Either no one's home or they aren't answering on purpose," Lulu said.

It was no use peering through the front windows facing the street, because the curtains were closed. I started down the porch stairs.

Lulu followed. "Where are we going?"

"To the back." I was desperate to see inside, as if that would give me insight into what was going on. Wooden privacy screens enclosed the back deck, which was high aboveground. I ran up the steps, but there was a door that I couldn't see through or over.

"Who has privacy screens all around a deck?" I asked, frustrated. "Isn't the point to see nature and the great outdoors?" In my experience, most people had screens on the sides to shield them from their neighbors but kept an unimpeded view of the backyard.

Lulu agreed. "Having a locked wooden gate to access the deck is also weird."

Trotting down the stairs, I circled the house, but the curtains were closed on every window on the ground level. I started back to the front porch. "I saw one of those small mailboxes by the front door."

"You're going to go through a stranger's mail?" Lulu looked around to see if anyone was watching. "Isn't that a federal offense?"

"My husband owns this house, and he's dead, so I guess that makes it mine now," I said harshly, tugging on the top of the black aluminum box. "Damn it!"

"What?" Lulu strained to see.

"This stupid thing has a lock on it. Who even knew you could lock a mailbox?" Although it made perfect sense. Especially when strangers on your front porch tried to snoop. Frustrated tears stung my eyes.

"Hello!" someone called out in a friendly Southern accent. "Are you looking for Mizz Darius?" A plump woman in her sixties stood by the gate with her leashed little black dog.

Miss Darius. Confirmation that a woman lived in Ali's house. *Oh my God.* The muscles in my stomach cramped. But Lulu didn't miss a beat. She spun around and delivered her most brilliant smile.

"Good afternoon!" she said to the woman. "Yes, we were hoping to catch her."

"Do you know when she'll be home?" I asked.

"Carol? She's such a nice young woman. I live just down the street. I'm afraid I haven't seen Carol for at least a week."

"Oh, that's too bad," Lulu said. "We hate to miss her."

Carol Darius. A nice young woman. I searched my memory. The name wasn't familiar.

"Are you leaving her a note?" the neighbor asked, holding tight to the leash as her dog tried to pull away.

"No, I don't think so," Lulu said. "We'll try to catch her another day."

Suspicion glinted on the woman's formerly friendly face. "Then why are you going through her mailbox?"

"Oh, we weren't—" Lulu began.

"She's an old friend of my husband's." I spoke over Lulu. They say the best lies are rooted in some truth. "We wanted to tell her in person that he passed away recently." My voice caught. I couldn't help it.

Surprise flashed on Lulu's face before she masked it. "Sad news like that should be delivered in person, don't you think?" she said to the woman.

Our inquisitor's expression softened. Whatever she saw on my face convinced her that my grief was real, even if the rest of it was a lie. Being a widow had few upsides. I wasn't above using my miserable new status to get some answers.

"Oh, dear," the woman said. "I am so very sorry for your loss."

The tears I blinked back were real. "Thank you," I croaked, hating how thready my voice sounded.

"You're so young. Much too young to be a widow," the woman added with an expectant expression, as if waiting to be filled in on the rest of the story. But I was there to satisfy my curiosity, not some stranger's.

"Let's go," I said to Lulu.

"Have a good day," my sister chirped at the neighbor before following me to the van. The woman watched us before finally allowing her impatient dog to tug her on their way.

"Well," Lulu said when we were back in the van driving. "I guess there's a widow card."

"No one is going to be mean to a widow." I pulled out my phone. "Time to find out everything there is to know about Carol Darius."

Chapter Seven

Before

"This is called injera," Ali told me about two months after we met. "You use it to scoop up the spicy stew."

We were at a trendy place in Adams Morgan, where Ali wanted to introduce me to Ethiopian food, which I'd never had. Trying out new cuisines, often at hole-in-the-wall places, was becoming our thing.

Ali ordered for us and explained the different dishes to me. He preferred the lamb, but I ended up reaching for the vegetarian options like lentils, chickpeas, and cabbage.

I followed the movement of his hands, which were big and tanned from all his outdoor activities. I loved watching him. From the twinkle in his eye when he smiled at me, to the purposeful, long strides when he walked. Honestly, I liked everything about him. I was in deep.

I eagerly embraced every part of our courtship. It was an old-fashioned word, but it applied to us. I'd never really dated. My Muslim parents strictly forbade it.

Lulu and I were both required to live at home while going to college so there was no real opportunity to go wild (although Lulu still managed to). Mama and Baba said there were plenty of good schools within driving distance, which was true. College was for studying and not an excuse to party. *Now, if you get into Harvard,* Baba had said, *we'll talk,* but Mama frowned when she heard that.

I mostly hung out with kids in the Arabic Club. Both Arab Americans like myself and FOBs, students who were fresh off the boat. The foreign students mostly came to get an education and planned to return home once they graduated.

If you seriously dated one of the Arabic Club guys, or any other student on campus, word got out, and you'd get a bad reputation. Then no one would marry you. That's why some parents, though not mine, thought it was better for their children to get married straight out of high school, after which the safely married couple could go to college and party together.

Ali and I never ran out of things to talk about. But, despite our far-ranging conversations over delicious meals, something about him remained unknowable. I chalked it up to him being a naturally reserved person. Besides, it was still early days in our relationship. We had plenty of time to really get to know each other. I couldn't wait to pull back some of those layers.

"Do you want to try Ethiopian coffee with dessert?" he asked. "It's a little strong."

"Sure."

He studied me, an expression of bemusement on his face.

"What?" I was paranoid something was stuck in my teeth. "Why are you looking at me like that?"

"Are you always this easygoing?"

I shrugged. "What is there to fight about?" I put up my hands. "Oh no, please don't make me eat delicious new dishes!"

He laughed in that quiet way of his. "I'm glad you were willing to try Ethiopian. This is one of my favorite places."

"I generally do go with the flow." I sipped my diet soda and shot him a mock-stern look. "As long as you don't cross me."

He chuckled. "I've been warned."

"Lulu is the type A in the family," I told him. "She's one of those annoying students who always has her school projects ready several days before they're due."

"That *is* annoying. What about you?"

"I always started working on my reports at the last minute. Sometimes, I'd be up all night finishing them. But I always got them in on time." I took another bite. "This lentil stew really is tasty."

"Some people are rigid about where to go and what to eat." He watched me scoop up the deep-red mixture. "It's a pleasure to be with someone who likes trying new things."

"I do." I flirted with a smile. "I especially like trying them with you."

His eyes sparked. We had major chemistry. I couldn't wait for him to kiss me again. I'd been slathering on the lip balm so that my mouth would be extra soft and kissable for any upcoming make-out session.

His expression became more serious. "I want to be completely honest with you," he said. "You deserve that."

It never occurred to me that he might be dumping me. Even though he hadn't tried to kiss me again, I felt the tug of something real and true between us.

He took a deep breath. "You know I went to JMU." When I nodded, he continued. "And obviously I dated some girls there."

His admission wasn't exactly a news flash. Of course, all the boys went out and dated, except for the truly devout ones. In our community, it was the girls, devout or not, who were supposed to be as pure and uncomplicated as fairy-tale princesses.

"Are you trying to tell me that you're not a virgin?" I joked, trying to lighten the mood. There was an undercurrent between us now that I had never detected before. It made me uneasy.

He didn't smile. "I dated a girl there."

"What was her name?"

He frowned. "What difference does it make? That's not important."

"If she's important enough for you to bring up, it's important enough for me to know her name." So much for being easygoing.

"Her name is Lizzie."

"Lizzie what?"

"Lizzie Martins. Why?"

"Don't worry, I'm not going to stalk her." But I was riled up. "Why are you telling me this? What do you want me to know about Lizzie Martins?"

"I dated her on and off for a few years."

A few *years*. Jealousy scoured my insides. "Did you want to marry her?"

He shook his head. "I was always straight with her. She understood that my parents would never accept me marrying someone who wasn't Muslim. Still, I felt"—he struggled to find the word—"an obligation to her."

"Why?"

He looked away. "She's had some hardship in her life, and I didn't want to hurt her if I could avoid it."

"Did you love her?"

"I think it's more accurate to say that I cared about her."

"What does that mean?" I struggled not to sound shrill. "Does that make me the girl you're settling for since you can't be with your one true love?"

"No. Being with you is most definitely not settling." He looked straight into my eyes. "I think you know that."

Suddenly, I felt very much like what I was—a twenty-one-year-old who'd never dated before. I was out of my depth. "Did you break up with her?"

"I did."

"What did you tell her?"

"The truth. She knew I had to explore the possibility of marrying within my culture. I'm my parents' only son, and I owe them that. But I don't think she expected me to find you. She assumed I'd go back to her."

"She knows about me?" I frowned. "You're still in touch?"

"You're the reason I broke up with her."

I felt sick. Surely I wasn't getting this right. "You were with that girl *while* you've been seeing me?"

"No, it wasn't like that," he said with a firm shake of his head. "We were taking time apart while I explored this. I've been completely honest and up-front with Lizzie. I tried to make a clean break months ago, but she resisted. Last week, I told her it was definitely over between me and her. I don't need more time to explore."

Of course, I couldn't help asking. "Why not?"

"Because I met you. I can see a future with you."

———

Later, when I told Lulu, her face twisted with disgust. "It's gross how he's stringing that girl along."

"He told her he was seeing me. They were taking time apart."

She shook her head. "Like I said, gross."

Lulu wasn't like me. I could see a lot of gray in situations, but my sister was more black and white. She had very definite ideas about how things should be. She thought the rules for Arab girls were stupid, so she didn't follow them. Lulu snuck out all the time, and I knew she'd kissed more than one boy. She got married a lot later than I did. Lulu was almost thirty by the time she met Khalid at a club.

"Don't listen to your sister," Mama said. "What does she know about the world? The boys fool around with the American girls. But when it's time to get married, they straighten up and look for a nice Arab Muslim girl."

Baba looked slightly more concerned when I asked his opinion. "Some of those boys, they stay with their girlfriends even after they get married."

Mama tsked. "Ali isn't like that. You can tell he's *hanoon*."

My mother wasn't easily swayed by people. If she thought Ali was kind and compassionate, it was easier for me to believe that he was. Besides, I wanted to believe in him.

I wanted to believe in us.

Chapter Eight

Now

Carol Darius did not exist.

At least not online. Lulu and I checked into our hotel and quickly settled on our double beds to do searches on our laptops. I googled Carol's name along with Durham. And then her name alone. Using every spelling combination I could think of, I searched her name and Ali's together.

There was no trace of Carol Darius in North Carolina. There was a Carol Darius in Cape Town, but I doubted she could be the Carol I was looking for. Another hit turned out to be an Irish singer who had died two years earlier. There were a couple of US-based Carol Dariuses in the Midwest, but they were in their late sixties. None of the other hits made any sense.

"How do we find someone if they have no online footprint?" I said as much to myself as I did to Lulu. There were no phone books, no other paper trails I could think to follow. "I'm so used to online searching for everything that I don't even remember how to look anything up in real life."

"Don't get mad at me," Lulu said haltingly, "but what was the name of that girl Ali was dating when he met you?"

"Lizzie Martins. Of course, my mind immediately went there too." I'd googled Lizzie Martins now and again over the years. She had a Facebook account that she stopped updating years ago. There was nothing on it, except some quotes about being true to yourself and signs of toxic people. There was no photo of her.

"Do you know what she looks like?"

"I made Ali show me her picture back then." It was stamped in my memory. Blond. Pale-blue eyes. Beautiful in the way that all young people are beautiful but don't realize that until they are old. Mostly, Lizzie Martins was a regular-looking girl. She and Ali were pictured in outdoor gear, the Shenandoah Valley behind them. I wasn't the only woman Ali took hiking.

We were both quiet as we worked on our laptops trying to track down the elusive Miss Darius. I called the city and county, trying to see if there was a way to find the deed to the house. Lulu called the utility companies. We both came up empty.

"There's no deed to the house on file," I said after getting off the phone.

Lulu looked up from her screen. "Who has the deed, then?"

"The county Register of Deeds office says they don't have to be filed."

Lulu made a face. "That doesn't seem to be very efficient."

"When I get back home, I need to go through all of Ali's papers." I had initially planned to delay that task indefinitely. Looking through Ali's things would stir up lots of emotions, and I had more than enough of those at the moment. "Maybe the deed is somewhere in the house."

The following morning, we went back out to Cozy Glenn. Again, no one was home. Tired and feeling defeated, I slid into a wood porch chair with white cushions that turned out to be very comfortable. It wasn't a cheap set. "How much do you think they paid for this furniture?"

"So we're doing this?" Lulu asked. "We're sitting on her porch like we own the place?"

"Don't we? I mean, don't *I*? Ali paid the mortgage. I'm his widow."

Lulu slipped into the seat opposite me. "If this is your house, why hasn't anyone told you? Ali died weeks ago."

"That's the latest in a long list of good questions we have no answer for."

"Did he have a will?"

I shook my head. "He didn't think it was necessary. Everything was in both our names. If one of us died, the other would get it." On Ali's last birthday, once he turned forty-eight and it sunk in that he was pushing fifty, he started thinking about wills and trusts, but he hadn't gotten around to doing anything about it.

"There has to be a simple way to figure out who pays taxes on the house." She started searching on her phone. While my sister tapped away on her device, I let my gaze wander, taking in the white-painted wooden porch floor and flowers beyond in the garden, the sweet scent of hydrangeas filling the softly humid air. I thought about the fluffy chair cushions coddling me.

Had Ali sat on this porch? In this very seat? Had he felt this comfortable? Ali was frugal. The kids and I teased him about it all the time. He would never have agreed to purchase outdoor furniture this nice. At least, he would have complained if I tried to buy it. Maybe there were different rules for Carol Darius.

"What for?" I could hear him saying as clearly as if he were sitting next to me sipping a glass of cold, sweetened iced tea. "It's a waste of money." He always had a pitcher of tea in the fridge, made with both real sugar and artificial sweeteners to get just the right combination. In that moment, I missed my husband with a burrowing longing that didn't feel survivable. Even though he'd had a secret house, and maybe even a questionable relationship with the woman who lived in it.

"What are you thinking?" Lulu asked.

I was afraid to tell her. As if saying the words out loud would make any emerging doubts more real. "Do you really believe Ali bought this house for his . . . for a woman . . . he might have been involved with?"

"Oh, Amira," she said, her voice full of feeling. "I hope not."

One of those trucks used by mowing services pulled up across the street. A man got out of the driver's side and crossed over. I watched him come up the walkway toward us, half expecting him to demand to know why Lulu and I were sitting on Carol Darius's front porch.

"Excuse me, miss?" he said in greeting, standing at the foot of the porch stairs. Startled, Lulu looked up from her phone.

"Yes?" I decided to act like I owned the place since there was a decent chance that I did.

"I'm Bob. I own the landscaping company that takes care of your lawn."

"Hi, Bob." I decided against sharing my name.

He shifted from one leg to the other. Bob was nervous. "I'm glad I caught you. I knocked on your door last week, but you didn't answer."

"I wasn't here." I wasn't going to actively impersonate Carol Darius, but I was OK with Bob the landscaper making assumptions that meant learning why my husband paid for this house.

"It's about the billing."

"The billing?"

"Yes, I haven't been paid in a month."

"My husband usually takes care of that," I lied. Or maybe it was true. "I'm not sure how he paid you."

"Do you have a number where I could reach him?"

"Unfortunately not. He passed away."

His expression shifted, shock followed by genuine sympathy—reactions I was becoming used to. "I'm sorry."

My throat constricted, but I pushed through. "I'm just starting to catch up on all of the things he used to take care of. I must have missed your bill. Do you recall how he paid you?"

"Let me see. It came from a company." He pulled out his phone to check. But I already knew what he was going to say. "Payment came from the Five *A*'s LLC."

I wasn't surprised. Ali's secret company owned the house, so it wasn't exactly shocking that it also paid some of the bills. But the revelation did chip away at the hope, still lodged deep inside me, that there was an easy, uncomplicated explanation for Ali's ownership of this house. "I'll have to look into it."

He paused. "Do you want me to mow the lawn today?"

Not if I had to pay him. "Maybe we should skip it for now. Do you have a card? I'll call you and settle everything once I've looked through the accounts."

"All right, then." He frowned, not seeming to appreciate the answer. He drew out a business card and advanced far enough onto the porch to hand it to me.

I empathized with Bob's need to get paid for his work, but there was zero chance I was going to pay this Carol person's bills. "Thank you, Bob."

He glanced between me and Lulu as if hoping for help from Lulu. When she just smiled at him, he sighed a little and said, "You two ladies have a nice day."

Chapter Nine

The first thing I did when we got back to Virginia was call Ali's cousin Nasser, a defense attorney. We met at his office near the courthouse at the end of his workday.

"Who is Carol Darius?" I asked, taking the seat opposite his desk. If anyone knew, it would be Nasser. He and Ali roomed together as undergrads and were close friends. Nasser was good-looking and knew it but pretended to be modest about his appeal to women. Never married, he used to show up at parties at our house with a succession of attractive women—some Arab, others not.

"I have no idea who Carol Darius is," Nasser told me. "I've never heard of her."

"Are you sure?" I pressed. "You were closer to him than just about anyone."

"I swear I have no idea." Nasser looked flabbergasted. "You don't think Ali was cheating on you, do you?"

"No, but he owned a whole house without telling me." Emotion clogged my throat. "Which means he *was* hiding something."

He slid his laptop in front of him. "What's the name of the LLC?"

"The Five *A*'s."

He punched a few keys. "Let's take a look."

"What are you doing?"

"Searching the Virginia Corporation Commission."

"What will that tell you?" I asked. "Can you see the operating agreement?"

"No, that's private." He focused on the screen. "But every LLC has to have a registered agent. Either a lawyer or a member of the LLC who lives in-state."

My pulse pounded. "What does it say?"

"Fred Perkins."

The name wasn't familiar. "Who's that?"

Nasser kept his eyes on the screen. "He's the registered agent."

"Have you ever heard of him?"

His face clouded. "No, but he's an attorney."

"I thought you were Ali's attorney."

"I am . . . I was."

"Why wouldn't Ali use you if he needed a lawyer?"

"That's a good question." Nasser exhaled. "Maybe Perkins specializes in real estate law or business law."

My mind churned. What if Ali had other reasons for not wanting Nasser involved in this particular transaction? I always thought my husband trusted his cousin implicitly. My stomach soured. Maybe Ali had a dirty little secret that he wanted to hide even from his closest friend.

Nasser shook his head, disbelief etched on his face. "There has to be a good reason for this."

"I agree. Now, I need to know what that good reason was."

"Maybe they had business together," Nasser suggested. "It's possible Perkins is a member of the LLC."

"How do we find out? Ali was paying the mortgage out of a joint account. Don't I own the house now that he's gone?"

"If you do, the agent, Fred Perkins, should have contacted you by now."

"I guess I'll have to reach out to him."

"Let me do it for you," Nasser offered.

"No." I refused a little too quickly, almost reflexively. "I'll do it myself."

"You don't trust me?" Hurt showed on Nasser's face. "*Wallahi*, I swear to God, I knew nothing about this. I wouldn't hurt you like that. And neither would Ali."

"I have to do this on my own." Something about the rawness of being a widow made me cut straight to the point. I no longer had the patience or energy to worry about how I framed my words. "I want to hear directly from the lawyer myself."

"Are you worried I might try to cover up any wrongdoing to spare you and the kids?"

"No." But if Ali hadn't trusted his cousin with this matter, neither would I. "I need to take more control of my life." I'd been too willing to blindly let Ali take the lead. He'd carried the weight of being the family's protector, the person ultimately responsible for the survival and well-being of our little tribe. I'd so eagerly yielded control of the finances that Ali was able to buy a *whole house* on the side.

I was done living in the dark. I needed to learn the truth. And I was going to go about it my way.

Chapter Ten

Before

Ali ceremoniously proposed during a hike at Great Falls.

"Shouldn't you be asking my dad?" I responded idiotically, completely surprised when Ali went down on one knee.

"I already have," he said.

"Then yes!" My heart felt like it would burst. I couldn't ever remember being as happy as I was in that moment. "Yes! Yes!" I could barely stand still while he slipped the ring onto my finger. It was perfect. A round-cut diamond in a platinum setting. Later, Lulu told me that she helped Ali select the ring. My sister knew exactly what kind of diamond I wanted.

Both sets of parents and our siblings emerged from their hiding places to congratulate us. "*Alf mabrouk*, a thousand congratulations." My mother kissed me hard on both cheeks, glowing with as much happiness as I felt. Afterward, Ali's parents took everyone out to eat, and talk turned to the *tulba*. During the official asking ceremony, Ali's family would bring their male elders to formally ask our family patriarchs for my hand in marriage.

"*Marhabobkum*. Welcome to you all," Ali's father said formally as we waited for our food to arrive. "We are very pleased to have another daughter in our family."

"*Marhaban bikum,*" Baba responded in kind. "How lucky we are to welcome a new son."

Ali's favorite sister, Julia, who sat next to me, lightly bumped her shoulder with mine. "My brother looks at you," she teased me and him, "like you're a juicy steak he can't wait to devour."

Sitting across from us, Ali shook his head. "I should have made sure you didn't sit next to Julia." But he said it with a mix of affection and humor. I loved the way he treated his sisters.

In the car with Ali on the way home, I studied the engagement pictures. They were spectacular against the backdrop of frothy sheets of water cascading over glistening boulders. I realized Ali had chosen the location because we both supposedly loved hiking. Guilt flashed through me. It was time to come clean.

"I have a confession to make before we get married."

He briefly took his eyes off the road to shoot me a glance. "That sounds ominous."

"I've sort of been lying to you."

"About what?"

I took a deep breath and confessed before I lost my nerve. "I don't love hiking, and I don't love the outdoors." But then I quickly added, "But I do love experiencing them with you."

"And?"

"And what? That's it." His flippant response surprised me. "I was pretending to be this outdoorsy girl, which I'm not."

He turned into a strip mall, pulling up to one of the parking spaces farthest from the shops. He turned off the engine and looked at me, his eyes glittering with amusement. "You could have just told me the truth."

I winked, relieved he wasn't mad or disappointed. "But I needed to make sure you bagged the prize."

He shook his head and laughed in that low-key way of his. I never stopped being pleased when he laughed at my jokes. "You're really something." He reached for me. "Time for me to claim my prize."

We met in the middle. It was awkward with the car console between us, but we made it work. Ali pulled me close and kissed me deeply, completely, without reservation. It was sensational. My little white lie earned me my first real kiss.

"Mmmm," I murmured when we briefly came up for air.

He nuzzled my neck. "That was totally worth the wait."

"Totally," I said dreamily, looking forward to another round. "Maybe I should lie more often."

"That kiss was for being honest. Not for lying." He kissed the tip of my nose before pulling away. "I need to get you home before your parents start wondering where you are."

"Since we're being honest and all, I do have a question for you."

"Shoot," he said, pulling onto the road in the direction of my house.

"What about Lizzie?"

I felt him stiffen. In the dark, he was mostly a shadowed outline. "What about her?"

"Does she know?"

"Yes. I told her." He'd been easy, gracious, and smiling all afternoon. Now his voice was distant. Hardened.

"How did she take it?"

"Not well." He blew out a breath. "But it's over."

I didn't want to ruin the joyous mood. Especially after that extraordinary kiss. But I needed to put the Lizzie issue completely to rest. I needed reassurance that I wasn't second best. I couldn't stand the thought of being the Arabic-girl compromise he made to please his parents. "Baba says some boys keep seeing their American girlfriends even after they get married."

"Is that what you think of me?"

"No." Then, because I felt bad for asking, I added, "Of course not."

He stopped at a traffic light and looked at me. His face shone from the glow of the nearby gas station.

"Listen to me. Lizzie is my past. I chose to put her there." He looked me straight in the eye. "You are my future. I would never ask you to marry me if I wanted it any other way. OK?"

I nodded, my throat tight, and hoped that was true.

"And another thing," he added. "I don't ever want to talk about Lizzie again. She has nothing to do with us."

"OK," I said, my voice barely a whisper.

I reached for his hand, which he immediately wrapped firmly around mine.

Chapter Eleven

Now

I was exhausted by the time I arrived home after seeing Nasser, even though it was barely dinnertime.

Everything tired me out these days. Grief was like a computer program that was always running in the background, constantly draining my battery. I drove into the garage, pulling up next to Ali's old Honda.

I'd cried when I picked up the dark-green sedan from the shop after Ali died. The thought that he'd never drive his car again tore my heart. It had been parked in the garage since. Next year, when Adam was allowed to have a car on campus, I'd let him take his father's car.

Dragging myself into the house, I toed off my shoes and put on house slippers. I padded around in the darkness, closing the curtains and switching all the lights on. I'd always liked bright spaces, and that was even more true now that I lived alone.

The house crackled, the upstairs floor groaning slightly. Uneasiness slithered through me. When would I get used to being alone at night? Surely I'd lived on my own long enough now to be slightly more accustomed to the symphony of unidentifiable noises.

The floor above me groaned again, followed by the unmistakable sound of muffled footsteps on the upstairs carpet. I stilled. Maybe it was the kids. Had one of them come home in the middle of the week?

"Hello?" I stood at the bottom of the stairs, calling up the dark staircase. "Ayla? Adam?"

Silence met me. Even the house seemed to be holding its breath. I paused for a few moments and, hearing nothing else, shook my head. My imagination was getting the better of me. I scurried up the stairs, turning on all the lights as I went, eager to reach the safety of my bedroom, where I could lock the door behind me.

Entering the primary bedroom, I slammed the door shut and pushed a comfortable stuffed chair up against it, which made me feel a little more protected. I stilled, listening, but the house was quiet.

With a slight breath of relief, I crossed over to the walk-in closet and pulled off my top. That's when I heard it again. Footsteps creaking along the floorboards. Coming from down the hall. This time, I couldn't pooh-pooh my fears. The sounds were undeniable.

Someone is in the house.

I froze, fear arrowing up my spine. Fighting the urge to panic, I dragged my shirt back over my head. There was no way to call for help. My mobile was downstairs, and we didn't have a landline in our bedroom. What if I made a run for it? But the primary bedroom was at the end of the hall. I'd have to go past all the other bedrooms to reach the stairs.

Think, Amira, think. I forced a calming breath, but it was more like a shallow huff. My heart slammed against my rib cage. How should I react if the intruder confronted me? I looked around wildly for something to protect myself with.

My gaze landed on the briefcase-like fireproof safe on the floor of Ali's closet. Ali stored titles to the cars and other important documents, like the passports and birth certificates, in the metal box. I grabbed it, clutching the handle, and imagined swinging the portable safe up to bash the intruder in the head. Maybe I'd stun him long enough to reach the stairs and escape to safety.

I stood completely still, listening for the intruder, although it was hard to hear anything over the pounding in my ears. The footsteps had stopped, the silence broken only by my breath sawing in and out of my chest. I crept toward the bedroom door, trying not to make a sound. Downstairs, a door slammed so hard, the windows shook.

"Help!" I screamed, assuming someone had just come in. It wasn't logical, but it was the first thought that came to me. "Someone broke in!"

The house was silent again. Offering no help. No hope or comfort. Had the intruder slammed the door on his way out? Maybe he was gone.

My legs were shaky as I shoved the chair away from the door and quietly pulled it open. I peered out of the window at the top of the stairs. I couldn't see much outside in the front yard, but movement near the street caught my eye. Someone running in the shadows. The intruder? I could barely make the figure out. No way to tell if it was a man or a woman.

Trying to regulate my breathing, I went to the nearest room, Ali's office. The light was on. The drawers were all pulled open, and what few papers had been on the desk were strewn across the floor. I backed away, shock rippling through me. This scene had nothing to do with my overactive imagination or paranoia. Someone had actually broken into my house. But why?

What were they looking for?

―――

"There's a sensor on every window," Nasser said a few hours later. After a couple of uniformed police officers left, he'd gone out to buy a security system. It was after ten o'clock by the time he finished installing it. "I've put the app on your phone. Any time a door or window opens, you'll get a notification."

Still rattled, I tried to focus on his instructions. "Do I have to turn it off and on?"

"No, you can leave it on all the time."

Needing something to keep my hands busy, I gathered the security packaging and went to the kitchen. "What do you think they wanted?"

"Since the intruder seemed to only focus on Ali's office, we have to assume they were after something Ali had."

"But what? He rarely worked from home or brought any business papers home."

"Maybe the officers who responded tonight will be able to come up with something."

Pulling open the disposal drawer in the island, I automatically separated the trash from the recyclables. I was still partially in shock. I couldn't believe someone had broken into my house. Had I interrupted a burglary? "This all seems unreal. Ali was just a regular guy, and suddenly I'm caught up in all this craziness."

He set a booklet down on the counter. "Here's the guide to the security system in case you need it. Tomorrow we'll see about installing a doorbell camera so you don't have to open the door to speak to strangers. Plus, it might be a good idea to install outdoor cameras."

I was on board with all of that. "The more security, the better. But I insist on paying you back for the security system you bought me today. I will not take no for an answer."

He raised his palms toward me. "I know better than to fight with you."

"Good, and I'm giving you dinner for installing it."

"That's not necessary. It's too late to eat—" he began.

I opened the fridge. "I have leftover *maklooba*."

He switched course. "You know I never turn down Arabic food."

"That's what I thought." I made us two plates of the rice, fried vegetable, and lamb dish that was cooked in a lamb broth, and heated it in the microwave.

The doorbell rang.

"Who's that?" Nasser asked, half standing.

"Why don't you sit down and eat while your food is hot. I'll get the door. It's probably Lulu."

"Make sure you check to see who it is before you open the door."

The instant she saw me, Lulu launched herself in my direction, enveloping me in a bear hug. "Are you OK? What the hell! You must have been so scared."

"It did freak me out," I admitted, relishing the warm comfort of her embrace. It felt like forever since I'd been held.

"You've got to come stay with me."

I was tempted to take her up on her offer, but moving out of the home Ali and I had shared for most of our marriage would confirm my worst fears about myself: that I was unworldly and dependent and couldn't make it without a man.

"No, thank you." I shook my head as I led her into the kitchen. "I like to sleep in my own house."

"That was before your husband died and someone broke in!" She spotted Nasser eating at the counter. "Maybe you can talk some sense into her."

He spoke around a mouthful of *maklooba*. "I agree that it would be safer for her to stay somewhere else."

I crossed my arms over my chest. "I'm not going anywhere. The kids have a short school break coming up, so I won't be alone."

"But you will be after they leave," Lulu pointed out.

"Nasser just installed a security system. And I'm going to have cameras put up outside." Maybe I was in denial, yet again, but whoever broke in didn't seem to be after me. The intruder ran away the minute they could, rather than confront me. Besides, I wasn't about to draw any potential danger to Lulu's house. She had young children.

"Aren't you afraid to sleep here alone?" she asked.

Yes. But I needed to prove to myself that I could stand on my own two feet. Besides, leaving the house would be like relinquishing another piece of my old life. Purchasing the house with Ali and making it into our home—a haven for us and our children—was core to our life as a couple. I wouldn't allow fear to push me out. I'd lost enough.

"I'll be OK now that I have a security system," I said, pretending to be braver than I felt. I looked to Nasser. "And maybe we could put a better lock on the door to the primary bedroom?"

"No problem. I'll take care of it first thing in the morning." Nasser rose and rinsed his plate off in the sink. "I'll leave you two ladies to it."

I followed him out. "Thanks for the security system."

"Anytime. Oh, I almost forgot." He reached into his jacket pocket and produced a small blue canister. "This is for you."

"What is it?"

"Pepper spray. Just in case," he said quickly. "It attaches to your key chain, but you can carry it separately in your purse."

"OK." I accepted his offering without protest. "Thanks. I'll keep it with me whenever I go out."

"Good." He reached for the door. "I'm glad you're being reasonable about security."

"Why wouldn't I be? I'm not a complete idiot."

What I didn't say was that I was my children's only surviving parent. I needed to stick around for them as long as I could.

After several days of trying, I finally got Fred Perkins on the phone.

"I didn't realize your husband had passed away," he said. "Please accept my condolences."

I asked about the house and whether, as Ali's spouse, it now belonged to me. After a long pause, Perkins finally answered.

"I have the operating agreement right here."

"And?" I pressed, my heart pounding hard. "What does it say?"

"I'm afraid I can't disclose that information. The contents of the operating agreement are private." He cleared his throat through the phone. "However, I can tell you that the house at 104 Cozy Glenn Lane does not belong to you."

"But . . . how can that be?" I was speechless. Flustered. Floored. "My husband paid for that property out of our joint savings account. Who gets the house?" I held my breath, waiting for him to utter Carol Darius's name.

"Unfortunately, that is also confidential. I am very sorry." And he did sound it. I could hear the sympathy in his voice.

"You're telling me that my husband used our jointly earned money to buy a house and now that he's dead I get nothing?"

Since Ali's death I'd felt mostly shock, followed by a numbness. I'd experienced the sensation of feeling disconnected from myself, all my emotions muted. But now, anger and frustration hammered through me. If there was any question whether I could still feel anything, learning my husband left a secret house that we paid for to someone else answered that question.

"Again, I am very sorry," Fred Perkins said. "All I can tell you is that another member of the LLC gets the house. There are provisions in the operating agreement that upon the death of one of the members, the other member would get the house."

The other member. "Does that mean there were only two members in the LLC? My husband and one other person?"

"It would not be appropriate for me to disclose anything further. Again, please accept my most sincere condolences for your loss."

My phone buzzed right after I hung up with Fred Perkins. I jumped, startled. I'd been on edge since the break-in. Especially whenever I was home alone.

My daughter's name popped up on the screen. Relief moved through me. I took the call. "Hi, honey."

"Hey, Mom."

"How's school?"

"It's a lot of work, as usual. What are you up to?"

"Nothing much," I lied. "Just working."

"How was that house you went to see in North Carolina?"

I stumbled. "How . . . was what?"

"The house you went to see in North Carolina?"

I swallowed. My throat felt like sandpaper. "How did you know about that house?"

"Mom?" Impatience tinged her words. "Are you OK? You told me you and Auntie Lulu were going to see the biggest house in the United States."

"Oh, you mean the Biltmore Estate." The tightness between my shoulder blades eased. "Yeah, it was fine."

"What else would I be talking about?"

"Sorry, I was in the middle of researching a new exhibit project," I lied. "I was distracted."

"Are you busy?" she asked. "Should I let you go?"

"No, no." I wanted to speak to my baby girl. Hearing her voice in the midst of all this chaos made my heart happy. "I can work on that later. How are you doing?"

"OK."

I doubted that, so I decided to be honest. "I'm worried about you."

"Don't be. I'm fine."

"You keep saying that, but you don't seem fine. You've lost weight. You're not yourself."

"Are any of us the same?" The words were sharp. "How can we be?"

"You're right. We can't." Tears stung my eyes. We'd lost so much, including the sense of safety that Ali provided. And my absolute belief in him as a faithful husband.

I fought to keep it together. The kids didn't need to know that my world was falling apart for a second time. As I spoke to my daughter, a crystal-clear thought formed in my mind, possibly the first completely lucid one since my husband's accident: I had to protect my kids at any cost. The last thing they needed was to share my confusion and growing doubts about their father. Once I figured out what was going on with the secret house, I'd explain everything to them.

Even if he left a house to his mistress? a voice inside me asked. I prayed I'd never have to cross that bridge. For now, at least, it had to be mentally healthier for our children to continue to believe in their dad.

Even if I wasn't sure how much I still did.

Chapter Twelve

Before

"I'm nervous," I admitted to Ali as we approached the sports bar where we were meeting his cousins to watch a football game.

I hadn't met any of them yet, but I knew they were all close. Ali was especially tight with the cousin he roomed with in college. "What if they don't like me?"

Ali squeezed my hand. Holding hands still felt very illicit. Our close family knew we were getting married, but our engagement wasn't official and wouldn't be public knowledge until after the formal asking ceremony, the *tulba*, in a couple of weeks.

"Why wouldn't they like you?" Ali asked. "Besides, what they think doesn't really matter because I like you." Winking, he squeezed my hand again. "Very, very, very much."

I smiled back, swallowing my nervousness. Pretending not to notice that he didn't use the L-word. Neither of us had. Other couples exchanged the L-word all the time. I knew that. We just hadn't gotten there. Yet.

But it was on my mind enough that, earlier that day, I'd mentioned to Mama and Lulu that Ali hadn't said the L-word yet.

"*Hetchee fathee,*" Mama proclaimed. "You don't need empty talk."

Lulu and I had been at the kitchen table making *maamoul* cookies, which would be frozen and served at the *tulba*. Mama stood at the counter prepping the date filling for the semolina butter cookies.

Lulu rolled a small ball of cookie dough. "Telling your future bride that you love them is empty talk?" she asked. "Do you mean Baba doesn't tell you he loves you when you're in bed at night being all lovey-dovey?"

"*Ist-hee a halick!*" Mama blushed and threw the kitchen towel she was holding at Lulu. "Have some shame."

Lulu easily caught it. "There's no shame in wanting your husband to be in love with you."

"Seriously," I said, agreeing. "But just because Ali hasn't said, 'I love you,' doesn't mean that he doesn't." He was definitely into me physically. And I felt his warmth and his fondness, that indescribable glow of something special between us.

"You don't have to love each other yet." Mama carried the date filling over to the table and heavily took a seat. Her apron was covered in flour, and curly gray-frosted tendrils of hair escaped her ponytail. "You *grow* to love each other."

Lulu scoffed. "Yeah, I intend to be in love *before* I get married, not after."

"Don't be such an American." Mama reached for a cookie-size dough ball and flattened it before spooning in the date filling.

"We are Americans," I reminded her.

Mama kept talking. "They are all in love when they get married, and then half of them end up divorced. Our way is much better."

"What way is that?" Lulu asked. "Marry a near stranger and hope you get along? It's like a one-night stand that lasts until death do us part."

Mama frowned at her. "We'll be lucky if we manage to marry you off. Men don't like girls with attitude."

Lulu winked at me and mouthed, *Some definitely do.*

"Our way," Mama continued, "is for the families to help you choose a good mate. We check his reputation and his family's reputation. We try to see if it's a good match, a sensible match."

Lulu grimaced. "I prefer a passionate love match."

I replayed Mama's words over in my head as Ali held the bar door open for me that evening. I didn't need to wait for love to grow. I was already in love. As for Ali, he was definitely in lust. And it was obvious that he enjoyed my company. But was he in love? I had no idea. But surely it was only a matter of time.

"There you are," said a heavyset guy with an appealing teddy bear quality about him.

Ali's cousins were an attractive group. They all had killer thick, dark lashes that required no mascara or eyelash curlers. He introduced me around. There were seven of them in all, four women and three guys, including his cousin Nasser, a handsome man who mostly kept his distance.

"This is Hamooda," Ali said, introducing me to the teddy bear cousin.

"So you're Lizzie, the girlfriend," Hamooda said. "I've heard a lot about you."

I froze. An arctic air swept through me.

"This is Amira," Ali said quickly. "My fiancée," he added, stamping the air with the firm words. "The girl I can't wait to marry."

"Oh! My bad." Hamooda looked both mortified and surprised. "You're engaged?" He looked to the others, who pretended not to notice the car crash happening in front of them. "Is this common knowledge? Am I the last to know?"

"Both," said the cousin named Shireen, a willowy girl with straightened long black hair. "If you'd ever return Mama's phone calls, you might learn something." She turned to me. "Amira, in order to survive this family, you have to ignore half of what these idiots say."

I forced a smile. "I'll keep that in mind."

But in my head, all I could think of was Hamooda mistaking me for Lizzie. I'd put her out of my mind after we got engaged, but for her name to pop up in this setting thrust her firmly back to center stage.

I've heard a lot about you.

What had he heard? Did all the cousins know Lizzie? Did they all think she was great? My insecurities about whether Ali had lingering feelings for his ex-girlfriend blazed back. Was I competing with her for his affection? And for that of his entire cousin group?

"Do you want something to drink?" Ali asked, his voice low and intense in my ear. I registered the tense lines around his mouth.

I ignored him. Instead, I plastered a teasing smile on my face, as if I were too confident to care about my fiancé's ex. "You've heard a lot about Lizzie?" I said too loudly, trying to be funny. "I haven't. Tell me everything."

For a brief moment, an uncomfortable silence hung over us.

"She was whatever." Shireen broke the silence. "Obviously a nobody. You're the soon-to-be wife. You're the winner."

"Does that make Ali the prize?" Hamooda said teasingly. "Poor girl."

I was tongue-tied, so unnerved by hearing Lizzie's name that I couldn't think of a clever way to engage in the banter.

The aloof cousin, the handsome one, subtly came to my rescue. "OK, everyone," Nasser said. "The game is about to start. Look at the menu, and let's order."

"I need some wings," one of the cousins said.

Shireen reached for a menu. "Should we order a bunch of appetizers for the group?"

"I'm going to get a burger," Hamooda said. "I haven't eaten since breakfast."

I exhaled, relieved the focus was no longer on me. My initial plan coming into the evening was to win over the cousins by being interesting and engaging. So much for that.

Once we were all eating and watching the game—I pretended to follow the action on the TV screen—Ali, who'd kept close tabs on me all evening, leaned in. He spoke into my ear so I could hear him above the din.

"Are you OK?"

"How well do they know Lizzie?"

"Not well. You heard Hamooda. He never met her."

"How *not well*?"

He released a breath. "She came out with us two or three times. Maybe more. Nasser was my roommate. He knew her the best."

Knew her the best. Liked her the best?

Ali placed his hand over mine and squeezed. "Forget about Lizzie. I promise you. She's ancient history."

Chapter Thirteen

Now

Nasser seemed pensive, but Lulu showed zero surprise when I filled them in on my conversation with Fred Perkins.

"Why are you sitting there acting like it's no big deal?" I asked my sister, even though I knew why.

Lulu bit into her carrot stick with a snap. "I'm not super surprised Ali didn't leave you the house, since he never told you about it in the first place."

We sat at my kitchen island nibbling mixed nuts and hummus with raw vegetables and pita bread. Feeling antsy, I got up and paced the wood kitchen floor, treading over nicks and dents from sixteen years of family living. I used to catch the kids rolling through the kitchen on their wheeled tennis shoes.

"I need to find out if that woman got the house," I told them. "I *have* to talk to her."

"Are you sure that's smart?" Nasser asked.

"I want to hear it from her mouth why Ali was paying for that house."

He winced. "I still don't believe Ali cheated on you."

"You're a lawyer," Lulu said sharply to him. "Shouldn't you consider all the evidence and reach the most logical conclusion?"

"I'm thinking like his best friend," Nasser returned. "Ali loved Amira. He wouldn't cheat on her." Just a few days ago I'd believed the same thing. But now? I didn't know what to think.

Lulu silently replenished our iced tea. Over the years, the extended family had come to appreciate Ali's tea recipe. Nasser gulped it down his throat, his biceps bulging in the short-sleeved button-down shirt he wore over jeans. His hair was wet. He'd just come from the gym.

"What we know so far doesn't look good, I'll give you that." He set the empty glass down. "But we don't have enough facts to reach any conclusions."

"That house is a pretty unassailable truth," I finally said.

Compassion filled Lulu's face. "The facts do seem to point to a pretty ugly reality."

Tears stung my eyes. "I was married to the man for more than two decades. I knew who he was, didn't I?"

"But you didn't know about the secret house in North Carolina," she gently reminded me.

"Yes, Ali lied. That's for sure." I took a breath, still holding on to hope. "But maybe there's another explanation for why he did that." *Please, God, let there be.*

Lulu dipped celery into the hummus. "I hope you're right. But I just want you to be prepared for the worst."

I would never be ready for that. "What if I sue her?"

Nasser poured himself more iced tea. "Who?"

"Carol Darius."

Doubt crossed Nasser's face. "You don't even know if Carol Darius got the house."

"Then I'll sue the LLC. I'd learn what I need to know during discovery, right?" I warmed to the idea. "Wouldn't they have to show me the operating agreement?"

"They might," Nasser admitted. "It could work, actually."

My phone buzzed. It was a text from Julia, Ali's sister. **Salam. Mama was wondering if you've ordered the headstone yet? Sorry to bother you but she keeps asking.**

I exhaled long and loud. "As if I don't have enough to worry about."

Lulu strained to see my phone screen. "What is it?"

"Ali's mom wants to know if I've ordered the headstone. The kids and I haven't decided what writing to put on it."

Nasser poured himself more tea. "You could just order the stone itself. And decide the writing later. That's what we did with *Sidi* when he died. It takes months for the stone to come in."

"I just can't deal with that at the moment." How could I know what headstone to order? A grand one fit for a loving husband and father? Or some cheap crap that was more appropriate for a cheating liar who kept a mistress? I also had to consider what the kids would want, how they'd want to honor their father. Fortunately, they hadn't asked about the tombstone yet.

"Don't let anyone rush you," Lulu advised.

I set my phone down, making a mental note to respond to Julia later. "What about it?" I said to Nasser. "Are you still my lawyer too? Or were you only Ali's attorney?"

"I'll help in any way I can," he responded, his voice gentle. "But maybe your sister is right. You might not like what you learn."

"I already know that." And then I added, "And I'm paying you your rate."

"Nope," he said. "I never charged Ali, and I'm not billing you." Arabs always fought over who picked up the tab, a habit ingrained in us even though we were born in America.

"That's not the same. Ali did the taxes for your law office," I protested. "You exchanged professional services." Nasser had a small legal practice. It was just him and two other attorneys.

Nasser held up a hand. "I'll let you pay any fees associated with any of the filings. But that's it."

"All right," I relented when I saw there was no arguing with him. "Let's do it."

"See?" Claudia said. "Doesn't it feel good to be out walking in the fresh air?"

I strode beside my neighbor, an effusive person who finally succeeded in badgering me into resuming our morning walks.

At least someone was still reaching out to me, even if she wasn't a close friend like Nicki and Rula, whose absence continued to hurt and make me feel even more alone. Especially after the phone call I'd had with Nicki a few days earlier.

"Why aren't you in touch more often?" I asked when Nicki finally reached out.

"What do you mean?"

"I never hear from you anymore."

"I don't know what you're talking about," she responded, acting completely oblivious.

Deflated, I let it go. She obviously wasn't up for an honest conversation. Death was an uncomfortable topic. Maybe Nicki and Rula kept their distance because they were afraid that my tragedy was contagious. Ali wasn't the only person who'd abandoned me. But at least he had no choice.

As we circled the cul-de-sac, I had a new appreciation for Claudia. At least she showed up for me. And it did feel good to be outside moving my body again for the first time since the accident.

"I hope you understand my going for a walk is a day-to-day decision," I said to her. "That's the most I can commit to."

"I'll take it!" she said cheerfully. "How's it been going? I feel like I never see you. I can imagine that losing Ali has been a lot."

"More than you know." I decided against telling her about the secret house. But she did live next door, and so, for her family's safety, I felt obligated to tell her about the break-in.

She shivered. "You were in the house with the guy? How are you so calm? I'd be freaking out."

"I'm freaking out on the inside." I only had so much freak-out energy left. Between losing Ali, discovering the secret house, and worrying about the possibility of another break-in, I was running on emotional fumes.

"What are you going to do?" Claudia had young kids. "How can you sleep by yourself in that big house?"

"We put in a security system. I feel a lot safer now." Not completely safe. But at least a little more secure.

"I don't know how you do it." We rounded a corner in the neighborhood. "You're so strong."

Little did she know. But I heard that a lot—how strong I'd been since Ali died. As if I had a choice. What was the alternative?

"You're a much braver person than I am," Claudia said as we picked up the pace. "If something happened to Matt, I think the kids and I would move in with my parents."

"I considered staying elsewhere, but my life has been upended enough already."

"Look." Claudia pointed to a house near the entrance to our neighborhood. "The Khans sold their house." We slowed down as we approached the "Under Contract" sign.

"I wonder where they're going." My first instinct was to text Ali to tell him and then ask how much he thought the house had sold for.

Sorrow bolted through me when I remembered that I couldn't. Another moment of grief, like so many others, that struck when I least expected, when there was no way to brace for the onslaught. Longing throbbed in the deepest part of me, despite the doubts I had about my husband. Losing Ali was like losing an arm or a leg. You could live without it, but something critical would always be missing.

I yearned for our throwaway, inconsequential, everyday conversations. Just like I missed that sense of safety that left when Ali did. But maybe all of that, what I thought we had, was an illusion. That was the way my mind worked these days. Sometimes, I was absolutely convinced there was no way Ali cheated on me. But during darker moments, I wondered.

How would I cope if my entire understanding of our life together turned out to be a lie?

Chapter Fourteen

Before

Lots of people come to Arab weddings.

Hundreds. In addition to dozens of aunts, uncles, and cousins on both sides, pretty much every immigrant family from our parents' native Palestinian town was on the guest list. Ali and I didn't know half of them. Luckily, our families were from the same town, so we didn't have to put another entire town of people on the guest list. Ali and I sent about twenty-five invitations each to our own friends and, in his case, colleagues.

Our tradition was for the groom and his family to pay for the wedding. Ali's mom, Um Ali (which translates to "Mother of Ali"), and his sister Julia made most of the arrangements but included me in the planning. That was when I first started to grow close to Julia, who was practical and pleasant and pretty much never had a mean word to say about anyone. Being around her made me want to be a better person.

In the spirit of inclusion and getting along, I invited Um Ali and Julia to go with me, along with Mama and Lulu, to pick out my wedding dress. It didn't take long for me to realize that I was fortunate in them. I'd heard nightmare stories about people's in-laws, but mine were genuinely kind.

"If you make my son happy, you make me happy," my mother-in-law liked to say.

About three weeks before the wedding, I was at my future in-laws' house with Julia finalizing the RSVPs and the seating chart when a name on the guest list caught my attention.

Ms. Elizabeth Martins.

I froze, staring at the name, unable to believe what I was seeing.

"What is it?" Julia asked.

"Do you know who this is?" I asked, unsure whether she was aware her brother had dated a white American girl for years.

She looked at the name I pointed to. Her expression grew serious. "You should talk to Ali about it."

"Do you think this is OK?" My neck burned. "To invite this woman to our wedding?" Julia was reasonable. She couldn't possibly approve. "Do you?"

"Amira," she said in a calm, quiet way that reminded me of Ali. "No matter what I think, I will never speak against my brother. Never."

"No matter what," I repeated, stung. "I thought we'd become close."

"I *am* your friend, and soon we'll be sisters-in-law," she said. "I would never speak against you either."

"If I was in the wrong, I'd want you to be honest, to tell me so," I said hotly.

"Speak to Ali." She moved away, returning to the other end of the dining table to continue what she was working on.

"I would if I ever saw him," I grumbled, mostly under my breath. It was tax season, which meant he worked long hours.

"I'm sure he'll explain everything."

"Fine." I grabbed my purse. "I'll see you later." I walked out, got into my car, and drove until their house was out of sight. Then I pulled over and forced myself to take several deep breaths.

I couldn't believe it. Ali invited his ex-girlfriend to our wedding without mentioning it to me? Without making sure I was OK with it? Maybe he thought I wouldn't care, that I understood that Lizzie Martins was in the past. But now doubt flooded me. Maybe Baba was right. Maybe Ali intended to keep Lizzie around as his sidepiece.

My face was hot, and my chest felt like there was a heavy brick lodged inside of it. I wanted someone to vent to, but I was too embarrassed to let anyone know that my fiancé invited his ex to our wedding without telling me.

My phone buzzed. It was Ali calling. I sent it to voicemail. The same with a second call. And a third. Then he texted.

Hey I'm trying to call you. Can you pick up?

I wanted to continue to ignore his texts. To keep him guessing for hours. Days, even. But I'd never been any good at playing the long game. I furiously pounded a response into my phone.

Me: Maybe you should call your girlfriend and see what she's wearing to the wedding I wonder if she'll wear white. What do you think?

Ali: Pick up the phone so we can talk

Me: NOW you want to talk???? I thought the subject of your girlfriend was off limits

Ali: If you just calm down I can explain

Me: Don't you dare tell me to calm down!!! You're the asshole here. Not me

Ali: Please pick up the phone so we can talk

I stopped responding to his texts and turned off my phone. I needed to think. What should I do? What *could* I do? The wedding was three weeks away. Everything was booked, the deposits paid. It would be a huge embarrassment for both families if I backed out now. I could just imagine the gossip. Everyone would probably assume that Ali dumped me.

Maybe she wasn't a virgin.
I heard that once he got to know her, he found her annoying.
She talked too much.

She didn't talk enough.
He's handsome and has a good job. He could marry anyone.
What a hamara. *Only a female donkey would think she could do better.*
She's not that young. Almost twenty-two.
They say she's mejnoona. *Crazy.*

I shoved the unconstructive thoughts out of my head. What I'd told Ali was true: I was basically a go-with-the-flow kind of person. But not if the flow included his ex. I wanted nothing to do with any girl he'd slept with. If the past was the past, then that's where Lizzie should stay. She definitely didn't belong at my wedding. I knew men could be idiots, but was Ali really *this* dumb?

I debated what to do. I didn't want to go home, and I didn't have a job to go to. I'd decided that if the museum job came through, great, but if not, I'd actively look for my first full-time position after we got married. I wanted to be free for wedding planning, and taking a new job right now would also limit the length of my honeymoon. In the meantime, college graduation cash gifts were my spending money.

Mama heartily approved of this decision to focus on my impending marriage, Baba was neutral, and Lulu just rolled her eyes. "Way to put your life on hold for a man," she said.

"I'm not focusing on a man. I'm focusing on my wedding," I told her. "You only get married once."

Now I wasn't sure I was getting married at all. Needing time alone to think, I went to a matinee—I had no idea what movie I saw—and then took myself to dinner. I texted my parents to tell them I was seeing a movie and eating out with friends so that they wouldn't worry. I somehow managed to keep my phone off. When I finally got home, it was after nine o'clock. Mama and Baba were watching cable TV news in the family room.

"There you are," Mama said, keeping her eyes on the screen. "Call Ali. He said he's been trying to call you but something is wrong with your phone."

"My phone is fine," I called back as I went up the stairs. "I just turned it off during the movie and forgot to turn it back on."

I reached the sanctuary of my room and stared at the full-size bed covered with an old floral comforter that I'd picked out in high school. Would I still be sleeping in this bed in three weeks? Or would I be on my honeymoon? I changed into my pajamas, washed my face, and brushed my teeth before climbing into bed. I kept my phone off.

Ali didn't track me down until the next morning as I was leaving the gym. Normally, I'd hate for him to see me at my worst, with sweaty hair and baggy clothes. I was never one of those girls who looked cute while working out.

"This is ridiculous," he said.

"Tell me about it." I walked past him toward the parking lot.

"Are you just not going to take my calls all the way up until the wedding?"

"*If* there's a wedding."

"Come on." His voice softened. "Don't talk like that."

"Don't tell me what to do." I reached my car and threw my gym bag in the trunk.

He followed me to the driver's side. "Are you really willing to throw all of this away?"

I rounded to face him, my back against the car door. "You threw it away by being a cheating liar."

"I've never been unfaithful to you. And I've never lied to you. Or anyone else. Ever."

"I guess I'll have to take your word for it."

"Julia told me you were upset to see Lizzie's name on the guest list."

I gritted my teeth. "If you tell me to calm down again, I swear I'll get in this car and run you over. Probably more than once."

"I didn't mean to invite her, but I screwed up. I asked Sara Carr, one of the girls in our JMU group, to email the addresses for our group to my sister Siham. Sara was basically our social coordinator in college. She planned every trip we took. She had all of our addresses. I never expected her to include Lizzie on the list."

"What are you saying?" I asked hopefully. "That you didn't know Lizzie was invited?"

"I found out after the fact, *after* the invitations went out. Siham didn't know about me and Lizzie, so she just added her to the guest list, no questions asked. I've been meaning to talk to you about it."

It was plausible that Siham didn't know about Lizzie. As Muslims, none of us were supposed to date, guys included. But many young men did, and most people, including their own parents, looked the other way, expecting their sons to ultimately come back into the fold by settling down with a nice Muslim girl. For a man like Ali to be quiet, even to his family, about dating an American girl made perfect sense.

But that didn't excuse the fact that Lizzie was *still* on the guest list.

"What exactly do you think there is to talk about?" I asked. "You should have picked up the phone, called Lizzie, and told her, 'Um, you're obviously not invited.' It's not rocket science."

"Actually, I did. I mean, I tried to, but Lizzie went ballistic. She said that it would embarrass her in front of our friend group to be left off the guest list."

"We wouldn't want your poor girlfriend to be embarrassed," I said acidly. "But hurting your future wife is OK, I guess."

"*Ex-girlfriend,*" he said pointedly. "Look, there are about seven people I was really tight with in college. Lizzie and I were both in the group. We told everyone the breakup was mutual, that we're still friends. Lizzie said if that's true, she should be invited."

I quelled an immediate urge to slap him. "Lizzie wants this. Lizzie feels bad about that. Maybe you need to step back and consider whether you're still into Lizzie."

"I'm not into her. In any way."

"Really? But you're so worried about her feelings. You know what I don't hear from you? Any concern, at all, about what *I* want. How *I* feel."

"All I care about is you." His voice was tender. He stared into my eyes in that way that made my knees turn to jelly. "I absolutely planned to tell you, but I've been so jammed at work. I needed to finish up a very challenging and time-consuming engagement and then focus on this. I didn't want to talk to you about it over the phone."

"That's a dumb excuse for such a smart man," I snapped. "When did you plan to tell me? After the wedding?"

"I know I made a mistake. I already texted Lizzie that she can't come. If it hurts her feelings or makes her lose face with our friends, she'll have to deal with it. I don't want us ever to have to talk about Lizzie again. I meant it when I said that she's in the past."

"Then why does her name keep popping up? I feel like I'm playing Old Girlfriend Whac-A-Mole." My tone was sharp. But even as I spoke, I felt myself softening. Ali was calm, as always, but I detected the note of desperation, the panic in his voice.

"I have never been sorrier about anything in my life. I know I effed up. The last thing I want to do is make you question how I feel about you or whether you can trust me. I am truly very sorry. I'll spend our entire honeymoon making it up to you."

"Oh really?" My anger dissolved as I ate up his apology. "What will that entail?"

"Anything you can think of." He leaned in. Slowly. Giving me time to push him away if I wanted.

But this desperate, almost-groveling version of Ali was crazy sexy. "I do like the sound of that."

Relief etched his face. "You're the only woman in the world who matters." And that's how he kissed me. Long and slow, deep and passionate, showing me what I meant to him with his mouth and tongue far more eloquently than words ever could.

I always thought the crazy chemistry between us was a lucky gift. But maybe it was a curse, because whenever Ali kissed me like that, with everything in him, I couldn't imagine ever letting him go. I was addicted to the way I felt when he kissed me. Beautiful, powerful, capable of anything.

"I want to go down on you," he said against my lips.

"That'll be some honeymoon," I responded, the blood rushing through my ears. My skin felt alive, every nerve ending titillated and eager for more.

"No." He kissed me again slowly, seductively, using his tongue to do things that made me lose my mind. "Now."

That wasn't going to happen. What I had going on down there was no fantasy. I wasn't groomed. I had an appointment for right before the wedding. "I just worked out. I can't."

"I don't care."

"I do. Plus, it's a jungle down there."

"Is it?" Interest lit his eyes. "Let me see."

"Absolutely not."

"Then at least let me feel." We were between cars, shielded by the wall I'd parked in front of. He shifted so that people driving by couldn't see me. His hand went to the waistband of my workout sweats.

"Oh!" I said at the electricity that shot through my body when he touched me. And there was no more talk, or thought, of my calling off the wedding.

Chapter Fifteen

Now

About seventeen years into our marriage, I had an epiphany about Ali.

During a yoga class meditation, we were asked to focus on the closest person to us, our truest love. My thinking mind immediately went to the children, but when I closed my eyes, I saw Ali's sweet face, the ever-present smile, the gentle expression, the understated laugh at one of my jokes.

Marriages, like people, are imperfect. There were times I actively disliked my husband, especially when his extreme cheapness made me feel constrained, hemmed in. We stopped seeing certain friends with expensive tastes because of it. Ali and I rarely fought about anything but money. The problem was that money touches everything in life. Where you live. Who you see. Where you go. What you do day-to-day.

But, that afternoon in the yoga class, the insight about the depth of my love for Ali felt like the truest thing. And I was glad, after he died, that I'd had that realization, that I knew what I had when I had it. That I didn't ever have to regret not loving Ali enough.

When I went home and told him, Ali said, "You only just now realized?" And we went upstairs and made love. Long and slow and sweet and tender. That afternoon stayed with me for a long time.

I couldn't remember Ali ever saying, "I love you." He showed it in the way he took care of me and the children. I never doubted his devotion. I assumed his reserve was a natural part of his personality. But maybe it was because he kept secrets from me.

Later, I compared the dates and realized that he'd already purchased the house on Cozy Glenn Lane by the time we made love that afternoon.

The morning after deciding to sue the LLC, I got my coffee and sat down to edit an exhibit script for a Missouri museum.

I'd developed a thriving freelance business, working with design firms hired by museums to put together new exhibits or update old ones. A lot of my work came via word of mouth. The museum world was tight knit.

But I couldn't concentrate. How long would it take to learn anything from the lawsuit? I was impatient to know more. My thoughts went to Ali's phone. I'd avoided going through his electronics up until now. In part because it still felt like snooping, even though Ali was dead. But maybe I'd find some clue about the woman who lived in the Cozy Glenn house.

I checked my work calendar. I had a meeting at eleven with a new client, a museum in Indiana that was being revamped and wanted me to write a new exhibit. It was a big job. But I had a couple of hours before the call, so I went upstairs to Adam's room, where Ali's phone was charging. Adam hadn't been happy when he came home to find his dad's phone dead. As though keeping Ali's phone charged was a way of keeping part of him alive.

I dialed in the security code—which Ali had never hidden from me. Tons of junk email had accumulated in the months since Ali died. I scrolled through, going back until the week of the accident, but found almost nothing personal. Ali had never texted much either, but there was one message that caught my attention. It was from Ian, one of Ali's JMU friends.

No one's heard from Lizzie in almost a year. I hope she's OK. Have you heard from her?

I checked the date. The text was more than a year old. Ali hadn't responded. Why not? Maybe he'd picked up the phone and called Ian to discuss Lizzie's mysterious absence.

Next, I went through Ali's tablet. Again nothing. No trace of Carol Darius, and he didn't even follow Lizzie online. I scrolled through Ali's Facebook account. He'd rarely posted.

I paused at a family photo of us at Thanksgiving from many years ago when the children were still in elementary school. I read through some of the comments. There was only one person I didn't recognize. Someone named Samantha Price. Her comment beneath the picture said, *Beautiful family*. Maybe she was a work colleague or some other acquaintance he'd met along the way. I clicked on her profile, but it was blank. No picture or biographical information. Ali hadn't responded to her or any of the other commenters.

The doorbell rang, startling me out of my ruminations. I set the tablet down, wondering who would show up unannounced on a weekday morning. It was Julia, Ali's sister. I hugged her hello.

"It's good to see you." I meant it. I'd missed my friend.

"Is it?" she asked.

"Of course." I led her into the kitchen and pulled the iced tea out of the fridge. Arabs never let guests leave without forcing food and drink on them whether they wanted it or not.

"Then why haven't you come to see Mama?"

I'd avoided my husband's family because I feared they'd sense my uncertainty about Ali. I wasn't sure I could hide my growing resentment at my husband for creating this situation and leaving me to deal with it. "Would you prefer coffee?" I asked.

"I would prefer that you stop what you're doing and talk to me."

I carefully set the tea pitcher on the counter. "I'll come and see Um Ali this weekend. I promise."

Julia crossed her arms over her chest. "Why are you avoiding us?"

"To be fair, I'm avoiding almost everyone." I searched for a plausible excuse. "People-ing is still a lot of work for me."

"You're obviously seeing some folks. Nasser mentioned that he saw you recently."

"He did?"

"He was trying to reassure Mama that you're OK. She's worried about you. You haven't come to see us. You haven't even called. Nasser told Mama he'd seen you and that you're fine."

"He's right. I am. I've just been busy."

"Doing what?" Julia didn't hide her agitation. "We're not dead, Amira. My brother died, and now you're acting like we're dead too."

My face crumpled. I couldn't help it. The pressure was too much. Julia immediately came around the island to hug me tight.

"We miss him too, *habibti*. We don't want to also lose you and the kids."

"You won't," I said through my tears. "That will never happen."

"What's really going on? Are you seeing a counselor? Maybe that would help."

I pulled away. "Did Ali ever tell you that he bought a house in the Raleigh area?"

"No." She tilted her head. "When did you guys get a house in North Carolina? And why?"

"Not us guys." I sighed and slipped into a chair at the kitchen table. "Just Ali."

"Wait." Julia plopped down opposite me. "What?"

"After Ali died, I found out he was paying the mortgage on a house in North Carolina."

"And you knew nothing about it? That's crazy." She looked dazed. "When did he supposedly buy this house?"

"Eight years ago."

Her eyes got bigger. "Is it a rental or something?"

I shook my head. "After he died, I think the house went to a woman named Carol Darius. Have you ever heard of her?"

"What?" Shock stamped her face. "I don't know that name. Who is she?"

"That's the million-dollar question." I knuckled my eyes. "All I know for sure is that Ali bought a house without my knowledge. And he left it to someone else."

Julia scoffed. "Impossible."

"I thought so too. But there's a paper trail. Money to pay for the house came out of one of our joint accounts."

"That's insanity. There's got to be a reasonable explanation."

"We haven't found one yet."

"Wait." Julia studied me. "You believe what? That Ali was having an affair with this woman?"

"I don't know what to believe."

Her face twisted. "You've already given up on him?" Accusation rang in each word. "You were married to the man. You know what a decent person my brother was. I can't believe you're so ready to believe the worst about him."

"How am I the bad guy?" It didn't feel like Julia and I were on the same team anymore, but then I remembered we never were. Suddenly, I was back in my in-laws' dining room staring at the wedding invitation with Lizzie's name on it. Ali's family would always close ranks around him, no matter what he did.

"I really thought you loved my brother," she said. "That you'd defend him and protect his memory until your dying day."

"He did invite his ex-girlfriend to our wedding without telling me," I retorted. "Oh, but I forgot, you condoned that."

"What?" Her face flushed. "I did not."

"You refused to even admit that it was wrong of him to invite her." I threw Julia's words from all those years ago back at her. "*I'll never speak against my brother, Amira.* That's what you said when I needed your support."

"You're still angry about that?" She looked flabbergasted. "After all these years?"

"What if he never gave any of his American girlfriends up?"

"That's impossible." Her cheeks flushed. "Are you saying he gave this Carol lady the house?"

"I don't know. The lawyer handling the LLC that owns the place won't tell me who got the house. He just confirmed it wasn't me."

"There must be a way to find out more."

"I'm working on it."

We both were calmer now, speaking in more measured tones, being careful with our words and each other.

"In the meantime, let's not mention this at Baba's birthday dinner," she said. "My parents don't need any more trauma around Ali's death."

"I won't say anything." The entire family planned to gather at my in-laws' later that month to mark my father-in-law's seventieth birthday. I was relieved that Ayla and Adam were coming down for the gathering. It would give me the opportunity to check in on them, especially Ayla.

"Baba didn't want to celebrate because of Ali, but he finally agreed to at least have dinner with the kids and grandkids."

"I'm not telling anyone outside of you, Lulu, and Nasser. The last thing I want is for Ayla and Adam to find out about this."

"You've told Nasser?" she asked. "Why?"

"He's helping me. We're threatening legal action if the LLC doesn't tell us who got the house."

Julia sipped her tea. "Hmm."

"Hmm what?" I asked.

"Nothing."

"Why do I get the feeling that you have something to say?"

She paused, considering her words. "Just be careful."

"Could you be more cryptic?"

"I know Ali loved Nasser like a brother," she said haltingly. "But I always got the sense that Nasser was jealous of Ali."

"Really?" This was news to me. "In what way?"

She shrugged. "Just be careful."

"That was quick," Nasser said over the phone a few days later. "They want to settle."

"Who does?" It took me a minute to focus. I was immersed in finalizing the draft for an exhibit that needed to go to the museum's curators by the end of the day.

"The LLC."

"Really?" I swiveled my chair away from my desk. "Is that even a thing? How do you settle something like this?"

He chuckled. "With money, what else? They're offering you a hundred thousand dollars to withdraw your lawsuit."

"That property is worth a lot more than that."

"I think it's a reflection of how much equity is actually in the house. In any case, it's a starting point for negotiation. I think we're in a pretty good position. The fact that they responded with a proposed settlement is a positive sign."

"How so?"

"It signals that they want this matter settled sooner rather than later," Nasser said. "I could tell them to double the offer."

"Double?" I shook my head even though he couldn't see me. "This is not about the money. Does the LLC have a lot of assets?"

"Nope. Just the house, according to Perkins, the lawyer for the LLC."

"Do you have the operating agreement yet?"

"Not exactly. The settlement is contingent on your taking the money and going away." He paused. "They don't want to show you the operating agreement."

"No deal," I said immediately. "The whole point of taking legal action was to see that document. Do you still think Ali had nothing to hide?"

"Does it really matter now?" he asked gently. "You could put two hundred K to good use. Invest it. Spoil yourself and take some fantastic vacations. Pay for Adam's wedding."

It *was* a lot of money. But the idea of never knowing the truth about Ali, Carol Darius, and that house would eat at me for the rest of my life. "I need to know what they're hiding. Why are they willing to pay a hundred thousand dollars for me to go away?"

"That's a valid question."

The doorbell rang. It was probably Jake with Ali's things from the office. "I have to go." I walked into the front hall. "There's someone at the door."

"OK. I'll tell Perkins that any settlement has to include giving you access to the operating agreement."

Jake smiled at me when I opened the front door, but behind the friendly expression, I sensed that same watchfulness as before.

"Here you go," he said, stepping inside the foyer to set a single box down. I hadn't invited him to come in, but he was obviously trying to be nice. He also carried one of Ali's suits on a hanger covered in plastic. "This was on Ali's office coatrack."

I nodded and took it from him, trying to keep my emotions under control. "He wore it to work that last day. He spilled some coffee on the lapel and changed at the office. Ali always kept a fresh suit at work, just in case." I folded the suit over my arm, resisting the urge to hug it to my chest and see if it still smelled of my husband.

Desperate for a distraction to avoid bursting into tears, I set the suit aside and focused on the box.

"It's just the one box?" Ali had worked at the firm for a decade. I expected a little more junk. "Is that all there is?"

"That's what they gave me," he said half apologetically. "Were you expecting more?"

"Not really, I guess." I thanked him. "Everyone has been so nice. Including people I'd never met who were friends of Ali's. Some from way back."

"I hope not too far back," he said lightly. "Some people should stay in the past if you ask me."

It was an odd thing to say. "What do you mean?"

"Nothing. I'm being silly." He chuckled. "I'd hate for my old girlfriends to come out of the woodwork after I'm gone."

I searched his face. Was he insinuating that he knew about Carol Darius? "Why?" I asked. "Did Ali mention an old girlfriend to you?"

"What?" The laughter died quickly in his eyes, and he looked away. "No. No, of course not. All the man ever talked about was you and the kids."

Uneasiness shivered through me. There was an aura around Jake, that watchfulness, that sense that he was hiding something, that made me uncomfortable. So I backed away. "I shouldn't have asked that. I'm sorry."

"Did that happen?" he asked with a frown. "Did an old girlfriend reach out to you?"

He asked in a casual manner, so much so that it seemed calculated. I shook my head. "No."

He hesitated and then said, "If someone is bothering you, I'd be happy to have a word with them. It's the last thing you need to worry about."

"Honestly, it's not serious." I wanted nothing more than for this awkward exchange to be over.

"No deranged fans who watched Ali on TV?"

I forced a smile. "He did get some strange fan emails."

"How did Ali land that gig anyway? I realize I never asked him. He was already a contributor to Channel Three when I started working at the firm."

"They interviewed him once for a story they were doing about the April fifteenth tax deadline. They said he was a natural."

"And he had a column on the station's website."

"Yes, people could ask questions there. He'd answer some of them on his semimonthly appearances on the five o'clock news."

"Like I said before, he was a good guy," Jake said. "It's a real loss."

"Thanks again for coming." I was eager to end the conversation. I also wanted to be alone to look through Ali's things.

"My pleasure. One more thing."

"Yes?" I said, masking my impatience.

"I know Ali occasionally worked from home. His manager asked me to pick up any documents Ali might have left here." He smiled apologetically. "I hate to bother you but—"

"It's fine." I cut him off. "I'll look around and give you a call if I find any work-related papers."

"Great. Thank you. And if you need anything, anything at all, please don't hesitate to call me."

I made sure to lock the door after Jake left. Then I contemplated the box as I would an adversary. Going through Ali's personal effects promised to be an emotional minefield. Who knew what I'd find that could set me off? But the answers I was looking for could be in that box.

What a lousy situation Ali left me in. Why had he hidden his purchase of Cozy Glenn Lane? My husband wasn't an idiot. He was a careful, deliberate guy. If he really had something to hide, he wouldn't have left a paper trail.

I took a breath and sat on the bottom step of the staircase. Pulling the box toward me, I tore the top open. Inside I found the detritus of a work life. Mundane yet completely personal. I pulled out certificates of completion for various professional development courses. Awards for successful projects. A small red stress ball with his company logo on it. There was no day planner or diary. No smoking gun. No references to Carol Darius or Cozy Glenn Lane.

But there were two pictures. One of Ayla and Adam at the pool many summers ago. Eyes squinting, cheeks red. They were about seven and five in the image. The other picture was of Ali and me on our honeymoon, tanned and relaxed, smiling and happy. Luminous in the way all young people are. The ache in my ribs intensified.

I longed to go back to that time.

Chapter Sixteen

Before

I was insecure at the start of our honeymoon in the Dominican Republic.

I've never been thin. My hips were round, and my stomach wasn't flat no matter how much core work I suffered through.

I insisted on making love in the dark our first time. Not only because no other man had ever seen me naked, but mostly because I remembered how lean and physically fit Lizzie Martins looked wearing those snug hiking tights in that photo.

Not that Ali gave me any reason to feel insecure. He gave every indication of being into me and my body. I certainly appreciated his body. He worked out regularly, and it showed. I loved looking at his naked form and had plenty of opportunity to do so. He had no insecurities or inhibitions about being naked around me. I enjoyed the view.

Being a man of few words, Ali never said much about my physical appearance. But he could be counted on to give me an appreciative glance or murmur whenever he liked how I looked in a particular swimsuit or outfit. During our honeymoon, he sometimes tugged me back to bed after we'd dressed for dinner and were ready to go out.

"It's interesting," he said after one of those spontaneous predinner encounters. We were lying on our backs, staring up at the ceiling after a frenzied round of sex. We were both still fully dressed except for his unzipped pants and my discarded underwear.

"What is?" I asked dreamily, still caught up in the residual sensations of our lovemaking.

"I never expected to have great sex with my wife."

I looked at him, my insecurities hitching up a notch. "You thought I'd be bad in bed?"

"Before I met you, I guess I assumed marrying a nice Arab girl from a Muslim family meant that we'd have nice, pleasant, polite sex."

"In other words, you thought you'd have to settle." I sat up and looked around for my underwear. "Let me guess, Lizzie was a maniac in bed." Had he thought of her when we were making love? Did he compare my body to hers?

"Whoa!" He sat up fast. "What?"

I immediately wished I could take the words back. I was furious at myself for uttering Lizzie's name and letting her intrude on our honeymoon.

He rubbed the back of his neck. "How am I supposed to be honest and talk openly if you're going to make anything I say now somehow about the women in my past?"

It was a fair question. The man wasn't talkative by nature, and the last thing I wanted to do was shut down what little conversation he did want to have. "I'm sorry. I'm a little insecure because I'm new at this."

He reached for my hand. "You can't really believe I'm thinking about anyone else when we're having mind-blowing sex."

"Mind-blowing?" That cheered me up. I always took pride in being an A student. "Tell me more."

"The best sex I've ever had." He dipped his head to kiss my neck. "Which I did not expect."

I shivered at the sensation of his lips gently nuzzling my nape. "Let that be a lesson to you that you can't put every Arab girl in a box."

"I wouldn't dare." His mouth trailed up to nibble my earlobe.

"You have no idea what it's like. We're brought up with the threat of total ruin, including parental alienation and community shunning, if we dare sex it up with a boy before marriage." I detested the idea of being thought of as a cold prude because I followed the rules, even though I chafed against them. "Just because we abstain, that doesn't mean we don't want sex as much as guys do. Or as much as white girls do."

"I never really thought about it, to be honest."

"And, by the way, while you were expecting boring sex with your wife, I was fantasizing about magical, fantastic sex with my husband."

"Were you?"

"Of course! If I'm only going to have sex with one man in my entire life, it has to be great sex, right?"

Amusement lit his handsome face. "That's a lot of pressure to put on a guy, expecting him to be the ultimate fantasy in bed."

I shrugged. "Hey, I didn't make the rules. I just play by them." I teasingly gave him a critical, exaggerated once-over. "I'll have to wait and see how it works out."

"What do you mean?"

"To determine whether the reality matches my fantasy. I haven't seen any unicorns and rainbows yet."

"Now you're going to give me performance anxiety."

I batted my eyelashes at him. "I think you might be up for the job. You're off to a good start."

"That's a relief." He chuckled, feathering his fingertips up my thigh. "I guess I'd better get back to work."

"So much for going to dinner," I said, lying back on the bed with a happy sigh.

Chapter Seventeen

Now

I was fast asleep when my phone blasted me awake.

The device vibrated, vigorously rattling on the bedside table like it was trying to wriggle out of its protective case. Alternating high- and low-pitched beeps blared into my ears.

"What the—" Still half out of it, I fumbled around the bedside table, feeling for my phone. I knocked something onto the carpet. It was the pepper spray Nasser had gotten me. I slept with it by my bed every night.

I always silenced my phone before I went to sleep, so why was it making that unnerving noise? My fingertips finally brushed cool metal. My phone. I grabbed it and squinted at the screen, my eyes trying to adjust to the light. The phone flashed the time. One twenty a.m.

Below the time stamp, a message pulsed in glaring red. As my vision cleared, I saw the warning was coming from the home security system. My heart slamming, I tapped repeatedly on the app to see what was happening. The alert buzzed, pulsing in capitalized letters.

INTRUDER ALERT! INTRUDER ALERT!

I shot up to a sitting position. Adrenaline blasted through my veins. Instantly awake, I scrutinized my phone for more information. It took a moment to figure out what I was looking at. One of the window sensors that Nasser installed had triggered. I forced myself to calm down enough to study the diagram to see which one. The window in the garage. One I'd never used and barely noticed. Had it been locked? I never checked that window.

At least the intruder wasn't in the house. Yet. I always double-checked and double-locked the door that led to the garage. Anyone trying to break in from the garage wouldn't easily access the house. My phone rang.

"Hello?" I whispered.

"Mrs. Abadi, this is First Shield Security calling; we have information that suggests an intruder has opened the window in your garage."

"What do I do now?" I whispered into the phone, relieved that I was no longer completely on my own.

"Secure yourself in an upstairs room with the door locked. The police are already on the way."

"OK. Thank you." I leaped out of bed to make sure the bolt Nasser had installed for me was firmly in place. "Now what?"

"Stay on the line with me," the security company agent said. "The police are six minutes away."

"Six minutes?" That sounded like an eternity. I closed my eyes and forced deep breaths. The entire situation felt surreal, like it was happening to someone else. I scrambled back to the bedside to snatch the pepper spray off the carpet. I clutched the small canister to my chest. If confronted, I wouldn't hesitate to use it.

"Are you still there?" The reassuring voice on the line calmed me a little.

"Yes," I whispered. "I'm here." Standing by my locked bedroom door, I strained to hear sounds of someone breaking into the house. But it was eerily silent. Until the house crackled, the floor settling somewhere. Or was it footsteps? Goose bumps prickled my skin. Where was the stranger? What did he want? More importantly, where the hell were the police?

"How much longer?" I whispered into the phone.

"They are two minutes away," she said. "Help is almost there."

I peeked through the curtains, watching the street for police vehicles. It seemed like forever, but a cruiser finally turned onto my street and came to a stop in front of my house.

"They're here." Relief whooshed through me, loosening my tense muscles.

"Hold tight while they secure the perimeter." A few minutes later, the security lady told me it was safe to come out of my room and meet with the officers. I joined them in the garage.

"What did they want?" I asked, surveying the garage to see if anything looked disturbed. Not that it would be easy to tell. The place was its usual mess, littered with old bikes, sleds, dusty lawn equipment, and other old stuff that the slight pack rat in me wasn't quite ready to throw away—in case I might need it in the future.

"It's hard to tell." Taking in the disarray around him, the officer probably wondered the same thing. "You have a security system, is that right?"

I nodded, wrapping my arms around myself. Shivering even though I wasn't cold, I showed him the app on my phone. We studied the camera views together. Unfortunately, there wasn't one aimed at the side of the garage. It never occurred to me that someone would try to come in that window.

"Can you tell if anything is missing?" the officer asked.

"Lots could be gone and I'd never know it," I admitted. "There's really nothing in this garage that's worth anything except the cars."

"We have had some incidents lately with teenagers breaking into cars and stealing items."

I checked the van, and it looked the same as when I'd last driven it. But the glove compartment in Ali's Honda was open, and the documents normally stored inside, the registration and car manual, were strewn on the floor of the passenger's side.

"Must be the kids again." The officer seemed convinced he'd cracked the case. "Did they take anything?"

I bit my lip. "Not that I can tell."

But the incident didn't strike me as a random break-in perpetuated by delinquent teenagers. Only Ali's car was tampered with, making the intrusion feel targeted. First someone had ransacked Ali's home office and now his car. What did Ali have that they wanted badly enough to break in not once but twice? How far would they go to get it?

Could it be related to Cozy Glenn? It was obvious that someone out there didn't want me to know what the deal was with that house. Maybe they thought Ali kept papers related to Cozy Glenn at home or in his car. Jake had asked for Ali's business papers too. Was that somehow related?

I told the officer about the previous break-in, and he conscientiously took detailed notes and promised to update me if they developed any leads. After the police left, I quickly locked up and scurried back to the safety of my bedroom.

I hated feeling unsafe in my own home. A place that had always been a sanctuary for me. I'd spent hours over the years choosing the right paint colors, furniture, and decor to make it the perfect home for me and my family. I took a lot of pride in the life that I'd made here with Ali and the kids.

But now, instead of feeling like my safe place, the house felt big and empty and scary. These days, I was always relieved whenever someone, like Lulu, Nasser, or Claudia, popped by so that I wasn't alone.

It took me a long time to fall asleep. I was too wired and couldn't call Lulu or Nasser. I didn't want to wake them up. Besides, they'd insist that I go stay somewhere else. But I still hated the idea of leaving the house.

Despite everything, while the world shifted around me, I continued to feel more grounded in the home where I'd lived with Ali and our family than anywhere else. The happiest times of my life had happened here. Besides, I'd already physically lost Ali. And now I faced losing the idea of who I thought he was. This house felt like one of the last touchstones left of my former life.

As I lay in bed, a million thoughts raced through my mind as unease trembled through me. The house had been broken into for a *second* time, and I still didn't know why. Giving in and going to Lulu's was tempting. I'd feel much more protected there. It was clear now that Ali had been my security blanket and that, on some level, I'd been living in fear since he died.

I'd found certainty in my roles of wife and mother. My identity was tied to being something to someone—wife to Ali, mother to Ayla and Adam—rather than a woman in my own right. The truth was that I'd been very reliant on my husband and was terrified of living the rest of my life without him.

Moving in with Lulu would be like admitting I couldn't make it on my own.

That left me with no choice. I *had* to stay put.

When I finally started to drift off, it was almost daylight. I felt secure in my decision. At least the new security system had kept me safe. It was comforting to know that a real live person somewhere out there was monitoring my house. Whoever the intruder was, he now knew I had a surveillance system. Maybe that would deter him. If not, I always had the pepper spray within reach.

But what if that wasn't enough?

"You look like hell," Lulu said that afternoon when she met me at the animal shelter in Falls Church.

"Gee." I suppressed a yawn after a fraught night with little sleep. "Thanks."

I still hadn't told her or Nasser about last night. If they discovered the truth, they'd pressure me to stay with my sister or a friend. But, even in the bright light of day, my feelings about leaving my house hadn't changed.

"I guess you're not sleeping well?" Lulu asked.

"Nope." I knuckled my tired eyes. "That's why we're here."

Her eyes widened when she realized what I was saying. "You're getting a dog?"

"You guessed it."

"You said you'd never get another dog after Hummus died."

"My circumstances have changed."

Ali and I had adopted Hummus, an adorable mixed breed, from a shelter when the kids were young. I'd grown up with dogs, but Ali had never had a pup and was eager to get one. We all loved Hummus, and the kids were devastated when he died of canine distemper when they were in elementary school.

We entered the kennel where shelter dogs available for adoption were kept. Excited barking and yelping echoed off the cement walls. Lulu pointed to a fluffy little black dog hiding in the corner of its pen.

"That one's cute."

"I'm not looking for cute." I kept moving. "Cute and fluffy isn't going to scare anyone."

"Hmm." She followed me, looking at the caged animals as we walked. "So, what you're looking for is a guard dog. There are lots of pit bulls. They can be vicious."

"I don't want a dog that scares me more than the bad guys."

"Are you still worried about the break-in? Please come stay with me. We'd love to have you."

I shook my head. "A security system and a dog should help. With Ali gone, I need to be able to stand on my own two feet."

"As long as you know that my offer still stands."

A shelter volunteer cleaning out a kennel ahead of us smiled in our direction. She was middle aged with wavy, gray-streaked curls. "Are you looking to adopt?"

"Yes, I hope so," I answered.

"What kind of animal are you looking for?"

"I was thinking of a big dog." My gaze caught on a large brown dog with patches of white and black sitting in the corner of its kennel wearing a forlorn expression.

"That's Binti," the volunteer said as she came to stand beside me. "She's a hound mix and a sweetheart."

Lulu's mouth twisted. "She looks so sad."

"Her owner was a woman in her forties who was deported suddenly," the volunteer informed us. "Poor girl has had a lot of upheaval and loss in a short period of time."

I could relate. "Can I pet her? Is she friendly?"

"She's very loving toward women, especially those who are the same age as her original owner. But she's very barky around strangers who trespass on her territory."

"Sounds like the perfect companion," I quipped. "Sweet to me and mean to strangers is exactly what I'm looking for."

"Amen," Lulu said. "She basically needs a security dog."

"This sweetheart is all bark and no bite," the volunteer assured me. "Mostly."

"As long as she seems scary, that'll work." I approached the dog, holding out the back of my hand so she could sniff me.

"Are you sure?" Lulu asked. "She seems so sad. Owning her could be depressing."

"Who better than me to understand what she's going through?" I tentatively petted the dog's soft head. "What did you say her name is?"

"Binti," the volunteer repeated.

Lulu chuckled. "Binti? Seriously? Maybe it's fate." We exchanged a laugh. In Arabic, "Binti" meant "my girl" or "my daughter."

The volunteer brought the pup out to a general play area where we could interact with her. I sat on the floor with crossed knees and smiled, talking to Binti in a gentle, encouraging voice. The dog immediately came over and licked my hand.

"Look at that," the volunteer crooned. "She went right to you."

Even Lulu was amused. "It's love at first sight."

The feeling was mutual. After Hummus, I hadn't wanted another dog because I didn't want to clean up after it and worry where to board the animal when we went out of town. But all those concerns went right out the window when Binti practically sat on my lap, stretching out and propping her chin on my knee. Petting her with long, slow strokes, I was overwhelmed with tenderness for this poor baby girl who'd suddenly lost everything.

"What do you say, girl?" I murmured. "Do you want to come home with me?"

―――

"I hope it's OK that I came by," Nasser said the day after I adopted Binti.

"Of course." I invited him in, always happier when another person was in the house with me. "You said on the phone that you have an update?"

Binti came running around the corner, erupting in animated barking when she spotted Nasser.

"Whoa." He backed away. "What is that?"

"Meet my new dog, Binti." I ran a hand over her silky head. "Good girl."

"When did you get a dog?"

"Yesterday. I feel a little safer with a big, noisy dog around."

"Well, that thing is definitely noisy." Nasser kept an eye on Binti. "She doesn't seem very friendly."

"She's not a fan of strangers."

"Do you know if she bites?"

"So far, she's all bark and no bite." I petted the dog vigorously. "It's OK, Binti. Nasser is our friend." I'd only had Binti for twenty-four hours. She was very loving and followed me everywhere. The volunteer said she didn't bite. I hoped she was right.

"Binti?" he asked. "As in 'my girl'?"

"Believe it or not, that was already her name." I patted Binti for a couple more minutes until she calmed down, then led Nasser to the kitchen to pour us some iced tea.

"Here's what they're offering." Nasser took a seat at the island. "They'll agree to let you view the operating agreement provided you sign an NDA."

"NDA?" I crossed my arms and leaned a hip against the counter. "NDA as in I can't talk about anything that's in the operating agreement?"

"Exactly. A nondisclosure agreement."

"Fine," I said immediately. "It's not like I want to steal company secrets."

"Signing a nondisclosure agreement means you can never speak about any names you learn as a result of what you see in the operating agreement," he clarified. "That includes never telling anyone who owns the Durham house."

"Who would I tell? It's not like I want the world to know that my husband left a secret house to another woman." I obviously didn't want the kids to find out before I knew the whole story. If ever.

Ayla was already troubled enough. To learn that Ali had some sort of secret life would crush both her and Adam. Thank goodness the kids were away at school. If they were around full time, I wasn't sure I'd be able to hide my doubts.

"What happens if I violate the terms of the NDA?" I asked Nasser.

"There's a financial penalty. You'll have to pay them fifty thousand dollars each time you violate the agreement."

I whistled. "They really want to keep their secrets, don't they?"

"What do you say?"

"I'll do it." I made an instant decision. "I'll sign the NDA."

"You're sure?"

"Positive. I have to know who got the house and what's up with the LLC." Like was it created to hide the fact that Ali had a relationship with the woman who lived there? A woman who probably got the house. It burned me up that Ali had not only had a possible affair but that he'd also used *our* money to pay for her house. Especially considering how thrifty Ali was. A woman would really have to matter to my husband for him to spend that kind of money.

"OK," Nasser said. "I'll let Perkins know."

"What about the cash?" I asked.

"What about it?"

"I still want it. Go ahead and ask for more, but I'll settle for the hundred thousand dollars they originally offered."

I registered the surprise in his voice. "I thought you didn't care about the money."

"It's not what's motivating me," I explained, "but I'm not stupid enough to turn down a boatload of cash. Besides, I want it just in case."

"In case of what?"

"You'll see," I answered. "But hopefully it won't come to that."

―――

It took another couple of weeks to hammer out a deal with Fred Perkins. Fourteen days that seemed to last forever. I couldn't stop wondering what else Ali might have bought for the woman in the secret house. Not knowing the whole truth gnawed at me. Everything felt like it was piling up.

I was perpetually worried about the kids, especially Ayla. Then there were the break-ins. Would there be another intrusion? The constant uncertainty made it even harder to sleep at night.

At least I now had Binti. Not only did she make me feel safer, but she was also good company, following me everywhere, quietly dozing in my office while I worked and happily curling up in her new dog bed beside me at night. Her presence made evenings more tolerable.

We'd quickly settled into a routine. A long walk first thing in the morning, followed by her breakfast. After lunch, it was time for another walk, this one shorter, just around the block. After dinner, we took a quick stroll up the street and back. Just before bed, I let her out for a few minutes to do her business before we turned in for the night.

As advertised, Binti barked noisily whenever an unknown person came to the door to deliver a package or on other business. In the past, I would have found a dog's constant barking at strangers very annoying. Now, I couldn't be happier.

I was learning to operate solo.

I left Binti at home in her crate when I went to meet Nasser in Reston, where Fred Perkins had an office. Perkins's law firm was situated in a high-rise that towered over a busy town center. Under the terms of the deal, Nasser and I were required to view the Five *A*'s operating agreement in Perkins's office. As soon as Nasser and I arrived, we were shown to a conference room with a glass wall that looked out on the corridor.

"Remember," Nasser said as we took our seats. "We're not allowed to take notes or pictures of the document."

"They're acting like they're the CIA or something. These people need to relax." Not that I could. My nerves were tight, and my heart thumped heavy against my ribs. Here it was. The moment of truth. After weeks of wondering, I'd finally begin to unearth the secrets about Cozy Glenn. I hoped with everything in me that the LLC papers would somehow exonerate Ali, leaving my memories of him intact. Not only because I needed Ali to be who I thought he was. But also because of what revelations about a secret girlfriend would say about how naive and easily duped I'd been.

An assistant brought the document in and set it on the table in front of Nasser. It was short, just a few pages. I inched closer while the assistant quietly departed, closing the glass door behind her. Nasser zeroed in on the key elements before I'd even started scanning the contract.

"Only two officers. One is Ali."

"And the other?" My eyes searched the written agreement, trying to see where Nasser was reading.

"Samantha Price."

"Who?" I didn't immediately compute his answer. "What?"

He pointed to her name on the paper. "See it there?"

"Who the hell is Samantha Price?" I burst out in frustrated disbelief. "First Carol Darius and now Samantha Price?" Instead of providing answers and closure, the operating agreement generated more questions and confusion. Tears rose in my throat; I swallowed them down.

"It doesn't say who she is," Nasser answered quietly, soothingly. "But she is the woman who got the house. You've never heard of her?"

"No. Never." Then I realized that wasn't true. "Wait . . . I may have seen the name before, but I can't remember where."

"Maybe it'll come to you."

"There's no mention of Carol Darius in the entire thing?"

"Let me make sure." He read the document to himself while I tried to compose myself. I didn't want to cry in front of Nasser and everyone at the Perkins firm who happened to pass by the conference room.

I blinked back tears. "This is unbelievable," I hissed, reaching into my purse for my phone.

"What are you doing?" Nasser put his large hand on my arm, firmly but gently stopping me from pulling my mobile out.

"What do you think? I'm going to google Samantha Price. Maybe that will jog my memory."

"Put the phone away." The words were decisive. Serious. "The terms of the agreement dictate that we not access our phones while we have the document."

"Oh." I left the phone where it was. "I forgot." While Nasser continued to study the contract, I racked my brain, trying to remember where I'd seen Samantha Price's name before. It was just on the edge of my memory. I'd seen the name in writing. I could picture it. But where? "Oh my God."

He looked up. "What is it?"

"I know where I've seen that name before. It was on one of Ali's Facebook posts. She left a comment on an old photo of us with the kids saying that he had a lovely family or something like that."

Nasser set the document down. "I wonder how he knew her."

"Her Facebook had almost no info on it."

"What the fuck was Ali doing?" He pinched the bridge of his nose. "A secret house. These women that nobody close to him has ever heard of. It's like I never knew the guy."

"Yeah, I know the feeling," I said bitterly. "Let's go." I never got headaches, but I felt one coming on. "I haven't eaten all day, and I owe you lunch."

It was a mild late-fall afternoon, so we walked over to get shawarma sandwiches at an eatery in the town center. We sat at one of a dozen tables scattered around a massive fountain. It was a cloudy day, which matched my mood. I texted Lulu the news.

WTF! Who is Samantha Price???? she responded. She was on a school field trip with one of her girls. **I'll call as soon as I can.**

"How are you feeling?" Nasser asked.

"Like I got run over by a bus." I set my phone down. "And you look like a kid who just found out Santa isn't real."

"Ali was practically a brother to me. But now with all this weird stuff we're learning, it's hard not to wonder who he really was."

I bit into my sandwich. "Tell me about it," I said miserably around the tender meat and garlicky white sauce filling my mouth. Ali had left Cozy Glenn to some strange woman. The man I thought I knew would never do that. Who was Ali, really? Did I know him at all? What else had been going on behind my back? Had he secretly laughed at my naivete?

Nasser reached across with a napkin and wiped the side of my mouth. "White sauce," he said by way of explanation.

I took the napkin from him to clean up my own lips. "I feel like an idiot. I'm still desperate to believe there's a reasonable explanation for all of this."

"Me too." He paused. "But, to be honest, I don't know how likely that is anymore."

My chest felt heavy as I set my sandwich down and reached for my phone. "OK. Samantha Price," I said as I searched her name online with clumsy fingers, "tell me who the hell you are." As much as I wanted—*needed*—to know the truth, I dreaded finding confirmation that I'd been an idiot, that my entire marriage was a lie.

There were dozens of Samantha Prices online. Frustration rippled through me. "This is going to take forever."

"I'll see if the researcher at the firm can turn up anything useful," Nasser said as he finished up his shawarma.

"Has your researcher looked up Carol Darius?"

"Yes."

"Did you find anything?"

He shook his head. "Nada."

"Then I don't hold out much hope that old Sammy will be any different."

"Did Ali even have time to cheat?" Nasser asked. "He didn't travel that much, did he?"

"Not a lot. Once or twice a month for a night or two here and there. Sometimes he stayed overnight if he went to the Baltimore office and the meetings ran late."

Now I wondered. Had he really been in Baltimore? Or had he been with Samantha Price? Were they lovers? Was she The One? For all I knew, she was just the latest in a long list of women my husband slept with during our marriage. The thought of multiple affairs made the food in my stomach turn rancid. I pushed the remainder of my meal away, the garlicky smell making me queasy.

"Well, at least I have some good news to share," Nasser said. "The settlement money should be wired to your bank account soon." Perkins hadn't budged on the $100,000 offer. Not that it mattered; any amount of money was a bonus.

I sipped my diet soda, hoping it would settle my stomach. "You should take your share of the settlement."

He set his jaw. "I'm not taking money away from Ali's kids."

I knew before offering that he would refuse. I thought about the logistics. "When will the money show up?"

"It was already wired to your account. The funds should show up in a couple of days. Perkins made a point of saying he hopes that means that our business is concluded. He has a meeting with his client this afternoon. He hopes you are both done with this matter."

"She would like that, wouldn't . . . wait." I sat up straight. "Perkins has an appointment with Samantha Price today? *This* afternoon?"

A wary expression crossed his face. "Why are you looking at me like that?"

I jumped to my feet. "Let's go."

"Where to?"

"We're going to sit outside that office building until we see Samantha Price."

"How will we know who she is? Do you plan to accost every woman who enters the building?"

"I haven't figured that part out yet." I started back in the direction of Perkins's office. "All I know is that this is the closest I've ever been to either Carol Darius or Samantha Price. I'll come up with a plan when we get there."

We took up a position on a knee-high landscaping wall that offered an excellent view of the doors leading into the office building. Several people came and went, some using the circular doors, others walking in the regular entrances flanking the revolving door.

"This isn't going to work," I said after keeping watch for about fifteen minutes.

"Agreed." Nasser stood up. "Let's go."

I started walking toward the building's entrance. "We have to be inside."

"What?" Nasser changed course to follow me. "Why?"

"I'm going to stand in the hallway outside Perkins's offices. That way, we'll be sure not to miss her."

"You can't be serious." He followed me through the revolving doors. "I'm an attorney of some standing in this county. I can't be stalking the client of a colleague."

I reached the elevator and pushed the up button. "You don't have to come."

"Leaving you alone is an even worse idea."

The elevator dinged, and the door opened. "Suit yourself." I stepped inside. He came with me even though I would have gone on my own.

I was fed up with feeling like a dupe. How long had I lived in the dark, completely oblivious to what was really going on in my marriage?

Nasser stood across the elevator from me. "Are you sure you don't want to rethink this?"

"It's the best plan I can come up with on short notice." Anticipation pumped through me. Was I minutes away from meeting Samantha Price? The prospect of finally getting some real answers made me jittery.

He shot me a wary look. "Even if you do somehow recognize her, what will you say to her?"

"I have no idea." I took in his tense posture. "Relax. It's not like I'm going to attack her. I just want to talk."

The elevator pinged. We'd reached our floor. I strode down the corridor and took up a position several feet before the glass double doors leading to the Perkins Law Group offices. I felt surer of myself than I had in a long time. I was taking concrete action to find the answers I needed.

"Now what?" Nasser looked up and down the corridor. "We can't just stand here in the middle of the hallway."

"Face me," I instructed, leaning a shoulder against the wall. Nasser did as I asked. "Good. Now we're just two people having a conversation."

"Are you planning to stand here all afternoon?"

"If that's what it takes. But it's already two o'clock. It can't be too much longer. How late would an afternoon meeting be scheduled?" I studied my husband's cousin. He had on a dark suit and wore it well with his wide shoulders and tapered waist. "You look very respectable. No one is going to think we're up to no good."

"Are we up to no good?"

"Of course not." The elevator dinged. An older couple got out and came down the corridor toward us. I had a good view of anyone getting off the elevator and going into Perkins's office. Every time the elevator sounded, it felt like a small animal leaped inside my chest. Twenty minutes stretched to thirty, then to forty-five.

"Shouldn't you be at work?" I asked Nasser.

"I cleared the day of appointments. Just in case."

"In case of what? Were you worried that we'd learn something today that would flip me out?"

The side of his mouth quirked up. "Something like that."

"You know, I never liked you very much."

He looked insulted. "That's a hell of a thing to say."

"Sorry. Being a widow has made me lose my filter. Obviously, I don't feel that way anymore. You've been amazing, and I'm so appreciative of everything you've done to help me find out the truth about Cozy Glenn."

His face softened. "It's the least I can do."

"I just meant to say that I always thought you were the kind of guy who didn't take life seriously. But I now know that's not true."

"It is up to a point." He shrugged. "I mean, what's the point of taking life too seriously? We aren't here for very long. Why not take some risks and have a good time?"

I considered his words. "Good point. Maybe the rule follower in me was envious that you did whatever you wanted."

"You married very young. Was that because you wanted to follow the rules?"

"Totally. God forbid I become an old maid. I was almost twenty-two."

He whistled low. "I could barely take care of myself at that age."

"I can't even begin to imagine Ayla getting married right now. She has so many plans for her future." At least she had before Ali died.

Worry zipped through me. I needed to call Ayla, and Adam, to check up on them. "She's always insisted that she's not getting married until her late twenties at the earliest."

"She has a good head on her shoulders. You and Ali did a great job raising those kids."

Any mention of the children put a smile on my face. I was so proud of them. Ali and I *did* do a good job with Ayla and Adam. But I agonized about what they might soon face. "What do you think Ali was up to?"

He avoided answering directly. "I always thought you and Ali were the perfect couple."

I guffawed lightly. "Believe me, there is no such thing."

"You weren't happy?"

"I was, but no marriage is perfect. For the most part, Ali was great. He was easygoing about most things, but sometimes dealing with him was like suddenly hitting a brick wall. Especially around issues related to money. And I would have liked to have socialized more as a couple. Ali was more of an introvert."

"Hmm. You and Ali made me believe in marriage. Watching how you two were together got me thinking that maybe it was something I could do. That I would actually want to do."

"We couldn't have been that convincing," I pointed out. "You're still not married."

He shrugged. "I haven't found the right woman."

"Have you ever come close?"

"There was a girl once, a long time ago, but she was already spoken for."

"You're running out of time. What are you? Forty-six? You don't want to be an old dad."

"Whoa," he said with a smile. "I didn't say anything about having kids."

"You don't want kids?" I thought everyone wanted children. It felt like the natural way of things.

"I used to think I did. I would be open to having kids if I married a woman who wanted them." Most of Nasser's family still lived in Ohio, where he was born. But he'd stayed in the DC area after finishing law school in the city.

The elevator pinged. I didn't immediately tense up. We'd been standing in the corridor for over an hour, and the elevator pinged a lot.

A woman in her forties with blondish hair emerged. She wore a sporty outfit yet still managed to look expensive and put together. Not super slim, she was obviously in good shape. Her face came into focus as she approached. I'd never met the woman, but I had seen her face before. As she walked by, a shadowy image from another lifetime crystallized into a real person.

I straightened abruptly, shock taking my breath away. The expression on my face prompted Nasser to look over his shoulder to see what I'd reacted to.

"Lizzie?" I spoke her name just loud enough to be heard.

Lizzie Martins did a double take, looking at me with a quizzical expression. Her eyes were big and blue. "I'm sorry. Do I know you?"

"No." My strained voice sounded alien to my ears. "But you knew my husband."

Her gaze flitted over to Nasser. It took a moment for recognition to flicker in her face. "Nass?" she said to Ali's cousin. "What is—?" She looked at me again, her eyes widening.

"Is she—?" Lizzie directed her questions at Nasser. "You're her lawyer?" she said as if Nasser had betrayed her.

She'd know a thing or two about betrayal. *My God.* Had the old girlfriend Ali supposedly gave up to please his parents been in the picture this whole time?

"Lizzie?" Nasser wore a stunned expression. "Where've you been all these years?"

"Are you Samantha Price?" I asked, my pulse slamming so hard in my ears that I could barely hear myself.

"I'm sorry, but my talking to you is not part of our deal." She looked like a deer caught in the headlights. "Please leave me alone. Take your money and go away. Please."

I lashed out at her. "It would have been nice if you'd left my husband alone for the past twenty years." My shock exploded into the outrage and fury that had been gathering force inside of me since I'd learned about the secret house. "I can see why you wouldn't want to talk about being my husband's sidepiece for twenty years. But I'm honestly curious. Did you even care that he was married? That he had children?"

"Please leave me alone," she said shakily, scurrying toward Perkins's office.

I reflexively went after her. She was pulling the glass doors open. I was losing my chance to speak to her. "Wait! I need to ask you—"

Nasser caught me. "You can't follow her in there." He looked as rattled as I felt. "You know that."

"That bastard." *It had been Lizzie all along.* She'd been like a jinn, invisible but always there, tainting my marriage. "What a liar Ali was." I didn't recognize my own voice. The guttural noises that escaped me sounded like they came from a wounded animal. My knees gave out. Nasser caught me. Strong arms closed around my waist, keeping me from crashing to the floor.

"*Yalla,*" he said. "Let's go home."

"What a piece of *khara*." I tossed my keys on the island with more force than necessary, still shaking from seeing Lizzie Martins in the flesh. "Do you think he had kids with that woman?"

"What? No!" Nasser slipped his shoes off and followed me into the kitchen. "No way." But he didn't sound totally convinced. He didn't know any more than me. And I didn't know anything anymore. Upstairs, Binti barked madly in her crate.

"It would make sense for him to leave one house to each of his families." I almost gagged at the thought.

Nasser noticed. "Sit down." He made sure I was seated on a counter stool before pulling the iced tea out of the fridge and pouring me a cup. "Drink this."

I was unsettled in a way I'd never experienced. As if my insides were untethered, flying haphazardly around within me, wild and out of control. Not even yoga breathing, which I tried on the car ride home, could calm my internal chaos.

"This has to mean that she *never* left. That lying, treacherous *hamar*," I hissed. "I was an idiot virgin bride who believed every lie that jackass ever fed me. I was a faithful wife. For twenty-three years, I never even *looked* at another man while he—he—"

"Ali always said he made the right choice by marrying you."

"But he didn't make a choice, did he?" My contemptuous laugh was shrill in my ears. "Or, I guess he did. He chose *both* of us. Me in this house. His girlfriend, his true love, in her stupid cozy house in North Carolina."

"You have every right to be upset. I know it looks bad. But we still don't know exactly what went on with—"

"Oh, shut up!" My body felt like an overfilled balloon that was about to burst. "Don't you dare defend him!" I hurled the glass, tea and all, at the nearest surface. It clunked against the cabinet and landed on the floor with a satisfying shattering noise. The tea splashed my arm, the ice-cold spray a welcome shock.

"I wasn't defending Ali." Nasser moved to pick up the glass shards. "We just don't know everything yet."

"Fuck him." I rose and went to the fridge to pull out the pitcher of iced tea. "Fuck him, and fuck his fucking girlfriend, and fuck his fucking iced tea." I pulled open the sliding glass door and flung the pitcher over the side of the deck. "I will never drink that crap again."

"Hopefully you didn't hit anyone," Nasser murmured. He pulled some paper towels off the roll and patted my neck and arm dry. I stood obediently still, like a child being toweled off by a parent after a bath, hurt and rage simmering through me. I studied him with a new perspective. My husband's playboy cousin.

"You've dated a lot of women."

He stayed focused on drying me off. "I wouldn't say *a lot*."

"Tell me honestly. What's wrong with me—from a man's perspective? I'm reasonably attractive, aren't I? Why wasn't I enough?"

He paused, bunching the paper towels in his fist. "You are incre—"

"Forget I asked," I interrupted. "It's an awkward thing to ask considering that I was married to your BFF cousin for twenty-three years. Besides, you'd never be mean enough, or rude enough, to say no."

"You're enough," he said quietly. "More than enough. Any man would be lucky to have you." He spoke with more depth of feeling and sincerity than I'd ever experienced from him. "It's just that Ali won the toss."

"What?"

"Ali won the toss."

I didn't understand. "What toss?"

He sighed. "We were both at that wedding when Ali first saw you." He paused. "I thought you were pretty hot too."

"Wait." I blinked. "You were there?"

"I was. But we were cousins, and we couldn't both go after you. That could've created a conflict between us, between our parents."

"How did I never know about this?" I was stunned. The story of Ali spotting me at a wedding was part of our lore as a couple. Nasser had never been part of that narrative.

"We flipped a coin. Ali won. He got to court you first. If he struck out, I would have my shot."

"You flipped a coin." As his words sank in, my vision went fuzzy at the edges. "Unbelievable."

"I always thought everything worked out for the best," he said. "You and Ali seemed happy together."

The air went out of my lungs. "All of our futures, our *lives*, determined by a coin toss." How many years had I lived my married life without context? Without knowing the whole story? Here was yet another thing that Ali had kept from me. What else didn't I know?

Nasser studied me. "You *were* happy with my cousin, right?"

"I thought I was." I stared at him, for the first time really looking at Nasser as a man who might have been my partner. My lover. Not someone from Ali's world, but a man who might have been central to mine.

"So, you see," he spoke into the awkward silence, "I have always thought that you were, and *are*, way more than enough. Ali was a very lucky man."

Somewhere inside me, a switch turned off. The lever that had always relegated Nasser to the friend zone deactivated. For the first time since meeting him more than two decades ago, I really observed Nasser as a man, a physically attractive man who'd apparently always wanted me, when perhaps my own husband hadn't. I took in the dark eyes and thick lashes, the wavy hair now liberally speckled with gray.

A new awareness tingled through me. I became acutely aware of my skin hunger—of being deprived of touch, of missing a man's emotional and corporeal companionship for months. Longing crashed through me. I craved physical contact and comfort.

But not from Nasser—even though he was appealing enough. I wanted it from the one person who could no longer give it to me. Tears stung my eyes, a crushing sensation bearing down on my chest.

I wanted Ali.

I needed my husband. Not the liar who left a secret house to his girlfriend. I craved the man I thought I knew, an extraordinary but normal guy with a tender touch and quiet, reassuring smile—a man Nasser could never measure up to.

Had that version of Ali ever been real?

Awkwardness stirred in the air. No matter what the truth about Ali was, whatever Nasser wanted from me was never going to happen.

I needed to be alone, to wrap my head around everything I'd learned today. If that was even possible. Binti was still barking. I needed to take her out.

"Thanks for seeing me home," I said to Nasser. "I know you must have lots of work to do."

"Gotcha." Nasser took my abrupt dismissal for what it was. A rejection. A door firmly being shut. "Call if you need anything."

Chapter Eighteen

Before

I first suspected I was pregnant when full crabs made me nauseous.

That had never happened before. Eating full crabs was a family tradition. We'd get bushels of them from the DC waterfront and eat them on someone's deck or patio. A trip to Ocean City was incomplete if we didn't go to our favorite all-you-can-eat crab place.

"Why aren't you eating?" Ali asked. He hadn't been big on full crabs back then, in the beginning. Too much work and not enough meat for the effort, he complained. But my husband came to enjoy them almost as much as I did. I marveled at how marriage brought new experiences into both of our lives. How, as a couple, our tastes often became synced, like Ali with the crabs, me with hiking, and my family requesting Ali's iced tea whenever they came over.

"I'm a little queasy." I swallowed against the sensation and tried not to breathe through my nose. The strong ocean smell of the crabs made my stomach feel worse.

Concern etched his face. "Maybe it was something you ate earlier today?"

I laughed. "It could be the boardwalk fries. Or the funnel cake. Or the custard ice cream." I always indulged on vacation. Any thoughts of healthy eating stayed home.

"You have gone a little crazy with the treats."

"But I couldn't not eat them," I protested. "They're an essential part of the Ocean City experience."

"If you're sick, we should get out of here."

I reluctantly agreed, and we left without getting our money's worth, which I didn't feel good about. But I couldn't stay in that place a minute longer. Once I breathed some fresh air, my queasiness eased. We walked back to our hotel holding hands, still firmly in the honeymoon stage. We'd only been married four months. By the time we got back to the room, I felt much better. Ali and I kissed as he edged me toward the bed. But when his hand went to my breast, I flinched.

He froze. "Did I hurt you?"

"No, it's just that my breasts feel so sore. Maybe I'm getting my period." But then the signs—nausea, tender breasts—made sudden sense. "Oh my God. What if I'm pregnant?"

His eyes widened. "Do you think you are?"

"Well, we're not always careful," I reminded him.

"No." He grinned. "We aren't."

Ali went out and came back with a pregnancy test. I stared at the stick, waiting to see if two lines showed up. And there it was, faint but proud. Undeniable. Two straight slivers of pink. A positive result.

I was pregnant.

We were giddy, surprised, and a little scared. I was going to be a young mother. It felt like a miracle, even though practically everyone we knew had kids.

"Are you OK with this?" he asked. "I know we talked about you working for at least a couple of years before trying to get pregnant."

I couldn't believe a child was growing inside of me. The initial shock gave way to elation. I burst into tears.

Alarm lit Ali's face. "I hope those are happy tears?"

I flung myself into his arms. "Yes," I sobbed. "I'm so happy."

Late that night in bed, we couldn't stop talking about the baby.

"What should we name it?" he asked. "I like Alia if it's a girl."

"And definitely Amir if it's a boy," I countered, suggesting the masculine form of my name to counter his feminized suggestion of his.

"As long as we keep it to all *A* names," he said.

He was half joking, but the longer I thought about it, the more I liked the idea. Both of our first names, and our last name, started with *A*. I liked the idea of all of us being connected in that way, a true family. A tight group.

Our bond solidified.

The way Ali made love to me that night—with exquisite tenderness and heightened emotional intensity—calmed something in me. Nothing in the past mattered anymore. A baby was coming. Ali and I were truly family.

Nothing, and no one, could come between us now.

Chapter Nineteen

Now

My father-in-law's birthday dinner was the usual boisterous affair with effusive greetings and too many people crowded about the table, the expected compliments to the chef, but also admonishments that my mother-in-law had worked too hard. In return, she insisted that everyone eat more.

Several cross conversations took place at the same time, siblings and in-laws talking over each other, some engaging in heated political discussions, others sharing the latest gossip or the most recent streaming series they'd binged.

There were few mentions of Ali, but we all felt his absence. Talking about the dead makes almost everyone uncomfortable, so people rarely brought Ali up. A normal widow might find that painful, but, given the circumstances, for me it was a reprieve. I didn't know if I'd be able to contain myself if the conversation turned to Ali and what a good person he was.

Ali's three sisters and their families were there. So was Nasser, who was always included in Ali's family's gatherings since his own parents and siblings lived in Ohio. He said hello to me in his usual friendly manner before retreating to the opposite side of the table. There was a new awkwardness between us now.

Ayla and Adam were at the far end of the table with the cousins their age. Ayla didn't seem to be talking much. My stomach knotted. She was already struggling. What would happen when my kids learned about their dad's old girlfriend and the house he bought for her? The disillusionment would be devastating.

My mother-in-law cooked a huge spread including *kousa mehshee*, the stuffed squash that was Adam's favorite, and *malfoof*, cabbage stuffed with rice and meat, which Ayla loved. The menu selection felt very intentional, a way to entice the kids to keep coming over to their grandparents' house now that Ali wasn't here to compel them to visit.

"*Wainick?*" Um Ali had said to me when I helped put the food out on the table before the meal. "Where've you been?"

"I mostly stay home," I answered. "I don't like to go out." I braced myself, expecting recriminations.

But all my mother-in-law said was, "I know it's not easy. But don't forget us," before moving away to flip the *malfoof* out of the pot. My bond with Ali's family seemed more tenuous now that the person who connected us was gone. We were like opposite sides of a riverbank with a collapsed bridge between us. I marveled at how easily connections forged over twenty-three years threatened to slip away.

As everyone ate and talked, my gaze traveled over each one of Ali's family members. Had any of them known about Ali's secret? Had they purposely kept the truth from me in order to preserve Ali's facade of respectability? The Arab community loved gossip, and news that Ali bought a house for a secret white girlfriend would easily fuel scandalous whispers for months.

I watched my mother-in-law fill another plate for someone. How far would she go to protect both her son and the family name?

When dinner finally ended, I escaped, excusing myself to go to the bathroom, but really just needing to sit quietly with myself for a few minutes. I ran into Nasser coming down the hall.

"Hey," he said.

"Hey yourself." I was determined to get past the discomfort between us. And to also keep Nasser firmly in the friend zone.

"You OK?" he asked.

"There's something I can't get out of my head."

Interest lit his eyes. "What is it?"

"If Lizzie Martins got the house, then who the hell is Samantha Price?"

What looked like disappointment flitted across his face before he quickly wiped it away. "According to Perkins, Lizzie's full name is Samantha Elizabeth Martins Price," he said in his normal approachable manner. "Price is her married name."

"She's *married*?"

"Divorced."

"How long has she been divorced?"

"I'm not sure, but I got the impression that it's been several years."

"I wonder if that's when Ali reconnected with her," I said more to myself than to Nasser. "Or maybe they had a thing this entire time, while both were married."

Julia came out of the kitchen, wiping her hands on a towel. "What else have you two learned about the secret house?"

I briefly considered lying. My natural instinct was to protect my husband, even in death. Shielding Ali's grieving family from the full extent of his duplicity was the noble thing to do. Unless they already knew everything. My bitterness overrode any fleeting notions of graciousness.

"He left it to Lizzie Martins, his old white girlfriend," I told her. "Imagine robbing your own kids of their inheritance by leaving an entire house to your mistress."

Julia paled. She looked to Nasser. "Is that true?"

"Do you think I'd lie about something like that?" I said too loudly.

Nasser dipped his chin. "He did leave the house to Lizzie Martins. We don't know anything else about the nature of their relationship."

"I think it's pretty obvious, don't you?" Hot tears pricked my eyes. "Ali wouldn't leave a house to just anyone. You'd have to really care about a person to leave them a significant property like that. And who knows what else Ali gave her when he was alive."

Julia looked pained. "I don't believe it."

"Did you know anything about Ali's involvement with the woman?" I asked. "Did you know that he was still seeing her?"

"You know I didn't." She looked hurt. "I would never hide something so duplicitous."

In my experience, Julia wasn't a liar, but I had no idea who or what to believe anymore.

Julia came over to embrace me. "Whatever the truth is, for sure Ali should have had zero contact with that woman after he married you. I'm so sorry. I just can't believe it."

I hugged her back, feeling for the first time that Julia might finally be on my side, at least a little.

"*Yalla*. Come on." My mother-in-law poked her head out of the kitchen. "Julia. It's time for the cake."

We all gathered in the family room with my father-in-law comfortably centered in his old leather recliner. When Julia brought the cake out, we sang "Happy Birthday" in English and then in Arabic before my father-in-law blew out the candles with help from his youngest grandchildren.

"Happy birthday, *Ummi*." I kissed him on each deeply grooved cheek and uttered the customary birthday greeting in Arabic. *"Meet senna inshallah."* May you live a hundred years, God willing.

I felt a stab of anguish that Ali would never be an old man. As disillusioned as I was with my husband, sorrow throbbed through me to know he wouldn't celebrate a single birthday surrounded by his children's offspring. He would never know his future grandchildren. And they wouldn't know him. As monumental as Ali had been in our lives, to his grandchildren, he'd only ever be a smiling stranger in old pictures and videos, so distant and abstract that he might as well have lived in another century.

But then again, despite having lived with Ali for more than half my life, I now wondered if I ever knew who he really was.

Samantha Elizabeth Martins Price.
"Let's find out who you are." The following morning, I typed Lizzie's full name into the search window, trying different variations of all her names until I found a Samantha Elizabeth Martins in an old obituary for her father.

Lawrence Robert Martins, age fifty-two, of Vienna, Virginia, died unexpectedly, leaving behind a wife, Martha Martins; a son, William Warren Martins; and a daughter, Samantha Elizabeth Martins. I calculated the dates. Lizzie's father died when she was in high school. There was little else online about Lizzie or her family members.

I called Nasser. He answered immediately. "Hey. What's up?"

"Did you know Lizzie Martins's family?"

"No, I only met Lizzie a couple of times before college."

"Wait. What?" Had I heard right? "You knew Lizzie before college? I thought she and Ali met in college."

"No," he said. "They went to high school together."

"They were a thing in both high school *and* college?" The revelation shook me. Their relationship was even more long standing than I'd thought. Here was yet another thing that Ali had never disclosed to me. "Why did I not know this?"

"I thought you did."

"They dated in high school and college?"

"I'm not sure they dated in high school. I had the impression that she had a crush on him and pursued him once they got to college. Ali was pretty sure she chose to attend JMU because that's where he was going."

"I guess she was determined to get her man."

"It always looked to me like Lizzie was way more into Ali than he was into her."

"If he wasn't that into her, why did he date her for so long?" It didn't add up. "He told me once that they went out for years."

I heard the shrug in Nasser's voice. "Ali was a nice guy. He didn't want to hurt Lizzie's feelings by dumping her. She was very dependent on him."

"In what way?"

"She always seemed very fragile. Like she could break at any time. She had the wounded-bird thing going on."

"Maybe because her father died when she was young, in high school?"

"Really?" I registered the surprise in his voice. "How'd he die?"

"I don't know. I found the obituary online. It just says that he died unexpectedly. Maybe it was super traumatic and that's why she was clingy?" I thought of the woman I'd encountered at the lawyer's office. She'd struck me as a fearful person. "Is there a way to get more information about how the dad died?"

"If the death was suspicious in any way, there might be a police report."

"Are those public?"

"Not generally," he answered. "By law, police are expected to provide information that the public has a right to know. But mostly only people directly impacted by an incident are allowed to see a police report."

"You're a lawyer. You must know some cops. Is there any way you can find out if there's a police report and, if so, what's in it?"

"I guess." He paused. "Why are you so interested?"

"I want to learn everything there is to know about Ali's relationship with that woman."

"Even if what you discover hurts you more?"

"All I know is that I'm going to be obsessed with this until I have all the answers."

Nasser paused. "OK," he finally said. "Let me see what I can do."

Chapter Twenty

Before

When the children were in elementary school, Ali's old JMU friend group managed to all be in the Washington area at the same time, so they arranged a mini reunion at a downtown bar.

My first inclination was to skip it. Old college friends form an impenetrable clique, having shared intimate formative experiences and frames of reference that outsiders can never truly understand. But Lizzie Martins was part of that friend group. If Ali's ex was going to be there, then so was I.

I paid a lot of attention to my appearance that night. I'd put on a few pounds from my pregnancies, but when I made an effort, I received appreciative looks from men. I was still young, barely thirty, and, if our active sex life was any indication, Ali seemed to find me as attractive as ever.

We dropped the kids for a sleepover at my parents' house before driving downtown. As soon as we walked into the bar, I automatically looked around for Lizzie Martins. I didn't spot her right away, but Nasser was there, and he waved at us before refocusing on a dark-haired girl he was talking to.

"Hey, Abadi, you made it." Ben Rodriguez came over to greet us. Ben had shared a dorm with Ali and Nasser during their freshman year at JMU. I first met him during our wedding weekend and remembered him as an outrageous but harmless flirt. I'd seen very little of him, or any of Ali's college friends, since our wedding.

Ali shook his hand. "Ben, you remember my wife, Amira."

"Sure, how are you?" Ben gave me an appreciative once-over. Quick and not leering, but I caught it. And so, apparently, did Ali.

"Watch it," he said genially. "I can still kick your ass."

"Whoa." Ben put up his hands like a surrendering prisoner of war. "Still jealous after, what is it? Ten years of marriage?"

"Eight and a half," I corrected. "It's good to see you again, Ben."

"You too. I see you are as fine as ever. Poor Lizzie never had a chance once Ali hooked up with you."

"Is Lizzie here?" The dark-haired girl who'd been with Nasser joined us.

"Hi, Sara." Ali greeted her with a kiss on the cheek. I remembered hearing that Sara Carr and Lizzie were close friends.

"Hell, no, Lizzie's not here," Ben told Sara. "After Ali dumped her, she pretty much vanished. Abadi broke her heart."

Sara shot me a sympathetic look. "Don't pay any attention to Ben. He's an asshole most of the time."

"Do you keep in touch with Lizzie?" Ben asked Sara.

"From time to time," she said. "Not that often."

I watched Ali's face. To my satisfaction, Ali barely reacted at the mention of his ex. I relaxed once I realized Lizzie wasn't at the gathering nor likely to show up later. I wanted to have a good time. Ali and I didn't get many nights out together now that we had kids. Especially not downtown. We got some drinks and chatted with Ali's friends. Someone ordered appetizers, and there was lots of chatter, catching up, and good-natured ribbing. At some point, we all ended up dancing to the music.

Ali and I took a break from the dance floor and sat at the bar. I was hot and thirsty and eagerly drank the cold water the bartender poured.

Nasser was dancing with Sara, his hands on her hips, which she moved in a sensual sway. "Did they hook up in college?" I asked.

Ali drank from his beer. "No idea."

"Liar," I said skeptically. "How many girls in your friend group has he slept with?"

Ali grinned. "No comment." But the way he said it made me think the true answer was, "All of them."

I rolled my eyes. "Your cousin really leaves no stone unturned."

"He's single. He likes to have a good time. The women are willing. He's not hurting anyone."

"I wonder if the women agree." Nasser was handsome and a successful lawyer. Surely some of those women wanted more than a fling.

One of the guys from the dance floor approached us. I didn't remember meeting him at the wedding. Ali introduced us.

"Amira, this is Ian Maxwell. He shared an apartment with me and Nasser during our senior year of college."

"Ian." We shook hands. "Nice to meet you."

"So, you're the girl who stole Ali away from us?" he said laughingly.

"I did?"

"Once our boy got married, we never saw him again."

"Bull," Ali interjected. "I'm here, aren't I?"

"Once in ten years?" Ian said. "Is that the best we can expect?"

"With work and the kids, it's not always easy to get away."

"Do you hear much from Lizzie?" Ian asked.

"Nope." Ali spoke in a decisive tone that warned against any follow-up questions. Ian got the hint, and he and Ali chatted for a little while before Ian wandered away.

"Does the group get together a lot?" I asked Ali once we were alone.

He shrugged. "Once or twice a year."

"Really? How come they don't invite you?"

"They do. I usually skip it."

"Why? I thought you enjoy getting together with your college buddies."

"Out of respect for you. There's no reason to risk running into Lizzie. Seeing the old college gang is not worth upsetting you."

I blinked. "You've skipped seeing your friends on my account?"

He shrugged. "It's no big deal."

"You didn't have to do that," I protested, but pleasure rushed through me.

"I'm all about self-preservation," he joked.

I should have felt a little guilty that my jealousy prompted Ali to distance himself from his old friends. Instead, I was thrilled. And turned on.

"I do think you deserve a nice reward for your loyalty and consideration," I said very suggestively.

He looked surprised. And interested. "What do you have in mind?"

I licked my lips and shot him a meaningful look.

He understood instantly. "Are you being serious right now?"

I leaned forward, putting my lips near his ear, and whispered something about letting him do a certain something during sex that I'd never been up for previously.

I felt the energy shoot through his body. "That's so effing hot." Ali never uttered bad words in front of me, although I knew he cussed around other people.

"And there are no kids at home," I reminded him. "Consider the possibilities."

"That's it." He grabbed my hand, pulling me off the barstool. "*Yalla*, let's go. We're leaving now."

Laughing, I protested, half stumbling off the stool. "But we haven't been here that long."

He made sure I was steady on my feet before practically dragging me toward the door. "Who cares?"

Certainly not me.

"Hey, Abadi," Rodriguez called out. "Where're you going?"

Ali didn't bother to turn around. "Home."

Several friends groaned. Another said, "We finally get you to come out and you're already leaving?"

"Yeah." Ali wasted no time pushing the door open. He motioned for me to go through, ladies first. "We've got better things to do tonight."

"You guys are goals," someone called after us. "Still hot for each other after all these years!"

Hooting and hollering followed as we spilled onto the busy city sidewalk. Just before the door closed behind us, I caught a fleeting glimpse of Nasser's pensive face, a moment before he smiled and raised his beer.

Once outside, Ali and I huddled together against the cold, laughing and rubbing up against each other as we went to find our car. Later, at home, I very enthusiastically delivered on my promise.

And I'm pretty sure that Lizzie Martins was the very last thing on his mind.

Chapter Twenty-One

Now

"Lawrence Martins died in a home accident," Nasser said over the phone.

I was at my computer writing an exhibit for the museum in Indiana when he called back a few hours later. Even though I was already way behind on the project, I welcomed the distraction. I couldn't concentrate. I wasn't sleeping well, and when I did manage to doze off, my jagged dreams kept the few hours I did get from feeling restful.

But Nasser's news injected new energy into my veins. "There is a police record? And you got your hands on it?"

"Yes, a report was filed but I haven't seen it. A law enforcement friend told me what's in it. It says Martins died at home after falling and hitting his head on the fireplace hearth. His death was ruled accidental."

"Remind me what part of the fireplace the hearth is," I said. "Is it the brick surrounding the firebox?"

"Sort of. It includes the raised part that surrounds the actual firebox. In this case, it was a raised stone hearth. The kind that's around the height of a low stool. You mostly see it in older houses."

"Hmm. I can see how that might mess Lizzie up if she witnessed his fall."

My home office desk was up against a window facing the road. Binti was upstairs sleeping in the warmth of the sun that poured in through my bedroom window in the late morning.

As I spoke, a gray sedan pulled up in front of the house. Two well-dressed people, a dark-skinned man with close-cut hair wearing a sharp navy suit and a redheaded, freckled woman in a forest-green pantsuit, exited the vehicle. I expected them to go to another residence, but they started walking toward my house, the woman's heels clicking on the poured concrete. "Someone is coming up my driveway."

"Who?" Nasser asked. "Do you recognize them?"

"No. It's two people. A man and a woman. Both are nicely dressed." I tracked them until they reached my front doorstep. "Maybe they're doing a security clearance on one of the neighbors."

It wasn't unusual for the feds to show up inquiring about some neighbor seeking a government security clearance. It had happened a couple of times since we'd lived in this house, and once back when we were in the townhome. The doorbell rang.

"They're at the door. I have to go."

"Keep the line open until you know for sure who they are," Nasser told me. "Don't hang up."

"OK." Phone in hand, I went to the door. Binti, roused from her sun-drenched nap, raced down the stairs to yell at the newcomers.

"Calm down, girl." I petted her gently. "It's OK." Grabbing hold of her collar, I opened the door.

The gentleman spoke first. "Good afternoon. Mrs. Abadi?"

"Yes?"

He smiled, revealing a dimple. Close up I could see just a sprinkling of gray in his cropped dark hair. He looked to be in his forties. Binti barked, and the man's smile vanished. "Does he bite?"

"It depends on who you are," I answered. "Who are you?"

"I'm Detective Isiah Lloyd, and this is Detective Sadie Fox."

The floor wobbled beneath my feet, and I forgot about Nasser on the phone and holding Binti's collar. Having law enforcement show up at my door would always recall the worst night of my life.

"May we come in?" the woman asked while keeping one eye on Binti, who stood next to me, tail on alert. The woman detective was about the same age as her colleague and wore a serious, no-nonsense expression.

"What is this about? Is it one of the kids?"

"No, nothing like that," Detective Lloyd reassured me with another dimpled smile.

"We're here about your husband," Detective Fox informed me. Her attention went to Binti. "Maybe you could put the dog away?"

"Can I see your ID?" I made a show of examining the silver-and-navy shields with the county police logo stamped on them. "You said you're here about my husband? He's deceased."

"Yes, we know," she said. "There's been a development that we'd like to speak with you about."

"What kind of development?" It had been months since the accident.

"We think it would be better if you sit while we have this discussion," the female detective said.

I opened the door wider to let them in. We sat in the formal living room that we almost never used. I set my phone aside. Binti settled near my feet. "She doesn't bite," I assured them. "What's going on?"

The woman brushed a bang off her eye. Her short, manicured nails were painted fiery red. She wore gold ring stacks on three of her fingers. "Whenever there is a serious car accident," she began, "it is standard to take blood from the deceased and send it to a lab for testing."

"OK." I waited for her to get to the point. "And?"

"Your husband's results were delayed for a bit. And when they did come in, they were, unfortunately, misplaced," she said. "The original officer on your husband's case retired, so the report was mislaid for a little while."

"When there is no reason to suspect foul play," the male detective added, "there isn't a big rush on the tox screen."

"The what?"

"Toxicology report." Fox, the woman detective, answered for him. "The results of the blood tests."

I remembered then that the police who visited shortly after Ali died mentioned running a blood test. "What were the results?"

"Since the results weren't routine," Fox said, "we have to investigate further before we close this case."

"Not routine? What does that mean?"

"Your husband had a significant amount of alprazolam in his system at the time of death," Detective Fox said.

"What is that?"

"It's more commonly known by its brand name," her partner, Lloyd, told me. "Xanax."

I shook my head. "There must be some mistake. Ali never took Xanax. He rarely even took over-the-counter pain relievers."

"Is it possible he took it without your knowing?" Detective Fox asked.

I was quickly learning that anything might be possible. Secretly taking antianxiety medicine could be the latest on the growing list of things that Ali didn't share with me. "I don't think he would hide something like that." At least the Ali I knew wouldn't.

Detective Lloyd referred to his phone. "Our report says that you previously mentioned being of the Muslim faith to our officers."

"Did I?" I didn't remember alluding to our religion. "I don't recall. How does that signify?"

"Isn't admitting you have mental health problems looked down upon in a conservative culture like yours?"

"We're American. We were both born here. I don't think less of people who need Xanax," I said flatly. "Obviously I can't know one hundred percent for sure that Ali didn't take Xanax, but it would surprise me very much if he did, given his general dislike of over-the-counter medicines."

Detective Lloyd gave me another kindly look. "We're not making any assumptions—"

"It sounds like you are."

"We're just trying to clear everything up," he finished.

Detective Fox scooted to the edge of her seat. "Did your husband have any sleeping issues?"

"How do you mean?"

"Did he have trouble falling and staying asleep?" She talked a lot with her hands, the red nails sweeping through the air. "People sometimes take Xanax to help them sleep."

"He seemed to sleep just fine. He never complained about not sleeping well. My husband was one of those outdoorsy guys who hated to use drugs. He wouldn't even take anything for a headache."

"Can you think of any reason for your husband to have this drug in his system?" Detective Lloyd asked.

"I honestly can't. Are you sure you didn't get the report mixed up?"

Detective Fox had a contemplative look on her face. "You are aware that your husband didn't brake before he hit that tree?"

"Yes." My muscles tensed. I knew where this was headed. "I'm aware."

"And the investigators felt it was possible that Mr. Abadi took his own life."

"I don't believe that."

"We don't mean to cause you any additional distress, Mrs. Abadi, but we have to be thorough in our investigation, and that means exploring all possibilities." She spoke in a brisk manner that gave the impression that I was holding her up. "Someone who felt suicidal might have anxiety, and he might take Xanax for that anxiety."

"What are you saying?" I retorted. "Did Ali drive into a tree because he wanted to kill himself? Or did he accidentally take too much Xanax, which caused him to crash?"

"As we said," Lloyd answered in a calm tone, "we have to explore all potential options."

Detective Fox seemed to lose her patience. She came to her feet. "Would you mind if we have a look inside your medicine cabinet?"

"What for?"

Detective Lloyd stood up. "Just to rule out that Mr. Abadi had Xanax in his possession."

"You can look, but we don't keep any medicine in the bathrooms. We keep it down here in the kitchen."

Detective Lloyd dimpled again. "Would you mind showing us?"

I led them into the kitchen and opened the cabinet where I kept meds like painkillers and allergy tablets, along with alcohol swabs and various sizes of Band-Aids. This cabinet saw a lot of action during the kids' years of scraped knees and grazed elbows.

"While Detective Fox looks through this cabinet, would you mind if I looked at the medicine cabinets?" Lloyd asked. "Just to be thorough."

I numbly showed him upstairs to look through the bathroom cabinets. Binti trailed after us. When we came down again, the doorbell rang.

"Are you expecting someone?" he asked.

"No, but I didn't know you were coming either."

I found Nasser on my doorstep wearing a dark tailored suit and a concerned look on his face. He didn't wait to be invited in.

"What are you doing here?" I asked at the same time Binti started barking.

Nasser focused on Detective Lloyd. "I'm Nasser Abadi."

The detective's brows lifted. "The eminent defense attorney?"

"That's right."

"Your reputation precedes you." His eyes narrowed as he contemplated Nasser's unexpected appearance. "Has Mrs. Abadi retained you as her counsel?"

Did the man think I'd hired a lawyer in the last ten minutes? Why would I?

The detective's face brightened. "You have the same last name. I take it that means you're related?"

Instead of answering, Nasser turned to me. "What are they doing right now?"

"The detectives say Ali had Xanax in his system."

"Xanax?" His face twisted with disbelief. "Ali?"

"Exactly." Nasser knew as well as I did that Ali would have had to have a serious medical issue in order to take any medication. "They're checking to see if we have anything like that in the house."

His face tightened. "We need to talk about this."

"No need." Detective Fox appeared. "We're finished here." She held up a plastic bag containing a couple of bottles of prescription medicine. "Do you mind if we take these with us for testing?"

I shrugged. "Those are old. I don't even remember what the prescriptions were for."

"We'll have the lab check it out, just to be sure," Detective Fox said.

"We'll be in touch." Her partner handed me his card on their way out. "Please call us if you have any questions or remember anything that might be useful. And, if I neglected to say it before, I'm very sorry for your loss."

"We both are," Fox put in.

"Thank you."

Nasser followed the detectives out and chatted with them by their car. After a few minutes, they all shook hands and the detectives drove off.

"What was that all about?" I asked when Nasser came back in. "How did you even know to come over?"

"I was listening on the phone, remember? I asked you to keep the line open."

I'd forgotten. "What did they say out there?"

"I don't want you speaking with the detectives without me present."

"Why?" I protested. "I'm not a little girl."

"I am your attorney. It would not be smart to speak with the police without me in the room."

"I've got nothing to hide."

"Just to be safe. It's very possible the drug found in Ali's bloodstream incapacitated him and caused the crash."

"But . . . I don't get it." I couldn't make sense of this new information. "Why would Ali have Xanax in his system? Do you think it's another thing he lied about?"

"I don't know. What we do know for sure is that Ali didn't brake before he hit that tree. It's plausible he crashed because the drug made him pass out."

"Could he have taken a Xanax by accident?" I grasped for an answer that computed. "Maybe he wanted a pain reliever for a bad headache or something and someone gave him Xanax by mistake."

"Until we know more, it's better that I be present whenever you talk to the police," Nasser said. "Ali was something of a local celebrity. I'm guessing the police want to do their due diligence in the event the tox report gets leaked. The reporters at Ali's TV station would be all over the story if foul play is suspected."

It was only later that I was able to process what Nasser didn't want to tell me outright. That if someone drugged Ali right before he got behind the wheel, his death might soon be investigated as a homicide. It wouldn't be long before the police went looking for suspects.

And anyone who watches detective shows knows that the first person they look at is the wife.

I drove straight to the kids' school right after Nasser and the detectives left. I might not be able to protect my children from the truth, but they deserved to at least hear it directly from me. Before leaving, I stopped to gas up, absentmindedly scanning the other cars at the pumps while I filled my tank and wondered how to tell Ayla and Adam that their dad had a strange drug in his system when he died. Naturally, I was especially concerned about how Ayla would take the news.

My gaze landed on a vintage-looking sports car. What drew my attention was its burnt-orange color. When I was little, my parents drove a station wagon in that same vibrant shade. People used to compliment the color all the time. I briefly wondered why manufacturers stopped making cars in fun colors. The gas nozzle clicked off. My tank was full. It was time to get on the road.

Two hours later, the kids and I were walking along a trail near the college.

"Did you drive all the way out here just to go for a walk in the park?" Ayla asked. She wore baggy sweats and looked like she'd forgotten to brush her hair that morning. Ayla had rarely appeared disheveled before her father died.

"I would prefer to go on a real hike," I answered. The college was nestled in Virginia's scenic Shenandoah Valley. Ali and I had always meant to come out for a hike with the kids. The one time we tried, it rained so hard that we went to lunch instead.

Adam trailed behind us holding Binti's leash. "I can't believe you got a dog after we left home." She and Adam had instantly become friends. Binti loved anyone who walked her.

"She's good company," I said.

"I'm glad you got her, Mom," Ayla said. "She's adorable."

"Why are you really here?" Adam paused to let Binti do her business. "If you came just to see if we're OK, as you can see, we are."

"How about you?" I looked at Ayla.

"I'm fine." She looked away. "Just leave it alone."

An obvious lie. "Have you thought any more about seeing a grief counselor? That might help. I could set it up."

"Mom," she snapped. "Stop."

I felt impotent. I wanted to assist my daughter, but she clearly wasn't ready yet. "OK, but if you change your mind about seeing a counselor—"

"I won't," she cut me off. "Are you going to tell us why you're here or not?"

I reluctantly let the subject drop. For now. "I know you two are strong and resilient." I swallowed hard, looking ahead. It was almost November. The leaves were beginning to fall, resulting in half-dressed trees lining the path. "Together, the three of us can get through anything." If I said it enough, maybe I'd start to believe it.

"It's not like we have any choice," Ayla said in a flat voice.

I inhaled long and deep. "I came because I have something to tell you."

Ayla halted. "Is it bad news?"

Adam came up behind us. "What's up?"

My throat was dry. I didn't know where to begin. I thought about the secret house. And now the Xanax. Lying to me was one thing, but how could Ali put the children in this position? I wanted to punch him.

Ayla watched me carefully. "What's going on, Mom?"

"It involves Dad." My voice cracked.

Ayla's eyes rounded. "Are you about to cry?"

My throat twisted. "Maybe."

"Why?" Adam cocked his head. "What's happened?"

I pointed to a nearby bench. "Let's sit."

"No, thank you." Ayla crossed her arms over her stomach. "Just say it."

I took a deep breath, forcing air into my deflated lungs. "I drove out here as soon as I found out. I wanted you both to hear it from me."

"What's up?" Adam asked. Binti seemed alerted to the change in atmosphere. She stood next to Adam, her tail high and still.

"Two detectives came to visit me today."

"Detectives?" he repeated.

Ayla was beyond pale. Her skin took on a grayish tint. "Why?"

"Apparently, whenever there is a fatal car accident, they test the person's blood. It turns out that your dad had a drug in his system."

Adam's mouth slackened. "Now you're saying Dad did drugs?"

"No," I said. "He—"

Ayla flushed. Two bright-red spots on her cheeks shone against the sickly tone of the rest of her face. "What kind of drugs?"

"Dad had Xanax in his system when he crashed."

A sound of surprise erupted from Ayla's lips. "Dad took Xanax? Since when?"

Adam's brows scrunched together. "What is that? I mean, I've heard of it, but what's it for?"

"It's an antianxiety medicine."

"Dad taking medicine?" Ayla looked totally thrown. And almost a little relieved. What had she thought I'd say?

"Why would he take anxiety meds?" Adam asked. "Was he anxious?"

I shook my head. "Not to my knowledge." But there was a lot I didn't know.

Adam dug his hands deep into the front pockets of his jeans. "It makes zero sense."

"For all we know, it could be a mistake." I looked from one of them to the other. "Maybe someone gave him a Xanax by accident. Maybe they thought they were giving him regular Tylenol or Advil."

"And Dad was driving," Ayla said. "Does Xanax make you sleepy?"

I nodded. "It can, yes. I looked it up. You're not supposed to drive after taking Xanax until you know for sure how it affects you." My legs didn't feel like they could hold me up for much longer, so I sank onto the bench. "Most people will feel the effects of the drug within an hour. Dad could have taken it right before he left to come home."

Ayla slumped onto the bench next to me. "Wow."

The three of us momentarily went quiet, trying to process this strange new development, until Adam broke the silence.

"Is that why he crashed?"

I hated not being able to protect these precious babies of mine. I dreaded the moment they learned about the secret house. "Possibly."

"I knew Dad was too good a driver," Ayla said, "to just go and crash into a tree. Even if he was in a hurry."

"Why would he be in a hurry?" Adam asked.

"I don't know." Ayla bit her thumbnail. Was this a new habit? A way to cope with stress? "To get home or whatever."

Adam looked my way. "What else did the cops say?"

"They're investigating. They'll trace all of your father's movements the night he died."

"And who he was with?" Ayla asked, her voice barely above a whisper.

I nodded. "Yes, and who he was with."

Adam kicked a pebble along the trail. "Do we really have to keep walking? This doesn't qualify as a hike. Not a Dad-quality hike."

I smiled. "He would say this trail is for suckers."

Ayla stared at the ground. "I don't feel like walking either."

I came to my feet. "Well, I'm already here, and if we have an early dinner, I'm buying."

I knew the appeal of a free meal to my college students. Ali had set a monthly food allowance for each of them when they moved out of campus housing. I'd maintained the payments since his death, although the kids usually had to remind me to send the money. Maybe Ayla would eat something if I was there to watch her.

Adam perked up. "Can we go to the Japanese steak house? Or is that too expensive?"

Ali would say it was too pricey. That something like the steak house was for special occasions. Well, he didn't make the rules anymore.

"Japanese steak house it is." I put my arm around my son's slim waist, pulling him in for a side hug. "Let's go. I'm starving."

Chapter Twenty-Two

Before

"The fridge is whining again," I complained to Ali the moment he walked into the kitchen. I was making our Saturday-morning coffee. The kids were fast asleep upstairs.

"I'll check the fan after breakfast." He opened the refrigerator and the grinding noise stopped.

"Should we just buy a new one?" The fridge had been rattling on and off for weeks. "Or at least call a repairman?"

Ali scoffed. "Do you know how much they charge just for the house call? That doesn't include the parts and service once they get here."

In fifteen years of marriage, spending money on big-ticket items was a constant push-pull. "The thing is obviously broken."

"It makes some noise. Big deal." He shut the fridge door. "It's only a couple of years old and still keeps everything cold." We'd picked out the appliance together, in keeping with Ali's mantra that it be nice but not too expensive.

"Listen to it! It sounds like we bought a lemon."

"It'll be fine once I check the fan. Something is probably obstructing it."

Irritation flared in my chest. "Why do you get to make all of the big money decisions?"

"Why would we pay for a new fridge when I'm willing to try to fix this one? It's not like I'm asking you to do the repairs."

I gave up. "What do you want to do for our anniversary?" I asked. "This is a big one."

"Fifteen years." Yawning, Ali carried his coffee to sit at the island. "Whatever you like. Except that it can't be next weekend."

"Why not?" This year's anniversary fell on a Thursday. We usually celebrated on the closest Saturday.

"I'm going on a golf weekend with some of the guys from work."

"Really?" I poured a little nondairy creamer into my coffee, turning the rich black color into a creamy brown. "Since when do you have golf weekends?"

"Since next weekend."

Coffee in hand, I leaned back against the counter. "That's weird."

"Why?"

"Because you've never gone away on a golf weekend before."

"Jake has some free tickets and invited a few of us to go." He studied me. "Do you prefer that I stay home?"

I sipped my coffee. "Where is this happening?"

"Someplace in North Carolina. It's supposed to be one of the nicest golf courses on the East Coast."

"You'd rather go golfing with the guys than celebrate our fifteenth anniversary with your devoted wife?" I teased him. "Just what are you boys planning to get up to?" Ali rarely took time to go out and have fun with the boys. We could easily celebrate our anniversary another weekend.

Ali's expression grew serious. "You do know that I would never cheat on you."

"Whoa. Where did that come from? I was kidding. Obviously." I often joked around with Ali. But he was clearly tense, his body rigid, his mouth contorted in a half grimace.

"I would never purposely hurt you," he insisted. "Never."

"I know. I was *kidding*." I put my hand on his arm, feeling the muscles in his forearm relax beneath my fingers. He seemed to want to say more, but I kissed him. He kissed me back like he meant it. A pretty intense kiss for a lazy Saturday morning.

When he pulled back, he said, "I don't have to go if you don't want me to." Then he shot me a playful look. "I don't want to spend the rest of my life hearing how I skipped out on our anniversary to go play golf with my buddies."

"I could get a lot of leverage out of that." I suggestively batted my eyelashes, relieved that we'd fallen back into our usual couple banter. "And here I was planning to cover myself in plastic wrap so you could 'open' me as an anniversary gift and we could have superhot sex."

He waggled his eyebrows. "Ooh, baby."

"At least now I'll save money on plastic wrap. That should make you happy."

He sipped his coffee. "Now you're *really* turning me on."

I laughed. Our sex life wasn't as active as it had once been, but we still made love once or twice a week. It was warm and lovely, comfortably satisfying. I viewed the decreased frequency as a natural ebbing for a busy couple that had been together a long time.

The refrigerator started rattling again. I rolled my eyes. "Pleeeease can we get a new refrigerator?"

"Sure," he replied, "as soon as this one breaks. Or if I can't get this thing to stop making noise."

"Fine. Go on your golf weekend." I straightened and took my coffee with me.

"Where are you going?" he asked.

"Away from that obnoxious refrigerator." I was much more irritated by the fridge than Ali's going away on the Saturday we'd normally celebrate our anniversary. "Maybe I'll make a unilateral decision and buy a new fridge while you're off golfing with your buddies."

"You could always welcome me back home with that plastic wrap idea," he called after me.

"Hah!" I snorted. "In your dreams."

Chapter Twenty-Three

Now

The detectives returned a few days later, after arranging the meeting through Nasser.

"Where's Cujo?" Nasser asked while we waited for the police to arrive.

"Her name is Binti and she's a sweetie. Don't worry, she's behind a closed door upstairs." I'd locked her up in my bedroom where she could sleep to her heart's content in her favorite ray of sunshine. "Why are you so dressed up?"

Nasser straightened the cuff of his expensive-looking navy suit. "It's part of the game. Detectives dress well. I dress well."

"What is this? A clothes-off?" I pulled open the refrigerator to pour Nasser a glass of water. "Are you trying to intimidate them?"

"Something like that."

"I'd be intimidated if I were going up against you."

He chuckled. "I doubt that."

We were settling back into a more comfortable rapport. We were friends and family, but nothing more. I handed him the water. "Why didn't they just call me directly?"

"When I walked them out the other day, I told them that I'm your attorney, which means any contact they want to make with you goes through me."

"Why?" I bristled a little. "I don't need to be taken care of." I'd let Ali call the shots most of the time, and look where that got me. I vowed never again to be so oblivious and trusting that my husband could buy an entire house from our joint account without my having a clue.

"I know that. But I'm a defense attorney. This is what I do. And it's what Ali would expect of me."

"Why are you being so protective?" I eyed him. "Are you worried the police think I've done something wrong?"

"I'm just being extra careful. I automatically tell all of my clients to speak to the police as little as possible."

"They can't really believe I did something to Ali, can they?" Maybe I was in denial because I hadn't taken this possibility seriously. Mostly because I didn't have the capacity to add another potential problem to my already-overflowing plate of troubles.

"If the detectives ask you any questions, answer calmly and succinctly. Try not to get emotional, and don't add anything extra. Just answer the direct question."

"I shouldn't be emotional that my husband's dead?"

The doorbell rang. Upstairs, Binti's barking erupted.

"My dog is right on cue."

I went to let the police in, eager to hear what they had to say. Maybe they'd learned how the Xanax got into Ali's bloodstream.

The two detectives stood on my doorstep looking as polished and well dressed as last time. There were polite greetings all around before I showed them into the living room.

Once we were all settled, Detective Lloyd pulled out his phone. "I'm going to record this. For my notes."

"I've no objection to that if Amira doesn't." Nasser retrieved his phone and started recording as well.

I stared at the dueling phone recorders. All of this felt completely surreal. "It's fine with me."

Detective Lloyd dipped his chin. "Great, let's get started, then."

"Before we do," Nasser interjected, "I'd like to request a copy of your recording of this interview."

"Noted, Counselor." The detective turned his attention to me. "Mrs. Abadi, do you know a woman named Samantha Price?"

I felt the blood rush from my face. I hadn't expected Lizzie Martins to be part of this conversation. "Um . . . yes."

"And how do you know her?"

"Well, I don't *know her*, know her." I swallowed hard. "I met her briefly once."

"I see," Detective Lloyd said. "How would you describe the nature of your relationship?"

I looked at Nasser, suddenly very grateful that he'd insisted on being present. He nodded almost imperceptibly.

"I don't have a relationship with her."

"So not friends," Detective Fox finally spoke up. "Enemies, then?"

"I don't know her well enough to like her or hate her." I might resent her. Was a little jealous of her. But hate? "Like I said, I've met her once, and it was very brief."

The detective kept her unwavering gaze on me. Her eyes were the palest green, so light you could practically see right through them. "To your knowledge, what was the nature of your husband's relationship with Ms. Price?"

I shifted in my chair. "She was Ali's college girlfriend."

"I see." Detective Fox's brows lifted ever so slightly. "And the nature of his relationship with her at the time of his death?"

Emotion twisted in my throat. "I can't say."

"Can't say or won't say?" she persisted.

"I honestly can't say." I released a long breath. "Before my husband died, I would have said that there was no relationship. To my understanding, Ali hadn't seen Lizzie . . . um . . . Mrs. Price in more than twenty years."

"I see." Detective Fox sat back in her chair. "It must have been quite a shock to learn that your husband left a house to his college girlfriend who, to your knowledge, had been out of the picture for decades."

So they knew about Cozy Glenn Lane. I shouldn't have been surprised. They were investigators, after all, with access to all kinds of information.

Nasser spoke up before I could. "Is there a question in there, Detective? Because I didn't hear one."

She gave him a tight-lipped smile. "Mrs. Abadi, how did you react when you found out your husband left a house to Mrs. Price?"

"I was shocked. And in complete and utter disbelief. Sometimes, I still think there has to be some misunderstanding."

Detective Lloyd leaned forward. "What sort of misunderstanding?"

"I know what the facts are. That Ali left a house to Samantha Price. I know that, but I don't understand it."

"Do you believe your husband was having an affair with Mrs. Price?" Detective Fox asked.

The bluntness of her question took me by surprise. "I don't know," I snapped. "Are you here to tell me that he was?"

"Easy," Nasser murmured under his breath while the two detectives exchanged a glance I couldn't interpret.

"No, we're not making any assumptions," Fox answered. "We're just asking questions. That's our job."

I forced myself to calm down. "I don't know when Ali would have had the time to conduct an affair. He rarely traveled. He usually came home straight from the office. He was busy coaching the kids' sports or attending their events in the evenings and on weekends. I just don't know when Ali would have had time to run to North Carolina to see that woman."

Both sets of eyes watched me intently as Fox asked her next question. "How would you describe the state of your marriage at the time of your husband's death?"

"We had a good marriage. Solid, loving." I couldn't help the bitterness that leaked into my words. "Or so I thought."

"What do you think now?" Fox asked.

"Beats me." I couldn't hide my agitation. "The man I thought I was married to would never, in a million years, cheat on me. But then how do you explain that house?"

"Did your husband's mood change in any way in the last weeks or even months before he died?" Detective Lloyd asked.

"No." I shook my head. "Not that I noticed."

Detective Lloyd checked to make sure his phone was still recording. "There was no indication that he was possibly hiding something from you or felt guilty about something?"

"No," I answered. "He seemed completely normal."

"How would you describe your husband?" Detective Fox asked.

I thought about Ali, envisioning his smile. The quiet, easy laughter. What he'd said to me after our first kiss. *I wondered if the chemistry was there. Wow. Just wow.*

It seemed like it happened yesterday. But also, forever ago. Yet my body still remembered the sensations, the excitement that sparkled through me when he kissed me for the first time.

"Mrs. Abadi?" Detective Fox's voice pried me away from my memories. "I asked how you would describe your husband."

"As one of the kindest people I've ever met. An excellent father to our kids. Ali was our protector." My voice thinned. I barely managed to choke the words out. "I mean, obviously he wasn't perfect, but I miss him every day."

It was silent for a moment, my grief, and my love for my husband, thickening the air. This roller coaster of emotions exhausted me. One minute I missed my husband with desperate longing. And then the next, I was so mad at him that I wished he were still alive so I could kill him myself.

"When did you find out that he left the house to his ex-girlfriend?" Detective Fox asked.

"After Ali died." I firmed my voice, determined to keep it together. "I didn't even know that house existed until I started trying to get a grip on our finances."

"Just a moment." Detective Fox held up a ring-laden, crimson-tipped finger. "You didn't know that the house existed?"

I shook my head, realizing how stupid and unaware that made me sound. "No idea."

Detective Lloyd gave me a sympathetic look. "How exactly was your husband able to purchase a house without your knowledge?"

I shrugged, feeling like an idiot. "He was an accountant. He handled all of the finances."

"Did you all have enough income, as far as you know, to afford a second house?" Detective Fox asked.

"I guess so. Ali was frugal. He was a saver." But not too cheap to buy his ex a house with the money he made me save. That stung.

"Hmm," was all Fox said, but I felt judged. "And do you work?"

"I'm a museum scriptwriter."

They both gave me a blank stare, a reaction I was used to. Few people had ever heard of my job.

"You know those cards displayed with artifacts in museums?" I said by way of explanation. "The labels that tell you about the item and its significance? I write those."

"Oh," Fox said. "I didn't know that was a job. I assumed curators did that."

"Curators are more accustomed to writing academic papers rather than labels normal people can understand."

"I see." Fox briskly returned to the business at hand. "So, both you and your husband had jobs. And you're sending two kids to college?"

"That's right."

"Are the kids taking out loans to cover the cost of tuition?" she asked.

"No." This was one financial question that I could answer. "We opened a college savings plan for each child when they were born. Tuition was all paid for by the time they started college."

Detective Fox watched me carefully. "I don't mean to be insensitive, but is it possible that Mrs. Price was your husband's second wife?"

"Excuse me?" I was incredulous.

"Marrying more than one woman is common in your religion, is it not?" Fox asked.

Lloyd interjected. "Your husband would have to be very connected to a woman in order to buy her a house."

I blew out an exasperated breath. "No. Having a second wife is not a common practice. It is exceedingly uncommon, not to mention illegal in the United States."

"But it is done in your culture?" Lloyd pressed.

"I'm forty-four years old and I've only ever met one much older man, who lives overseas in the Palestinian Territories, who married a second wife. So no, taking a second wife is not very common in my experience."

Nasser cleared his throat. "Maybe we could stay on track with the facts rather than waste my client's time on outlandish cultural assumptions."

Lloyd acknowledged Nasser with a sharp nod. "Mrs. Abadi," he said, "did your husband have good friends, coworkers, or family who might have known about the relationship with Mrs. Price or the purchase of the North Carolina house?"

I shook my head. "I don't think anyone knew." I declined to mention my suspicions that Ali's family might have been in on the secret.

"Mr. Abadi was my cousin and we were tight," Nasser put in. "I would venture to say I was one of his closest friends. And he never mentioned anything to me. I was as shocked to hear about the house as Mrs. Abadi was."

"Aside from Nasser, Ali had his work friends and his college friends," I added.

"I see," Detective Lloyd said. "We'd like to get their information if possible."

"I can put you in touch with the college friends," Nasser told them.

"Mrs. Abadi"—this from Detective Fox—"do you have access to your husband's phone, email, and any other devices that we could look through?"

"For what purpose?" Nasser interjected.

"Just to be thorough, you understand." Detective Lloyd spoke in an almost-breezy tone as if we were talking about the weather and not the suspicious death of my husband. "We'd like to look for evidence of a relationship, to see if it's possible that Mr. Abadi was being blackmailed. To see if someone had it out for him."

Nasser frowned. "I don't think—"

"Yes," I interrupted. "I'll give you access to my husband's phone and email. Whatever you need. I just want to know what happened."

The detectives both looked Nasser's way, but he didn't react. His face remained expressionless. But that changed once the detectives left.

"You gave them an opening," he said, clearly worried. "You don't know what they might find in Ali's email and his phone."

"I've already looked; there's nothing there."

He ran the flat of his hand over his mouth and chin. I knew by now the gesture meant Nasser was worried. "With their resources, the police will be able to find a lot more information than you."

"Good!" I exclaimed. "Why do you think I gave them that stuff? Because I want to know what they find."

He shook his head, exasperated. "You might have just opened up a whole can of worms."

"I have my reservations about the police, that's for sure." First, they painted the picture of a suicidal Ali, and now they wanted to know if my husband was a bigamist. "But Ali's dead. They can't hurt him. I'm still alive and I want the truth. I'm willing to do whatever I have to do to find it."

The next day I went to visit Ali.

For a cemetery, the place I'd chosen to bury my husband was beautiful. It was a serene old burial ground where some markers dated back to the 1800s. The graves were nestled among towering old trees, silent witnesses to generations of grief and loss. I could feel the history of the place whenever I walked through it.

We'd laid Ali to rest next to an old oak tree. I liked the idea of its massive branches sheltering him from the hot summer sun. I'd come by regularly after his death, until I discovered the existence of the second mortgage and life went into a tailspin. It had been more than a month since I last visited.

I don't know what compelled me to visit, but something drew me there. I was a mess of tangled emotions and didn't know what I believed anymore. The cemetery was a peaceful, almost meditative place. Maybe visiting Ali's burial site would calm my inner turmoil and help me see things more rationally. I'd do just about anything to get some clarity.

I made my way toward Ali's grave. There was no solemn granite marker to identify the spot, just a paper nameplate encased in plastic. I still hadn't selected a headstone, which also made me feel delinquent in my duties. Installing a marker—the final physical testament that Ali had lived and died on this earth, that he'd had a family that loved him—was my last obligation to him as his wife. No matter what he'd done.

But I couldn't summon the energy to pick out a tombstone. I still had no idea what his epitaph should be. How could I compose a proper tribute when I wasn't sure who Ali truly was? Devoted husband and father? Lying low-life cheater? I'd been married to the man for twenty-three years, yet I couldn't say.

As I came around a tree, I caught sight of someone kneeling at Ali's grave. I paused, at first thinking I was in the wrong section of the cemetery, momentarily confused about the grave's location. It *had* been a while since I'd visited. But then the figure came into focus.

Fury rippled through me. "What the hell are you doing here?"

Lizzie Martins looked up, her face pale and narrow. As I got closer, I realized she was crying. Tears streamed down her face. My stomach coiled. If I needed proof that Ali meant a great deal to Lizzie Martins, the evidence was sobbing right in front of me.

"I'm sorry, I shouldn't be here," she said in a watery voice. "I don't want to bother you."

"Why are you here?" I kept my voice calm, almost soothing. I didn't want to risk having her run off again like she had at the lawyer's office.

A sob escaped her. "I just heard that Ali had drugs in his system. That he might have tried to kill himself."

I stiffened. "Where did you hear that?"

She blew her nose. "The police came to see me."

"They told you Ali killed himself?" Who else had they shared their theory with? Fury shot through me. What if the kids heard?

"They said it was possible." She crumpled the tissue in her fist. "They also said he had drugs in his system."

Something rustled, and I thought I saw a shadow move in the corner of my eye. I looked toward an old tree but didn't see anyone. The small cemetery appeared mostly empty except for a few cars pulled off to the side where people attended to their loved ones' graves.

I was mildly surprised to see a familiar-looking vehicle parked nearby. It was the orange sports car I'd noticed at the gas station a few days earlier. The gas station and cemetery were located within a few miles of each other. The sports car owner must live in the area.

"I'm sorry," Lizzie said to me, "very, very sorry about Ali. Did you realize that he was having . . . emotional troubles?"

"He seemed to be doing fine."

Lizzie looked at me, squinting her eyes like she was staring into the sun's glare. "We don't always know the people we love."

"I thought I knew Ali. But now I have no idea what the truth is. And I'm definitely in the dark about why he bought you that house. Will you tell me?"

Instead of answering, she said, "The last time I saw him, he seemed off. As if he had something on his mind."

Her words hit me like a punch in the ribs. Had they met regularly? "When did you last see Ali?"

"I don't remember exactly. Maybe a month or so before he died. I ran into him by accident when I was in town visiting my mother. I told the police."

"What exactly did you tell them?"

"The truth. That Ali seemed worried. I had the impression it had something to do with his work."

I scoured my mind. I couldn't remember anything out of the ordinary in the weeks before Ali's accident. "He seemed fine to me."

She moved restlessly, like a skittish horse. "Why did you give my name to the police?"

"I didn't. They found out about you on their own. They want to know why Ali left you a house."

She shook her head. "They've got it all wrong. I explained everything to them."

"It would be nice if you'd extend the same courtesy to me."

"They also asked me if my children could be Ali's."

Shock rippled through me. I felt sick. "Could they be?"

Her eyes flashed. Disgust twisted her features. "How can you even ask me that?"

"How could I not?" I lost my cool. "He supposedly gave you up to marry me. But here you are, twenty-three years later, sobbing at his grave and the proud owner of a house that Ali and I paid for. And you tell me *nothing*. You offer no explanations."

She shook her head, her contempt obvious. *Her* contempt. For *me*. The *nerve*. "Ali gave up so much for you and you still doubt him?"

"Gave up so much?" I choked on the words. "Like what? Are you referring to yourself?"

"You never deserved him," she said sadly. "He was the most decent guy in the world." And then Lizzie Martins did what threatened to become a habit whenever the two of us came face-to-face.

She bolted.

Chapter Twenty-Four

"Just let it go," Lulu advised.

"Please turn over," her masseuse ordered. Lulu flipped over on her back, tucking the sheet neatly under her arms. I was on my stomach a few feet away getting pummeled by my masseuse, Suzie, a small woman with mighty hands and elbows with pinpoint precision.

It was Saturday, a couple of days after I ran into Lizzie at the cemetery. Lulu had turned up before I'd even finished my morning coffee, insisting that I needed a self-care day after all I'd been through. She booked massages and afternoon tea at a quaint shop in Old Town that served the tastiest tiny sandwiches. The latter was a concession from my sister, who preferred tea at the Ritz but knew I favored the Alexandria waterfront.

Lulu and I were each naked under our sheets, our cots a few feet apart as we received side-by-side massages in the couples room. Ali and I had never gotten a couples massage, and it occurred to me that now we never could. Not that Ali would have been into it. I'd never bothered to suggest we get one because I knew he'd dismiss it as a waste of money.

"Let what go?" I asked my sister.

"Try to put that woman in your past. Look forward."

"Would you just let it go if your husband left a house to an ex-girlfriend?" I winced as the masseuse's elbow zeroed in on a tender spot near my shoulder blade. "Or would you try to find out everything there was to know about her and why he did that?"

Jenny murmured something in Mandarin. Suzie replied with an affirmative-sounding, "Mmm."

Lulu released an exasperated sigh. "What do you hope to achieve?"

"Some closure. I really want to talk to Lizzie again."

"You're in la-la land if you really think that can happen."

I opened one eye to look at her. "Why?"

She turned her head to meet my gaze. "Your husband dumped that girl to marry you. She's not going to be super fond of you."

This time, Suzie murmured something to Jenny. Then the two women traded a few quiet words back and forth. They were obviously talking about us. In the same way Lulu and I often switched to Arabic for the same purpose. But I didn't have the energy to care what Suzie and Jenny overheard.

"She doesn't have to like me," I told my sister. "I just want to know the truth."

"Even if she wasn't sleeping with Ali, she could easily tell you that she was, just to hurt you. To get back at you for stealing him from her." More words between the masseuses. "You'll never know if what Lizzie Martins tells you is the truth."

"I have to at least try."

"I think you should focus on what was good and real between you and Ali," Lulu said. "He was a caring husband and father. He made you feel loved and appreciated."

Tears stung my eyes. I closed them, pretending to focus on the sensations provoked by Suzie's expert fingers. "I have to make it make sense. I don't want to wonder about Ali's involvement with Lizzie for the rest of my life."

Jenny and Suzie exchanged more quiet words.

"I read somewhere that your life has many seasons," Lulu said. "Your season with Ali has come to an end. You're entering a new season. See a therapist. Figure out what that means."

Her advice made sense. I'd been in constant upheaval since Ali died. Maybe a grief counselor could help me sort out the tangle of emotions clogging my insides. But I felt like I needed to resolve this Cozy Glenn business before doing anything else.

The timer went off, signaling the end of our massage. The masseuses pounded our backs a few more times before leaving us, quietly closing the door behind them. As we were pulling our clothes on, Lulu got a call from Khalid.

"We can take our time and go shopping after tea if you want. I don't need to get home to the kids," she said when she hung up. "Khalid was supposed to meet up with Nasser, but Nasser apparently forgot he has a thing with his JMU friends."

I swung my head toward her. "He's meeting his college friends?"

"Yeah." She gave me a wary look. "Why?"

"No reason."

I enjoyed the tea and happily indulged in warm scones, delicate sandwiches, and tiny decadent desserts. After we sufficiently gorged ourselves, Lulu and I went shopping. We sampled different creams and eye shadows at the makeup counter and tried on ridiculously expensive loafers in the shoe department. By the time I got home at the end of the day, I was happily worn out.

My mood soured as soon as I entered the kitchen. The refrigerator was buzzing. It wasn't the full-fledged rumble that drove me crazy all those years ago, but it didn't sound good.

Something about that noise jolted me back to the past. To Ali. And made me think of the time he fixed the refrigerator. These days it was hard to think of my husband without my mind immediately going to why he'd kept secrets from me.

I reached for my phone and called Nasser.

"Are you sure you're up for this?" Nasser asked as we walked up to a tidy white brick cottage in Arlington. The get-together was at Sara Carr's place.

"Why not? What could be worse than losing my husband and finding out he had a secret house?"

He cracked a smile. "When you put it that way."

"Maybe they can give me some of the answers that Lizzie won't provide. Or, who knows, maybe Lizzie will turn up."

I *was* nervous. I'd rarely interacted with this group in the dozen years since Ali and I had left the bar early. Most of the JMU friends had reached out in some way after Ali died. Some made it to the burial; others didn't because we laid Ali to rest less than twenty-four hours after the accident.

Sara greeted me with a hug. "How are you doing? And the kids, how are they?" I was drawn to Sara and could see us being friends. Her warmth felt genuine. She'd gotten married since we'd last met at the JMU reunion. Her husband was an earnest guy with boy-next-door vibes.

One by one, Ali's old friends approached me with hugs and words of support. To be here with Ali so conspicuously absent felt surreal. But surprisingly, it wasn't awkward. These people embraced me because of the love they'd had for my husband.

There was a lot of talk about Ali at dinner—old college stories I hadn't heard before that made me smile. When Muslims bury their dead, there are prayers at the mosque followed by the burial. We don't generally do memorial services, but that night at Sara's, reminiscing with people who loved Ali, felt like one.

Throughout the evening, as I watched them laugh and eat and top off their wine, I couldn't help but wonder if any of them, or maybe the whole group, knew about Lizzie. After all, she'd been part of their inner circle since college. Maybe they all saw me as the gullible wife who fell for every lie Ali fed me.

"Do any of you stay in touch with Lizzie Martins?" I asked as we finished coffee and dessert.

"I was wondering about her too," Ian said. "I didn't see her at Ali's funeral."

Sara sipped her wine. "I haven't talked to Lizzie in seven or eight years."

"What was she up to when you last talked to her?" I asked.

The people at the table exchanged glances.

I was so desperate for information that I decided to be honest. "Ali left a house to Lizzie."

Sara almost choked on her wine. "A what?"

"A house that I never knew he owned. It's in North Carolina." I hated how high and thin my voice got. "I found out about the property after he died."

The shock in the room was palpable. Everyone went quiet.

"Are you sure?" Ben asked after a long pause.

"Positive." I pressed my lips inward, trying to keep my emotions in check. "I saw her briefly."

"Who?" Ian asked. "Lizzie? Where did you see her?"

"At her lawyer's office and at the cemetery. I found her visiting Ali's grave site."

"Lizzie was in town?" Ian set his coffee down. "For how long? Is she still here?"

I shrugged. "I have no idea."

Sara reached for her wine. "Did you ask her about the house?"

"I tried, but she wouldn't talk about it." I blinked back tears. I managed to keep it together most of the time, but now all my emotions were snowballing. "All I know for sure is that she got a house that Ali made payments on from one of our joint accounts."

"My God," Sara breathed.

Ben blinked. "That dirty dog!"

Nasser scowled at him. "Watch it, Rodriguez."

Ian studied me. "Did you have any idea that Ali and Lizzie were still in touch?"

"No." I sipped the dregs of my decaf coffee to calm my emotions. "Naturally, I have a lot of questions. If anyone here knows anything, please tell me."

"He seemed so into you," Ben said wonderingly. "I find it hard to believe Lizzie was still in the picture."

My heart lifted to hear one of my husband's oldest friends express his belief that Ali had truly loved me. It gave me a sliver of hope that the caring, faithful version of Ali could still be real.

"I agree," Sara chimed in after a beat. "I can't wrap my head around it. Ali wasn't the cheating type."

"With all due respect," Ian said, his tone a little harsh, "all men are the cheating type given the right circumstances."

Nasser shot him an amused look. "Sounds like someone is speaking for himself."

"All men and women are the cheating type," Ian retorted. "It's human nature."

"The Ali affair theory has a major flaw," Ben pointed out.

"Which is?" Sara asked.

"If a man wants to hook up with his sidepiece, he doesn't buy her a house in another state. He gets her something close by, where he can see her regularly."

I took a deep breath. "Why else would Ali buy Lizzie a house?"

"Where exactly is this property?" Ian asked.

"In Durham, near Duke University."

"The last time I spoke to Lizzie, her marriage had just broken up," Sara told me. "She did mention that she was moving away, but she didn't say where to."

"And this was about eight years ago?"

Sara nodded. "About that. Yes." She paused. "I was shocked to hear she was getting a divorce. I thought that she was happy with her husband."

I ran a finger around the rim of my mug. "How long was she married?"

"A long time," Sara said. "Ten, eleven years. We kept in touch back then but, after her divorce, it's like she vanished."

Later in the car on the way home, Nasser scolded me. "You do realize that you just violated the terms of the NDA you signed?"

"I didn't even think about the NDA." I wasn't thinking about the nondisclosure agreement because my thoughts were consumed with what Sara had told us. "Lizzie's marriage broke up about eight years ago. The timeline fits with the purchase of Cozy Glenn."

I pulled out my phone to see if I could find any details about Lizzie's divorce. Now that I knew her full name maybe I'd have better luck. "Her marriage breaks up." I typed her name into my phone as I spoke. "Maybe she was low on money and asked Ali to help her out?"

Nasser kept his eyes on the road. "Without telling his wife?"

"I don't know if Ali cheated, but we do know that he wasn't a saint. He lied to me about Cozy Glenn, at least by omission."

"Please try to remember not to talk about the North Carolina house or its owner in the future. Slipping up like you did could be a very costly mistake."

"What are your college friends going to do?" I scoffed. "Alert the media?"

"Just be careful, Amira. Please."

Chapter Twenty-Five

The next morning, the refrigerator started rumbling again.

I heard the commotion from my bedroom. It actually woke me up, along with Binti, who trailed me down the stairs and into the kitchen.

"You stupid piece of crap." I yawned at the chrome refrigerator, thinking back to that morning years ago when it last sounded like it was dying. Whatever Ali did to fix it that day, the noise had stopped permanently. Until now.

I pulled the door open. That killed the sound because the fan stopped whenever the door wasn't closed. I shut it, and the rumbling restarted.

I sighed. My immediate instinct was to ask Ali what we should do about it. He'd say he'd fix the fan or that maybe the fridge wasn't level, I'd grumble about how he was too cheap to buy a new one, and we'd go on about our day, with me confident that Ali would take care of everything.

But Ali wasn't here to fix the refrigerator. Or anything else. Shit. Feeling sorry for myself, I swallowed the urge to cry.

Yawning, and muttering to myself about how much life sucked, I went to my office and powered up my laptop, intent on searching for how to stop the refrigerator commotion. But the screen seemed frozen. I checked the internet connection. There wasn't any.

Great.

I looked at the tangle of wires and boxes on the floor by my desk. It was pathetic, but I wasn't even sure which one was the modem. Whenever this happened, Ali or one of the kids would reset it. But there was no one else here to do it. So, feeling very inept and sorry for myself, I knelt down and investigated. Once I was reasonably sure that I'd identified the modem, I tried turning it on and off. Nothing.

Resisting the instinct to scream about how everything was falling apart, I went upstairs to retrieve my phone. I searched for info on how to stop the stupid rumbling. If only I'd paid attention when Ali fixed the thing. I couldn't stand the noise.

Then it hit me. Ali wasn't here anymore. I could buy the new fridge I'd been wanting for years. I didn't have to ask for anyone's permission. There was nothing to stop me from ordering the appliance online and scheduling delivery.

How old was the fridge? I thought back to when Ali had fixed it. I remembered it was around our fifteenth anniversary. Then realization dawned, slamming into me with such force that I almost dropped my phone.

Eight years ago.

Our fifteenth wedding anniversary. The weekend he went away. The supposed golf trip to North Carolina. Lizzie Martins moved into her North Carolina house eight years ago. And there'd never been another golf trip after that.

"Seriously?" I muttered into the silence. Had Ali missed our anniversary dinner in order to help move his ex-girlfriend into her house? I choked on a breath. My chest felt like it was caving in. I was such a sucker that I hadn't been suspicious about his plans for that weekend. I'd been more upset about a stupid refrigerator than Ali going away on the Saturday we were supposed to celebrate our anniversary.

I should have bought the new fridge when Ali left that weekend as I'd fake threatened to do. Well, there was no time like the present. I searched the word "refrigerator" on my phone. Several came up. A world of possibilities laid out before me, with no one hovering over my shoulder telling me which one I could buy.

I picked the brand and model I liked best—stainless with French doors, a dual ice maker, and twin freezer drawers—without worrying about the price, which would make Ali roll in his grave. Punching in my address and payment information, I hit "Complete Order."

There.

It was done. I'd have a new refrigerator within the week. Adrenaline surged through me. It was the most expensive thing I'd ever ordered on my own. I'd just made my first major purchasing decision at the age of forty-four. I really was a neophyte.

But as the buyer's high wore off, thoughts of the weekend Ali went away consumed me. I couldn't stand not knowing the truth. I was ready to burst out of my skin. There was only one person alive who could give me the answers, and I'd do whatever it took to get her talking.

I might not know much about Lizzie Martins, but I had learned one important thing. And I would use that information to force that woman into telling me what I needed to know.

I drove to Durham without telling anyone. A major advantage of living alone was that people never knew your business. As long as I answered my phone, no one would worry. I made good time, stopping only once to use the restroom, buy some coffee, and take Binti for a quick walk at a rest area. She'd happily hopped in the van when we left home. She must have ridden in cars with her previous owner.

Dread slithered through me once I turned onto Cozy Glenn Lane. I had a passing moment of doubt. Intuitively, a part of me was afraid of the truth. What could have been so important to Ali that he was willing to lie to me? What was he hiding? Why hadn't he trusted me with the truth?

As I drove up, the figure of a woman closed the gate in front of the house. I slowed, pulling over a couple of houses away. I was in luck. If you could call it that. Lizzie was actually home for once.

She got into a navy Volvo sedan and pulled out, driving slowly through the neighborhood. I followed, my heart pounding, maintaining a reasonable distance but staying close enough to keep her in my sights. Just when I started worrying about losing track of the Volvo, Lizzie pulled over. It was a cemetery.

I watched her park and cross through the grass amid the sea of gravestones. She had a canvas bag slung over her shoulder and wore a gray sweatshirt with dark leggings that showed off her legs. She still had good legs.

Lizzie stopped at one of the graves and knelt to pull some weeds. Reaching into her bag, she withdrew a cloth and some sort of cleaner. She sprayed and buffed the soft gray marble stone. Then she sat for a while, legs crossed. It looked like she was talking to whoever was buried there. After about twenty minutes, Lizzie grabbed her tote, got up, and strode back to her Volvo.

I'd make a lousy detective because I lost her in traffic a few minutes later, but it didn't matter. I knew where she lived. I'd catch up with her eventually. Curiosity compelled me to circle back to the cemetery. Whose grave had Lizzie so lovingly attended to? Retracing her steps, I found the tidy, shiny headstone and read the name.

CARYL DARYUS
1936–2013
LOVING WIFE, MOTHER AND GRANDMOTHER

I almost laughed when the meaning of what I was looking at hit me. The reason I couldn't find Carol Darius online was that I'd misspelled both her first and last names. Not to mention that the woman lived most of her life before the internet, dying at the age of seventy-seven in 2013. And yet,

Carol Darius was the spelling the landscaper had given me when he wanted to be paid for mowing the lawn at Cozy Glenn Lane.

Pulling out my phone, I easily brought up the obituary. Caryl Daryus, mother of five, grandmother of fourteen, including Samantha Martins Price. Lizzie.

Why had Lizzie assumed her dead grandmother's name? I still had so many questions. But at least now I knew that Lizzie Martins and Caryl Daryus were the same person.

I went back to Lizzie's and parked a couple of houses down to wait for her to come home. She showed up about forty-five minutes later, carrying a couple of overloaded grocery bags inside. I sat in my van, forearms resting on the steering wheel, contemplating whether to knock on the door. Before I had a chance to decide, she came back out, climbed into her car, and drove off again.

This time, I followed her more closely, determined not to lose her. She eventually pulled into the parking lot of a state park. She got out and headed toward a hiking trail. I jumped out of my van and hurried to follow. Binti barked after me in protest, unhappy about being left behind in the van. I'd cracked the windows open so she'd have fresh air. Plus, I didn't plan to be gone for long.

Quickening my pace, I tried to catch up with Lizzie. There was no telling how long her hike would take, and I didn't want to spend the night in Durham. Once I got what I came for, I'd get back on the road. I had every intention of sleeping in my bed that night.

Luckily, I was wearing tennis shoes. Not the sort for long trail hikes, but they'd do the job. Lizzie was a brisk walker; she moved in long, sure strides and was much faster and more agile than me. I hadn't hit a real trail since before Ali died.

She looked back a couple of times, seeming hyperaware of her surroundings, but she didn't recognize me from a distance. At least not at first. When I got close enough, she finally spotted me.

She shrank away. "What are you doing here? Please leave me alone."

"I'm not here to hurt you or for anything bad." I approached slowly so that she wouldn't take off running into the woods. "I just need to know why Ali bought you a house."

"You should trust him," she said quietly. "He was a good man."

I stopped about five feet from her, giving Lizzie her space so she wouldn't feel cornered. "I just need to know about the house. Why did he buy it for you?"

"He didn't. He was just trying to help me out."

"Why?"

She shrugged. "I don't know." There was a desperate tone in her voice. "For old times' sake, maybe."

"I think you do know. Why won't you just tell me the truth?"

"Because sometimes the truth is overrated. Believe me," she pleaded. "You don't want to hear the truth."

"But I do. I can't properly mourn Ali and move on until I find out."

"You don't understand. This has nothing to do with you. At *all*."

"Of course it does. Surely you can see that."

"I can't see anything except that you're asking for trouble. Just let it go." She turned to walk away.

I followed. "It's not that easy."

She picked up speed. "I paid you a lot of money so that I wouldn't have to talk about it."

"Why?" I demanded, trying to catch my breath. "What are you hiding?"

"That's none of your business."

"It is if it involves my husband."

"None of this has anything to do with Ali. Go away and leave me alone."

I hurried after her. "Just tell me why he bought you a house and I'll disappear forever."

"He didn't."

Did she think I was a complete idiot? "I saw the payments. They came out of our joint bank account."

She waved me off. "I don't know anything about that. Just go away. Please."

I struggled to keep up. "I'll tell everyone. I'll call the TV station where Ali worked."

Halting abruptly, she faced me. "Ali always said you are very smart. And that would be a stupid thing to do. That's why you signed the NDA."

"Why do you think I took the one hundred thousand dollars from you?" She frowned when I answered my own question. "So I can violate the NDA and give back what you paid me."

Lizzie paled. "You won't do that."

"I just want the truth," I said gently.

I could see her struggling, sizing me up, both fear and panic emanating from her. "You would tell the world that your husband died and left a house to his old girlfriend."

"That's right," I said with a firm shake of my chin. "The Washington gossip columns will have a field day."

"You would subject your children to that?"

She caught me off guard with that, and she knew it.

"That's what I thought." She turned to stride off, veering from the trail. "If I were you, I'd take the trail back to the parking lot. You don't want to get lost."

"I hiked all the time with Ali."

"So did I," she said, disappearing into the brush. "I'm the one who introduced him to hiking in the first place. When we first met, it was a struggle to coax him outside, but he eventually took to it."

Stunned, I stared dumbly after her. Lizzie Martins had put her stamp on my family without my even knowing it. The Ali I knew was an avid outdoorsman who got me and the children into hiking. To discover that it all started with Lizzie, to know her likes were so firmly implanted in the family I made with Ali, made me sick. And livid.

After Ali died, I naturally assumed I'd always think of him whenever I wandered into nature. Now I knew I'd never hike again without thinking of Lizzie Martins.

I made my way back to the van, and took an indignant Binti for a quick walk before heading home. I called Nasser while Binti sniffed her way down a park path, being picky about where to relieve herself.

"Was Ali always an outdoorsy guy?" I asked when he picked up. "You grew up with him."

He paused. "Uh, hello to you too."

"Sorry, I just saw Lizzie, and she told me that she's the one who got Ali into hiking."

"Wait. Back up. Where did you see Lizzie?"

"In Durham. I needed to talk to her. But as usual, I came away with more questions than answers."

"You drove to Durham?"

"Yes, and I'm on my way back now. Was Ali outdoorsy?"

"Technically, I didn't grow up with him. I grew up in Youngstown, but we saw each other for weeks at a time during the summer. We played outside like most kids. But by the time we got to college, he was more of a city lights guy."

"Not a hiker, then. I guess Lizzie was telling the truth."

"So what? Why does that upset you?"

Emotion welled in my throat. "It's hard to explain. It's like another thing I thought I knew about Ali that's not exactly the whole truth. I thought he was this outdoorsy guy—"

"He *was* by the time you met him. That was real. He loved hiking and camping. You knew that."

"But he got it from *her*. He passed that love on to our children. It's like Lizzie was a bigger part of his life than I ever realized. In a way, she asserted herself in our lives without my knowing it."

"We're all the products of our life experiences," he said. "Lots of different things influenced who Ali was by the time you met him."

"Ali got a clean slate in me, because he was my first and only romantic relationship."

"Hiking is a good habit, a healthy habit," he pointed out. "It made Ali happy. He would probably have discovered his love for nature at some point along the way. It's not like Lizzie forced him. She simply introduced him to the natural world."

"You're right, I guess."

"I am," he said. "Now please be careful driving home."

"I will."

As I walked Binti back to the van, I couldn't help wondering what else I didn't know.

Chapter Twenty-Six

Before

"Do you think they have a happy marriage?" I asked Ali as I watched my old friend Rula dancing to Arabic music with her husband, Marwan. We'd met in high school and attended college together.

Ali cut into his prime rib. "He's definitely cheating on her."

"What?" I asked, both shocked and intrigued by this unexpected tidbit from my husband, who never gossiped.

We were at a wedding for Rula's younger sister. My other university friends were also there with their husbands. Hanan, the bride, was much younger than me and the last in our extended group to tie the knot. The rest of us had been married for years by then. Ali and I were celebrating our eighteenth anniversary the following month.

I watched him cut his meat. "What do you mean he's definitely cheating on her?"

Rula still felt like one of my closest friends, even though we both had busy lives and moved in different circles and didn't see each other much.

Ali shrugged. "You can just tell with some men."

"How can you tell?" I pressed.

"Just by the way they talk."

I studied Marwan. When I first met him, he did have what my mother would call a white eye. *"Aina baitha,"* she would say, meaning that he looked at women inappropriately. The literal translation being that the white of his eyes showed too much because he looked at women with overly wide eyes.

But I'd always found Marwan to be a harmless flirt and a good match for Rula. He seemed devoted to her.

"By the way they talk?" I persisted. "Why? How does Marwan talk?" Were there special code words that men used with each other?

"I don't know."

"*Marhaba*, cousin," a voice said from behind me. I looked up to see Hamza, my second cousin, smiling down at us.

"Hamza!" I got up to greet him with an air-kiss on each cheek. "What are you doing here?"

Hamza gestured toward his dark suit jacket. "I'm the banquet manager." He shook hands with Ali, who'd also gotten to his feet. "Is my crew doing a good job tonight?"

"They've been great. Excellent service," I said. "Obviously their boss has whipped them into shape."

"Good to see you, man," Ali said to him. "How long have you been working here?"

"A few months. I'm in the management training program. *Inshallah*, I'll be the general manager one day."

"*Inshallah*," Ali and I both repeated. God willing. We chatted briefly, catching up on his family and promising to make plans to get together soon.

"Good to see you both," Hamza said before getting back to work.

Later, as we waited for the hotel valet to bring our car around after the wedding, the conversation about Rula and Marwan played over in my mind. "What would you do if I cheated?"

"Why?" He shot me an amused sidelong look. "Am I boring you?"

"Hah! As if that could ever happen." Besides me genuinely liking my husband as a person, the physical attraction between us remained strong. "Why are you asking?"

"I was just thinking about what you said about our friends earlier." I didn't want to mention Rula and Marwan by name in case any of their family and friends walked by and overheard. "If he does cheat, I wonder if she knows and pretends to be oblivious."

He chuckled. "I could never get away with that with you."

"I'm glad you realize that, buddy."

"One woman is enough trouble for me."

"How romantic."

He grinned. "All I need is you, baby."

I considered his words. "What if we stopped having sex?" I lowered my voice as the crowd around us grew with people waiting for their cars.

"Why would we stop having sex?"

"Just hypothetically," I said. "Would you cheat then?"

"I guess it would depend."

"On what?"

"On why we weren't having sex. If you were sick, God forbid, obviously I would never cheat. But if you just suddenly arbitrarily decided you weren't into it anymore, I don't know what I'd do."

Ali liked to have sex regularly, so I understood where he was coming from. "You're saying I have nothing to worry about as long as we keep it moving in the bedroom?"

"You have nothing to worry about period." His tone turned more serious. "Some men are the cheating type and others aren't. I'm not the cheating type."

"Lucky for me because I don't think I could handle it if you were unfaithful," I told him. "I wonder if I'd leave you." That last part I said more to myself than to him.

"Is it even a question?"

"It would be hard to let another woman sink her claws into you. It might be easier to shoot you."

He laughed. "So you'd murder me. Got it."

"Yes, I think I'd rather you were dead than with someone else."

"I'm learning so much about you. I never took you for the jealous type."

I wasn't. Or at least I hadn't been. "We've been together so long now that I guess I've become territorial." I lightly pinched his upper arm. "You're mine, and don't you forget it."

"Right back at you. I'd kill any guy who tried to lay a hand on you."

"Ha! Look at the difference between us. I'd kill you, and you'd kill the man."

We watched the valet bring our car around. "Luckily, it's a moot point because neither of us is a cheater."

"I know." I smiled, feeling a rush of love and gratitude to be in a secure marriage. "Thank God."

After he tipped the valet and we were in the car, Ali looked at me with that smug expression that I knew so well. "Now let's get home and keep it moving in the bedroom, shall we?"

Chapter Twenty-Seven

Now

The kids noticed the new surveillance equipment when they came back for the university's fall break, which really amounted to a long weekend. They also spotted the new refrigerator.

"Nice," Adam said while using the internal water dispenser. "How much did this cost?"

"Too much," I responded.

He nodded his approval. "It's about time we got a decent fridge."

I was thrilled to have them home. They might not have bothered to come back for such a short break before Ali died. But now they showed up whenever they could. I was always happy to see them, mostly because I could check on them. Also, the house seemed a lot less scary.

Adam was pretty much his usual self, while Ayla still mostly kept to herself and rarely initiated conversation. They both assumed I installed the new security system because I lived alone. I didn't tell them about the intrusions.

"Mom, when are we supposed to get a marker for Dad's grave?" Adam asked while we ate take-out kebab from a nearby Persian place.

"Soon." The bite of grilled chicken turned rubbery in my mouth. "I need to do that."

"We went by the cemetery on the way home," he told me. "Dad deserves better than the little plastic name tag."

Did he, though? "Yeah, I'll need to order it soon."

"Well, *I* visited Dad," he clarified, "while Ayla stayed in the car. She wouldn't even get out to see Dad." Accusation rang out in each word.

Ayla put her plastic fork down. "Whatever," she mumbled.

Unease squeezed my chest. "Ayla, why didn't you get out?" I asked. "I mean, I know Dad's loss has been really hard on you."

"What's the big deal?" she retorted. "It's not like it matters to him anymore."

"It's a sign of respect," Adam said. "He deserves for us to show that we care."

Acid rose in my throat. How would Adam react if he found out about Lizzie Martins and the secret house? I'd hide the truth from them forever if I could. But it didn't take long for me to learn that as hard as I tried, I couldn't keep my children in a protective bubble indefinitely.

The following morning, I was wiping down the kitchen counters when I heard someone coming down the stairs. From the weight and pace of the tread, I could tell it was my son.

"Wow," I called out, my focus on an unidentified pink counter stain, "you're up early. It's not even eleven o'clock in the morning yet."

"Is it true?" Adam's voice quavered.

I turned to face him. He wore sweats and a hoodie. His face was ashen, his beautiful dark eyes rimmed in red.

"*Habibi*, what's wrong?" Alarm filtered through me. "Is what true?"

"About Dad buying a house for his mistress."

I felt like I'd been slammed against the wall. "Where did you hear that?"

"From an article on a DC gossip site."

Dread coiled through me. "It's online?"

He teared up. "So it is true?" His face contorted. "How could you not tell us?"

"Tell us what?" Ayla padded into the kitchen in her baggy red-and-black plaid pajama bottoms topped with a white T-shirt. I noted the dark circles under her bleary eyes. "What's going on?"

Adam handed her his phone. "Read it."

My mind slowed to the point of almost stopping. How was I in yet another unfathomable situation? Where was Ali when I needed him? And then I remembered that he was to blame for putting me in this position.

The beat of my heart throbbed in my ears. "Can I see?"

"You've known all along," Adam said accusingly. I watched helplessly as whatever innocence my son had left, whatever naivete remained after his father's sudden departure from his life, drained away.

Ayla's face transformed as she took in the contents on her brother's phone. It was like watching a house implode, shrinking into itself, closing and shuttering all its windows. I silently cursed Ali for breaking our little girl's heart.

She looked at me. "How did they find out?"

"What the fuck is going on, Mom?" Adam demanded to know.

Normally I'd come down hard on my children for using curse words. Swearing was always unacceptable in our house. But that was before. Our lives would forever be cut into two parts now. The before, when Ali was alive. And the after, the vast space of time ahead of us that we were supposed to live without him. College graduations. Marriages. Births. Celebrations. Revelations. All faced without him. One era ended. Another beginning. In this new era, profanity didn't even register. We lived on a different planet now.

"I'm still trying to figure everything out," I said to my children. "I was going to tell you after I had all the answers."

"What is there to figure out?" Adam demanded, his face red. "This is crazy. There's no way it's true."

Ayla studied my face for what felt like forever. "It's not bullshit." Her voice was almost a whisper.

Tears filled my eyes. Their shock and disappointment, their hurt, was a physical pain inside my body, a knife twisting in an open wound. "I didn't know." My voice faltered. "I had no idea."

"About what?" Horror spread across Adam's face.

I reached for his hand. "Oh, *habibi*."

He backed away. "What are you saying?"

"Just spit it out, Mom," Ayla said sharply. "The article says Dad left a house to his old girlfriend and that you found out after he died and sued her to get it back."

I was trapped. What could I do except tell them the truth? Even if it shattered everything they thought they knew about their father. "For the most part, yes."

"That fucker!" Adam burst out.

My voice trembled. "Whatever your father's faults, he loved you two more than anything."

"Apparently not more than his girlfriend," Ayla retorted. "She got a whole house to herself. The three of us get to share this one."

"Who is this lady?" Adam asked. "The story doesn't mention her name."

"She's an old girlfriend. Dad was dating her when he met me."

Ayla's eyes narrowed. "He dated you and this lady at the same time?"

"No, he broke up with her after he met me." *Supposedly.* "He knew your grandparents would never accept him marrying a non-Muslim."

"If he broke up with her, why did he leave her a house?" Adam asked. "An *entire* house."

I shook my head helplessly. "I don't know. I only learned about the house after Dad died."

"What the hell?" Adam asked, incredulous.

"Where's the love nest?" Ayla asked with a bitter twist to her lips.

"The what?"

"The house Dad gave his old girlfriend. Or maybe not-so-old girlfriend."

I forced myself to stay calm. To keep breathing. "It's in North Carolina."

"Have you seen it?" she asked.

"From the outside, yes."

"What's it like?"

"It's not big," I told her. "It's just a nice, normal-size house."

"Who cares how big it is!" Adam burst out. "This whole thing is fucked up. Screw this." He stormed out of the kitchen. I heard him going up the stairs and slamming the door to his bedroom.

"I know this doesn't make any sense right now," I said to my daughter. "But we need to reserve judgment until—"

"Stop." Ayla backed away, hands over her ears. "I don't want to talk about it."

The phone calls and texts started coming in almost immediately. My parents called from the West Bank, where they spent several months a year now that Baba was retired.

"Is it true?" Mama asked. "I can't believe it."

Baba's irate voice sounded in the background. "I told you it's not good to marry a boy who has a girlfriend. You and your mother should have listened to me."

"He shamed his whole family," Mama declared. "They have no honor now."

"Maybe they knew," Baba said. "Maybe Ali's family kept his secret."

"Baba," I said, "I don't think they knew."

"Maybe." His skeptical voice was tinny in the background. "I knew a guy who disappeared for nine years and the family pretended not to know where he was, but they knew. They always know!"

"It's not true," Um Ali insisted over the phone when she called later. "My son wasn't like that. It's a lie."

She truly seemed shocked. Maybe Ali's family hadn't known? I couldn't reassure her, so I kept it vague. "I'll figure everything out. *Wallah*. I swear."

I did appreciate it when Claudia reached out to ask how she could help. But annoyance flashed through me when Nicki and Rula, who had basically been MIA since Ali died, texted to see if I was OK and ask if it was true that my husband left a house to his mistress. I ignored their messages. I was learning that maybe friendships, even the longest and deepest ones, had a season, and ours had come to an end. I would be cordial when I saw them, but my inner circle had shifted. Ali's death had realigned my relationships.

Lulu and Nasser came over right away.

"Well, this is pretty messed up," Lulu proclaimed as she made hot mint Arabic tea for us.

"How do you think this happened?" I asked Nasser. "How did it get out?"

"I asked around. I haven't heard back yet. But you did tell people," he reminded me.

"You *did*?" Lulu slid a steaming mug in front of me. "Who did you tell?"

My head throbbed like I had the worst caffeine headache in the world. But a thousand cups of coffee wouldn't cure this disaster. "I mentioned it at dinner with some of Ali's college friends. I thought they might know something."

Lulu handed Nasser a coffee. "Would your college friends call a gossip column?"

He shrugged. "It's DC. Word gets around."

I swiped a tear away. "If only Ali had never gotten that stupid TV gig. This wouldn't have made a local gossip column if he was a boring accountant that no one had ever heard of." Not that Ali had ever been boring.

Nasser's phone pinged. He studied it. "Well, that answers the question of how the local gossip website found out."

Nausea stirred in my stomach. "It's my fault, isn't it?"

His mouth stretched into a grim line. "It came from Ian."

"Who's Ian?" Lulu asked.

"A college friend," Nasser answered.

"No!" I said at the same time. "How?"

"His sister lives with a guy whose cousin's wife writes for the website," Nasser told us. "It looks like Ian told his sister, who told the boyfriend, who told his cousin, who told his wife, who then wrote about it online."

"That's one hell of a game of telephone," Lulu remarked.

Tears filled my eyes. "I'm such a big mouth. Now I've gone and ruined everything for the kids. As if they weren't already traumatized enough." The worst part was that I had no idea how to comfort them. I was barely able to keep it together myself, much less help the kids navigate this catastrophe.

"Playing the blame game doesn't serve anyone," Nasser said. "We have to focus on damage control."

"What does that even mean?" I asked miserably. "The only people I care about protecting already know the truth."

"I expect to hear from Lizzie's attorney," he said. "She'll want you to pay for violating the NDA."

"Whatever." I sighed. The world seemed to be closing in. "That's the least of my problems."

Later, I forced the kids to come out of their rooms so we could eat dinner together.

"It's the stupid way we get married," Adam said. "That's why Dad had a girlfriend."

I stared at my son. "Excuse me?" Was he making allowances for his father's behavior?

Ayla stared down at her full plate, which remained virtually untouched. "Why do we have to marry someone who's Arab and Muslim? It's dumb. What's the purpose of that? It's not like we're religious. Adam and I can't even speak Arabic."

"You're culturally Arab American and Muslim," I countered. "There are nuances to Palestinian culture and ethnicity that most non-Arabs can't understand. It's easier to marry someone who is like you."

"All I know is that Dad dated that woman way back in college," she said. "And twenty years later, she's still in the picture? Obviously, he never got over her."

Her words, uttered so matter-of-factly, were a punch in the stomach. I knew her father's death had hit my daughter hard. But it was difficult to reconcile this bitter, skeptical version of Ayla with the complete daddy's girl she'd been just a few months earlier.

"He was probably into her this whole time," Ayla continued, resentment in her voice, "while he lied to us and pretended we were this perfect family."

"What if that Lizzie woman was the love of Dad's life?" Adam asked.

My children's complete lack of sensitivity took my breath away. Did all kids believe their parents were emotionally invincible? I took a shaky breath. "Why don't you two just take turns stabbing me in the heart with a kitchen knife?"

Ayla's expression hardened. "But, Mom, we're talking about you too. If Dad had been allowed to marry the love of his life, then you could have found the love of your life too."

"Oh, Ayla. Don't you get it?" Sorrow jetted through my body. "Your dad *was* the love of my life."

"Lizzie's attorney contacted me this morning," Nasser said over the phone a couple of days after the kids went back to school. "They want you to pay the fine for violating the NDA."

"This isn't exactly a surprise." Still, the thought of writing Lizzie Martins a check irritated me. "How am I supposed to pay her? Do I wire the money?"

"Slow down," he advised. "We're not just going to hand the money over."

"We're not? Why not? I obviously violated the agreement."

"We're going to make them prove it first. If Lizzie and her lawyer want fifty thousand dollars from you, they need to show proof that you actually violated the agreement."

"That shouldn't be too hard. All they have to do is talk to the people who were at Sara's dinner party."

"Exactly. And until they do, until they formally submit the request for payment, along with proof of violation, we sit tight."

I almost smiled. "I have to admit that I like the idea of making them work for the money." Especially after Lizzie's continual refusal to answer the most basic questions that could give me peace of mind.

"It's really just a delay tactic on our part," Nasser said, "but we're going to make them cross all of the t's and dot all of the i's before they get a penny."

"I'm good with that. If that's all, I've got to run."

"Going somewhere?" he asked.

"I tracked down Lizzie's ex-husband. I'm going to meet him now."

Once I learned Lizzie's full name, it hadn't been hard to track down her ex-husband. Sean Price lived in Maryland and agreed to talk with me in person, suggesting Frederick, an hour's drive from me, as a meeting point.

"Why do you want to talk to Lizzie's ex?"

"Maybe he'll have some insight into Ali and Lizzie's relationship. I can't help feeling that there's a missing piece to this puzzle. Once I find it, maybe everything will make more sense."

"Are you sure it's safe?" Nasser asked. "This guy's a stranger."

"Don't worry. We're meeting during the day at a coffee shop," I reassured him. "And I've got my pepper spray."

"Good," he said. "Keep it close."

When I entered the quaint coffee shop in the historic section of town in Frederick, Maryland, I scanned the tables for Lizzie's former husband. The place was mostly empty. It was four in the afternoon, long past the lunch rush and too early for happy hour. A man with a rumpled-professor look stood up as I approached.

"Amira?" he asked.

"Sean?" We shook hands. "It's nice to meet you."

"I knew there was an ex-boyfriend," he told me after we ordered coffee. "I had no idea he was still in the picture until he visited her at her apartment after we separated."

"He did?" My stomach dropped. "Are you sure?"

"I didn't know who it was at the time. Now I assume the man who came to see her was your husband."

"Did you get a look at him?"

He shook his head. "No. After Elizabeth moved out, I dropped by the apartment she'd rented to pick up something. I saw a man's athletic shoes and bomber jacket in her foyer. He was obviously inside the apartment, but I didn't see him."

My heart thumped. "Did you ask her who it was?"

"When she realized I'd seen the man's things, she volunteered that an old college friend was visiting for the day. I'd already gathered that, since the bomber jacket had the university logo on it and was a distinctive color."

"Purple and gold," I said. The university's colors. I fought to keep my composure. Ali had a bomber jacket like that somewhere in the back of his closet, even though he rarely wore it. And it wouldn't have been hard for him to get up to Frederick to see Lizzie. "After my husband died, I found out that he left her a house."

"You mentioned that on the phone." He frowned. "That's very surprising. Elizabeth doesn't need financial help. She came into some money when her father died. The family received a sizable life insurance payout, and she makes an excellent salary."

"She does?" I hadn't thought of Lizzie as someone with a career. "What does she do?"

"She's a very talented interior designer."

That explained the beautiful front-porch furniture at the house on Cozy Glenn Lane. "And you never suspected there was another man before you saw a man's things in her apartment?"

"Not once. My wife and I just grew apart." He paused for the server to pour our coffee before continuing. "Elizabeth definitely became more distracted, more distant, after we separated. But we didn't have an acrimonious breakup. My parents had a terrible divorce. It was extremely difficult for me as a child. My experience made me determined to keep things amicable for our children."

"How many kids do you have?"

"Three. Two girls and a boy."

I hadn't given much thought to Lizzie as a mother. I'd never considered her as a fully rounded person. To me, she was frozen in the one-dimensional role of girlfriend with good legs who Ali might have loved more than me.

"How old are your children?" I asked.

"Payne, our son, is seventeen. The girls, Emma and Amanda, are twins. They're fifteen." He paused, sipping his coffee. "Elizabeth has always been a little high strung, but, after the divorce, she really started behaving in ways that were out of character."

"How so?"

"At first, we decided to share equal time with the children. But then Elizabeth changed her mind and gave me full custody."

"Your children live with you?" What kind of mother would voluntarily give her kids up?

He nodded. "And then, not long after that, she moved five hours away. The Elizabeth I thought I knew, who was devoted to her children, would never relocate so far from them. They were still quite young when she left."

I did a quick calculation. The oldest child would have been nine and the twin girls just seven when Lizzie left. "Do you know why she decided to settle in North Carolina?"

"Her grandmother once lived there, but there's no family left in the area. Honestly, I have no idea why she's in Durham."

"Does she see the children?"

"Not nearly as much as they'd like."

"I'm sorry." I couldn't imagine moving to another state and leaving my children behind, especially not when they were that young. Or even as adults. Ali and I used to joke with a horrified Ayla and Adam that they'd never be rid of us. We intended to retire wherever they moved to be close to our grandchildren.

"It is what it is," Sean said with a sigh. "I've given up trying to figure my ex-wife out."

"She's definitely an enigma."

"I drove myself half crazy trying to understand the choices she's made. Elizabeth has always been a bit selfish, but she was also, for the most part, a loving mother. Why would she choose to hurt our kids like that?"

"Did you come up with any answers?"

He shook his head. "I finally realized that I might never know what drives Elizabeth. She's become even more flighty over time. Sometimes we just have to accept that we'll never find all of the answers to our questions."

"I suppose it could have been another man," Lulu said when I called her on my way home. "A million people who went to JMU have those bomber jackets."

"What do you think the chances of that are?"

"I honestly think it could go either way." A child chattered in the background. "Yara, go do your homework. I'll be right there." Lulu sounded far away. "I'm back," Lulu said, her voice loud and clear. "Where were we? What were we saying?"

"You were saying bomber jacket boy might not be Ali."

"Oh yeah, that's right. You said yourself that their college friend group is very tight. It could have been any of those guys."

"And, of course, she's a talented interior designer," I grumbled. "She couldn't have a boring normal job."

"What kind of mother hands her kids to her ex-husband and moves away?" In the background, I could hear her girls fighting. Lulu raised her voice to be heard over the racket. "I mean, we all dream of dumping our kids to get some peace and quiet, but none of us actually does it."

"Her husband said she was a devoted mother until they separated. Then she suddenly relocates and barely sees her kids." I released a long, frustrated breath. "It's yet another story that doesn't add up."

"Do you think the guy who broke in and ransacked Ali's office is related to this Lizzie business?" She only knew about the intruder who'd searched Ali's office. I still hadn't told anyone about the garage breach.

"I have no idea." I beeped at a pickup that almost veered into my lane. "I really don't know what to think."

"Maybe the break-in is completely unrelated."

"Maybe. All we can say for sure is that Ali kept secrets from me." Checking my rearview mirror, I prepared to change lanes to get away from the speeding pickup. The last thing I needed was for him to swipe my van. I did a double take when I caught sight of a vintage sports car behind me, a couple of lanes over, its burnt-orange color catching the sun's glare.

"Are you still there?" Lulu asked.

"Yes." The back of my neck tingled as I kept my eye on the sports car. Seeing the vehicle around my neighborhood was one thing, but what was it doing in Maryland? The likelihood of the vehicle being a different car seemed small. Was I being followed?

"What about Ali taking Xanax?" Lulu asked. "Could that be another thing he kept from you?"

I focused on the road ahead of me. "I have to at least consider that possibility."

"So much about all of this doesn't add up."

"That's why I have to keep digging. To make it all make sense." I checked my rearview mirror again.

The orange sports car was gone.

Chapter Twenty-Eight

Before

"Honey, I'm home!" I called out as soon as I came in through the back door from the garage.

It was a familiar ritual between us. Me jokingly parroting the old TV husbands, whose perfectly coiffed stay-at-home wives doted on them the moment they got home from work.

Ali always had the same reply. "Welcome home." But he said it warmly, like he meant it, which never failed to make me feel cared for.

He stood at the sink rinsing plates and neatly arranging them in the dishwasher. He still wore his work clothes, but in a deconstructed way that never failed to turn me on. His tie and suit jacket were discarded, the sleeves of his white dress shirt rolled to his elbows and still tucked into his belted navy suit pants. I always loved the way dress pants draped over his hips.

He smiled at me over his shoulder. "How was your girls' night out?"

"Good. I think Iman is doing Botox. She looks amazing." I set my purse on the built-in kitchen desktop. I'd had dinner with old girlfriends that I'd met at the Arab student club during college. "I was surprised to see your car parked outside. You're home early."

"Something came up."

"What could possibly come up to send you home early in April?" Ali always worked late during tax season. "Or," I teased, "are you too big a TV star now to work long hours?" A week earlier, Ali had appeared on a local TV news segment offering tips on preparing income tax returns.

"You're never going to believe this." Closing the dishwasher, he reached for the kitchen towel to dry his hands. "Channel Three wants me to become a regular contributor."

"A regular contributor of what?"

"They want me to appear a couple of times a month and give financial advice, answer money-related questions, that sort of thing."

I dipped my chin. "Are you kidding?"

He chuckled. "It's crazy, right?"

"How did that happen?"

"The news director called the firm today. He says I have a good TV presence, whatever that means."

"It means you've still got it. You hottie, you." I went in for a hug and was rewarded with a very sweet welcome-home kiss. "We need to go out and celebrate. Where should we go?"

"I don't know," he answered. "Somewhere nice but—"

"Not too expensive," I finished for him since I knew where that particular sentence always ended.

He shrugged. "Who knows if it'll work out. They want to do a few test runs over the next couple of months and see how it goes."

My arms still around him, I slid my hands lower to squeeze Ali's butt. "How could they resist you?"

"Gross." Fifteen-year-old Ayla walked into the kitchen. "Do you have to do that in public?"

"Your dad's about to become a massive TV star," I told her.

In the end, the trial run went well, and Ali became a regular contributor on Channel 3 news. I wasn't surprised. After all, Ali's good looks and quiet charisma reeled me in from the moment I met him.

But I *was* caught off guard when people started recognizing Ali while we ran errands or ate out. That was the only way Ali's new side gig impacted our everyday lives. I started making sure to look halfway decent whenever we went out. I didn't want random people thinking Ali had a sloppy wife.

Meanwhile, the kids took Ali's new minicelebrity status in stride.

"Whatever, Dad" was Adam's response when he heard. Most people his age didn't watch local television news. But Adam's enthusiasm skyrocketed once Ali started getting VIP passes to the Washington football team's training camp. Then came the occasional free tickets, always for great seats, to other local professional sports events. After that, Adam informed Ali that he could never quit his TV gig.

"Never?" Ali teased him. "How about once you're in college?"

"Never," Adam reiterated. "Cuz I'm still gonna love sports even when I'm in college. And basically all of my life. Until I'm old like you."

"Before you know it," I said to my husband, "you'll be taking both Adam *and* his kids to games."

"How fun is that going to be?" Ali smiled at the thought. "I can't wait."

Chapter Twenty-Nine

Now

"Again?" I asked when Nasser called from his car to tell me the detectives wanted to meet with me. I closed the door to Adam's room, where Binti was napping. "What is it now?"

"They say there are new developments they want to share with you."

Instantly nervous, I pinched the skin on my throat. Did the cops still think I was a suspect? "What kind of new developments?"

"I don't know. Maybe they found something on Ali's devices. Listen, I was a little delayed by a client meeting, but I'm on my way to your house now." Beeping sounded in the background. "Get out of the way, asshole," Nasser muttered under his breath.

"Don't crash in your hurry to get here," I said before realizing how that sounded. Before I remembered that Ali died in a crash. There was momentary silence.

"I'll be careful," Nasser promised. "If the detectives get there before me, listen to what they have to say, but don't answer any questions until I get there."

"Why?" I asked, bitterness in my voice. "Because they think I might have killed Ali?"

"Listen, I don't want you to worry about that. There's no evidence that you did anything wrong. The cops always look at the spouse. Just be smart about what you say to them. The less said, the better."

The doorbell rang. "It looks like they beat you," I said before hanging up and going to let the police in.

"Nasser said you have new information. Is it related to my husband's death?" I said once we were all seated in the living room. "Is it significant?"

"It could be." Detective Fox's crimson-tipped fingers brushed a feather from one of my decorative pillows from her tailored tweed slacks. "It's an avenue we're exploring."

"What's the news?" I crossed my legs and then uncrossed them. I hadn't done anything wrong, but knowing that the police suspected otherwise made me nervous.

Detective Lloyd glanced toward the front door. "Is your counsel not joining us?"

"He's on his way, but I don't want to wait," I said impatiently. "I'd like to hear whatever it is you came to tell me now."

"OK." Detective Fox gave me a perfunctory smile that didn't come close to reaching her eyes. "Your husband had a web page on the Channel Three website."

"Yes, I know. It was set up so viewers could send in their financial questions."

"And make comments," Detective Lloyd added.

Detective Fox continued. "Your husband received threatening messages through that site."

I gaped at her. "He did?" Ali never mentioned receiving menacing emails. "What kind of threats?"

"Threats of bodily harm. Death threats."

"Seriously?" It was hard to get my head around anyone threatening Ali, who really was as close to a mild-mannered accountant as you could get. You couldn't take advantage of the man, but Ali wasn't the type of guy to get into altercations unless pushed to his limits. "And you think those were real threats and not some wack job saying stupid stuff on the web where he can be anonymous?"

"The threats were pretty specific," Detective Fox informed me. "Your husband was warned to stay away from Mrs. Price."

I sucked in a breath. "What?" Someone out there knew Ali was involved with Lizzie Martins before he died. Who?

Detective Fox kept her unwavering gaze fixed on my face. "It appears that the perpetrator believed your husband was engaged in a relationship of some sort with Mrs. Price."

My heart dropped. There it was. More evidence pointing to an affair. The possibility that Ali's involvement with Lizzie had led to his death floored me. Someone out there was mad enough about their liaison to kill? I thought about the orange sports car. Should I tell the police about it? Or was I being paranoid?

"We have to take every lead seriously," Detective Lloyd said. "Especially considering that your husband might have been unknowingly drugged. These threats suggest that someone out there might have had a motive to do your husband harm."

"You think he was targeted?"

"Possibly. Mrs. Abadi," Detective Fox began, "it would help us tremendously if—"

"Have you asked Lizzie about it?" I interrupted. "Does she have a boyfriend who might have been jealous of Ali?"

"We intend to talk to her after speaking with you," Detective Fox said. "As his wife, you deserved to hear this information first."

"I see." It was natural for the police to acknowledge my primary place in Ali's life. But then it hit me that, to the cops, Lizzie was right behind me in importance. They intended to speak to her next. In death, as in life, that woman was everywhere, all over my life like a bad case of poison ivy. I pressed a fist against my lips as a bitter tang filled my mouth.

Detective Fox had a sympathetic look on her face. "The thing is, this investigation would move much faster if we could search your house."

"For what?"

"To rule you completely out as a person of interest," she said.

My stomach muscles tightened. "*I'm* a person of interest?" Hearing them say it out loud sent a wave of panic through me.

"We just need to establish that there's no Xanax, or anything else that's pertinent to the case, in your possession," she said.

"It's helpful to rule out the spouse as early into an investigation as possible," Detective Lloyd added.

"Do it." I stood up. I couldn't handle the added stress of being a suspect along with everything else. "Go ahead and look."

The detectives exchanged glances.

Detective Fox came to her feet. "Mrs. Abadi, just to be clear, do you consent to having us search your house?"

"Yes, I do," I said. "Let's get this over with."

They got to work right away, the two of them, methodically combing through every room. I followed them around. They moved quickly and efficiently. Nasser texted that he was stuck in traffic.

To my relief, Detective Fox went through my bedroom. Better to have her look through my underwear rather than her partner. She spent a lot of time combing through Ali's closet. Emotion roiled in my chest as the detective went through my husband's things—his favorite sweatshirt for lounging on weekends, the old jeans he wore to mow the lawn, the polo with his firm's name on it that he sometimes wore to the office on casual Fridays. I kept Ali's closet door firmly closed most of the time. There were too many painful memories nestled among the hanging blazers and neatly folded khakis.

"What time did you say your attorney was supposed to arrive?" Detective Fox asked as she sifted through Ali's T-shirts.

"He should be here any minute." I knew exactly why she asked. "You'd better hurry."

Nasser showed up just as the detectives were leaving. He exploded when he heard about the search.

"I leave you alone with them for fifteen minutes and you give the cops permission to search your house?"

The sounds of Binti barking from Adam's room flowed down the stairs. I'd never seen Nasser so worked up, but I held my ground. "That's right."

"But why?" Anger flashed in his dark eyes. "How could you be so reckless?"

"Because I've got nothing to hide," I retorted, my face heating up. "I'm not going to hold the police up just because I can. I want them to rule me out as a potential suspect so they can focus on finding out if someone actually drugged Ali on purpose."

He took a deep breath, his hands flat on the top of his head. "Do you know why they had to talk you into it? Because no judge will approve a search warrant. There's not enough probable cause."

"The police didn't talk me into anything. They didn't have to. The detectives asked and I agreed. They were actually very nice about it."

"Of course they were nice!" he thundered. "That's their technique. If law enforcement can't get a judge to sign off on a search warrant, they sweet-talk someone like you into doing something that isn't in your best interest."

Someone like me. Stupid? Gullible? *The kind of woman everyone assumed got cheated on.* My temper flared. "Don't tell me what is or isn't in my best interest," I snapped. "I want answers. About it all. Lizzie, the Xanax, what really caused the car accident. I can't live with not knowing. It's eating me up."

"Don't you see that this is not the way to get answers? They are looking for evidence in this house to hold against you. Don't you get that I'm trying to do right by you?"

"Doesn't it make sense to let them search? Once they don't find anything suspicious, they'll look for the real culprit."

He blew out a breath. "Sometimes you can be very naive."

I knew he wasn't just talking about the police. But Nasser was wrong. I was done being lied to and taken advantage of. I might have been a gullible fool before. But that version of Amira no longer existed.

Jake called late the following afternoon while I was getting my van inspected. I'd noticed earlier that day that it was a month overdue. Ali used to take care of everything related to the cars, another chore that I'd never paid any attention to before. As annoying as the task was, handling the inspection gave me a sense of empowerment. Taking the reins, even on the most mundane tasks, made me feel less helpless.

"I'm sorry to bother you," Jake said, "but some old notebooks were found in Ali's desk."

"What kind of notebooks?" I envisioned pages filled with math equations even though I knew that wasn't how accountants work.

"The kind you take notes in, with the spiral at the top." Car horns sounded in the background. He must have called from the road. "I don't know what they're called."

I got up from the sitting area, where a couple of other people were also waiting for their vehicles. "And he wrote in them?" I asked as I walked outside.

"It looks like it. Just notes that were jotted down here and there. I didn't look at them too closely."

"Who found the notebooks?"

He paused, clearing his throat. I sensed his discomfort. "The gentleman who, ah, now uses Ali's office."

Sorrow panged in my chest. A stranger had taken over Ali's desk. His place at the firm. I shouldn't have felt surprised or wounded by the change, but I was. "Oh."

"Whoever initially cleaned out Ali's desk left them in a bottom drawer," Jake told me. "I guess they're not technically part of Ali's personal effects. But when I noticed they had Ali's writing in them, I thought I should check to see if you want them. I mean, maybe you don't—"

"I do," I interrupted. "I do want them." The pages might be full of inconsequential notes, but whatever he'd jotted down would be something new from Ali.

"I'm on my way home from work," he said. "I can drop them by in a few minutes."

"I'm not home right now."

"I'll leave them on your front doorstep."

As soon as the van was ready, I drove straight home, eager to see the notebooks. There were three of them, nondescript with slightly worn gray covers. I sat at the kitchen table paging through them. I felt a pang to see the familiar writing, indiscriminate scratches that ignored the lines on the ruled paper. There were some formulas, jargon, that meant nothing to me. Short work-related to-do lists.

And then I saw it.

Lizzie. 2 p.m. Angelino's.

I felt lightheaded. There it was. *In writing.* A meeting with Lizzie. I'd never heard of Angelino's, but a quick search on my phone turned up a tucked-away Italian place by Lake Anne in Reston. A location that was just out of the way enough not to be seen by anyone we knew. I scoured the other two notebooks but found nothing else related to Lizzie.

When had they met? How long ago? I looked at the pages before and after the Lizzie notation to try to gauge when they'd gotten together at Angelino's and why. There was no indication. I went to my laptop and pulled up the credit card records. I sorted through a year's worth. And then the two years before that. No credit charge at Angelino's. Which didn't necessarily mean anything. If Ali wanted to be discreet about the meeting, he could easily have paid cash.

I went back to the notebook, to the page with Lizzie's name on it. The name "Comstock" was scrawled across the top of the page. The notes suggested it was a client account Ali had worked on. I reached for my phone to call Jake but then hesitated. It would be easier for Jake to brush aside my questions over the phone. Maybe I'd get more answers in person.

The following morning, I showered and dressed with care, putting on slacks and a blazer, a uniform that made me feel more confident. Going to Ali's office, knowing he wasn't there and never would be again, wasn't easy. I'd only visited the firm a handful of times over the years, because holiday parties and other work events were usually held off-site. Once I pulled up to the building, I sat in my car for a few minutes staring at the place where Ali had spent so much time.

It was no surprise that I didn't recognize the young woman in reception once I entered Ali's firm, and she obviously had no idea who I was.

"May I help you?" she asked with a polite smile.

"Yes, I'm here to see Jake Barnes."

"Is he expecting you? Do you have an appointment?"

"I do not have an appointment. My name is Amira Abadi. I just need a few minutes of his time."

"Abadi?" A somber expression came over the receptionist's face. "Are you Ali's wife?"

"Yes." I struggled not to show the emotion aching in my throat.

"I'm so very sorry for your loss," she said with feeling. "We all loved your husband. He was always so pleasant and thoughtful."

Had Ali fooled everyone else too? Or, despite evidence to the contrary, did I have everything wrong now? Maybe I was still an idiot, but a growing part of me felt there had to be more to the story, that Ali really was who I—and everyone who knew him—thought he was.

"Thank you," I said. "He really enjoyed everyone he worked with here at the firm. Would you mind seeing if Jake can spare me a few minutes?"

"Of course not!" she said. "I'll call him right now. Would you like to have a seat? Can I get you anything? Water, coffee, tea?"

I shook my head. "No, but thank you." A few minutes later, a man I didn't recognize appeared and spoke briefly with the receptionist, who pointed him in my direction.

"Mrs. Abadi? Is it OK if I call you Amira?" he said as he approached. The man was tall with reddish hair and a close-cropped beard. "Ali talked about you and the kids so much over the years that I feel like I know you."

"Did you work closely with my husband?"

He looked perplexed. "Very closely. And my boys appreciated all of the hand-me-down bikes and skateboards that we got from you."

I blinked. Ali gave hand-me-down toys to this man too? "And your name is?"

He shot me a strange look. "I thought you asked to see me? I'm Jake Barnes." He put out his hand to shake mine. "It's nice to finally meet you in the flesh."

Chapter Thirty

Before

For our twentieth wedding anniversary, Ali and I went back to the Dominican Republic for a second honeymoon. It was our first real holiday alone since having kids.

Something about being on vacation brought out the sexy in us. We made love a lot that week. Not nearly as much as on the honeymoon, but plenty for a seasoned couple twenty years in, with all the emotional bumps and scrapes to prove it.

During the day, we relaxed in loungers by the beach, indulging in fruity drinks and ordering a variety of appetizers, rather than full meals, to snack on. At night, we went to dinner and sometimes stayed out long enough to dance to the live entertainment.

Once we had children, nothing was about us anymore. But during that week in the DR, we felt like ourselves again, like in the beginning. And we started to see how our life would change once Adam joined his sister at college.

"We'll be able to do more traveling," Ali pointed out, his long body stretched out on the lounger, his skin glowing bronze in the sun. We were both older, a little heavier and less toned, but Ali never stopped being attractive to me. He continued to hike and work out regularly. Up until the end, I saw the version of him that I married and still got a thrill whenever I saw him naked.

I dipped a chip into salsa and then guacamole. "We won't be confined to planning all of our travel around the kids' school schedules. Think of all the deals we can get in the offseason," I teased, knowing how much my husband loved a bargain.

"I can't wait."

"Where do you want to go?" I asked.

"Anywhere." He sipped his drink. "I'll go anywhere with you, baby." The words were more playful than hot.

Adam had protested after hearing our plans to travel more once we became empty nesters. "Why are you guys going to start doing all of the fun stuff after we leave?"

"That's the point, son." Ali had playfully wrapped Adam in a headlock, which the boy easily twisted out of. "We put in the time raising you and your sister. Now it's time for Mom and me to have some fun."

"It'll be just the two of us," I said now to Ali as we lounged on the beach. "Like in the beginning."

"Lucky me," he said like he meant it.

"Ireland looks beautiful." I reclined on my lounger, feeling completely self-indulgent, relishing the nurturing warmth of the sun on my skin. "Let's go there."

"Ireland?" He paused. "You've never shown any interest in Ireland before."

"The pictures Ayla took of cycling along the coast, those gorgeous cliffs, changed my mind." Our daughter had visited Ireland with a student group back in high school. "The hiking views must be insane."

"I'd rather push Ireland down the list."

"Why?"

"Since I've already been there."

"You have? When?"

He didn't answer right away. "Right after college," he finally said. "With a friend."

"How could you not mention that? Ayla went to Ireland and you never once brought up that you'd been there."

"Because I went with an old girlfriend."

"That must mean you went with Lizzie." Thinking about Ali with his ex still made me a little crazy, but I wasn't about to admit it. "That was a long time ago." I forced a casual tone. I didn't want the specter of that woman intruding on our second honeymoon the way it had the first. "I'm too old to worry about college girlfriends."

"Hallelujah!" His surprised gaze met mine. "That only took twenty years."

I shrugged, pretending to be much more nonchalant than I felt. "By the time we hit our thirtieth anniversary, I won't even remember her name."

"That would be nice. I barely remember it myself."

I sipped my frozen drink. "You were such an idiot to invite her to the wedding," I couldn't resist adding, recalling my devastation when I spotted Lizzie's name on the guest list.

"If you recall, I didn't mean to invite her. But, yes, it was stupid of me not to check the guest list."

"I wonder what happened to her. Does the group ever hear from her?"

"I don't know, and I don't ask. She knows I don't want to hear from her. I mean," he amended, "I don't wish her any ill will." He spoke haltingly. "If she were in deep trouble and desperately needed help, obviously I would do what I could."

Irritation rippled through me. As if that were his place. But I forced a playful tone. "Hero complex much? You dated twenty years ago," I reminded him. "If she got into trouble, she probably has other big strong men in her life to come to her rescue."

"Why are we even talking about this?" He got up. "I'm going in. You want to come?"

I smiled up at him, surprised to note the tense lines around his mouth. "No, thanks. Maybe later."

"Come on." He reached for my hand. "Come into the water with me."

I relented. We waded into the cool water, and once we were deep enough, he pulled me into him. It was unusual for Ali to get handsy in public.

"We can go to Ireland if you want," he said.

"No, that's OK. There are a million other places I'd like to see." Places that would be new to both of us. Enjoying the water's buoyancy, I wrapped my legs around his waist and looped my arms around his neck. "Is there any other country you visited with an ex-girlfriend that we should avoid?"

"Nope." He studied my face for what seemed like a long time. "You know that I would never do anything to hurt you, right?"

"Of course." I could feel the tension in his body. He'd been so relaxed until the subject of the old girlfriend came up.

"I want you to know that I never loved anyone more than I love you," he said. "What we have, you and I, is on a whole other level. We've built a life together. Nothing means more to me than you and our family."

"I know." I tried not to dwell on it, but sometimes I still wondered if I had been Ali's second choice. But I also knew my husband never said anything he didn't mean. I feathered my fingers over the frown lines in his forehead, longing to erase them. "It's in the past."

"I'm so relieved that you understand that." He paused as if measuring his words. "Lizzie was—"

"Why are we even talking about her?" I interrupted, wanting to forget about his ex and get back to our indulgently romantic holiday, to our own little world.

"I just want to be clear with you regarding—"

"It's clear." I kissed him. "You love me. I'm your wife. That woman is twenty years in the past. Let's leave her there. Now, loosen up. We're on vacation."

He paused, but then his face cleared. "You know what would loosen me up?" He waggled his brows and kissed me deeply. Heat rolled through me. "Do you want to go back to the room?" he asked against my lips.

"As if you have to ask."

It had been a long time since Ali used the chemistry between us to create a diversion. Only this time was different. Instead of attempting to divert me, it felt like Ali was trying to distract himself.

Chapter Thirty-One

Now

I stared at the stranger standing in front of me. "You're Jake Barnes?"

"In the flesh." He examined my face. "Are you OK?"

Was I losing my mind? "That's not possible. I've met Jake Barnes."

His brow lowered. "I don't think we've ever actually met. Would you like to sit down? You look a little pale."

I shook my head in little frantic motions. "I'm . . . I'm a bit confused." The elevator dinged, and a group of men in suits got off, talking loudly, joking about the most recent Washington football game.

"Come," the man claiming to be Jake said kindly, putting a light hand to my elbow to guide me past the reception desk. "Let's go where we can talk in private." He showed me to the conference room and pulled out a wheeled leather chair for me.

"Thank you," I rasped as reality sank in. If this was the real Jake, then who was Fake Jake? Who was the total stranger that I had allowed into my house?

"Let me get you some water." He returned with a bottle and pulled out a chair to sit opposite me.

"Do you want to tell me what's going on?" he asked. "Maybe I can help."

"I don't know where to start." I took a sip of the cold water to settle myself.

"How about at the beginning? Why did you come to see me?"

"A few weeks ago, a man who said he was Jake Barnes called. He wanted to come by and pick up Ali's computer."

I registered the doubt in his face.

"Are you sure he said his name was Jake Barnes?"

"I'm positive." I took a breath and told him everything about my interactions with Fake Jake since Ali died. How he'd picked up the computer and dropped off the contents of Ali's desk.

"Well, that obviously wasn't me," he said with a frown. "And I definitely don't like the idea of someone impersonating me."

"But how did this person come to have the contents of Ali's desk? And he just recently dropped off some notebooks Ali wrote in. Did the firm ever get Ali's laptop back?"

"We did. I think Bill Warren picked it up."

"Who's Bill Warren?"

"One of our colleagues."

I remembered that I had an office number for Fake Jake. I fumbled around in my purse for my phone. "Here it is." I pulled up the contact and showed it to the real Jake.

"Hold on." He pulled up some sort of office directory on his phone. His brow furrowed. "That's Bill Warren's extension."

I released a relieved breath. "So it is someone who works here. But why would this Bill person pretend to be you?"

"That's a very good question." He studied me for a moment. "I'm surprised you've never heard of Bill Warren."

"Why?"

"Ali never mentioned him to you?"

"Not that I can recall. Ali did talk about a few of his coworkers that he was close to, like you. But he never brought up Bill Warren."

"Hmm. I assumed Ali was pretty close to Warren. He fought hard to get him a job here. Ali vouched for him. The firm took a chance on Warren because they respected Ali's opinion."

"He must be very good at his job for Ali to recommend him so highly."

Jake didn't respond, but the way he twisted his mouth spoke volumes.

"What's wrong with him? I mean, aside from pretending to be someone he's not."

"I really shouldn't discuss firm business. But, just between us, Warren's a nice enough guy, but he's not a very good accountant."

"Ali took pride in his work," I protested. "He would never champion someone who was incompetent."

"That's exactly why I assumed they were close. Ali acknowledged there were problems with Warren's work but agreed to take Warren onto his team to bring him up to speed. He said he and Warren went way back."

If Bill Warren was a longtime friend, why had Ali never mentioned him to me, even in passing? It didn't make any sense. "Ali told you that he and Warren were old friends?"

"He didn't say how close they were. Just that he'd known the man since college."

"Where is Bill Warren now? Can we bring him in here and get to the bottom of why he pretended to be you?"

"I wish we could, but he's on vacation with his family in Mexico right now."

"He has a family?"

Jake nodded. "He's married with four kids."

"Oh." Someone who had a family seemed less scary than a loner who lived in his mother's basement.

"When Bill gets back, you can be sure that I will talk to him."

I exhaled. "So many things have happened since Ali died that don't add up."

He paused. "I was shocked when I heard Ali had another house," he said, choosing his words carefully. "Everyone here thought he was a devoted family man. For what it's worth, I find it hard to believe that Ali led any kind of double life."

I smiled gratefully. "I hope that's true. Can I ask you something?"

"Of course."

"Did you ever go on a golfing weekend to North Carolina with Ali?"

"Once. About eight years ago. We had a great time."

The tension between my shoulder blades loosened a little. At least Ali hadn't lied about going golfing on the weekend we should have celebrated our anniversary.

Jake cleared his throat. "Do you mind if I ask why you came to see Bill Warren today?"

"I wanted to know when Ali would have worked on the Comstock account. Can you tell me?"

"I'm sure you are aware that I can't talk about clients," he said carefully. "That's confidential."

"Of course," I said. "I'm just asking *when* Ali would have worked on that account. I don't want to know anything about the account itself." When he was silent, I added, "Please, Jake. This is very important to me."

He relented. "Comstock is a relatively new client. Ali started working with them about two years ago."

"I see." That meant Ali had met with Lizzie sometime in the past two years. My phone buzzed. It was Nasser.

"The police want to see you. They have some pictures to show you."

"When?" I asked.

"Can you do it now?"

Nasser was waiting for me when I arrived at police headquarters.

"What are the pictures of?" I asked as we walked into the newish building composed of sharp angles and reflective windows.

"I'm not sure." He emptied his pockets, preparing to go through security. "All I know is they're retracing Ali's final interactions on the day he died and they have some questions for you."

We'd agreed to meet at the police station because it was close to Nasser's office and he had a packed schedule. "You didn't have to come with me," I told him after we got through security. "I know you're busy."

"They said it wouldn't take long." He pushed the elevator button for the sixth floor.

"I'm glad you're here." I tapped my foot, my nerves getting the better of me. "Especially since they might consider me a suspect."

"I'm relieved you understand that we need to be careful. The last time I left you alone with the police, you gave them carte blanche to search your entire house."

"It was my decision to make, and I still think it was the right way to go." It was about time that I started making big decisions beyond purchasing a refrigerator. Looking back, I could see clearly how I'd automatically allowed Ali to take the lead in our marriage, ceding final say on all the major decisions. It's not that he was some hard-ass who'd demanded complete control. I'd just automatically relinquished it.

Maybe that was because I'd never truly been on my own before now. I'd gone directly from my father's house to my husband's. Given that I lived at home during college, when would I have had the chance to develop my independence? If Ali's secret house taught me anything, it was how badly I needed to take control of my life.

"I let them have Ali's phone and tablet and they didn't find anything fishy, did they?" I pointed out. The police had updated us that there was nothing of interest on Ali's devices or among the things they'd taken from my house.

"I'm advising you the same as I would any client," Nasser said. "I'm not the enemy."

I flushed, feeling bad considering all Nasser had done for me and how much time he'd taken away from paying clients to help me. "I'm sorry for snapping at you."

"You don't have to apologize."

"There's something I need to tell you that just happened—"

The elevator pinged. "It'll have to wait," he said as the doors opened to a massive open-plan workspace with high ceilings and lots of curved desks and edges. About half the desks had people sitting at them.

Detective Fox met us at the elevator. She wore a dark pantsuit with a cream button-down blouse underneath. Detective Lloyd wasn't with her, and she didn't explain his absence. The detective escorted us to what looked like a standard conference room with gray chairs surrounding a glossy wood table.

"Thank you for coming," Detective Fox said. She laid out a series of pictures. "These images were taken at Waterman's Grill in DC. That's the establishment where Channel Three threw the party for advertisers that your husband attended on the night he died."

The photos were black-and-white surveillance images. Ali was in most of them, the last photos ever taken of him. Shots of him from the back, the side, full on. Sorrow blossomed behind my ribs as I drank in the sight of my husband. It was like unexpectedly seeing Ali again when I'd anticipated never having anything fresh or new of him. For an instant, he came alive and belonged to the present, rather than the past.

The images were grainy, but I could make out his smile. It was his polite smile, not a genuine expression, which was rare for my husband. In other shots, he listened intently to others but looked preoccupied.

What were you thinking, Ali? What was going through your mind?

"It's hard to fathom that just an hour or so after these were taken," I said, my throat aching, "Ali would be dead."

"You OK?" Nasser asked. I met his gaze and registered the emotion in his eyes. Nasser had loved Ali too. I nodded.

"We've analyzed the security footage and identified almost everyone who was around your husband that evening," Detective Fox said in a crisp voice. "The cameras don't cover every part of the restaurant, so it's possible that Mr. Abadi interacted with other people that evening that the cameras didn't capture."

I continued to stare at the last images of my husband. "Can I have copies of these?" I asked. "I'd like to show them to my children." But would they want to see the photos now that they knew about the secret house? I'd called them every day since they'd found out about Lizzie Martins. Ayla barely picked up. Adam was always in a hurry to get off the phone.

"I'm sure that can be arranged." She pointed to one photo with a red-tipped nail. "As I said, we've been able to identify almost everyone." She tapped the face of a man next to Ali. "Do you know this man?"

He was a stranger to me. "No, I've never seen him." My gaze slid over the photo until it landed on a familiar face. I scrutinized the image more closely, the baldness on top and band of dark hair curving around the sides. Chills scattered through me.

"I do know this man. But what was Bill Warren doing at a Channel Three event? He worked with Ali at the accounting firm. He had nothing to do with the TV station."

"Who is Bill Warren?" Nasser asked.

I explained about Bill Warren and Fake Jake.

Nasser shifted in his seat. "Why didn't you tell me this before?"

"I tried to on the elevator."

"What exactly happened?" Detective Fox interjected.

"Bill Warren came to my house on two separate occasions. You can ask my sister." I looked to Nasser. "Lulu was there the first time this guy came over. She saw him. He picked up Ali's computer and dropped off things from his desk."

"He said he was a friend from college?" Nasser seemed to search his memory. "I've never heard of the guy and I was Ali's roommate all four years at school. I think I would have met him."

Detective Fox scribbled some notes on a notepad. "Mrs. Abadi, did Bill Warren ask you for anything else or bring you anything else?"

I thought back. "He did ask if there were any of Ali's work papers at the house. I looked but I didn't find any."

She stood up. "If you'll excuse me for just a minute. I need to check something."

After she left, I looked at Nasser. "Why would Ali's coworker lie about who he is?"

"I can't think of an aboveboard reason. Can you?"

"No." I picked up the photo. As I stared at the grainy image of the only man I'd ever loved romantically, countless interactions with Ali flashed through my mind. The mundane. The loving. His smile. The way his mouth tightened when he was mad. How cherished he made me feel. How I could always depend on him. The depth of my love for him.

You know that I would never do anything to hurt you, right? His words from our second honeymoon came back to me. *I never loved anyone more than I love you. Nothing means more to me than you and our family.*

The common thread of reflections from the people who knew him best—Nasser, his college friends, and even his colleagues—flooded my thoughts.

Ali wasn't the cheating type.
Ali loved Amira.
He wouldn't cheat on her.
Seemed so into you.
Always so pleasant and thoughtful.
All Ali ever talked about was you and the kids.
Everyone thought he was a devoted family man.
Hard to believe that Ali led any kind of double life.

Something clicked in my brain and it was like I'd known the truth all along. If only I'd trusted my instincts from the beginning. Ali would never cheat on me. I *knew* it in my bones. I sagged into the chair, relief flooding me. I felt light, almost giddy. But I still needed to prove what I knew in my gut, and to fully restore and protect Ali's reputation, especially for his children.

Nasser's voice broke into my thoughts. "Cuz looks good," he said, peering over my shoulder.

I soaked in my husband's face. The smile I missed so much. The man I knew had been true to me. "He looks preoccupied." My throat clogged. "I hope his last hours were good ones."

"He loved you," Nasser said softly. "You made him happy."

The image swam before my eyes. "I did, didn't I? But there are so many unanswered questions. Like Cozy Glenn and Lizzie. And why was there Xanax in his system?"

He blew out a breath. "I wish I knew."

"What about this Fake Jake business? Do you think it's connected to the break-in?"

"It's possible. The police will find out."

Detective Fox returned a short time later. "We've arranged to obtain Mr. Abadi's laptop. We're going to examine the device to see what Bill Warren might be searching for."

My gaze darted between them. "You think he wanted to go through Ali's computer before mailing it back?"

"We'll look into it," Detective Fox said. "Now, in regards to your husband's work things, Bill Warren apparently told the firm that you asked him to bring the contents of Mr. Abadi's desk to your house."

"I did no such thing. I've never heard the man's name before today. He called me, as Fake Jake, and said he was going to deliver a box packed up from my husband's desk." A shiver ran down my spine. It had never occurred to me to question Fake Jake's identity. "I thought he was the real Jake. And the real Jake was someone I sort of felt like I knew because Ali talked about him a lot."

Nasser leaned forward. "When will you speak with Mr. Warren about this new information?"

"He is out of the country at the moment. We'll interview him as soon as he's back in the US."

"Do you believe my client is at any risk from him?"

"I have no reason to believe Mrs. Abadi is in danger. Mr. Warren's interest seems to lie in Mr. Abadi's computer and whatever information he believes is on the device," Detective Fox said. "If he wanted to harm Mrs. Abadi, he's had ample time and opportunity to do so before now."

"That's good to hear," I said, some of my anxiety easing.

Nasser came to his feet. "If that's all—"

"Actually," Detective Fox said. "I have some more questions for Mrs. Abadi."

Nasser settled back in his seat.

"Yes?" I said.

"In interviewing some of Mr. Abadi's friends and acquaintances, it has come to our attention that you threatened to kill your husband if he ever cheated on you."

An incredulous laugh erupted from my throat. "That's ridiculous."

She watched me carefully. "Do you deny threatening to kill your husband?"

"Of course I deny it! I never threatened Ali."

"This would have been a few years ago when you were leaving a friend's wedding."

"We're Arabs. We go to a lot of weddings," I retorted. "You'll have to be more specific."

"This was a wedding at the Parkview Hotel. You were waiting for the valet to bring your car around, and a wedding guest overheard you threatening your husband with death if he was unfaithful to you."

I tried to remember back and realized she was talking about the time we went to Rula's sister's wedding. When Ali said that he thought her husband, Marwan, slept around.

It would be hard to let another woman sink her claws into you, I remembered telling him. *It might be easier to shoot you.*

He'd laughed. *So you'd murder me. Got it.*

A chill went through me. Were the police seriously asking me if I'd wanted to kill my husband? "We were joking around," I told the detective. "I said I'd shoot Ali if he cheated, and he threatened to kill any man I cheated with. Neither of us was serious. It was just . . . couple bantering."

Her steady gaze remained fixed on my face. "And you're sure that's all it was?"

My cheeks were hot. "I'm positive."

Nasser stood again. "Mrs. Abadi has answered your questions. I think we're done here."

I jumped to my feet, eager to follow Nasser out.

"Am I being paranoid," I asked him once we were alone in the elevator, "or are the cops really out to get me?"

"Like I said, the spouse is often the perpetrator in situations like this," he said. "Law enforcement is predisposed to thinking you're the guilty party."

My stomach turned over. "That's just great."

"That's why I don't want you talking to the police when I'm not there."

I nodded. "You won't have to tell me again."

Anger flared in my gut. I was fed up, tired of being unjustly accused, of having my home broken into and being harassed by people like Fake Jake. I was determined to learn the truth, to prove that Ali wasn't a cheating jerk. And nothing and no one was going to stop me.

Chapter Thirty-Two

"Sorry to show up unannounced," Julia said when I answered the door later that afternoon. "But Mama made *kenafa* and asked me to bring it over."

"Never apologize for bringing me my favorite Arabic dessert." I embraced Ali's sister.

"Where's the new dog?" she asked warily.

"She's at the groomer's. I have to go get her in an hour."

"Plenty of time to enjoy your *kenafa*."

I blew out a long breath. "After the day I've had, I could use some *kenafa* therapy."

"Why?" Julia slipped off her shoes. "What's happening?"

I took the foil-covered plate and led her into the kitchen. "The cops want to know if I killed Ali."

"Shut up. Are you serious?"

"I wish I wasn't. As if I don't have enough worries."

"Are you really concerned that they think you did something?"

"Nasser says I shouldn't stress out because they have no evidence against me. But I can't help being nervous."

"That's understandable."

I took out a couple of dessert plates. "Since misery loves company, you have to have some *kenafa* with me."

"You twisted my arm." She adjusted her navy headscarf, which matched her maxi-length floral-print dress. "Tell me what's going on."

I set a bright-orange square of the cheesy treat, made with homemade dough, on each plate and microwaved them for about thirty seconds.

"Maybe they should focus less on you and more on how Ali was drugged," she said after I caught her up on the investigation. "What else did they ask you?"

"Nothing. Nasser shut them down once they asked if I wanted to kill Ali. He got me out of there pretty fast after that."

We sat at the counter and took turns soaking our desserts with simple syrup. It had been too long since I'd had a chance to spend time with my sister-in-law. Especially now that I trusted in Ali and no longer suspected that his family was hiding a dark secret about him.

"Anything new on the drugging situation?" she asked between bites.

I shook my head. "No, but there have been some weird new developments." I filled her in on Fake Jake.

Her eyes widened. "That's so creepy."

"It's a good thing I have a security system and Binti," I said around a generous bite of *kenafa*.

"Are you sure you want to stay in the house? I'd be afraid to live alone."

"This is my home." I sipped some cold water and tried to sound bolder than I felt. "I've already lost enough."

There was a brief silence while our forks scraped across our plates.

"I don't want to be a pest," Julia said, "but have you given any thought to the headstone yet?"

I set my fork down. "Not yet, but I will."

"When?" she pressed. "It's been months since Ali passed. *Allah yerhamo.*"

"Soon." I'd been so mad at Ali that I hadn't trusted myself to give him a proper headstone and inscription. Now I needed his epitaph to be a perfect reflection of the man I'd lost. But I couldn't focus on that until I cleared Ali's name and found out who was harassing me. "I promise."

"Baba and Mama say they're happy to do it. They'll even pay for the installation."

I shook my head. "I feel like it's my final duty to Ali, as his wife, to get his headstone installed. But I promise that I won't finalize anything until we all agree on a design."

"I know you're going through a lot," Julia said.

"I am." I sipped from the glass of cold water. "We all are. I'll get it done soon."

Our conversation moved on to other topics. Relatives, community gossip, and how our kids were doing. After about an hour, Julia reluctantly got up to leave. I followed her into the foyer, sorry to see her go.

"Please thank your mom for the *kenafa*," I said. "I'll call Um Ali too. I appreciate your bringing it over."

"No problem." After a beat, she asked, "What do you think of Nasser?"

"That's a weird question."

"You seem to be spending a lot of time with him."

"Only when it pertains to legal matters."

She slipped her shoes on. "You do know that he had a crush on you before you were married."

I stared at her. "Did everyone know about that except me?"

"Not *everyone*. But we knew, my family. Ali told us even before we met you, after he and Nasser saw you at that wedding."

I handed her coat over. "Seems like someone should have mentioned that to me a long time ago."

"How did you find out that Nasser was into you?" She watched me closely as she pulled on her coat. "Did he tell you?"

"Not that it matters." My cheeks burned. "I doubt I'll ever be able to look at another man in a romantic way."

"I'm not suggesting that you are doing anything wrong." She zipped up her coat. "I know you loved Ali."

"Then what *are* you asking me?"

"Actually, Mama and Baba wanted me to tell you that they'd be OK with it."

"OK with what? Are you telling me that your parents think something is going on between me and Nasser?" The thought horrified me.

"No, but if, in the future, you decide to remarry, they think you should marry Nasser."

"Whoa! Where did *that* come from?"

"You're still young." Julia adjusted her hijab. "If you marry Nasser, Mama and Baba say that would keep you and the kids close to us."

"I don't need to marry Nasser in order to maintain strong bonds with you. I hope you and your parents know that."

I shouldn't have been surprised by my in-laws' matchmaking scheme. It wasn't uncommon for a widowed Arab man to marry his late wife's sister, the idea being that she'd love her deceased sister's children more fully than a stranger would and integrate more naturally into the extended family.

"Mama says you're still young enough to give Nasser a son and that every man should have a son."

"Gross." I pulled the door open. "I'm still mourning my husband."

"Ali loved you a lot. I hope you believe that."

"I do. This whole secret house thing really threw me. It made me question everything about my marriage." I tried to put my shifting feelings into words. "But the more I think about it, about the kind of person Ali was, the less I believe he lived some sort of secret life. That's just not who he was."

"Exactly." Julia looked relieved. "That's why none of this makes sense."

"Especially the part about him leaving a secret house to his ex-girlfriend."

"What does Nasser say? Is he encouraging you to think the worst about Ali?"

"He doesn't know what to think."

Her lip curled. "I'll bet."

I registered the distaste on her face. "You really don't like Nasser."

"I always felt like he was competitive with my brother, maybe even a little jealous of him, but Ali was too *hanoon* to see it. I don't trust Nasser." She kissed me on both cheeks as she said goodbye. "I think you should be careful."

"Nothing yet," Detective Fox said when I called her a couple of days later for an update on Fake Jake. "But we plan to talk with Bill Warren as soon as he gets back tomorrow."

"What about whoever broke into my house and went through Ali's office? Or the garage situation? Could it be Bill Warren?"

"Anything is possible and we are investigating. There is another matter I'd like to discuss with you."

The muscles across the backs of my shoulders tightened. "Do I need to get my lawyer on the phone for this?" Being accused of wanting to kill my husband did not foster trust.

"No, that's not necessary," she said. "I want to update you on the investigation."

"There's an update?"

"Yes, we have reason to believe that your husband did not go straight home after leaving the Channel Three event at Waterman's Grill."

My thoughts scattered. "Where did he go?"

"We're still trying to retrace his movements. He left Waterman's at eleven p.m., and the accident was at eleven forty-eight p.m. The accident site is just fifteen minutes from Waterman's. That leaves about forty minutes unaccounted for."

"But where would Ali go that late after a long and busy day?" I spoke more to myself than to her.

"That is what we'd like to know." She paused. "Your husband didn't happen to mention going somewhere else that night, did he?"

I thought back to the last time I saw Ali alive. He ran late that final morning. I could picture him going out the door, still looking sharp despite the coffee stain developing on his lapel. He hadn't closed his travel mug tightly enough. *I'll change at the office.* He always kept an extra suit at work for emergencies. *Don't forget I've got that Channel Three thing tonight. It might run late. Don't wait up.*

I hadn't waited up, and he never came home. It still gnawed at me that I was fast asleep the moment Ali left this earth. How could I have slept through such a life-shattering event? It felt like a failure on my part.

"No, Ali didn't say he was going anywhere else. He just mentioned the work event. Nothing else."

"OK. Sit tight," she said. "Detective Lloyd and I are retracing Mr. Abadi's steps from that night. We're hoping security cameras along the nearby streets will offer some clues."

"What about his phone? Can't you track his movements on that?"

"Your husband had location services turned off. We can still find the information, but it'll take longer."

"You'll let me know if you learn anything?" I asked.

"Absolutely."

Thanking her, I hung up and stared out the window, watching the postal truck come to a stop in front of my house. After the letter carrier drove away, I went out to get the mail, barely noticing the chill, my mind focused on Ali's last hours. Where would he have gone at eleven o'clock on a work night?

"Amira? Um . . . Mrs. Abadi?"

Someone came up behind me. I didn't immediately place the voice. I turned from the mailbox and found myself staring at Fake Jake.

"Oh my God." My heart spasmed. The cops said Bill Warren wasn't supposed to be back until tomorrow. I glanced toward the house to see if I could make a run for safety, but my front door seemed a million miles away. As did Binti and the pepper spray Nasser gave me. All my vigilance since the break-ins, getting a dog and my insistence on always having the pepper spray with me, meant nothing now that this man had caught me alone and unprepared.

I backed away. "What do you want?"

"I don't want to scare you." He held out his arms in front of him, palms down, trying to placate me.

"Then get the hell away from me." I glanced down the empty street. It was midafternoon. The neighborhood was quiet, but someone was bound to come walking by with their dog or on their afternoon run.

"I'll call the police," I warned him. An empty threat because my phone was in the house, along with my pepper spray.

"I've already called the cops," Bill Warren said. "I have an appointment to talk with some detectives later this afternoon. But I owe it to you to tell you the truth first. You've been through enough."

"Why did you lie about being Jake Barnes?" I backed up in the direction of the house as I spoke.

"I figured you'd give Ali's computer to Jake Barnes, no questions asked. But you might hesitate to hand it over to someone you've never heard of."

He wasn't wrong. "Why did you want my husband's computer?"

The man looked down before meeting my gaze. "Because I've done things I'm not proud of."

"Oh my God." I felt the blood rush from my head. "You drugged Ali."

"What? Ali was drugged?" Shock stamped his face. "I had nothing to do with that. I would never."

"What was on Ali's computer that was so important that you were willing to lie to his grieving widow to get it?"

He took a long breath. "Ali and I worked together on an engagement. He was the manager on the project. As the senior, I reported to him."

"And?" I kept inching backward toward the house.

"I made a serious mistake on a final report for the client. One that could cost me my job."

Up the street, Claudia appeared with her dog on a leash coming back from a walk. I waved to make sure she saw me. Just in case I needed help. She waved back, her curious gaze falling on Fake Jake.

"What does your mistake have to do with Ali's computer?" I asked him.

"I wanted to delete our chat history and any emails that implicated me in the mistake. I swear I only wanted to read Ali's business emails to see if he'd told any of the higher-ups at the firm about my error."

Barking erupted from inside the house; Binti was at a downstairs window watching us.

"And?" I pressed. "Had he?"

"No. That's why I went by Waterman's, to ask him, to beg him, to give me more time. He said he needed to tell the partners, that he couldn't wait any longer. But then the accident happened."

"What a lucky coincidence." I felt sick to my stomach. "How convenient that my husband did you the favor of dying right before he could tell the firm about your screwup."

He looked stricken. "I'm very sorry about your husband's death. I liked Ali. Everyone did. He was a good guy."

"But that didn't stop you from trying to turn his death to your advantage."

"I admit that I did see a chance to save my job." Beads of perspiration glistened on Bill Warren's upper lip, despite the brisk day. "In a way that wouldn't hurt Ali or his family."

"What was the plan?" I asked. "To erase any evidence of your mistake, and then what? Blame it on Ali?"

He had the decency to look ashamed. "Ali was dead. It wouldn't hurt him."

"Your lie would have damaged his reputation even more," I snapped, losing any fear. "People already believe that Ali bought a house for his secret girlfriend. But you didn't care about anything but yourself."

"I'm sorry." He pulled a handkerchief from his jacket and mopped his face with it. "I was desperate."

"Is that why you delivered the things that were in his desk?"

"Yes, I wanted to look through them to make sure there was nothing in there that implicated me."

"And the notebooks? Why did you even bother to give those to me?"

"I honestly thought you might want them."

"After you looked through them, I assume. Did you do it?" I asked harshly. "Did you pin the blame on Ali for your mistake?"

"I'll make it right." He pocketed his handkerchief. "I promise. I will tell the partners the truth."

"Who were you to my husband?" I wanted to know. "Why did Ali push so hard to get you a job at the firm?"

His eyes slid away. "We were old friends from school."

"Really? But not close enough for him to ever mention you to me." I'd made it to my front door, but this agitated, perspiring man no longer felt like a threat. "And his college roommate has never heard of you. That's a little strange, don't you think?"

He shrugged. "I don't know what to tell you."

"Just how close were you and my husband before he got you the job?" I pressed. "Did you meet up occasionally?"

"No, we just stayed in touch via occasional texts." He glanced at his phone. "I really have to go. I'm meeting with the police in less than an hour."

He was lying. It was obvious. This man had no intention of telling me the whole truth. Maybe Fox and Lloyd could get more out of Bill Warren. "Well, don't let me keep you from the police."

"I don't expect you to forgive me—" he began.

"Good." I pushed open the front door and slammed it hard behind me. So forcefully that you'd think Fake Jake was responsible for murdering my husband and stealing my life.

Chapter Thirty-Three

Before

"Why are you weeding alone?" I asked Ali, offering him a tall glass of iced tea.

"Someone's got to do it." His face glistening, he drank down half the iced tea in one go. "I've got an issuance that has to be filed by next Monday, so I might have to work next weekend."

He set the glass down and went back to pulling weeds. I sat on the doorstep and sipped my drink. "I thought Adam was helping you."

Ali tugged on a weed. "I told him I'd finish it up."

"Why? You're the dad. He should be the one to finish up."

"He's having a hard time."

"I did notice that he seems kind of flat lately." Adam was in his junior year and spent his weeks in a bustle of school activities. He was part of the student government at his high school and was always on the go. But he'd been listless for the past couple of days. "What's going on? Do you know?"

"I think it's girl trouble."

"Uh-oh. What happened?"

"I think that girl Gina that he liked broke up with him."

"Broke up with him? Were they officially an item?"

Ali dumped his collection of pulled weeds into a paper lawn bag. "I guess."

"Did you ask him what happened?" Ali was maddening in that he never asked for, nor gave, any details.

"Nah. What difference does it make? It's not like they were getting married or anything. It's kid stuff."

I sat in silence for a moment and then asked, "Do you think the kids are going to do what we did and marry Muslims?"

He tied up the bag. "Who knows?"

"What do you think?" I called after him as he carried the bag to the curb for Monday's pickup. "Is it important to you that they do?"

"It's up to them." He returned, pulling his work gloves off. "It's not my life."

"We're their parents. We're supposed to give them guidance."

He reached for his tea. "What would you tell them?"

"I honestly think they'd be happier marrying someone who is more like them," I said. "Marriage is hard enough without throwing religious and cultural differences into the mix."

"We can't mandate who they marry." He emptied his glass. "I'm not going to be like our parents and threaten to disown them if they don't do what we want. They need to do what *they* want."

It felt like we were skirting the edges of talking about his decision to give Lizzie Martins up in order to marry me. It's not like I constantly thought about Ali's ex, but from time to time I did wonder. I didn't press the matter. Nothing constructive could come of dredging that up again. It wasn't like he'd admit to having regrets.

So I adopted a teasing tone. "What are you saying? That you were forced to marry me?"

"Yes. Thank God." He pushed in to kiss me, sweaty and all.

"Gross." I leaned back out of his reach. "Can you do that after you've showered? This is not my idea of hot and sweaty sex."

He pulled away with a chuckle.

"It's not like you'd actually admit to being sorry you married me," I noted.

"I wouldn't want anyone else to call me Cheapo Depot."

"To be fair, the kids came up with that." But I did think it was funny.

"Anyway," he added, "our kids are never going to be Arab enough or Muslim enough for some people."

I didn't need to ask what he meant. Although we'd sent Ayla and Adam to weekly religious classes to learn the basics of Islam when they were younger, we were more culturally Muslim than devoted followers of our faith. And the kids barely spoke Arabic, which would leave them feeling like outsiders in a family full of fluent speakers. They could look like fools sitting in a room with everyone talking in a language they didn't understand, possibly even speaking negatively about them while they nodded and smiled and had no idea what was being said.

"I don't want them to ever feel that way in a marriage." I handed him my half-full glass for him to finish. "Marrying the traditional way worked for us. I'd at least want them to try it."

"I'm sure my mom and sisters are standing by to be matchmakers." He poured my tea down his throat. "OK. I'm going to mow the lawn now."

The subject came up a few weeks later at a barbecue celebrating Ali's nephew Jamal's high school graduation. It was a big group, about sixty people, mingling inside the house and out on the back deck. We found the graduate's mother standing with a group of Ali's cousins, including Shireen and Hamooda.

"*Mabrook,*" I said to the graduate's mother, Ali's sister Siham. "Congratulations."

"Thank you." She greeted me with a kiss on each cheek. "*Inshallah*, God willing, we'll be celebrating Adam's graduation soon."

"That's coming up, isn't it?" Shireen asked.

I nodded. "Just one more year to go."

Ali scanned the groups of people on the deck. "Where's the graduate?"

Siham gestured toward the backyard. "He's out there with his high school friends." Jamal was sitting with a group of boys. And a young blond woman in a crop top.

"Who's the blonde?" Hamooda asked.

"That's Jamal's girlfriend," Siham said.

"Girlfriend?" I echoed. Although most parents among our cousins knew their boys dated on the sly, this was the first time anyone in our generation was totally open about it.

Siham shrugged. "Yeah, they've been together since last summer. Why lie about it?"

"I don't see a problem with it," Ali said later. "It's inevitable that this generation is going to marry out."

"Why inevitable?" I asked.

"Come on, these kids, like our own children, were born to parents who were also born here," he said. "The attachment to the culture and traditions of our ancestral homeland, a place we never lived, are bound to ease."

"I guess that's what assimilation is all about." I wondered what it would be like to marry anyone you wanted, and not just the narrow group of people who shared the culture and religion of your forefathers. "It makes me sad, though, to think this generation will lose so many of the traditions we grew up with."

"It is sad," Ali agreed. "But the idea of being able to do whatever you want also sounds very freeing."

Chapter Thirty-Four

Now

My heart turned over in my chest every time I walked by Ali's closet.

Like his home office, it was one of the places in the house so intrinsically tied to Ali that I could still feel his presence among the jumble of clothes and shoes. Even mundane things like underwear and socks took on a poignant edge. On the closet floor, a lifetime of select papers, pictures, and memories filled an old leather briefcase that I'd never seen Ali actually use. The presence of these objects drove home again and again how strange it was to have all of Ali's worldly goods here while he was in another dimension.

Going through his closet made me feel like an interloper. This was Ali's personal space. I'd always stayed out of it. After his death, the closet became a constant reminder of a loss that remained so incomprehensible that I still couldn't quite believe it.

I couldn't bear to get rid of his belongings. Now that my faith in my husband was restored, it was much too early to contemplate giving away yet another piece of him. But I did need his possessions out of my room, safely tucked away for me to revisit when I wanted to, rather than being assaulted by my loss every time I walked past his closet.

Besides, Adam and Ayla might want some of Ali's things to remember him by once they both fully believed in him again. I'd taken to wearing an old navy sweatshirt Ali used to wear around the house. I went out to pick up some plastic bins at the store and got to work as soon as I returned home. I'd put my husband's belongings away until the kids and I were ready to sort through them together. Packing away Ali's things made me more determined than ever to exonerate my husband, especially in the eyes of our children.

I worked methodically, going through the pockets, pulling out old receipts and parking stubs. There wasn't a lot to clean out. Ali was good at emptying his pockets at the end of the day. When I came to Ali's suits, I lingered on the one that was still covered in plastic, the coffee-stained jacket Ali wore to work on his last day.

I drew off the plastic and inhaled the suit's scent, which was a musty closet smell with no lingering traces of Ali. I sighed and emptied the pockets. One contained a wadded-up sticker name tag. I smoothed it out to make sure I wasn't throwing away anything important.

Ali's name was written on the tag in red marker. It was from a place called the Meadows, which I'd never heard of. But what caught my attention was the date. Adrenaline streaked through my veins.

July 23.

The day Ali died.

What was this place? Why would Ali be there on a workday? Maybe there had been some sort of professional meeting at the Meadows. I immediately texted Jake, the real one, to see if there'd been a work event that day at a place called the Meadows. He replied almost immediately.

Jake: Hi Amira. Good to hear from you. I've never heard of the place.

Me: Could one of your clients be associated with the Meadows?

Jake: I'd have to check.

Me: Do you know if Ali left the office during work on the day that he died?

Jake: Let me check on both points. Give me a few minutes.

I folded more clothes while waiting to hear back from Jake. On that last day, Ali had reminded me of his evening work event but hadn't mentioned going anywhere else. The phone pinged, and I practically lunged for it.

Jake: I couldn't find any firm associations with any place called the Meadows. But it does look like Ali left the office for a couple of hours on July 23

Me: Did he say where he was going?

Jake: The receptionist remembers Ali talking about having an appointment

Me: OK. Thanks for checking

Jake: No problem. Also, I asked around and no one at the office knows what the Meadows is

I immediately pulled out my laptop to search the Meadows. A Meadows Ice Cream Shop popped up, along with a Meadows Condominiums. The only thing that popped up with the "The" before it was an eldercare facility in Arlington. I found the facility's website and clicked around inside, trying to find a reason Ali would have visited the place during a workday.

The facility had an online newsletter. I clicked through the pages; some welcomed smiley new arrivals, while others featured shots of seniors in exercise class. Some residents were gray haired and weathered; others sported coiffed dyed hair and stylish outfits.

I was about to give up when a name in the birthdays section caught my attention. The posted group photo was of residents who had upcoming birthdays. I zeroed in on one name. *Martha Martins.*

Could it be? I went back to the old online obituary for Lizzie's father. And there it was. *Survived by his wife Martha Martins.* Ali went to see Lizzie's mother on the day he died?

Why?

There was only one way to find out.

"You'd like to see Mrs. Martins?" The receptionist greeted me with a welcoming smile. "She'll be thrilled. Miss Martha loves to have visitors."

I'd picked up flowers at the grocery store on the way over to the Meadows, which turned out to be a bright, airy place with pale lemon walls trimmed in white.

"Is she expecting you?" the receptionist asked.

"Not exactly." I embellished a little. "She knew my late husband quite well. He visited her here."

She reached for the phone and pounded a few buttons.

"Yes, Miss Martha? This is Bernice at reception. There's a nice young lady here to visit with you. She says you knew her husband." I could hear the muffled voice on the other line.

"I'll check," Bernice said into the receiver before catching my eye. "What is your husband's name?"

"His name was Ali. Ali Abadi."

"Ali Abadi," Bernice repeated into the phone. More from the muffled voice. She smiled and hung up. "Go on through. Room 204. She's excited to see you."

My heart pounded behind my ribs. "Thank you."

When I reached room 204, I found the door open and Mrs. Martins waiting for me on the threshold. She looked older and far frailer than I'd expected. Her curly hair was completely gray, her skin lined and colorless.

"My dear." To my surprise, she enveloped me in a warm hug. "How nice of you to come."

"Thank you for seeing me." I handed her the bouquet. "These are for you."

Her lined eyes crinkled. "They're beautiful. Come in, please."

I followed her into the room, a generous space with a bedroom area with a cheerful sitting area. She set the flowers on a side table and settled on an old leather lounger, gesturing for me to take the sofa. "Aren't you as pretty as a picture? Ali is a lucky man."

I smiled, noting how she referred to Ali in the present tense. "I was lucky to be his wife."

"Oh yes, such a decent and devoted young man. He didn't deserve what happened to him."

"It's a terrible loss," I agreed, wrestling with my emotions, determined to keep my composure.

"If you know Ali, you must also know my daughter, Elizabeth?"

"I have met Lizzie, yes."

"And my son, have you met him too?"

"I'm afraid I haven't had the pleasure."

A puzzled expression crossed her face. "That's very surprising."

"It is?" I asked. "Why?"

"Because of how Ali—"

She was interrupted by a knock on the door, followed by the appearance of a nurse wearing colorful floral scrubs. "Miss Martha, it's time for your medication."

The older woman frowned. "But I just took them."

"No, dear, you haven't had your meds yet today."

Martha regarded the woman with suspicion. "Are you sure?"

"I'm positive," she said, her voice upbeat. "Would I lie to you?"

Mrs. Martins looked dismayed. "I keep forgetting so much lately."

"We all have days like that," the nurse said in a soothing tone. "Here you go."

I looked around the room to give Mrs. Martins some privacy while she took her medications. A grouping of family photos on the side table caught my eye. Lizzie looked the same as now, just older. But I didn't immediately recognize Mrs. Martins. She looked much younger in the picture, smiling and vibrant, worlds apart from the frail older woman sitting across from me. My gaze caught on the third person in the photo. My pulse spiked as I stared at the familiar face.

"There you go, Miss Martha," the nurse said to Mrs. Martins as she finished giving her medication. "You call if you need anything."

After the nurse left, I struggled to stay calm. I didn't want to do anything to alarm Mrs. Martins. "Are these your children?" I asked, keeping my voice as steady as possible.

"Yes, that's Elizabeth, who, of course, you know. And that's my son, William."

My heart kicked. "Bill Warren is your son?"

Her rheumy eyes lit up. "So you *do* know my Billy?" She shot me a puzzled look. "I thought you said you didn't know him."

"I guess I forgot that he was Lizzie's brother," I blustered. "I think the association slipped my mind because they don't have the same last name. Why is that?"

"Didn't you know?" she said. "Billy is the product of my first marriage. Lizzie is the child from my second marriage to Lawrence."

Shock rippled through me. Lizzie and Bill Warren were half siblings. What did that mean? Why hadn't Bill Warren mentioned the connection?

"If you'd come this morning, you could have seen Lizzie," Mrs. Martins said.

"Lizzie visited you today?" I asked. "She's in town?"

She nodded. "Oh yes. When she's in Virginia, she books a room at the extended-stay hotel down the street."

"And does she visit you often?"

"Yes. No." She scrunched up her face. "I think so. Maybe. Sometimes it's hard to remember."

My stomach dipped. I desperately needed Mrs. Martins to remember her meeting with Ali. "My husband came to see you on the day he died. I was wondering why. Did he visit often?"

"Ali?" She shook her head. "No, he never came. That was the first time. I asked him to come because—" She abruptly halted mid-sentence. "What do you mean? On the day he died? What's happened to Ali?"

It was my turn to be confused. "I assumed your daughter would have told you." Lizzie came to visit often and never told her mother about Ali's death? "He died in a car accident a few months ago."

Shock rippled across her face. "On the same day he came to see me?"

"I'm afraid so."

"No, no, no," she moaned, shaking her head, breaking into heaving sobs.

Alarmed, I came to my feet and crossed over to put a light hand on her shoulder. "Mrs. Martins, please don't be so upset. Is there anything I can get you?"

Instead of being comforted, the old woman sobbed even louder.

The door opened, and two staff members rushed in. The young man and the nurse who'd administered Mrs. Martins's meds hurried to the woman's side. "Mrs. Martins, calm down. Everything is going to be OK."

I backed away to give them room.

"Is my husband coming to see me?" she asked, tears streaming down her face. "I want Lawrence right now." She huddled over, rocking herself back and forth.

The nurse looked at me. "What did you say to her?"

I felt her recrimination. "I told her that my husband died. They're . . . I guess you could say . . . old family friends."

Her face hardened. "In her condition, the last thing Mrs. Martins needs is to be upset by visitors."

I briefly wondered what the state of Mrs. Martins's health was. "I didn't realize that she hadn't been told."

The man straightened to face me, speaking loudly over the old woman's moaning. "I think you should leave now. Mrs. Martins needs to rest."

His voice was kind but firm, leaving me no choice but to gather up my things. I scurried out of Mrs. Martins's room, guilt rippling through me, even though I'd done nothing wrong. My mind zigzagged in all directions. Bill and Lizzie were siblings. And their mother said she was sorry about Ali.

He didn't deserve what happened to him.

I'd assumed that she was referring to the accident, but if the crash was news to her, what had she meant?

I climbed into my van. A shot of orange flickered in my peripheral vision. When I turned toward it, an orange sports car pulled out of the parking lot and sped away. I shivered. That car showing up in random places no longer seemed like a coincidence. Could somebody actually be following me?

Maybe I was being ridiculous. Maybe orange sports cars were the latest rage. Still, I dialed Detective Fox.

"You don't know for sure that you're being followed, is that right?" she said after I told her about the vehicle.

"What are the chances that we both just happened to be in the same place that often?"

"It's hard to look up without a license plate," she told me. "Try to get the license plate number if the car shows up again. And I'll see what I can do."

Chapter Thirty-Five

"What are you doing here?" Lizzie asked as I marched into her hotel suite.

"We need to talk, and I'm not leaving until I get some answers. Real answers this time."

She closed the door and regarded me warily. "How did you find me?"

It wasn't hard. The extended-stay hotel was less than a mile from the facility Mrs. Martins lived in. For the first time in my life, I'd actually bribed someone, giving a hotel maid fifty dollars to tell me which room Lizzie was in.

I surveyed her space, which was more like a one-bedroom apartment. Beyond the small kitchen near the entrance was a sitting room with a door that led to a sleeping area containing a king-size bed. "Nice place."

She crossed her arms, rounding her shoulders so that she caved into herself. "How did you know which room I'm in?"

"That's not how this is going to go," I told her. "I'm going to ask the questions."

"Please." Her eyes watered. "There's honestly nothing to say. Please just go and leave me alone."

"I'm not going anywhere until you tell me why Ali bought you a house."

"I'm going to call the police if you don't leave," she said, her voice shaky. "Please don't make me."

"I just came from seeing your mother. I learned some very interesting things."

"You saw my mother?" Her face paled. "Where? When?"

"At the Meadows. It seems like a nice place."

"You had no right to bother my mother."

"She was very happy to see me." At least at first. "She even hugged me. Your mother says you visit often but that you didn't mention Ali's death. That's strange. Why is that?"

Something flashed across Lizzie's face before vanishing. Was it fear? "I didn't want to upset her."

"Why would she be upset about an old college boyfriend who broke up with you more than twenty years ago? And why would Ali visit your mother on the day he died?"

"I have no idea." Lizzie exhaled. "My mother knew Ali was helping me."

"Helping you how?"

She paused. "I'll tell you everything as long as you promise not to bother my mother again."

I didn't trust that she would, but still I agreed. "Go on, then."

"Ali didn't pay for the Cozy Glenn house. I sent him the money, and he made the payments so that ownership of the house couldn't be traced back to me."

"Traced by whom? You make it sound like you're laundering money or something. What were you hiding?"

She exhaled, dragging two hands down her face. "You might as well take a seat."

I was too agitated to sit. "Thank you, but I'll stand."

"I've been stalked by a man who terrorized me for years." Lizzie slid into a chair, looking like she'd lost all strength in her legs. "It began almost as soon as I separated from my husband. The harassment started with dead flowers left on my doorstep. And once someone chalked the word 'bitch' on my apartment door. When this person started threatening my children, leaving notes that said I didn't deserve to be a mother, I moved far away and stopped seeing them, my own flesh and blood"—her voice shook—"to remove them from any potential danger."

"Someone is stalking you?" Suddenly, Lizzie's jumpiness, her constant state of fear or being on edge, made sense. "How did Ali figure into this?"

"I begged him to help me. He was an accountant, so I figured he'd know how to set up a payment system to hide my ownership. I didn't want the stalker to find me."

I sat in the chair opposite her. "And he eventually agreed to make the payments for you."

She nodded. "You'll see that I regularly transferred money into one of Ali's bank accounts to cover the house payments."

"Why didn't Ali tell me about this?"

"He wanted to. But I begged him not to. I was petrified of anyone finding out about Cozy Glenn. It was the only truly safe space that I had." She shivered. "The stalker always seems to know what I'm doing, where I'm going."

I turned this new information over in my mind. "Even if you are telling the truth, Ali still should have told me."

"I am not lying. Check your bank account. You'll see a clear record of my payments for the house."

I stood, eager to check right away. "Don't worry. I will."

She followed me to the door. "And, Amira."

I faced her. "Yes?"

"Please don't tell anyone where my mother is."

"Are you still being stalked?"

"Sort of." Lizzie shook her head. "I recently discovered who it is. He tracked me after all of that publicity about your suing me about the house. After he found me in Durham, I left in the middle of the night and drove here. I checked into this hotel and have been here ever since. But he traced me again. He came here to my hotel just a few days ago. He keeps showing up everywhere I go."

I felt a stab of guilt. "Did you call the police on him?"

"Yes, but he hasn't broken any laws yet."

"I thought you said he made threats against your children? Is that legal?"

"I didn't report the early incidents in Maryland. There's no proof that he's done anything wrong. The cops told him to stay away from me."

"I wish you'd told me the truth from the start," I said. "I wouldn't have had to sue you."

"At least now you know everything."

If only that were true. "What about Caryl Daryus?"

"It's my grandmother's name. I used different names and spellings in different places to make it harder for anyone to track me."

"Another thing," I said. "Why didn't you tell me that Bill Warren is your brother?"

Her mouth fell open. "You know Billy?"

"He works at my husband's firm. You must know that."

"I didn't realize you'd met him. It's not as if you and I have ever had a reason to talk about my brother."

"Are you two close?"

"Not super close. But we are siblings," she said. "We always have each other's backs."

"Meaning that you look out for each other?"

"Yes," she affirmed. "Always. Are you satisfied? Will you go away now?"

The more time I spent with this woman, the more I felt I could trust my instincts, which screamed that Ali hadn't been unfaithful to me with her or anyone else. But I still had questions.

"I can't understand why Ali risked our marriage to help you when he could have sworn me to secrecy."

"What does it matter?" she asked wearily. "He loved you. There was never anything intimate or sexual between us once he met you. Ali would never be unfaithful once he made a commitment."

"I do know that." Satisfaction washed through me to hear her confirm what I already knew in my heart. There'd been no affair. Ali was faithful to me. Our mutually loving marriage was real.

"I was devastated when Ali broke up with me," Lizzie told me. "Is that what you want to hear?"

"I want the truth. That's what I've always wanted."

"The truth is that I wasn't all that surprised when Ali broke up with me. I always knew I loved him more than he ever loved me."

The words reverberated through me. "You're not the one that got away," I said.

"I was never the one," Lizzie said coolly. "I always thought *you* were."

"Do you believe her?" Ayla asked when I FaceTimed the kids from the parking lot of Lizzie's hotel. "Maybe she's just telling you what you want to hear so you'll leave her alone."

"That's possible." I actually felt a little happy for the first time since Ali died. "But I do believe her."

"So do I." Relief etched Adam's face. "I never could imagine Dad cheating."

"Right." Ayla made a face. "Because Dad was such a saint."

Her scornful reaction worried me. It was almost as if she wanted—needed—for the worst to be true. "Why aren't you happy, Ayla?" I asked her. "This is good news. It means your dad was, for the most part, who we always thought he was."

Her lip curled. "You believe this Lizzie person because you want to believe her. You *need* to believe her."

"What's your problem?" Adam snapped at his sister. "It's almost like you're disappointed Dad didn't have a side chick."

"Or maybe I'm the only one here who's being realistic," Ayla shot back. "If Dad was so innocent, why didn't he tell Mom about the secret house?"

She had a point. "I told you that Lizzie begged him not to," I said. "But he should have told me. I'm not saying Dad was perfect. I'm just saying I believe he didn't cheat. His coworkers, his college friends, Uncle Nasser, they also don't believe that Dad would be unfaithful."

"Whatever," Ayla said. "I have to go. I have a class." She disconnected before I even had a chance to say goodbye, leaving me feeling a little deflated. I had FaceTimed the kids expecting them to be as pleased as I was.

"She's psycho," Adam said after Ayla was gone. "She's been so weird since Dad died."

"We have to be patient with her. We all grieve in our own way."

"It looks like Ayla's way of grieving is to believe Dad was an asshole so she can stay mad at him."

"Maybe that's what she needs to do right now in order to be able to cope."

As relieved as I was about Ali, I was now more worried than ever about Ayla. It felt like something else was going on with her. I needed to find out what it was before she spiraled and was beyond help.

"I know why you're here." Bill Warren slipped into the coffee shop booth across from me the following afternoon. "Lizzie texted me after she spoke to you, so I wasn't surprised when you reached out."

"She did say that you siblings always have each other's backs."

"Having Lizzie's back can be a lot of work." His words had an edge. Not exactly the demeanor of a loving brother. "You may have noticed that my sister is on the needy side. As her big brother, I'm used to being called in to save the day."

"Why didn't you tell me that Lizzie was your sister?"

"What was the point of telling you? It had no bearing on anything."

"Most people would naturally mention something like that."

"Being in Lizzie's orbit can be a lot. I don't make a habit of talking about my sister. Besides, I knew you'd ask me about the North Carolina house and I wanted to stay out of it."

"Your sister claims that her romantic relationship with my husband ended before he got married."

"I'm sure that's true. As far as I knew, they barely had anything to do with each other after you married him."

Bill Warren might not be a trustworthy person, but hearing him confirm what Lizzie said still made me feel better. "Is your connection to Lizzie the reason Ali got you the job at his firm?"

"Probably. I never asked him directly, but I'm not an idiot. I assumed that's why he wanted to help me."

Bill Warren made a show of being open and transparent, but I still felt there was something else behind the facade. More he wasn't saying.

"Do you still have a job?" I asked.

"I'm on probation pending an investigation. I don't expect things to go my way." He shrugged. "I would never have gotten the job in the first place if Ali hadn't gone to bat for me."

"Why did he?" Ali had risked our marriage by keeping me in the dark about Lizzie's house, and he'd risked his professional reputation to help Lizzie's incompetent brother. It didn't make sense. Ali never was a risk taker. He took pride in being careful and deliberate. "Why would Ali go out on a limb to get you a job at the firm?"

"Beats me. Now you're asking me things that I can't answer. All I can say is that Ali was a good guy."

But he wasn't an idiot. And yet he'd gone out of his way to help both Lizzie and Bill Warren—at his own expense. It almost seemed like Ali had felt beholden to Lizzie and, by extension, her brother.

But why?

Chapter Thirty-Six

Before

Bits of the conversation on the back deck drifted up through my open bedroom window.

"Are you ever gonna get married?" I overheard Ben Rodriguez ask. "You're the lone holdout in our group."

I assumed he was talking to Ian, because the only other person hanging out on our deck was Ali, who obviously had a wife.

The three friends were out back smoking cigars, a habit Ali picked up after turning forty. He'd have one or two people over, primarily neighbors but also old friends—when their schedules allowed. I usually stayed out of sight on those evenings, not only because I hated the smell of cigars but also because Ali deserved some guy time. He rarely went out with his friends, and I knew how much he enjoyed the occasional relaxing cigar night.

I was reading in bed when the pungent scent of smoke wafted in the open window. I'd crossed over to close the window when I overheard Ben's question.

"I'm not the only holdout. Nasser isn't married yet either," Ian pointed out. "Has he even come close?"

"Not that I know of." Ali's voice. "What about you?"

"Not yet," Ian answered.

"You don't know what you're missing," Ali told him.

"Yeah?" Ian asked. "What's it like—being married and having a family?"

"There's nothing like it. Amira's essentially my best friend. We always have each other's backs. And the kids"—I heard the love in my husband's voice—"they just take life to a different level. It's a feeling that I can't describe."

Warmth blossomed inside my chest. I knew Ali loved me and our family, but I enjoyed hearing him say it. He was a man of few words, especially when it came to expressing his feelings.

Ben snorted. "It's also having no time to yourself, always running after kids, getting no sleep because they're up at the crack of dawn, and being too tired to fuck your wife at the end of the day."

I heard Ali's quiet laugh. "Your kids are still young. It gets much better once you start getting enough sleep again." Ali had been the first to get married in his friend group. Ayla and Adam were already in middle school by the time Ben got married.

"I thought I came close to snagging 'the one' a couple of times," Ian said. "But it hasn't worked out yet."

"Yet?" Ben echoed. "She's still in the picture?"

"We've been on and off for years."

"Years?" Ben snorted. "I see you're still having trouble closing the deal."

"From what I hear, Lizzie is single now," Ian remarked, in what sounded like an obvious attempt to shift focus away from his lackluster love life. "I wonder what she's been up to."

"I heard she hooked up with someone right after her divorce," Ben said. "But nothing after that."

"Who did she hook up with?" Ian asked.

"No idea," Ben answered. "But I think it lasted a little while."

"How about you, Ali?" Ian's voice again. "Have you heard anything?"

"Nope." I could hear the shrug in his answer.

"You two were so close," Ian said. "Do you seriously not stay in touch at all?"

"I'm a happily married man," Ali said. "And I intend to remain that way."

"Are you worried that Lizzie might tempt you if you were to see her again?" Ian persisted.

"Fuck off." Ali's voice was calm but cold. "My wife is inside the house. Have some respect."

Ben laughed. "Ian's trying to distract us from the fact that he still can't close the deal. I remember you and Nass got all the action back when you three roomed together. Ian was lucky to get your leftovers."

The chatter continued but I stopped listening. I quietly closed the window and went back to bed, savoring Ali's words about marriage and family.

Chapter Thirty-Seven

Now

"I'm surprised you wanted to come tonight," Nasser said as we pulled up to a hot new downtown restaurant to celebrate Sara Carr's birthday.

"I like her," I said. "It was nice of her to personally reach out and ask me to come." Plus, there were some questions I needed to ask her.

Sara's party was in a private room at the back of the restaurant. It was a small gathering. I recognized the core group of college friends. Ben was there but I didn't see Ian, and there was a handful of other people I didn't know. I briefly pondered whether Lizzie would attend since she was in town. But I didn't spot her.

"I'm so glad you came." Sara hugged me as I handed her my gift. We chatted briefly, but the birthday girl had to see to her other guests. I mingled a little, trying some of the Japanese-inspired appetizers. Most of what I sampled was new to me. As we got older, Ali became a less adventurous eater, so we mostly stuck to restaurants that we knew we liked.

I purposely didn't seek Nasser out. I needed to learn how to be in the world on my own. Now was as good a time as any to start finding my legs. Nasser didn't approach me either. He mingled and laughed and had a couple of drinks. It felt natural to go to him, but I held myself back. I sensed his continuing interest in me and didn't want to give him the wrong idea.

At dinner, I was flattered to find myself seated next to Sara. "This way we'll have time to chat," she said as we took our places. She asked me about the kids and work, taking care to integrate me into conversations with her other friends seated nearby.

"Do you know Lizzie's brother?" I asked Sara midway through the meal. "His name is Bill Warren."

"I've met him a couple of times."

"Are they close?"

"I don't think so. He mostly seemed exasperated by her whenever I saw them together. Why do you ask?"

"No reason." I didn't want to go into it during the party when the focus needed to be on Sara. But later, after dinner was over and we'd cut the cake, Sara and I sat off to the side alone, and she raised the issue again.

"I think Lizzie's brother gets annoyed with her always being so emotional and distracted," Sara said. "But she's got good reason to be."

"Why is that?"

"I actually spoke to Lizzie recently. She called me out of the blue." Sara poured the last of the wine bottle into her glass. "Lizzie is dealing with a situation."

"What kind of situation?"

"Someone is stalking her."

"She told me. Do you believe her?"

"Why would she lie? That's why she's been so off the radar and never shows up to anything." Sara sipped her wine. "Apparently this stalker has been relentless since she got divorced. She never told her ex about it because she didn't want him or the kids to get involved."

"She said she knows who he is now. That he found her after all the publicity about my lawsuit and the North Carolina house. Do you know the man?"

"Yes, but she swore me to secrecy. She doesn't want to provoke the guy."

For the first time, I felt the stirrings of real empathy for Lizzie. If her story was true. "What a terrible way to live."

"Especially since it was someone in our college group," Sara said in a dramatic whisper before bottoming out her wineglass.

"What? Can you tell me who it is?" I cajoled, hoping the alcohol lubricated her tongue enough to spill confidences she might otherwise keep. I still wasn't sure I believed the stalker story. "I won't tell anyone."

"It was Ian!" Her eyes sparkled, and her cheeks were flushed. "Can you believe that?"

"*Ian*, Ian?" I gaped at her. "Seriously? Is that why he's not here tonight?" We were interrupted by a trio of guests who came to say goodbye. Sara stood and hugged each guest lavishly. "Thank you so, so much for coming."

Her husband came to her side, chuckling. "Sara is very effusive when she's had more than two glasses of wine."

With a wave in my direction, Sara disappeared into her crowd of friends.

On the way home, Nasser was disbelieving when I told him about Lizzie's supposed stalker. "Ian? I don't believe it."

"That's what Lizzie told Sara."

"Maybe she's mistaken."

"Maybe, but that would partially explain why Ali helped Lizzie conceal the purchase of her house."

"Why partially?"

"Ali helping Lizzie conceal her purchase of Cozy Glenn to protect her from a stalker is absolutely something Ali would do. But the Ali I knew wouldn't break my trust by keeping such a big secret. He would have told me about the situation and sworn me to secrecy."

"You believe in Ali again." Nasser's face was in the shadows. "What's changed? Have you learned something new that I don't know about?"

"No, I just finally got my head on straight. Once I stopped doubting my memories and started trusting my judgment, I realized that I *did* know the real Ali. And he wasn't a cheater. Or a liar."

He was quiet for a moment. "If that's the case, then what's your theory regarding Cozy Glenn?"

"I think there's more to it. Something pretty extreme had to happen for Ali to hide the house from me. I feel like Lizzie and her brother know what it is. They're still hiding something."

"Like what?" He glanced over at me before refocusing on the road. "Uh-oh. I don't like that look on your face."

"What look?"

"One that suggests you have a plan."

I did have a plan. But I was keeping it to myself at the moment because Nasser definitely would not approve.

"I don't want to be a pest, but I worry about you." He lowered his voice. "I care about you."

Anxiety arrowed through me. That slight discomfort, the uneasy awareness, still lingered between us. I was afraid of losing Nasser as a friend if he openly confessed to having feelings for me. But he couldn't be anything more. I might be a widow, but I was still married to Ali's memory. I couldn't imagine ever being ready to move on.

"I need to create a little space to make my own decisions," I told him. It was past time for me to be completely true to myself, for once, even if that meant losing people who were important to me. "I hope you can understand that."

"I know you want some breathing room," he said. "But can you blame me for being protective when your house has been broken into twice?"

"What?" I swung my head toward him. "How do you know about the second break-in?"

He paused. "You told me."

"No, I didn't. I absolutely did not tell you," I insisted. "In fact, I made a point of keeping it from both you and Lulu."

He was quiet, his eyes on the road. Uneasiness twinged through me. Nasser was the one who installed the security system. The intruder came in through the unlocked window in the garage. Nasser would have seen that window was unlocked when he installed the sensors. *He could have even unlocked it himself.*

"Well?" I pressed, my voice a little shaky. "How did you know about the garage break-in?"

"I have friends on the police force. I asked them to keep me posted if there were any incidents related to your case."

"But the break-ins happened even before I met Detectives Fox and Lloyd. You were keeping an eye on me before we knew Ali's death might not have been an accident?"

"I wanted to make sure you were safe."

I thought back to Julia's warning not to trust Nasser. I'd pretty much blown off her advice, but now I wondered.

———

"What if Nasser was behind both break-ins?" I asked Lulu, who I called as soon as I got home. The creepiness of that possibility shivered through me.

"I can't believe you kept that second break-in a secret until now," Lulu complained. "Why would you do that? I tell you everything." She actually sounded hurt.

"Can we just focus on Nasser right now?" I asked as I went around the house making sure all the windows and doors were locked.

"Fine," she said with attitude. "Why would Nasser break into Ali's car and office?"

"What if Nasser was up to something shady financially? Ali did do the taxes for Nasser's law firm. Maybe he had proof."

"Do you really think Ali would risk his CPA license to cover up Nasser's shady dealings?"

"No, Ali was a straight arrow, especially about accounting." I racked my brain. "What if Nasser just wanted to scare me?"

"Why would he do that?"

"We know he's had a thing for me. What if he wanted me to be so afraid that I needed him to come over and protect me bodyguard-style?"

"He'd have to be a real sicko to do that. Did Julia say why she's suspicious of Nasser?"

"She just said she doesn't trust him, that he was jealous of Ali."

"I mean anything is possible—"

"My God." A thought suddenly came to me. "Nasser has my security code."

"He does? Have you changed it yet?"

"No, but I'm doing it right now," I said determinedly. "If Nasser thinks he can scare me out of my home, he's got another think coming."

"Calm down. We don't even know it's him. An attorney caught breaking into someone's house would probably lose his license, wouldn't he?"

"I'm not saying it is Nasser for sure. But I am changing the code. Just to be safe." The ground beneath my feet felt shaky again. Had I been wrong to place my faith in Nasser? Who else couldn't I trust? I sighed, fatigue settling into my bones. I wanted nothing more than to crawl into bed and hide out from the world for a few hours. "OK. Let me go. I'm meeting Ian for brunch tomorrow."

"What?" she asked. "You're meeting the stalker?"

"In a public place. It'll be fine."

"Are you completely *mejnoona*?" Lulu went ballistic. "Who invites a known stalker to coffee? It's like you're trying to become his next obsession!"

"There are still so many unanswered questions. I need to find out whether Ian has some of the answers."

"Yes," Ian confirmed after agreeing to meet me at a busy lunch place in Arlington. I'd found his number on Ali's mobile. "I was the guy at Lizzie's apartment in Maryland. She wanted me to stay out of sight when her estranged husband visited."

Something inside of me relaxed a little more. For another person to confirm that Ali hadn't been involved with Lizzie solidified the truth for me. Ali loved me. Whatever else he kept from me, at least he wasn't unfaithful.

"Is it true that you stalked Lizzie?"

He grimaced. "'Stalked' is a little strong. Lizzie has always been a melodramatic girl. I didn't do half the things that she accused me of. But I am working on my issues with a therapist."

"Therapist?" I wrapped my hands around my mug, soaking in its warmth. "What made you decide to seek counseling?"

"Lizzie called the police on me. Seeing a counselor was a condition of having any potential charges dropped." He spoke around a healthy bite of roast beef sandwich. "I did get too caught up. I needed the wake-up call."

"How did this thing with you and Lizzie start?"

"Lizzie messed with my head." He crunched on a potato chip. "She was happy to sleep with me when Ali dumped her to marry you."

Surprise rippled through me. "You and Lizzie hooked up?"

"But, after a couple of weeks, she decided it was a rebound thing. Apparently, I wasn't good enough. Then she went off and married her professor."

"She did have a right to marry whoever she wanted." How many guys slept with girls for a couple of weeks and then dumped them?

"Now you sound like my therapist." He swiped some crumbs off his mouth with a white paper napkin. "But you're right. I let it go the first time."

"The first time? There was a second time?"

He nodded. "After her marriage broke up, we started seeing each other again. So I think to myself, 'This is finally our time. Lizzie finally sees it.'" His voice rose in anger. "And then she dumps me *again*? Tells me *yet again*, 'Oh, sorry, you're just a rebound fuck.'"

"I'm sure she didn't say it that way."

"She might as well have."

It took a moment to fully digest the fact that Lizzie and Ian had hooked up repeatedly. "Did Ali know you and Lizzie had gotten involved?"

"Nobody did." He slurped soda thorough a paper straw. "Lizzie wanted to keep it quiet."

"Do you know why?"

He shrugged. "No idea, but Lizzie insisted that she never meant to hurt me." He stuffed several more chips into his mouth. "There I was, ready to marry her like a complete asshole while she was thinking we were just two old friends with occasional benefits."

"What did you do after Lizzie said she didn't want anything serious with you?"

"After she dumped me a second time, I started following her." He held up a hand. "Before you say anything, I know it was wrong. And guess who she met up with? Good old Ali. Mr. Perfect screwing around on his wife."

It hit me. "You're the person who left threatening emails for Ali on the Channel Three website, aren't you?"

He paused. "I'm not going to say anything to incriminate myself."

"Do I look like a prosecutor to you?"

"You should thank me." He crunched on another chip. "You didn't want Ali seeing her, did you?"

"I'll take that as a yes."

He flushed. "It wasn't my finest moment. I was jealous."

"He wasn't having an affair with Lizzie," I told him. "It was business. He just helped her buy the house."

"Privately, right?" Ian said. "So that I wouldn't know where she lived. I think she exaggerated her stalking accusations so that Ali would feel sorry for her."

That wouldn't surprise me. But I wasn't about to let Ian off the hook. "You just admitted that you wouldn't leave her alone."

Ian's eyes darkened. "That's because I believed that Lizzie and I belonged together. Even though she's a cocktease who's jerked me around since college. I can't believe I wasted so many years waiting for that b—for Lizzie . . . to realize I was the one. I'm an idiot."

Anger radiated off him. I leaned back in my chair. "You found Lizzie because of me, didn't you?"

"Yeah, it worked out great." He finished off the first half of his sandwich and reached for the second. "I thought Lizzie would come to Ali's funeral but she didn't bother to show up. Luckily for me, your lawsuit helped me find the information I needed."

That didn't track. "The lawsuit never went to trial, and the settlement was private. That can't be how you found the address to the Durham house."

Ian flushed. "Listen, I'm not proud of my behavior—"

"Wait. Wait a minute." The revelation burst through me. "You're the person who's been following me!"

He pressed his lips together. "I don't know what you're talking about."

"Are you sure?" I prodded. "You know, it won't be hard to find out if you own a vintage orange sports car."

"It could have been a coincidence that we ended up at the same place at the same time."

"I was right." Anger rushed through my veins. "It is your car."

He gave me a wary look. "I don't need any more trouble with the cops."

"You scared the hell out of me! My husband died five minutes ago and you decide it's a good idea to freak me out even more by following me all over town?"

A sheepish look came over his face. "I didn't mean to scare you, I swear. *If* I followed you, I might have hoped you'd lead me to Lizzie."

I thought back to the moments when I'd felt someone was watching me. "You were at the cemetery."

He was silent.

"Have the decency to tell me the truth," I snapped.

"I happened to be there to pay my respects to Ali."

What an obvious liar. "How lucky for you that Lizzie happened to be there when I got to the cemetery. You followed her after that, didn't you?"

"I might have lost her in traffic when she drove away."

"Did you follow me to Durham when I went to see Lizzie?"

"Maybe," he said, still being cagey. "But then she vanished again."

"Did you tail me to the eldercare facility? And eventually from there to Lizzie's hotel?"

"Again, I'm sure you appreciate that I can't say anything that might incriminate me."

"You're a creep." I spat the words.

His expression softened. "I never meant to hurt or scare you. I'm truly sorry."

I was quiet for a moment, processing this new information. "Did you break into my garage and my house?"

"What?" He frowned while he chewed. "Why would I? Someone broke into your house? What were they after?"

"I don't know." I couldn't think of a good reason for Ian to want to get into my house. I wanted nothing more to do with this lowlife, but I still had questions that needed answering.

"So," I continued, "after you followed me to Lizzie's hotel, what happened?"

"She called the police on me. I have to stay away from her now."

"And will you?"

"I'm definitely not going to jail for that"—his lips twitched—"person. Did you know that Ali and Nasser always got all the girls at school? They used to come in and out of the apartment at all hours. Lizzie wasn't Ali's first, but I wanted her the minute I saw her. I knew it wouldn't last between her and Ali. I just had to wait."

"What made you think Ali and Lizzie wouldn't go the distance?"

"Ali said once that the only reason he slept with Lizzie was because he got hammered out of his mind at some fraternity party. He didn't feel like he could break up with her after he slept with her. He laid off the sauce permanently after that night."

My world tilted. Lizzie was the reason Ali stopped drinking? "Are you sure that's how they got together? They did know each other in high school."

"They went on a couple of casual dates his senior year, from what I heard. That was it."

"But I was always under the impression that he really cared about Lizzie."

"Maybe he did, but it was more like he felt responsible for her." He swallowed the last of his soda. "You were a totally different case. From the beginning, it was obvious to all of us how crazy Ali was about you."

"But he stayed with Lizzie for a few years before he met me."

"Marrying you was Ali's escape," he told me. "You were basically his get-out-of-jail card. You freed him from Lizzie."

"I have to ask you a question," I said when Lizzie opened her hotel room door shortly after my meeting with Ian.

"Another one?" She shot me an exasperated look. "I thought I answered all your questions. No, your husband didn't buy me a house. No, I was not having an affair with your husband. What else could you want to know?"

"I just saw Ian. He pretty much confirmed that he was stalking you."

"You reached out to Ian?" She opened the door wider. "Why? You didn't believe me?"

"I don't know you that well. Let's just say I wanted to hear it from a second source."

She threw up her hands. "OK, then . . . If Ian confirmed what I told you, then why are you here? What else do you need to know?"

"One question has really been nagging at me. I still don't know why Ali visited your mother on the day he died."

"Neither do I." She exhaled loudly. "You might as well come in. I'm making a salad."

I followed her into the kitchen area, where a cutting board and vegetables for salad were laid out on the counter.

Leaning against the wall, I crossed my arms over my chest. "Your mother said it was a shame what happened to Ali."

"What's wrong with that?" She diced a carrot, making sharp thwacking noises each time the knife hit the wooden cutting board. "It *is* a shame that he died in the car accident."

"Yes, but the thing is that your mother said that *before* I told her that Ali was dead."

"Amira," Lizzie said in a way that suggested I was testing her patience but she was still trying to be nice about it. "My mother is very ill. She is easily confused and very forgetful. The meds she takes for her illness don't exactly promote mental clarity. I can't tell you what she meant by that. I honestly have no idea."

"Don't you think it's strange that Ali suddenly decided to visit your mother after, what . . . twenty-three years of not being in touch with her?"

She scooped the carrots into a metal mixing bowl. "Maybe he visited her regularly. He had a bond with my mother. They were very fond of each other."

I watched her movements. "Your mom said he'd never visited before."

"Like I said, Mother is forgetful." She paused to look at me. "Why is this so important?"

"My husband died suddenly and had Xanax in his system." My throat clogged with emotion. "The man never took anxiety meds. I would have known if he was anxious. Maybe if I visit your mother again, she'll be able to tell me why Ali went to visit her."

Lizzie went very still. "I wish you would let it go. If Ali wanted you to know why he was anxious, he would have told you."

"Wanted me to know what?" I straightened. "What do you know?"

Her eyes slid away. "I don't know if Ali was hiding something." She started cutting a cucumber. A methodical chop, chop, chop. "I'm just saying that, if he was, maybe he had a good reason for it."

There was something she wasn't saying. As usual. But what was different this time was that I sensed that Lizzie actually seemed on the verge of telling me the truth.

"Please just tell me. There are too many unanswered questions," I pleaded. "I can't rest until I know everything."

Lizzie paused, staring down at the round slices of cucumber. "I won't allow you to visit my mother because your presence will upset her."

"Why? She barely knows me."

She set the knife down. "Because she associates you with Ali, and he was responsible for the biggest tragedy in her life."

Chapter Thirty-Eight

"What are you talking about?" I braced for more lies, but then it registered that this was the first time Lizzie wasn't fidgeting or on edge around me. Instead, she seemed resigned.

"It was an accident," she said with quiet resolve. "Ali didn't mean it. He was just trying to protect me."

My scalp tingled. "Protect you from what?"

"My father." She walked into the sitting room and over to the window. I followed her. "Daddy was overprotective, and he had a temper, especially when he drank. And he drank a lot. Too much. He caught Ali kissing me."

"What happened?"

"Daddy walked in on Ali kissing me in our family room when I was seventeen. It was just a kiss. An innocent teenage thing." Her blue eyes filled. "Ali and I were sitting on the fireplace hearth—you know, that built-in brick bench in front of the fire—"

"I know what a hearth is." I remembered Nasser telling me about the police report and how Lawrence Martins had died at home after accidentally falling and hitting his head on the raised hearth. "Go on."

"That's why I've been avoiding you," she said quietly. "Ali took his secret to the grave. I thought it wasn't my place to tell you."

Dread trickled through me. "Tell me what?"

"He protected me when I needed it." She swiped a tear away. "I felt that the least I could do was protect Ali in death."

"What happened?" My voice came out as a whisper. I cleared my throat. "I need to know. Tell me."

"We jumped up as soon as my dad tore into the room, calling me a whore—" She bit her lip, trying to keep her composure. "He was coming at me. I think he was going to hit me. Ali instinctively stepped between us and shoved my father away. That's when Daddy fell and hit his head."

I recoiled as though she'd punched me. "No. You're not saying—" I couldn't bring myself to put words to the thought.

"It wasn't like it was a hard push or anything," she said. "But Ali was an eighteen-year-old high school athlete. Daddy was an out-of-shape man in his fifties. He stumbled backward and tripped over our shoes, which we'd taken off. He fell and hit his head."

"On the fireplace." My voice cracked.

"Sit down," she said gently, coming over and guiding me into the nearest chair. "You don't look very good. You've lost all the color in your face."

I slumped into the chair, my legs giving out. "Keep going. I need to hear everything."

Sitting opposite me, Lizzie told me the rest. Lawrence Martins was knocked unconscious by the fall. Her mother came into the room and told Lizzie to call 911. And then Mrs. Martins turned to Ali and told him to go home. Her husband would already be furious when he woke up, and seeing Ali would make things worse. *It's OK,* she'd said to Ali. *He's had too much to drink. And the paramedics are on their way. They'll check him out. Everything is fine.* So Ali, a scared teenager in way over his head, had done what Mrs. Martins asked.

"But then the paramedics came," Lizzie said. "And it was worse than we thought. My father had stopped breathing. They transported him to the hospital, but there was nothing to be done. It was too late."

"No." I shook my head, not wanting to believe what I was hearing. "No."

When Ali heard the news the next day, he told Mrs. Martins that he was going to tell the police the truth. *It was an accident,* he said. *I'll explain it all to them.* But Mrs. Martins had insisted that Ali stay silent.

"We'd already lied to police," Lizzie said to me. "How would it look if we told them, after the fact, that Ali was there when my father fell, that he pushed him?"

My throat was dry. Poor Ali. "He wanted to tell the truth." Of course he had. That was the man I knew.

"My mother begged Ali to say nothing. We would all look like liars, like we were guilty of something. There was also an insurance policy." She hauled a decorative pillow into her lap, her fingers toying with the fringed trim. "We were going to need that money to live on after Daddy died. If there were any questions surrounding his death, we risked losing everything—the house, the ability to pay for college, *everything*. Mom told Ali that he'd do even more damage to my family if he went to the police. And we'd already been hurt enough with Daddy's death."

"All this time." Nausea stirred in my stomach. "Ali lived his *entire* adult life with this horrible secret?"

"It was the only way. He was eighteen. His life could have been ruined."

My heart ached for what Ali had endured. To keep a secret like that, to be unable to seek public exoneration, had to have eaten away at him. "It was wrong of your mother to make him lie."

"Was it?" she asked. "Mom reminded him that he was his parents' only son. It would have killed them to have their son accused of murder. It could have ruined Ali's future."

"Or maybe you did it to save yourselves because the only real adult in the room, your mother, chose to lie to the police from the beginning." Anger flared in my belly. "And then she forced a decent, naive kid to go against his principles so that she could get her insurance money."

"I know this is a shock. It's hard to think rationally at a time like this." Empathy coated every word. "Once you've thought it through, you'll have a different view. Who would it have served if Ali came forward? No one, that's who."

"It might have been the best thing for Ali," I choked out. "For his conscience."

"Maybe. That's easy for you to say now. But think about it." She toyed with the pillow trim. "His life would have been ruined. He could have been found guilty of involuntary manslaughter. That's a felony conviction. It would have hurt Ali's chances of going to college. And do you think that fancy accounting firm of his would hire a convicted felon?"

"No, probably not." But still, what they'd done to Ali was wrong. I tried to think rationally. To give Mrs. Martins the benefit of the doubt. She'd just lost her husband. Maybe she truly believed she was protecting Ali. Had they really acted in his best interest? Or had they sacrificed him for the insurance money?

"We were all in a state of panic and fear and confusion." Lizzie released a long, trembling breath. "My father had just died. Everything was crazy. Maybe what my mother did was wrong, but she made the best decision she could at the time. She wanted to protect all of us, including Ali."

I could only imagine the damage keeping that horrible secret had done to Ali's conscience. "You mentioned he seemed anxious when you saw him several weeks before the accident."

"We met very occasionally because I was the only person that he could talk openly with about what happened to my father. That was the only lasting bond we shared."

"And when you had lunch together in Reston? What was that about?"

"Where?" Her brow crinkled momentarily but then cleared. "Oh, you're talking about when we met at that restaurant by Lake Anne. That was near the anniversary of Daddy's death. The anniversary always hit Ali hard. And me too, of course."

"Did he go see you in North Carolina?"

"Once, when we needed to sign some documents related to the mortgage. He was on a golfing trip with his buddies. I only saw Ali for a couple of hours."

"But you two talked regularly?"

"Not often. More so in the years since I bought the house on Cozy Glenn, when the secret seemed to fester in Ali. He'd call me to talk or meet up when he needed to unburden himself."

Queasiness coated my stomach. I swallowed down against the rising bile. But it was no use. I surged to my feet and bolted to the bathroom. Slamming the door behind me, I barely made it to the toilet before I vomited. My belly heaved and I retched, the sour taste filling my mouth as I emptied the contents of my stomach into the bowl.

Tears stung my eyes. My head pounded. I gagged until there was nothing left but dry heaves, my body trying to rid itself of a truth that there was no escaping.

Weak and spent, I slid to the porcelain floor, the chill of the tiles bleeding through my pants. I leaned back against the wall, taking a few deep breaths, shaking my head against the thoughts ricocheting in my mind.

I pictured Adam, our tall and gangly son still fighting the pimples that plagued him in high school. Adam was nineteen, no longer a boy but not yet a man. Ali had been a year younger when Lizzie's father died, an unseasoned teenager faced with an unthinkable situation.

I believed Lizzie. It made sense for guilt to drive Ali to help both Lizzie and her brother. That sense of obligation, the idea that he owed them for killing their father, explained why Ali had risked his professional reputation to help Bill Warren. Why he'd put our marriage, and potentially his own happiness, on the line to help Lizzie buy her house.

There was a light tap on the door. "Amira?" Lizzie's gentle voice. "Are you OK? Can I get you anything?"

"No," I croaked, my throat burning. "Just give me a minute, please." I hauled myself up and over to the sink. Turning on the water, I tried to rinse the bitterness out of my mouth. I scanned the personal-care products scattered on the bathroom counter. Maybe Lizzie had something that would chase away the acrid taste on my tongue. Among the cosmetics, vials of prescription meds, and skin-care paraphernalia, I spotted a plastic bottle of green breath freshener.

Pouring some mouthwash into my cupped hand, I sucked it and gargled. My gaze wandered over the products on the counter as I swished the minty liquid around while silently counting to sixty. Lizzie took her beauty seriously. There were lots of eyeshadows and lipsticks, balms and lotions. All high end. I didn't recognize any of the meds, which had long medical names I couldn't begin to pronounce: escitalopram, alprazolam, citalopram. Why was Lizzie on so much medication?

When my count reached sixty, I spit out the mouthwash. At least my breath was a little fresher now. I splattered cold water on my flushed face, relishing the coolness against my hot cheeks. Grabbing a clean folded white washcloth, I mopped my face. I took a deep breath to fortify myself and went back out to join Lizzie. "I don't want you to think this was easy on any of us," she said. "I started having severe stomach problems after Daddy died. I still have to take all sorts of prescription meds to calm my digestive tract."

It was hard to feel sympathy for her in that moment. People lost loved ones every day and it was a tragedy. I knew that as well as anyone. What wasn't common was for a good man to live with the guilt of having killed someone as a teenager and never having the chance to defend himself.

I looked at Lizzie and found her watching me closely. I needed to escape. From her at least, since there was no getting away from the awful truth.

I grabbed my purse. "I have to go."

Chapter Thirty-Nine

"I'm coming over," Lulu said over the phone.

"No." I groaned. "Don't." The last thing I wanted was for my sister to show up at my house. One look at my face and she'd know something was very wrong.

"You're not yourself," Lulu continued. "You haven't left the house in what? Three days now?"

"I think I'm getting sick."

Sick to my stomach. The truth about Ali kept me in a constant state of nausea. The throbbing headache pounding behind my left eye didn't help. And I hadn't had a decent night's sleep in the two days since I'd learned the truth. When I did manage to fall asleep, it was in short, jagged, restless spurts. I wanted to dream of Ali. To see him again, to comfort him, at least in my dreams. But he never showed.

"The last thing you need is to catch something from me," I told her, "and give it to Khalid and the girls."

"No problem. I'll wear a face mask."

"Listen, Lulu. Take a hint." My voice hardened. "I lost my husband not four months ago. I deserve time to grieve in whatever form that takes without you jumping down my throat."

"Oh." Her tone gentled. "Is that what this is?"

Tears stung my eyes. Not exactly. But I was in mourning. Despairing that Ali had endured his guilt alone. If only he'd shared the burden. Maybe I could have eased it. What happened with Lizzie's dad was an accident, and Ali was a kid caught in an impossible situation. A scared teenager who followed the directions of the only adult in the room.

That teenage boy must have been so frightened. The adult he became had to have been riddled with guilt. Lying by omission, hiding the truth, went against everything Ali was as a person. I believed Lizzie about Ali feeling the need to talk to her about what happened. Part of me was actually grateful she'd been there for him.

"Just let me be in my feelings," I said to my sister, fatigue weighing me down. The truth drained everything from me. "I promise I'm OK."

"Are you sure? I'm worried."

"I'm sure. The only way through this is to let myself experience all of the emotions. I'm not going to let anything happen to me. I'd never hurt the kids that way. You? Maybe," I said, making a faint joke. "But not my babies."

"If you're sure."

"I am. I promise I'll call you tomorrow."

As I disconnected the call, my phone pinged. A text from an unfamiliar number.

> It's Lizzie. I'm just checking in to make sure you're OK.

How had she gotten my number? From her brother probably. I pushed myself out of bed. Binti lazily stretched on her nearby dog bed. A museum project was due soon, and I never missed a deadline. But my head felt too cottony to tackle anything harder than making a cup of coffee. I trudged into the kitchen, with Binti on my heels. I selected a coffee pod. Normally I went for decaf, but I needed a full shot of caffeine to make it through the day. Turning on the kitchen faucet, I filled the coffee machine's water tank.

Yawning, I stood by as the machine whirred, dripping the steaming dark liquid into my coffee cup, the deep, nutty aroma floating through the kitchen. I'd started using Ali's favorite cup. He wasn't one for huge thick mugs. He preferred the thinner, smaller ones and drank his coffee to the last drop, while I barely got through half of mine.

I gave Binti her breakfast and refreshed her water. Watching her eat, I sipped the hot, bitter coffee. Black with no cream or sugar. One of the hardest parts of learning the truth was not being able to talk to anyone about it. I normally told Lulu everything. But Ali had taken the secret to his death. Telling anyone would be a betrayal of my husband and his memory.

Reaching for my phone, I called the last person I ever imagined turning to for comfort. Lizzie picked up almost right away.

"Are you all right?" she asked immediately. "I've been worried about you."

I'd had a lot of time over the last few days to think about Lizzie's culpability in all this. When I thought of Ayla at age seventeen, I knew I couldn't blame Lizzie. She'd been just a kid at the time too. It was even hard to find fault with her mother's initial instinct to send Ali home to spare them all from her husband's anger. Martha Martins couldn't have known what she was setting in motion.

I exhaled into the phone. "It's a pretty heavy thing to carry. I hate that Ali had to bear it for all of his adult life."

She was silent for a long moment. "It is hard. That's why I tried to keep you from learning the truth. It serves no purpose except to haunt you like it does my family."

"But I was like a dog with a bone."

She gave a quiet laugh. "You are very persistent."

"Everything finally makes sense now about why Ali helped you and your brother."

"My brother?" I registered the frown in her voice. "What does Billy have to do with this?"

"Ali got him a position at his firm."

"He did? Billy never told me that. He shouldn't have asked Ali to help him. My brother's not great at holding down a job." Her exasperation came through the phone. "But who am I to talk? I convinced Ali to help me hide my purchase of the Cozy Glenn house. I'm sorry about keeping it a secret from you. He truly didn't want to."

"None of that feels like it matters now," I responded. "But I reserve the right to be mad about it later."

"Noted," she said with another light chuckle.

"About the Xanax," I said slowly, bringing up one last unresolved question. "Do you think Ali was taking it?"

Lizzie paused before answering. "I honestly don't know. I mean, he was obviously bothered by the events surrounding Daddy's death. Maybe he wanted something to take the edge off."

My phone buzzed. I had an incoming call. It was Detective Fox.

"I have to go. I have another call. A business call." I'm not sure why I lied to Lizzie about the police being on the other line. But it was my first instinct.

"I'll let you go, then. No problem." She talked fast. "Listen, Amira. Call anytime you need to talk."

"Thanks," I said, eager to switch over to pick up Detective Fox's call.

"I mean it. It's the least I can do for you . . . and Ali."

Thanking her again, I clicked over to pick up the detective's call.

"We have a new development," Detective Fox said.

My stomach twisted. "What is it?" Irrationally, I jumped to the conclusion that she suddenly knew about Ali's role in Lawrence Martins's death.

"Surveillance footage near the Parkview Hotel in Rosslyn shows the loaner car your husband was driving pulling into the hotel parking lot on the evening of the accident."

"The Parkview?" I repeated. "What was he doing there?"

"That's what I was going to ask you. Can you think of any reason Mr. Abadi would have to visit the hotel after leaving the Channel Three work event at Waterman's Grill?"

"None. We've been to a few weddings there, but he'd otherwise have no reason to be there. How long was he at the hotel?"

"Not long. According to our timeline, your husband left Waterman's at eleven o'clock, and the accident scene is only fifteen minutes from Waterman's. We think Mr. Abadi was at the hotel for less than twenty minutes."

What had Ali been doing there? "Is there any surveillance tape from inside the hotel?"

"We're checking, but it could take some time. Hotels like to protect their guests' privacy. They don't willingly share surveillance tape unless a crime has actually been committed on their property."

"How long could it take to get the tape?"

"If we have to go through the formal process? It could take weeks, unfortunately."

I hung up, completely bewildered. I could think of no reason for Ali to go to that hotel. I needed to see that surveillance tape, possibly the last footage ever taken of him. I couldn't bear the thought of waiting weeks for that to happen. There had to be a way to see it sooner. Who could I call? How could I get that tape? Would Nasser have any special pull?

But just as quickly, I backed away from the notion of asking Nasser. I was still uneasy that he'd known about the second break-in. I wasn't sure I could trust him now. Or if I ever should have. Maybe I was being overly suspicious. But I needed to rely on myself to figure this out.

Then I remembered running into my second cousin Hamza the last time we attended a wedding at the hotel. I searched my memory. He was some sort of manager over there. Did he still have a position at the hotel? I'd seen Hamza at Ali's funeral, but we hadn't talked much beyond him offering condolences. I went through my contacts and pulled up his number.

"Hamza," I said when he picked up. "I need a favor."

"Anything for you," he said right away. I'd learned that many people jumped at any opportunity to make a widow feel better. Hamza was clearly one of them. "What can I do?"

"Do you still work at the Parkview Hotel?"

"No, I've moved to another property. I'm the assistant general manager at the Parkview location in Fair Oaks."

My heart sank. "Oh."

"Why? What's going on?"

I told him about Ali being at the Rosslyn hotel on the night he died. "Do you guys even hold on to surveillance tape for that long?"

"Only if there's some reason to keep it."

"Like what?"

"If there's some sort of accident or altercation. It's a liability issue, so they keep the footage just in case."

"I guess I'm out of luck if you don't work there anymore."

"It's still a sister property. A friend of mine is the banquet manager over there. Let me call him. Tell me the date again?"

I was in luck. Hamza's friend, Mahmoud, was willing to help. Hamza arranged for me to meet the man the following evening, when Mahmoud would be the manager on duty. He was waiting for me in the lobby when I arrived at the agreed-upon time.

"Salam alaykum," Mahmoud said.

"Alaykum a-salam," I responded. "I'm sorry to impose on you."

"Ma-a-lish. It is nothing," he said graciously. "It is always my pleasure to help a sister." Mahmoud was an Egyptian immigrant, a fellow Arab, so there was an immediate unspoken fellowship between us.

"I'm sorry to hear about your husband. *Allah yerhamo.* May God have mercy on him."

"Ameen. Thank you so much."

"The luck is with us," he told me in a tangled mix of English and Arabic as he led me past the security room where several black-and-white monitors showed various parts of the hotel. "We did keep the tape from July twenty-third."

"You did?" Excitement strummed through me. "I thought you recycled the tapes."

"We do unless there's some sort of incident."

"There was an incident?" My pulse beat faster. "What happened?"

"You'll see it on the footage. A man had a run-in with a very agitated young woman."

We came to an office. A windowless, compact space with just enough room for a desk and chair. He set up a laptop on the desk. A grainy black-and-white image popped up.

"Here you go. That's the video. Just press the arrow." He showed me how to hit play, freeze the video, and rewind. "I'll give you some privacy. Take your time."

I waited until he was gone. And then, with anticipation zipping through my veins, I pushed play.

I was instantly mesmerized by the moving images on the screen. Emotion roiled through me the minute I spotted Ali. He paced across the lobby in his dark work suit, the images too distant and grainy to reveal the expression on his face. But I recognized that walk—the no-nonsense stride, the determined set of his shoulders. He was agitated. But why?

"What are you doing there?" I whispered at the screen. The setting abruptly switched to the hotel bar, where Ali approached a small round table. A woman was seated with her back to the camera, with deep shadows further obscuring her from view. I couldn't tell what she looked like, who she was. Ali halted abruptly, staring down at the woman with his hands planted on his hips. I distinguished that stance too. This was no romantic assignation. Ali was furious.

The woman shook her head in frantic side-to-side motions. She gestured with her hands, palms down, trying to calm him. Why? What was Ali so upset about on what would be his last night on earth? He paused before taking a seat at the woman's table.

He sat spine straight, shoulders back, still on alert, almost as if he was humoring her while waiting for her to get to the point. She started to cry. Ali got up and went to the bar. The woman watched him leave and then turned to reach for her purse. She retrieved a bunched tissue from a leopard-print handbag and fumbled with it for a moment before dabbing her eyes.

I watched as Ali returned with two glasses. The woman sipped from hers while Ali looked on. He removed his suit jacket and tossed it over the back of his chair. He sat again, arms crossed over his chest, and said something with a sharp tilt of his head. I could imagine him saying, "Well?" His body language suggested he was waiting for an answer.

She started talking. Ali listened for a few minutes, his body posture stiff. He abruptly leaned forward with a sharp wave of his hand. He was doing the talking now. The woman leaned away from him, as if his words stung.

But then another woman entered the frame. This one was young, with wild dark curls. Ali immediately jumped to his feet, his body language now compliant, rather than hostile. He forgot about the woman at the table. His complete focus was on the young woman who was gesturing wildly, obviously upset.

The back of my neck tingled because I recognized the new arrival. It was Ayla.

Disbelief rippled through me. What was my daughter doing there? Ayla had never mentioned seeing Ali on the night he died.

Turning my attention back to the monitor, I watched my baby girl storm out of the bar. The tape switched back to the lobby, where Ali followed his daughter. He reached for Ayla's arm, but she jerked it away.

Frustration slammed through me because it was impossible to know what they'd said to each other.

Shaking, Ayla backed away from him. He reached out to her with one placating arm. But she shook her head violently before pivoting and running out of the hotel.

I was riveted. "Go after her," I pleaded with my husband's image on the screen. "What are you doing?" How could he let Ayla drive away when she was that upset? It wasn't safe for her to be on the road.

But instead of following our daughter, Ali returned to the bar. He said something to the woman, who was still seated at the table. From his tense posture, it was clear Ali's anger had returned in full force. His fists were clenched. He did not sit. Pointing at the woman, he shook his head and appeared to speak sharply. I had never seen my husband so animated in his anger. Who was the woman? Why was he so mad?

When Ali finished talking, he reached for his glass and poured it down his throat. I assumed it was water because Ali never drank. Then he grabbed his jacket off the back of his seat and left. The woman jumped to her feet and appeared to call him back. Ali ignored her. When he reached the lobby, he was sprinting.

About time, I thought. He was finally going after Ayla.

———

Shaking, I replayed the tape again and again. What did it mean? Who was the mystery woman? Why was Ayla so upset with her dad? What made Ali so furious at the woman in the hotel lounge?

I thought about Ayla's behavior since Ali died. How withdrawn she'd been, how morose and willing to assume the worst about her father. I'd assumed her changed demeanor was a reaction to Ali's death. Now I knew better. A powerful urge to protect my daughter washed over me.

I had no idea what Ayla knew, but I sensed how badly she needed me. My insides quivered. I was afraid for my daughter. I grabbed my bag and bolted out of the office.

I had to find her.

Chapter Forty

"OK, I'm here." Ayla dropped her backpack by the front door and toed off her sneakers. "What is so important that I had to come home in the middle of the week?"

Binti trotted over to Ayla, waggling her body, her tail swiping left and right. Ayla crouched down to greet the dog. "How's my good girl?" she crooned while rubbing the dog's ears. Binti looked like she was in heaven.

I drank in the sight of my daughter, my tense muscles relaxing a fraction now that we were in the same room, even though she was far too thin, her face even more drawn than the last time I saw her. I'd made Ayla drive back from college because this was a conversation that needed to be done in person, and in the comfort of the home she grew up in.

"I have something important to talk with you about," I said softly.

She looked up, her gaze wary. "Don't tell me there's a new revelation about Dad. Are you going to reveal that he had a second wife and a whole other set of children?" Ayla's uncharacteristically negative attitude toward her father now made sense. She'd been furious with him on the surveillance tape.

I shook my head. "No, it's nothing like that. Come and sit down."

She grimaced as she stood up, forgetting all about Binti, who looked seriously disappointed. "OK, now you're scaring me. Why are you so intense?"

"Come on." I ushered her into the family room, where we sat on the sectional, her favorite place to hang out other than in her bedroom.

"So?" she said impatiently after we were settled. Binti nudged Ayla's leg with her nose, still craving attention. But Ayla's eyes were on me. "What is it?"

"First of all, I love you and your brother more than anything on the planet, including myself and even your dad."

"Okaaay." She waited for me to continue.

"And I'm not here to judge you or blame you for anything. I want to protect you and make sure you're OK."

"Why wouldn't I be?"

Binti gave up her quest for attention and settled at Ayla's feet for a nap.

I took a breath, my heart throbbing. "I just saw a surveillance tape from the Parkview Hotel from the night Dad died."

Ayla paled. "There's surveillance tape?"

"You didn't do anything wrong." I took hold of her hand. "I just want to understand why you were there. Can you tell me why you were so mad at Dad?"

"Isn't it obvious?" She burst into tears. "Dad was cheating on you! I confronted him."

"How did you know he'd be at the hotel that night?"

"Earlier that day, I was here at home using Dad's tablet because mine wasn't charged." She gulped between sobs. "I saw the whole text exchange between him and that woman."

Ali's tablet was connected to his phone. "But I went through Dad's tablet after he died. I didn't see anything weird or suspicious."

"I deleted the whole text exchange after I read it. I even deleted the app from the tablet. I didn't want you to see it."

My throat ached at the thought of Ayla trying to protect me from a devastating revelation. "What did the texts say?"

"That he needed to see her immediately." She sniffled. "How gross is that?"

"I can see why that would be upsetting. How did the woman respond?"

"She asked if it could wait, that she was busy, but he texted back that he needed to see her right away." Disgust waved over her face. "She answered that she was staying at the Parkview and he could come there. I wanted to gag."

"Did they arrange a time to meet?"

"Dad told her that he had a work thing and could come over after, at around eleven o'clock. That he'd text her when he was on the way."

"Did you recognize the woman? I couldn't see her face on the surveillance tape." I wasn't worried about another potential affair now that my faith in Ali was completely restored.

She shook her head. "No, I'd never seen her before. But you're way prettier than she is."

I impulsively hugged her for her staunch defense of me. "What about on the text chain? What was her name on Dad's tablet?"

"No name. Just initials."

"What were they?"

She blinked, another tear falling down her cheek. "LM."

Lizzie Martins. The last person to talk to Ali before he died. And she'd never mentioned seeing Ali that night. Fury flared in my belly. What was she still hiding?

I squeezed Ayla's hand. "It might not feel like it now, but everything is going to be OK. I promise."

"No, it's not. It'll never be OK." She started to sob. "It's my fault that Dad's dead."

"What?" I froze. "No, it's not!"

"I said horrible things to him, Mom," she cried, her face swollen and red, "really horrible things. And now that woman says they never had an affair. That makes everything worse."

I gave her a side hug. "He would understand. You know Dad."

"I asked him if you knew he was meeting another woman late at night at a hotel."

"And what did he say?"

"That you didn't know but that it wasn't what it looked like. He said he just needed to talk to the woman. I told him it was gross, what he was doing, and that I hated him. Then I ran out. He followed me into the lobby and told me that it wasn't safe to drive when I was so upset. When I got to my car, I was crying so hard that I couldn't see anything. I just sat there for a couple of minutes trying to calm down."

I felt a wave of gratitude that one of Ali's last acts was an attempt to protect our daughter. "Thank goodness that you did."

"But then I saw Dad run out of the hotel and get into that loaner he was driving. I started my car right away to get away from him. I knew he was coming after me because I was upset." Tears streamed down Ayla's face, grief contorting her features to the extent that she was almost unrecognizable. "Dad died because of me. Because he was chasing after me. He was probably driving too fast and that's what caused the accident."

"Oh, *habibti*, no, it's not your fault." I hugged her hard, my heart breaking for all the months she'd secretly lived with misplaced guilt about her father's death.

"You're just saying that to make me feel better," she said between hiccupy sobs. "I'm so messed up. I can't sleep; I can't study."

"I am not just saying that to cheer you up." My voice was firm. "The police did not say that speed was a factor in the accident. And remember that Dad had Xanax in his system that might have caused him to fall asleep at the wheel. You *did not* do this."

"When I first heard that Dad had Xanax in his system, I was a little relieved. I thought maybe it wasn't my fault that Dad crashed after all."

"*It wasn't,*" I reiterated.

"But then I thought about how he rushed out after me. Maybe the drug impaired his judgment and he was already worried and upset, and who knows—"

"Stop," I said gently. "You're spiraling. You are not responsible for the sequence of events that led to Dad's death."

"I wish I could believe that." She looked at me with red, watery eyes. "But we'll never know for sure, will we?"

I held my daughter while the tears flowed. My heart contracted painfully as I rocked her and hummed the old lullaby that I used to sing to Ayla when she was little and I could shield her from the world's horrors.

———

"You're a liar." The words were out of my mouth before Lizzie shut her hotel room door behind me.

"It's nice to see you too." She faced me. "What's going on?"

"Why didn't you tell me that you saw Ali the night he died?" My voice rose. "Aside from Ayla, you were very likely the last person to see him alive." I'd left Ayla asleep on the couch and asked Lulu to come over and stay with her while I went to see Lizzie.

Her expression softened. "Your daughter finally told you."

"I saw the surveillance tape."

"What surveillance tape?"

"At the Parkview. There is tape of Ali looking very upset."

She nodded. "He was upset. He went to see Mother that day because the guilt about what happened to Daddy was eating away at him. He wanted to make sure Mother forgave him."

"And did she?"

"Of course. She never blamed Ali. You've seen for yourself how fond of him she still is. We all knew Daddy's death was a terrible accident."

"Why was Ali so desperate to see you on the night he died?"

"He'd had enough of the secrecy. He wanted to come clean with you, to tell you everything."

Tears stung my eyes. If only he had confided in me earlier. I could have helped him through it. "And what did you say?"

"I told him it wasn't my call. But I questioned whether it was fair to put his burden on you."

"You didn't want him to tell me."

"Honestly? No, I didn't. We'd kept everything quiet for so long that I didn't see the point in telling anyone else."

"How do I know that you're not lying now? For all I know, you hate me. Or you're still jealous that Ali broke up with you to marry me."

"Because, if you think back, you'll realize that I've never lied to you. Yes, I avoided telling you the truth about how Daddy died—for obvious reasons." Her mouth twisted into a sad smile. "But if I hated you or were jealous, why wouldn't I lie and say, 'Yes, Ali did buy me a house. Yes, we were madly in love and had an affair for all of these years.'"

She had a point. As much as I hated to admit it.

Lizzie went on. "To be honest, seeing Ali wasn't easy. It always took me back to that awful night. I didn't blame Ali, but, in my mind, he was forever connected to the most horrible thing that's ever happened to me."

"Why would you hide the fact that you saw Ali the night he died?"

"Because of your daughter."

I blinked. "What about her?"

"She arrived and immediately misinterpreted everything. She was upset, and he ran off after her. I was trying to protect her."

"By withholding the truth?"

"I was trying to shield your daughter the way I think Ali would have wanted me to." She paused. "I didn't want you to blame Ayla for killing her father."

"She didn't kill him," I snapped. "It was an accident."

"I'm not saying she did, but I didn't know you. I had no idea how you'd react. When I realized your daughter hadn't said anything to you about seeing her father on the night he died, I decided to keep quiet. I thought she had a valid reason for not saying anything."

"It was wrong of you to keep the truth from me." My voice trembled with emotion. "When I think of the guilt she's had to bear all of these months—" My voice caught. "There's no telling what kind of emotional damage has been done to her."

Lizzie's lower lip quivered. "I'm sorry if I made the wrong decision. I've lived in fear of people learning the truth about how Daddy died for so long that I've become such a guarded person. I paid for that with my marriage." She exhaled long and loud. "A habit that develops over the course of almost three decades is not easy to break."

Emotion roiled inside my chest. If only Ali had never met Lizzie or her family. The decades-old secret they forced him to keep had not only rotted through my husband's life but crossed generations and damaged our daughter. I no longer cared about Lizzie, her mother, or her brother, or what their true motivations were.

My daughter needed me. And I wasn't going to let her down.

———

Ayla stayed home for a couple of days. I spent that time encouraging her to open up and, in true Arab-mother style, cooking her favorite foods. Binti rarely left her side, and Ayla seemed comforted to have the dog nearby. To my relief, the more time we spent together, the more Ayla opened up to me.

She told me she was only sleeping three or four hours a night and the constant fatigue made it difficult to focus on school. She also felt anxious most of the time. Hearing what she'd been going through gutted me. Why hadn't I done more earlier? I'd known my daughter was suffering.

"Mom, you were dealing with your own stuff," Ayla reminded me as she ate some rolled grape leaves stuffed with rice and lamb that I made for her. Binti, ever hopeful of being treated to some scraps, sat alertly by Ayla's chair. "Not just Dad's accident but then everything with the secret house."

I added a few more rolls to her plate. "Thank you for letting me off the hook, but one of a mother's primary roles is to protect her children from harm, and I've done a lousy job of that."

"We're pretty much grown up," she reminded me. "You can't protect us forever."

"Maybe, but I'll never stop trying."

She put her plate aside. I was satisfied to see that she'd eaten reasonably well. "You still believe in Dad? That he didn't cheat?"

"I do." I told her about Lizzie and the stalker. "The main reason Dad helped Lizzie is because he was there when Lizzie's father died and that bonded them."

Her eyes rounded. "What?"

I chose my words carefully, explaining how Lizzie's father had tripped and hit his head on the hearth, a death that was ruled accidental. Ayla probably needed to know at least part of the truth in order to begin healing her emotional wounds.

"So," I said after sharing a sanitized version of events, "that's why Dad helped Lizzie out when she told him she was being stalked, because of what they'd been through together as teenagers."

"But why keep it a secret from you?"

"Lizzie was afraid that I might blab and that the stalker would somehow find her. She wanted as few people as possible to know about the house."

She set her mouth. "Dad still should have told you."

"I agree. According to Lizzie, he intended to share everything with me right before he died. That's why he saw her that night." I checked my phone. "Come on. It's time to go or we'll be late for your appointment."

Part of ensuring that Ayla was healthy both physically and emotionally involved scheduling time with a grief counselor and our primary care doctor. The first appointment was with Dr. Macias, our family doctor, who'd treated all of us for years. She examined Ayla and spoke to her about her issues.

"You've been through a lot," Dr. Macias said near the end of the appointment. "I'm going to prescribe an antianxiety medicine."

"OK," Ayla said.

"How long will she have to take it?" I asked, not knowing anything about medicines used to treat anxiety. "Is it addictive?"

"This is only for the short term," Dr. Macias reassured us both. "Right now, Ayla is dealing with the aftereffects of trauma and grief. When she is feeling especially anxious or overwhelmed, taking alprazolam will help take the edge off."

"That sounds good," Ayla said abruptly. "I'll take it."

"Are you sure?" I asked her.

She gave a firm nod. "Yes."

I had my own misgivings, but I needed to let Ayla do what she thought was best for her.

On the way home, we stopped to pick up the prescription at the grocery store pharmacy. We waited in a short line until it was our turn, and the clerk punched Ayla's name and date of birth into the computer.

The clerk stared at the screen. "It says here that the pharmacist would like to speak with you."

"Why?" I asked. "Is there a problem? Did the doctor's office not call in the prescription?"

"No, that's not it. We have the order."

"Miss Abadi?" Overhearing the conversation, the pharmacist, who was in the dispensing area on a raised platform behind the counter, gestured for us to meet her over at the consultation window.

"Who is this for?" she asked, looking between me and Ayla.

"It's for me," Ayla said. "This is my mom."

"We do have your prescription, which is for the generic form of this medication. But I won't have generic until the day after tomorrow." She handed a bottle over to Ayla. "So I'm giving you a few tablets of the brand name until then."

"And it's the exact same thing?" I asked.

She nodded. "Yes, it contains the same active ingredient."

"Can I see?" I asked, and Ayla promptly handed the medicine over. I examined the three light-blue oval-shaped pills inside and read the label. "This says these are Xanax?"

"Really?" Ayla said. We exchanged a surprised glance. We were both thinking of Ali.

"Yes," the pharmacist said. "Your doctor prescribed alprazolam, which is the active ingredient in Xanax. It's the same thing. It's just that one is generic and the other is name brand. I'll have the generic by the day after tomorrow."

Despite an uneasy feeling, we thanked her and walked out to the van.

"It's weird to be taking Xanax after what happened to Dad," Ayla said. "Do you think he took antianxiety meds without telling you?"

"I really don't know." I supposed it was possible now that I knew how stressed and guilt ridden Ali must have been. But something still felt off. It was like having a word on the tip of my tongue, just beyond my grasp.

"My friend Rachel from college is coming over when we get home," Ayla said once we were back in the van heading home. "She came down because she had a scheduled dental appointment. We'll probably order in dinner."

"Are you sure you feel up to it?"

"Yes, it'll be a nice distraction."

"OK. I'll try to stay out of your way."

She groaned. "Go out, Mom. I'm OK. Or at least on my way to being OK. You've been home with me twenty-four seven. Get out of the house."

"Fine." I mock pouted. "I know when I'm not wanted."

She smiled at me. "Helicopter Mom needs to take some time off from hovering or else she'll run out of gas."

"If you insist." Seeing that Ayla needed a little space and would be occupied for the next couple of hours, I made a decision. "I'll let you off at home, and then I'll go out for a little while."

"Hey, stranger." Claudia was out by her mailbox when we got home. I'd dropped Ayla and was pulling out of the driveway. "We're due for another walk."

I rolled down the window. "Ayla's home for a few days, so I've been busy with her."

"Isn't it the middle of the semester? Or is she here to see your brother?"

"My brother? I don't have a brother."

"You don't? I could have sworn the man I met in your backyard told me that he was your brother."

I stilled. "You saw a man walking around my backyard? When?"

"He was in a suit, walking around kind of looking at the windows. I thought he was checking out security for you. Maybe he said he was your brother-in-law and I didn't hear him right."

I pulled out my phone and scrolled through my photos until I found a shot of Khalid. "Is this the man you saw?"

"No." She shook her head. "That's not him."

Was it Nasser? He was the person who put in the security system to start with. I pulled up Nasser's photo from his law firm website.

"Wow, he's cute. I'd definitely remember him," Claudia said as she inspected the photo. "No, it wasn't him."

A low hum of anxiety settled in. "Maybe there's an innocent reason that man was in my yard. It's just that I've been on edge since the break-ins—"

"Break-*ins*?" Claudia cut in. "As in plural? Did you have another break-in?"

I nodded. "Besides the guy who went through Ali's office, someone broke into the garage, too, but my security cameras don't have a view of the side of the garage."

She paused. "Mine might."

"Yours? Since when do you have security cameras?"

"Since you came home alone and found a man in your house. Matt said we shouldn't take any chances. Do you want to come in and see if our cameras caught anything?"

I looked at the time on my phone, debating with myself. "I've really got to be somewhere. Can we do it tonight?"

"Sure," Claudia said. "When did the second break-in happen? I can look up the date and have the footage ready for you when you get back."

I gave her the date. "I'd appreciate that."

She shook her head in confusion. "I really thought I saw you talking to the guy who said he was your brother."

"You did?" I was perplexed. "When?"

"The other day when I was walking Buddy, you were out by your mailbox talking to the man. We waved at each other. Don't you remember?"

It took me a minute to place the scene she referred to. But then it hit me. She saw me talking to Bill Warren when he came to explain why he'd pretended to be Fake Jake. "Are you sure it was the same man?"

"Pretty sure. Who is he?"

"Definitely not my brother or even a friend."

Her eyebrows went up. "OK, then. I'll check our security cameras to see if there's a picture of him."

"That would be great. Thank you." I pulled out of my driveway and set the GPS to my destination.

Normally I would have jumped at the chance to see Claudia's footage to confirm Bill Warren had been sneaking around my backyard so I could call the detectives. But nothing felt more critical than the mission I was on.

Chapter Forty-One

I drove straight to the Meadows to see Mrs. Martins again.

There was one thing I couldn't get out of my mind: how agitated Ali had been on the surveillance tape. In twenty-three years of marriage, I'd never seen him appear so disturbed. His demeanor unsettled me. He'd almost looked distraught. Lizzie's explanation, that they argued over telling me the truth, didn't sit right with me. Mrs. Martins talked to Ali on his last day. Maybe she could fill in some of the blanks.

Once I arrived, I parked and went inside, approaching a shaggy-haired young man who looked like he belonged on a surfboard rather than behind a reception desk.

"Sorry," he said after I told him my name, "but you are not authorized to see Mrs. Martins."

I frowned, surprised by this unexpected stumbling block. "What kind of authorization do I need?"

He looked perplexed. "Huh?"

"There must be a mistake." My car keys jingled as I fidgeted with them. "I visited Mrs. Martins two weeks ago. She was very happy to see me." Until, of course, she became so upset that medical personnel had needed to rush in and tend to her.

He shrugged. "I don't know what to tell you, but there's a note on Mrs. Martins's file that you can't visit her. You did say your name is Amira Abadi, right?"

"That's right," I confirmed. "Did the doctors make the decision? Can I speak to one of them?" I needed to speak with Martha Martins, and I wasn't going to let Surfer Dude deter me.

"Nope. The doctors have nothing to do with it. The family makes the no-visit list."

"The family?" I stopped jingling my keys. "Are you saying that Mrs. Martins's son or daughter specifically asked that I not be allowed to visit her?"

He squinted at the computer. "It says here that the son, Bill Warren, made the request."

I stiffened. Why would Bill Warren ban me from seeing his mother? Had he learned that my last visit had upset her, or was he still hiding something? "Can you tell me if all visitors are limited, or is it just me?"

"Yep. Looks like just you," he said. "Sorry about that, but you can't see her."

He didn't seem very sorry at all, but I thanked him. I got back to my van and sat there, still in some disbelief, staring at the redbrick facility with its darkened windows accented by forest-green valances. It seemed like an impenetrable fortress now. I needed to get inside. But how?

A woman crossed in front of the van on her way into the facility. She looked vaguely familiar. It took me a minute to place her. It was Bernice, the lady who'd manned the reception desk the first time I visited Martha Martins.

I sat in the van for another half hour, contemplating ways to see Mrs. Martins. Knocking on one of her windows could work—if I could find the right one. But then I imagined someone calling the police to report a peeper at the old folks' home.

While I thought about other ways to sneak into the facility, Surfer Dude emerged from the front sliding doors. I watched him climb into a beat-up Chevy and drive away. I considered my options. Maybe having Bernice at the front desk would improve my chances of getting in. I didn't have any better ideas.

Taking a deep breath, I exited my van and walked back into the Meadows with my heart beating in my ears. I immediately spotted Bernice alone behind the reception desk. I exhaled. Maybe things were finally going my way.

"Why hello there," Bernice greeted as I approached.

"Do you remember me?" I asked.

"I never forget a face," she said with a warm smile. "I suppose you're here to see Mrs. Martins?"

"Yes." I cleared my throat. "I'm really looking forward to visiting with her again today."

"Great. Let's check you in." My heart sank as her fingers tapped the keyboard. She read the screen and then gave me an assessing look. "I am terrible with names. Tell me your name again?"

I made a split-second decision. "Grace Mansour." It wasn't a complete lie. The name on my birth certificate was Amira Grace Mansour. I even had a Social Security card in my wallet to prove it. My parents opted to give me a more Americanized middle name in case the adult me decided to utilize it for professional purposes. I had never used it before now.

"Grace." The way she studied my face made me sure Bernice could see right through my pathetic attempt at subterfuge. Pasting a smile on my face, I held her gaze and tried not to squirm. I'd read somewhere that liars always look away. My armpits were getting damp.

"That's a pretty name," she finally said.

Relief whooshed through me. "Thank you."

She reached for a red marker to write the name down on a visitor's tag. "Don't stay too long. Mrs. Martins needs her rest."

"I promise not to tire her out."

"Have a nice visit." She handed me the name tag. "You remember the way?"

I assured her that I did and got out of the reception area as fast as I could without looking like a prison inmate making her escape. I went down the corridor, passing an older gentleman scuffing along with a walker and a couple of staffers. I finally reached Mrs. Martins's room and tapped on the door.

Silence. I shifted my weight from foot to foot. *Come on. Answer. Please be here.*

Finally a trembling voice sounded from inside. "Coming."

The doorknob jiggled and Mrs. Martins appeared, looking gaunter than before, her sunken eyes lined with dark smudges. It had been barely two weeks since my last visit. I was stunned by the visible physical deterioration.

"Hello, my dear?" She stared blankly at me. "Do I know you?"

Was this some sort of dementia? "How are you?" I asked gently. "We met earlier this month. I'm Ali Abadi's wife. Remember?"

She studied me with cloudy eyes. Then she smiled. "Of course. How are you?"

I exhaled. At least she knew who I was. "May I come in?"

"Yes, yes." She moved aside to allow me to enter. "I'm forgetting my manners along with many other things."

We settled in the same seats as we had at our previous visit. "How are you?" I began, eager to get to the point before someone discovered that Mrs. Martins had a forbidden visitor.

"Billy said you moved to another state and would no longer be coming to see me."

"Excuse me?" It took a moment to process her words. "Your son told you that I moved away?"

"But I'm so happy you're here," she continued. "I've been asking to see you."

"You have? No one told me." What was Bill Warren up to? Why take steps to ban me from seeing his mother and then lie to her about me relocating? "If I had known you wanted to see me, I would have come right away."

Confusion filled her gaze. "But Billy promised to tell you."

"I guess he forgot," I said as kindly as I could, determined to avoid upsetting her like last time. "But I'm here now. What did you want to talk with me about?"

Her gaze wandered over to the window. "That's why I called Ali at work the day he came to see me. I didn't want Billy to know."

My skin prickled. "Why not?"

She continued as if she hadn't heard me. "I knew Ali worked where my Billy worked, so Bernice helped me find Ali's work number."

"That was nice of Bernice. Why did you call Ali?"

"I wanted him to come and see me." She sighed heavily, as if releasing years of suppressed emotions. "It was wrong what I did to him after my Lawrence died."

"Did you ask Ali to come and see you so you could apologize?"

She shook her head. "I didn't deserve his forgiveness. What I did to that young man was far worse than he could imagine. Ali had no idea what really happened the night Lawrence died."

"I don't understand." Had the woman become confused again? "Ali saw what happened because he was there the night your husband died."

"He was there *before* my husband died," she corrected me.

What did she mean? "Do you remember Ali pushing your husband, causing him to stumble and hit his head on the fireplace?"

"Yes." She teared up. "I remember. I'll never forget."

"What did you tell Ali the day he came to see you?"

"Do you know that I'm dying?"

I sucked in a breath. "No. I had no idea."

"It's cancer. Slow moving, the doctors tell me, but it will eventually get me."

"I'm very sorry to hear that."

"That's why I need to talk to you before it's too late."

"I'm here," I prodded, hoping she'd get to the point before we were interrupted. "And I'm listening. Please go ahead."

"After Lawrence hit his head, he lost consciousness, and I told Ali to go home. I thought everything would be all right . . ." Her voice wandered off. She turned her head to stare out the window again.

"But everything didn't turn out OK—" I prompted.

She looked at me. "That's right. As soon as her father fell, I told Elizabeth to call 911. While she was on the phone with them, giving them our address and such, I convinced Ali to go home so that my husband wouldn't wake up and find him there." She paused, blinking, like a computer that was short-circuiting.

"What happened after Ali left?" I asked, eager to keep her on track.

"Oh." She seemed to come back to herself. "I wondered what was taking the ambulance so long, so I went to the kitchen to call them again. I told Elizabeth to get her father a pillow for under his head so that he'd be more comfortable."

"And then?" I prodded.

"When I called 911, they said no one from our address had called for an ambulance. I was annoyed by the mix-up and told them to please send an ambulance as quickly as possible because my husband stumbled and fell and hit his head on the hearth." A tear slipped down her cheek. "When I went back to the family room—" Her face crumpled with emotion. "That's when I saw what Elizabeth had done."

The hair on the back of my neck tingled. "What had she done?"

"She had the pillow over her father's face." She began openly crying. "She smothered the life out of him."

I blinked. "What?" Did the old lady know what she was saying? "Are you sure?"

She reached for a tissue and blew her nose in a loud snort. "I'll never forget it."

"Lizzie killed her father? Is that what you're telling me? She suffocated him?" As a seventeen-year-old girl? The horror of it was too much to contemplate.

"What could I do?" She twisted the tissue in her lap. "You're a mother. Surely you understand that I had to protect my daughter."

I closed my eyes, fully absorbing just how monstrous Martha Martins's actions had been. Sacrificing Ali's mental well-being in order to save her daughter. Nausea swirled in my belly. "You protected Lizzie at Ali's expense."

"Yes," she said simply. "I had to choose between Ali and Elizabeth. I chose my daughter."

"That's obscene." Disbelief trembled through me. "You allowed Ali to be tormented by a horrible lie for his entire adult life, to let him believe he'd done something unspeakable. What kind of people are you?"

The reality that Lizzie had killed her own father, and that her family deliberately let Ali believe he was to blame, left me speechless with outrage. I couldn't find the words.

"I thought my guilt would ease over the years, but it deepened." Mrs. Martins reached for another tissue from the box on the side table. "I called Ali because I needed him to know the truth before I died."

"And did you share what you've just told me?"

She nodded. "I told him everything. Lawrence didn't die from the blow to his head. He died by suffocation. I was terrified for my daughter. That's why I told police that my husband stumbled and fell."

I wanted to throttle the woman for what she'd done to my husband, for how she'd made him suffer *for decades* in order to protect her daughter. And herself. "How could you let an innocent teenager think he killed a man?"

"What could I do? Elizabeth was crying hysterically. She said we were finally free of him. That he'd never boss either of us around. She was tired of him being so strict with her. Of him never letting her go out with her friends. What could I do?"

I gritted my teeth. "You could have done the right thing. Which is tell the truth."

"My husband was . . . a challenging person. Lawrence was very uncompromising with Elizabeth. She couldn't go out much at night like other teenagers, and she resented it. He believed a young lady shouldn't date until she turned eighteen."

How bad had it been? "Did your husband beat Lizzie?"

"He slapped her once after discovering she snuck out of the house to go to a party. That's the only time Lawrence laid a hand on her. But Lizzie has always been high strung and very emotional."

"Your lie infected Ali's entire adulthood." My voice trembled. "And you let a murderer walk free."

"That's why I told Ali the truth the day he came to see me." She was twisting the tissues again. They came apart, little white bits littering her lap. "I needed to make things right."

"You could never properly atone for what you did to him."

"I know. But at least Ali knew the truth before he died. He was very relieved."

Tears stung my eyes. "What did he say? How else did he react?"

"He was very relieved but also very upset. After he left, I called Lizzie to warn her that Ali knew the truth."

Lizzie. *A murderess.* How many times had I been alone with her while she repeatedly lied straight to my face? "What did Lizzie say when you told her Ali knew she killed her father?"

"She told me not to worry. That she would take care of everything."

"How—" I began but was interrupted by a knock on the door.

A nurse came in. "Time for your meds, Mrs. Martins." She looked from me to the older woman. "Is everything all right?"

"No, it's not," I said bitterly. "But I'm done here."

I strode out of the room without another glance. I couldn't bear to look at the old woman. I was overwhelmed, still in disbelief.

"How did your visit go?" someone inquired when I reached the lobby.

I blinked through my haze to see that it was Bernice. "Fine," I croaked, the stale nursing home scent filling my nostrils.

She met my gaze. "She's been asking to see you, but her family wouldn't allow it."

I gaped at her. "You know who I am? Why did you let me in to see her?"

"Because I couldn't let that nice old lady die without her final wish being fulfilled."

Bile rose in my throat. I turned away, careening toward the automatic sliding doors that led to the parking lot. When I stepped out, a blast of brisk fresh air hit my bare face.

I couldn't breathe. Leaning over, hands on my knees, I forced air into my lungs. Once I'd settled a little, I managed to make it back to my van. Still feeling sickened, I leaned my head against the headrest, forcing more deep breaths. How was any of this possible?

My phone buzzed. A photo from Claudia. I read her text.

Here's a screen grab of the guy who was in your backyard.

I tapped the picture, impatiently waiting for it to enlarge. A familiar face popped up. My stomach turned over. It *was* Bill Warren. The man was always showing up where he didn't belong. Had he broken in because he wanted Ali's papers? It made sense. But how was all of this related?

My conversation with Mrs. Martins played over in my mind. Flashes from the last few days ricocheted in my head. Lizzie's face contorted in an expression of false sympathy. Ali on the surveillance tape confronting her. Mrs. Martins crying. Ayla challenging her father at the hotel. Picking up her prescription.

Xanax.

Alprazolam.

Ali.

The accident.

Realization slammed into me. Nausea tunneled its way up into my throat. I gagged, but there was nothing there. My stomach was empty.

Shock twisted through my insides. How had I missed the truth? Now that I saw the connection, I couldn't unsee it. I had to confront Lizzie. But first, I needed to make a call. I dialed the number, but it went to voicemail. I left an urgent message for Detective Fox.

Then I started my van and headed to the extended-stay hotel down the street.

Chapter Forty-Two

I paused in front of the door to Lizzie's hotel room to take a breath and steady myself.

Reaching into my purse, I pulled out my phone and set up the voice recorder. I often taped my interviews and meetings with clients. I patted my coat pocket. All was as it should be. I used the recordings as notes that I could refer back to. I even had backups in case something went wrong with the first taping.

I knocked. A moment later the door opened to reveal a perspiring, red-faced Lizzie wearing leggings and carrying a hot-pink weight in one hand. The sounds of an exercise tutorial with up-tempo music played on the TV behind her. A woman's voice chirped instructions.

"*Exhale as you press up. Keep your wrists straight.*"

"Amira," Lizzie said with a welcoming smile. "I was just working out. This is an unexpected surprise."

"Yeah, there seem to be a lot of those lately." This entire day felt entirely surreal. Maybe that was why I felt strangely calm. "Can I come in?"

"Of course." She stepped aside, opening the door wider. "I'm glad you stopped by. I've been worried about you."

"What exactly were you worried about?" I walked into the sitting room area and then turned to face her. "Me finding out the truth?"

She tilted her head. "What do you mean?"

"I just came from visiting your mother."

"What?" She closed the door. "That's not possible. Mother can't have visitors."

"Don't you mean to say that I am the only person who can't visit her? The Meadows said they were specifically instructed not to allow me in to see your mother."

"Can you blame us?" she asked in a reasonable tone. "You *did* upset Mother the last time you saw her."

I marveled at her cool restraint, the ease with which she lied. "Was it me who upset her?" I asked. "Or was it the fact that Ali died on the same day she told him the truth?"

"Control the weights up and down," the instructor trilled in the background. *"Focus on taking your time."*

"Mother is not herself." Lizzie smiled, but the way it didn't reach her eyes sent an icy arrow down my spine. "She can be very confused and muddled in her thinking."

"She was very cogent with me. And very clear about what happened the night your father died."

Lizzie's gaze narrowed. "What did she tell you?"

"That you killed your father."

"Me?" Lizzie gave an abrupt laugh. "Surely you realize how ridiculous that sounds."

"It *is* hard to fathom, but I think Ali believed your mother. That's the real reason he confronted you at the Parkview, isn't it?"

Her expression hardened. "I already told you that we met because the secret was eating away at Ali and he insisted that you had to know the truth."

"I don't believe you." I held her gaze. "I knew there was something off about the way Ali looked on the surveillance tape. The way he reacted . . . something extraordinarily awful had to have happened for him to be that upset."

"You can believe what you want—"

"Oh, I will," I interrupted. "I think Ali was so upset, more distraught than I'd ever seen him, because he realized that you let him take the blame for a murder that you committed."

Lizzie's composure slipped. "It was a horrible lie." Her bottom lip quivered. "Mother is confused. Nothing happened beyond what I've told you."

"Halfway there," the instructor said in a singsong voice. *"Keep going! Stay strong!"*

"This is all ancient history." The volume of her voice hiked. "Why are you here? Do you intend to report me to the police for the murder of my father? Do you think they'll believe you?"

"Not necessarily. But they might believe me about the Xanax."

"Make sure your arms stay close to your body as you bend your elbows."

Keeping her eyes glued to me, Lizzie slowly reached for the remote and aimed it at the TV. The training video clicked off, bathing the room in silence.

"What about the Xanax?" she asked.

"I saw it on your bathroom counter when I was here before."

The muffled sounds of closing doors and retreating footsteps echoed down the corridor.

"I don't know what you're talking about," Lizzie said. "I don't take Xanax."

"No, but you do take alprazolam, which is the active ingredient in Xanax."

She uttered an incredulous laugh. "You think I gave Ali Xanax?"

"Yes, actually, I do."

"Why would I do that?"

"Because he learned a pretty damning secret about who you really are and what you're capable of. That's why you wanted me to believe Ali was mentally unstable, to hide your complicity, to make me think he needed medication."

"What's wrong with taking Xanax?"

"Absolutely nothing. I'm sure it helps people who need it. But Ali didn't take Xanax because he needed it. You drugged him with your Xanax."

She threw up one hand. The other one was still carrying the dumbbell. "You're out of your mind. I don't take Xanax or alpha . . . whatever you called it."

"I saw the bottle, Lizzie."

"I don't know what you think you saw, but you're welcome to look at the meds on my counter. I told you that I take all sorts of things for my stomach."

"I know what I saw."

"Do you really?" Exasperation rippled through each word. "Then be my guest and go get the incriminating evidence and take it straight to the police."

I studied her, wondering what to believe.

"Maybe you want me to go get this mystery medicine?" She darted into the bathroom. Panic streaked through me. Was she getting rid of evidence? I barreled after her. When I burst into the bathroom, Lizzie was nowhere in sight. That's when I realized my mistake. A noise came from behind me. I started to turn around.

Pain exploded against my head before everything went black.

"You fucking killed her?" A man's furious voice drifted through the darkness.

"Relax." A woman's voice. Lizzie. She sounded far away. "I just hit her with a weight."

"Jesus. Just?" the man said incredulously. "You're fucking nuts."

The sounds of their conversation echoed in my ears. My head throbbed, pain pulsing between my temples. I felt like someone had struck me in the head with a bowling ball. I struggled to open my eyes, but my eyelids were too heavy.

"You have to hit me," Lizzie's voice said.

"What?" the man's voice retorted. "Why?"

"The police have to believe Amira and I struggled. I'll say that I was working out and she came in and attacked me. I had to hit her with the weight. It was self-defense."

I grappled to make sense of my surroundings. Where was I? Then I remembered. Lizzie's hotel. We argued—I couldn't remember why—and then she'd . . . ambushed me?

"Why would Amira Abadi attack you?" the man said. "Who's going to believe that idiotic story?"

"The cops bought it when we told them about Daddy, didn't they? They'll buy our story this time too."

"*Our* story?" he retorted. "It's *your* story."

"Whatever," Lizzie said dismissively. "I'll say Amira lost it and came after me in a rage over my affair with her husband."

"In your dreams." He scoffed. "You weren't fucking Ali. He wanted nothing to do with you."

"Shut up!" Her voice grew shrill. "He would have married me if his parents hadn't insisted he marry his own kind. They're so backward."

A heavy sigh. "Keep deluding yourself."

"Come on," she cajoled. "Hit me. You know you want to. Now's your chance."

The tile was cold beneath my cheek. I finally managed to blink my eyes open. I was on my side. Lizzie had her back to me, obscuring my view of her companion.

"And then what?" the man asked. "You'll kill her the same way you offed Dad and Amira's husband? You can't just go around killing people."

Lizzie did drug Ali. I closed my eyes as the truth crashed over me again. Tears welled in my throat. *Oh, Ali. What these people did to you.* I wanted to howl at the injustice of it.

Lizzie walked over, towering above me. I kept my eyes closed. "Amira is a huge problem. She keeps asking questions. Butting her nose where it doesn't belong. I can't let her tell people her ridiculous theory that I killed Daddy."

Another long sigh. "She can't prove anything."

"Do you think my clients are going to want anything to do with me if they think I killed my own father? What about my kids?"

"What about them? It's not like you're the mother of the year."

"I love my children. I didn't want Ian to hurt them."

"Mm-hmm. So you've said."

Lizzie nudged my inert body with her foot. I stayed perfectly still. I wasn't sure I could move if I wanted to. "I can hit her in the head again with the weight." Lizzie talked fast. Energy buzzed from her. "Or I can smother her."

He made a sound of disgust. "You really are twisted. How many people do you plan to kill?"

"Shut up. You know I didn't mean to hurt Ali. How was I supposed to know that he was going to race out of the hotel to chase after that kid of his?"

"Did you really drug him?"

"What choice did I have? When I realized Mother told him the truth, I ground up some Xanax and stirred it into his water when he ran after his daughter in the lobby. I knew that, at some point, he'd come back for his jacket. When he did, he drank the water before running back out after the girl."

The man exhaled long and loud. "How is this happening all over again?"

"It's not!" she insisted. "Ali wasn't supposed to die. I thought he'd sleep it off in my hotel room while I figured out what to do."

"Listen, Lizzie." The man's voice took on a menacing tone. "I am tired of cleaning up your messes."

"As if you're so innocent," she scoffed. "At least I'm not breaking into people's houses and garages."

"That's completely different. I didn't hurt Amira or anyone else. I just needed to see if Ali had any documents in his office or car that might make me lose my job. I certainly didn't kill anyone."

"Ha! Keep making excuses for yourself."

The voices floated farther and farther away. The pain in my head was agonizing. Blackness seeped over me, offering a respite. *No.* I panicked. I had to stay awake. I had to do something. I couldn't leave Ayla and Adam alone in the world.

A smacking sound jolted me from the edge of sleep. I blinked against the light. The man was slapping Lizzie.

"Use your fists, but not too hard," she directed him. "It has to look like I was in a fight with a woman."

I squinted, sharpening my gaze on the man. As I'd surmised by now, it was Bill Warren. I began to tremble as the reality of my situation settled over me. Lizzie was dangerous, a murderer. And she'd attacked me. I thought of my children. What would happen to them?

Something rustled beside me, pulled on me. A shadowy outline of Lizzie rifling through my crossbody, which was still on me.

Don't touch me. I itched to swat her hands away, but my arms were too heavy to move. My heart raced. I had to stop her. I couldn't allow Lizzie to get away with what she'd done to Ali. I couldn't let her destroy my family even more than she already had.

"Ha!" Lizzie pulled out my phone. "She was trying to record our conversation. She's a real Nancy Drew. There." She tapped the phone a few times. "That should take care of that. Now we have to decide what to do with her."

———

Who was pounding on the door? My headache was excruciating. I moaned. The door banged open, sending a fresh wave of pain blasting through my head.

"Where's my mother?" a female voice demanded. "I know she's here."

Horror bolted through me. I would recognize that voice anywhere.

"Hello, Ayla," Lizzie greeted my daughter.

I struggled to open my eyes. The urge to protect my child racked my body. *Run!* I silently pleaded. *Run. Ayla, run.*

"I have no idea where Amira is." Lizzie's voice. "Did she tell you she was coming here?"

"No, but I tracked her phone. I know she's here."

No, Ayla. Save yourself. Don't come in. Get as far away as you can! Desperation clawed at me. I tried to drag myself into a sitting position. I had to help Ayla. My daughter needed me.

"You got me," Lizzie's voice said as I drifted away. "Your mom *is* here."

No! I tried to yell. But it came out as a whimper.

Run, Ayla, run! Lizzie murdered your dad! But my warnings were silent screams blasting into a void of nothingness. I needed to get up, to help her. Then I remembered.

My crossbody was still slung across my shoulder. I forced my hands to move. It was a herculean effort; each arm felt like a fifty-pound weight. Luckily, Lizzie had left my bag unzipped. I fumbled around inside until my fingers wrapped around what I was looking for.

Darkness was gaining on me again, but I battled against the fatigue. If I went to sleep, who would save my little girl?

"I want to see my mom *right now*," Ayla said.

"Calm down. Like I said, your mom is inside," Lizzie said. "Wait here while I see if she wants to talk to you."

"Nice try." Ayla's skeptical voice. "Why wouldn't she want to see me?"

"She knows that you were involved in your dad's death. She's pretty upset about it. Now wait while I check."

Witch! How dare she say that to Ayla?

And was she getting something to hurt my daughter with? I struggled against the lethargy, which was like quicksand slowly pulling me under.

"Lizzie!" I croaked. I cleared my throat. *Louder,* I bullied myself. *For Ayla.* "Lizzie!"

Lizzie stood over me. "What?" she hissed. "Now your brat is here. See what you've done."

"I have proof of what you did in my purse . . ."

"Thanks for the tip, but I already took care of your phone."

"Second phone," I gasped. "Also recording."

"You're lying. I didn't see a second phone." Still, she leaned closer to reach for my bag.

My heart rate spiked. It was now or never. Gathering every bit of strength I could summon, I dragged the small canister out of my purse and blasted Lizzie in the face with pepper spray.

As I drifted off, her screams filled my ears.

"Amira! Amira! Wake up." A man's voice wafted over me. *Ali?* Relief rushed through me. Ali was here to help me save our baby girl!

"An ambulance is on the way," the man said. "You're going to be OK."

I fought to open my eyes. "Ayla," I croaked, trying to sit up. Bill Warren might hurt her. "Have to help her."

"Easy." The man's firm but gentle hand on my shoulder kept me in place. "Ayla is fine. She's safe. But you need to lie still until the paramedics get here."

"I'm here, Mommy." Ayla's voice. When was the last time she'd called me "Mommy"? "I'm not hurt." Relief whooshed through me. My girl was OK.

I dragged my eyes open. Ayla's concerned face hovered over me. Nasser knelt beside her.

"How did you find me?" I whispered to keep my head pain from skyrocketing.

"I knew you were too worried about me to stay gone this long," Ayla said. "Once I figured something was wrong, I tracked your phone."

"I turned off location services." My voice was barely audible.

"Adam and I can tell when you turn them off, you know. We just turned them back on the next time we were home."

"So sneaky," I breathed.

"We were worried about you," Ayla said. "Why do you think we've been home so much since Dad died?"

My heart contracted painfully. Despite everything that Ayla had been going through, she'd still been concerned about me? "And I thought you came home because you needed to be with your mommy," I said hazily. "How did Nasser get here?"

"I called him on my drive over."

"That's not your job, to worry about me," I whispered. Loud sounds hurt too much. Especially ones coming from inside my head.

"Oh, Mommy." Tears filled her big dark eyes, droplets catching in her lush eyelashes. She had Ali's lashes. "I'm so glad you're OK."

Another blurry face appeared behind Nasser and Ayla. The features sharpened into focus. "Detective Fox?"

"I'm sorry I missed your call. I came as soon as I got your message." She wore her usual humorless expression. "How are you feeling?"

"Like someone hit me over the head with a weight."

She cracked a smile. "We're interviewing Bill Warren and Lizzie Martins. They both say you're the one who attacked Lizzie first with pepper spray."

My throat was so dry. "I recorded our conversation," I rasped.

Behind her, Detective Lloyd appeared with my phone and looked through it. "I checked the voice notes. You didn't record anything today."

"Not that phone. Check my jacket pocket."

Ayla went through my pockets and pulled out the device. "Why do you have Dad's phone?"

"I always double record my interviews," I explained as Ayla handed the phone to Detective Lloyd. "In case one of them messes up."

"Poor Dad," Adam said. "What assholes those people were to let Dad think he'd killed someone." He'd driven down from school after Ayla called to tell him what happened.

"Definitely a very troubled family." I was lying on a gurney in the emergency room, where I'd been taken from Lizzie's hotel room. So far I'd had a CT scan and other tests. We were waiting for the ER doc to come in to talk with me.

"And they arrested this Lizzie person and her brother?" he asked.

"Yes," Ayla said. "I was afraid the brother was going to come after me after Mom pepper sprayed his sister, but Uncle Nasser showed up. And the police came right after."

"Thank goodness." I rubbed my aching head. "Hopefully they'll lock both of them up and throw away the key."

Adam looked relieved. "I knew Dad wasn't some loser who'd buy a house for his girlfriend. Seriously, Dad wasn't cool enough to have a side piece. He was kind of a nerd."

"Thank goodness for that," I murmured.

"Adam, don't be an idiot." Ayla rolled her eyes. "Cheating on your wife isn't cool."

He dismissed her. "You know what I mean."

"Whatever. Here." She handed me some water. "Maybe you should drink some more."

"Thank you, *rohee*." My soul. These beautiful children were my heart and soul, and I was beyond grateful that the three of us were safe and together. I took the water even though I feared it would make me more nauseated. "How are you doing?"

She shrugged. "I feel sad about what Dad went through. I feel bad that I was such a bitch to him that last time I saw him."

"You know your dad. He would understand. He'd never blame you. You came to a natural conclusion when you saw him secretly meeting a strange woman late at night at a hotel. You have to give yourself some grace."

"At least I don't feel like I killed him."

"Whoa! What?" Adam's gaze ricocheted between the two of us. "What are you talking about?"

"You've missed some things." I closed my eyes to quiet my throbbing head. "Ayla will have to fill you in."

Chapter Forty-Three

"Mrs. Price claims that she did not intend to kill your husband," Detective Fox said when she and Detective Lloyd stopped by the house five days later to brief me. Nasser was also there.

My face heated. "She still drugged my husband right before he got behind the wheel. Ali wouldn't be dead if it weren't for Lizzie's actions."

Nasser set a hand on my forearm. "You have a concussion," he reminded me. "You're not supposed to get upset. You should be resting."

I withdrew my arm. "Resting in a dark, quiet room for almost a week is what the doctor ordered." I was lucky to be recovering so nicely. Fortunately, Lizzie had bad aim and the hand weight she used hadn't landed as lethally as it could have.

I focused my attention on the detectives. "Lizzie also smothered her own father."

Detective Fox nodded sympathetically. "Maybe she did, but we cannot prove that Mrs. Price killed her father. She doesn't admit to it on the tape."

"So that's it?" I threw up my hands. "She literally gets away with two murders?"

"No," Detective Fox replied in the most soothing voice I'd ever heard from her. "The suggestion that Mrs. Price killed her father does give her a motive for trying to murder your husband. She could have been fearful he'd publicly accuse her of the crime."

Nasser shifted forward. "Is that how prosecutors plan to pursue the case?"

"You'll have to speak with the prosecution about that," Detective Lloyd answered. "Someone from their office should be getting in touch with Mrs. Abadi soon."

"Ultimately," Detective Fox added, "it's up to county prosecutors to decide what to charge her with."

"What about her attack on me?" I pressed. "She can't get away with slamming me on the head with a weight."

"She's been charged with assault," Nasser reminded me. He was closely following both cases. "In Virginia, that means she acted with the intent to do bodily harm."

"She told her brother that she intended to kill me." I looked from him to the detectives. "It's all on the recording."

"The county prosecutor will take his time building the case," Nasser said. "Lizzie could eventually face additional charges. Her brother could face charges as an accessory."

I peppered the detectives with several more questions, which they patiently answered before eventually getting up to leave. "We'll be in touch," Detective Fox said.

I walked the detectives to the door and embraced each of them. "Thank you for everything."

"Just doing our jobs," Detective Lloyd said.

Detective Fox patted me awkwardly on the back. "Take care now."

"You need to rest," Nasser said the minute I rejoined him in the living room.

"How long is this process going to take? The whole bringing charges, court proceedings, all of it?"

"It depends on what Lizzie does. If she takes a plea deal, the case will be over much sooner than if she decides to take her chances in court."

I exhaled long and loud through my nostrils. "I hate the idea of this dragging on indefinitely. For me, obviously, but mostly for the kids.

They're so young. It's not fair to lose your dad and then have to deal with all of this trauma on top of everything."

"Kids are resilient," he reassured me. "Or at least that's what I've heard."

"I worry they'll be even more damaged by all of this."

"You and Ali raised good, strong, resourceful kids. And they've got you looking after them."

"At least they know the full truth about their dad."

"You were right. Toward the end there, you were pretty convinced that Ali would never cheat on you."

"Did you believe he would?"

He shrugged. "The circumstantial evidence didn't appear to be in his favor." He paused. "A man would have to be crazy to be unfaithful to you."

I knew I couldn't avoid the elephant in the room any longer. "Nasser—" I began.

"I'm here for you," he said. "You know that, right?"

It wouldn't be hard to fall into the same pattern with Nasser as I had with Ali. To allow a loving, protective male to care for me and make me feel safe again. Not too long ago, that was all I wanted. To feel like I had before, with Ali. But there was no going back.

"I don't want to hurt you, but I do think we should take a little time apart." I spoke as gently as I could. "It would be so easy for me to just let you take care of me."

"Is that such a bad thing?" he asked with a sad smile. "Before you, I never wanted to be even partially responsible for someone else's happiness."

I crossed over to sit next to him on the sofa. "I need to know that I can be OK on my own. I went from Baba's house to my husband's house. In a way, I've never felt like a true grown-up."

"Do any of us ever really feel like real adults? Sometimes I feel like a kid playacting the part of a big, important lawyer."

"You are significant to me as my friend." I reached for his hand. "The thing is, I haven't properly mourned Ali yet. I've been so busy being angry and confused about how Lizzie fit into the picture. Now that I've proven that my life with Ali was real, I need to give myself time and space to grieve."

"I can understand that."

I stared at our clasped hands. "I need to figure out who I am on my own, to prove to myself that I can make it alone."

"I respect that." I registered the resignation in his tone. "I'll still be around, if you want to call me in a few months."

My first instinct was to reassure him. The wife and mother in me was so used to making sure everyone around me was OK. Sometimes at my own expense. But I still couldn't envision myself with any other man, especially not Nasser. I associated him too closely with the person he could never compare to.

Besides, I had no idea who I would be once I sorted myself out. The role of wife and mother had been my core identity for most of my adult life. Who was I without a husband or children to look after? I was in no position to make any decisions until I figured that out.

Nasser laughed quietly to himself.

"What's funny?" I asked.

"I think this is the first time I've been dumped by a woman," he admitted. "I'm generally considered a catch. I'm not sure my ego can handle rejection."

"You *are* a catch," I said. "I'm just not ready to cast my net for anyone yet."

"Mom, don't you think it's a little cold to be hiking?" Ayla asked several weeks later when the kids were home for the weekend.

"I think Dad would say it's never too cold to hike." The brisk temperature definitely didn't bother me. I was just happy to be fully recovered and able to exercise. I'd chosen a relatively easy trek not far from home, along the Appalachian Trail. Our first family hike without Ali felt like a tribute to him and the family we'd made together.

The irony was not lost on me. When Ali was alive, he used to force us out of bed for morning hikes. Now I was the one dragging the kids along. Reaching the observation point, the kids and I paused to appreciate the view beyond the mountain ridge overlooking wide swaths of farmland. Binti trotted around exploring the rugged terrain.

Adam stared out at the golden-red morning sky. "If Dad were here, he'd say, 'Look at that view. Is that beautiful or what?'"

I smiled. "That's exactly what he would say."

Adam sat on a rock formation. "It's hard to think about living an entire life without Dad. It seems so . . ." He shook his head. "I don't know . . . forever is a long time."

I settled next to him. "We can keep him with us in our own way. I don't know about you, but I can hear Dad in my head all of the time."

"Me too." Ayla sat on my other side. "When I'm in a challenging situation, I always imagine what Dad would say, the advice he'd give me."

"I was putting together a desk chair at school," Adam told us, "and I picked up my phone to call him to ask him for help . . . you know . . . to give me directions over the phone. And I realized I couldn't."

"I'm sorry this is so hard." I ached for all my children had lost. Their father would be a memory longer than he'd been an actual living presence in their lives. It was so unfair that Ali couldn't be there to see these two ripen into full-blown adults. "I would do anything to spare both of you from this heartbreak."

"After I figured out how to put the chair together," Adam continued, "I wanted to call Dad to tell him about how I did it all on my own."

"He would be proud of you, for sure."

I hated that Adam and Ali would never know each other as men. Ali should have lived long enough to share that kind of adult male bond with his son. A connection I'd never fully understand.

"It almost feels like Dad is here with us," Ayla said. "I feel his energy."

"Yeah," Adam agreed, "me too."

I studied my children, their cheeks bright from the cold. Ayla had her father's thick lashes and bone structure. Adam's round eyes were so like Ali's. Their father might not be physically present, but they weren't fatherless. Ali would always be their dad. Everything he'd instilled in them was still there and would forever be part of who they were. Ali would always light the way for them.

I breathed in a lungful of the crisp, cold air. For the first time since Ali died, I actually believed we were going to be OK.

Chapter Forty-Four

Before

A couple of weeks after Adam went to college and we became empty nesters, Ali and I were on the back deck smoking hookah.

We used to enjoy the occasional *sheesha* session before we had kids, but we stopped after Ayla was born because we didn't want our children to think smoking was acceptable. Even though, in recent years, Ali had started having the occasional cigar on the back deck. I wondered if all parents became less themselves in order to transform into the role models they think their children need.

Now that Ayla and Adam were both at college, Ali and I had started to regain our rhythm as a couple. He exhaled a neat column of smoke.

"I could get used to this."

I took the hose from him and inhaled deeply. "Me too."

I'd expected to miss the kids terribly once they went to college, and I did. But it also felt like Ayla and Adam went out into the world at an appropriate stage in their lives. By the time each of them reached their senior year of high school, they had started to chafe at the parameters of home life. They'd outgrown the family routine that defined their childhoods.

For me and Ali, it meant that we didn't have to try to keep track of who would be home for dinner when, and what we should cook that the children would eat. Now we could fry up some eggs, add sliced cucumbers, some labne and a few olives, and call it a day. We'd gone back to being just the two of us. A sweetness that was the past and the future all at once.

"What about Virginia Beach?" he said. We'd talked about getting a second place, a weekend and vacation home. But, at that point, we were still in the dreaming-of-it stage.

"The waves are so rough there." I exhaled, watching the smoke dissipate into the night. "Have you forgotten that Jamal dislocated his shoulder when he went there for spring break? Old people like us need calm water."

"OK, Grandma. How about a lake?" he suggested. "Maybe Lake Anna."

I made a face. "Next to the nuclear power plant? Talk about the wrong kind of glow-up."

He chuckled. "So maybe not Lake Anna."

"What kind of place do you want?" I asked. "A condo, a house?"

"Whatever you prefer. We should get something nice but not too expensive."

I laughed. "That should be your epitaph."

His brow crinkled. "What should?"

"'Something nice but not too expensive' is basically your motto."

"You'll be glad after I'm dead that I saved so much money for you and the kids."

"I might die before you," I pointed out. "And then all of that scrimping will have been for nothing."

"God, I hope not." Then Ali uttered what was probably the most romantic thing he'd ever said to me. "*Ya'aburnee*. I hope you bury me."

It was an Arabic saying, an expression of hope that the person you loved would outlive you because you couldn't bear to live without them.

In the end, of course, Ali got his wish.

And I was thrust out into the world alone, left to live without the man who'd loved me completely and gave me my first real sense of belonging in the world.

Chapter Forty-Five

Now

The morning after my hike with the kids, I picked up the phone, finally ready to do something that I'd been avoiding: my last act as Ali's wife. My final duty to my husband.

"SJ Memorials," a man answered. "How may I help you?"

"Yes, hi." My throat closed a little. Ali had been dead for months, but this was like putting a period at the end of the sentence that had been his life.

I knew it was time for me to start writing the next chapter, the one without Ali in it. My life with my husband was like a permanent museum exhibit. I could enjoy revisiting it, but not much would change. A new memory might pop up occasionally, but there wouldn't be many updates.

Most marriages, like exhibits, were collaborations, but I would write this next phase alone. "I'd like to make an appointment to order a tombstone for my late husband," I said.

"Of course. I'd be happy to help you with that. I'm very sorry for your loss." His voice was gentle and sympathetic. "Do you have a particular type of stone in mind? Like, say, marble or granite?"

"Not really." I smiled as Ali's words immediately formed in my head. I knew exactly what he would say, what he would want. In that moment, he was with me again and we were making this final decision together.

"I want something nice," I told the man, "but not too expensive."

Acknowledgments

This book would never have been published if it weren't for the editorial insight and professional generosity of Megha Parekh, who saw something worthwhile in my original manuscript and helped shape it into the novel it was meant to be. I'm eternally grateful to Megha for sharing my manuscript with Mindy Kaling. It's an honor and a thrill to be published by Mindy's Book Studio and to have Mindy, whose writing I admire so deeply, take the time to craft a thoughtful introduction. Thank you, Mindy.

My sincere gratitude goes to the teams at Mindy's Book Studio and Amazon, especially Tiffany Yates Martin, who worked tirelessly to whip this manuscript into shape, and also Karah Nichols, Joanne O'Neill, and everyone else behind the scenes who had a role in bringing this novel fully to life.

My brother, Sameer Hasan, attorney at law, patiently answered my legal questions about LLCs, operating agreements, and nondisclosure agreements. Any errors are my own. My colleague and friend Sharon Shahid let me borrow her real-life job as a museum scriptwriter for my protagonist. And Shannon Collier's (MA, MS) wise reflections on grief resonate on many of these pages.

If this book weren't dedicated to my late husband, that distinction would belong to Sophie Jordan, who was literally there every page of the way, cheering me on and offering perceptive suggestions. Joanna Shupe is always available for a brainstorm, read-through, or whatever else I need. And Sarah MacLean generously shares her vast knowledge of all aspects of publishing.

To my sons, Zacharia and Laith, thank you for being the extraordinary men you've become. Your resilience, quest for excellence, and genuine decency make this mom very proud. You honor your father's memory by living your lives with such purpose and grace.

About the Author

Photo © 2025 Shelley Larrabee

Diana Awad is an Arab American who grew up all over the world as the daughter of a United States Foreign Service Officer. After college, she became a local television journalist and often covered stories about violent crimes and mysterious disappearances. She eventually decided to write her own stories with unexpected endings. Diana also writes historical romance as Diana Quincy and historical mystery as D. M. Quincy. She is now happily settled in Virginia but still gets the itch to explore far-off places. When she's not bent over her laptop, Diana reads, devours streaming thriller series, and plots her next travel adventure. For more information, visit www.dianaawad.com.